"Open it," Khadem instructed one of his men. He drew his own stunner up to the ready position and hit the 'charge' button on its grip.

Stanford imitated the Marshal and felt a reassuring hum from the weapon as it cycled up its charge chamber.

The selected MP stepped up next to the door and hit the panel that should have opened it. The security door failed to respond. The MP turned his gaze towards it, focusing on it for a moment, and then turned back to Khadem.

"Standard overrides aren't working, sir," he told his boss. "It's locked down under the Commodore's personal code."

The Lieutenant-Major nodded grimly, stepping up to the panel and tapping the golden badge of his office, a layered block of molecular circuitry that could override almost any lock in the Navy, against it.

The panel flashed bright red, and then slowly conceded to the police override. The door slid silently open, revealing the last sight that Stanford had been expecting to see.

The office was the same as it had been when Larson had threatened him. The viewscreen behind the desk still showed Avalon – only now it was spattered with blood.

Second Edition November 2016

Space Carrier Avalon Copyright 2015 Glynn Stewart

Illustration © Tom Edwards

TomEdwardsDesign.com

ISBN-13: 978-1-988035-09-3

ISBN-10: 1-988035-09-0

Printed in the United States of America

SPACE CARRIER AVALON

GLYNN STEWART

CHAPTER 1

New Amazon System, Castle Federation
18:00 July 5, 2735 Earth Standard Meridian Date/Time
On approach to DSC-001 Avalon

Wing Commander Kyle Roberts did not enjoy being flown by someone else. It was always a struggle for the red-haired pilot to keep his hands and implants away from the controls and overrides when he was a passenger in a shuttle. To make everyone's lives easier, he normally stayed out of the cockpit.

Today, however, he wasn't feeling quite so magnanimous, and had unceremoniously shunted the small craft's normal co-pilot into the bucket seat that was supposed to be reserved for an observer like him. The burly Commander already felt a little bit guilty over that, but that slipped from his mind as the shuttle began its final approach and *Avalon* came into view.

"There she is, sir," the pilot told him, her amused tone revealing at least some understanding of her much-senior passenger's anticipation.

Avalon would not be the first of the Castle Federation's Deep Space Carriers that Kyle had served on – but she was the first whose starfighter group he'd command in its entirety. *Avalon* was a legend, the first modern space carrier ever built by *anyone*, and her SFG-001 had a list of battle honors as long as Kyle's arm.

The abbreviated arrowhead of the carrier slowly grew in his vision, and he twigged his implants to zoom in on her. The computer in his head happily threw up stats and numbers as he scanned along the length of his new home.

The carrier was small compared to her modern sisters, a mere eight hundred meters from her two hundred meter wide prow to her four hundred meter wide base, angling from a hundred meters thick at the prow to two hundred meters at the base. She was smoother than more recent ships as well, with her weapons and sensors clustered together in the breaks in her now-obsolete neutronium armor.

Several of those clusters were currently open to space, weapons dating back two and three decades, according to his brief, being ripped out for replacement with the super-modern systems delivered by the transport he'd arrived on.

"I never expected to see *Avalon* fly again," the co-pilot observed from behind Kyle. "Rumor had it that her assignment as guardship here was just a quiet way of placing her in the Reserve."

Kyle nodded his silent agreement. He'd heard the same rumors, and he'd seen the rough brief of the work they were doing to make her fit for duty. If nothing else, *Avalon* was a *carrier*, and the starfighters she'd carried had been three generations out of date.

That was his job to fix, of course. He'd spent his trip babying six entire squadrons – forty-eight ships – of brand new, barely out of prototype, *Falcon*-type starfighters. The new ships strapped mass manipulators and engines rated for five hundred gravities to four three-shot launchers firing short-range missiles with gigaton antimatter warheads and a positron lance rated for fifty kilotons per second.

The number of ships told the story of *Avalon*'s age, though. His last command, the fighter wing aboard the battlecruiser *Alamo*, had also been forty-eight ships. That ship, however, been almost *thirteen* hundred meters long, and had carried a broadside of ten half-megaton-per-second positron lances in each of the four sides of her arrowhead shape, plus missile launchers and the seventy-kiloton-per-second lances generally used as anti-fighter guns.

Avalon was less than two thirds the size of modern ships, as the technology behind the Alcubierre-Stetson Drive had advanced significantly in the forty years since she had been built. Past her, he could see the twelve ships of the Castle Federation's New Amazon

Reserve Flotilla – the smallest and oldest of them twenty years newer than *Avalon*, and a quarter again her size.

"She's a special case," Kyle said finally, continuing to eye the old carrier. "The Navy's Old Lady, gussied up one last time."

After that, Kyle was silent, considering his new ship and his new command. One last time was true – rumor had it that the tour of the Alliance that they'd been assigned to carry out was *Avalon's* last mission. Once they were done, they would deliver the old lady to the shipyards of the Castle system itself, where she would be gently laid to rest.

New Amazon System, Castle Federation
19:00, July 5, 2735 Earth Standard Meridian Date/Time
DSC-001 Avalon – *Flight Deck*

Exiting the shuttle, followed closely by the two Flight Commanders he'd brought with him, Kyle found the ship's Captain waiting. He was a tall, gaunt man with iron-gray hair who looked like he'd gone best out of three with Death – and the Reaper had kept an eye.

Modern prostheses could be almost indistinguishable from the real thing, but Captain Blair's was an older model, an emergency implant Kyle had most commonly seen on men and women injured in the War who were proud of the plain but extremely functional metal eye.

"Welcome aboard *Avalon*, Wing Commander Roberts," the Captain greeted him with an extended hand. Like Kyle, he wore the standard shipsuit that, despite imitating the appearance of slacks and a turtleneck, was a single piece garment capable of sealing against vacuum and sustaining the wearer for at least six hours, underneath his formal uniform jacket – piped with gold in the Captain's case for Navy, blue for the Space Force in Kyle's.

"I am Captain Malcolm Blair," Kyle's new commanding officer continued. "I wanted to welcome you aboard in person, though your Flight Group is waiting to show you the song and dance."

Blair gestured slightly behind him, where the four Flight Commanders leading the squadrons currently aboard the carrier stood at rigid attention.

"Thank you for the welcome, Captain," Kyle replied. "I understand we have our work cut out for us."

"We do," Blair confirmed. "Uniform of the day is shipsuits until further notice," he continued cheerfully with a tug at the gold-banded sleeves of his uniform. "We have enough work going on throughout the ship that an accidental loss of pressure isn't impossible."

"Understood, sir," the Wing Commander replied, glancing past the Captain again to the men and women he would command.

"Allow me to introduce you to your Flight Commanders," Blair asked, stepping aside and leading Kyle and his two trailing officers forwards to where the Flight Group waited. "Your senior squadron leader is Flight Commander James Randall."

Randall stepped forward with an Academy-precise salute and inclined his head slightly.

"Welcome aboard, Wing Commander Roberts," he said smoothly. "May I say that it's an honor to serve under the hero of *Ansem Gulf*?"

Kyle shook Randall's hand calmly, gauging the man with an appraising eye. The Commander was blond, blue-eyed, and easily ten years older than Kyle himself. His uniform jacket was decorated with the neat blue and gold square ribbon of the Space Force Combat Badge, a badge only earned by flying a starfighter under fire. Technically, Kyle's jacket should have borne the same badge, next to the tiny gold icon of the Federation Star of Heroism, their second highest award for valor, but only dress uniform required even the ribbons.

"Thank you," Kyle said quietly, and turned to the remaining officers.

"Flight Commander Michael Stanford," Blair continued after allowing the silence to drag a moment too long. "Flight Commander Russell Rokos. Flight Commander Shannon Lancet."

Stanford was a short, pale man with a firm grip and watery blue eyes. He met Kyle's gaze levelly and nodded his silent greetings. Rokos and Lancet each murmured pleasantries, the former a stocky man of Kyle's own bulk without the height, and the latter a willowy blond woman.

"These are Flight Commander Wang Zhao and Jose Mendez," Kyle told the assembled officers, introducing the woman and man who had arrived with him. Wang shared Lancet's height, but was dark-skinned and haired to the other officer's fair blondness. Mendez, despite his name, shared every ounce and inch of Kyle's own imposing height and bulk, with close-cropped blond hair and the brown eyes of his Hispanic ancestors. "Both are recently of SFG-074, aboard *Alamo*."

"I will leave you to the formalities of your command," Blair told Kyle. "Once you've read yourself in and the Commanders have given you the tour, please do me the courtesy of stopping by my office."

"Of course, Captain Blair," Kyle confirmed. With a firm nod, the gaunt Captain drifted away from the group as Kyle turned to face his command.

The Flight Commanders had managed to gather up all ninety-six of the flight crew for the four squadrons already aboard *Avalon*, and those officers had been waiting in relatively graceful silence as the Captain had introduced their squadron leaders. Along with Kyle and his two squadron leaders, six more members of the two squadrons he'd arrived with had arrived on the shuttle with him. As they saw Kyle draw up to face the Flight Group, all eight of the new officers quietly moved over to join its ranks.

"Deck Chief, please report," Kyle said calmly and clearly, projecting his voice across the deck. The projection was unnecessary, as the Senior Chief currently responsible for the Flight Deck had been hovering about ten feet away since he'd stepped off the shuttle.

"Senior Chief Marshal Hammond, sir," the burly and grizzled non-commissioned officer, a stereotype of any space navy for all that the man wore the blue piping of the Space Force.

"Please record for the log," Kyle instructed, pulling a sheet of archaic parchment from inside his jacket. Under the parchment was an electronic chip that he would deliver to the Captain when they met later, but for tradition, the parchment was vital.

"To Wing Commander Kyle Roberts from Vice Admiral Mohammed Kane, Joint Department of Space Personnel, June Twentieth, year Two Thousand Seven Hundred Thirty Five Earth Standard," he read crisply. "Upon receipt of these orders, you are hereby directed and required to proceed to the New Amazon system and report aboard the Deep Space Carrier *Avalon,* hull number DSC – Zero Zero One, there to take upon yourself the duties and responsibilities of commanding officer of Starfighter Group Zero Zero One in the service of the Castle Federation. Fail not in this charge at your peril."

At the completion of the formal words, every officer standing in front of Kyle seemed to relax slightly except for Randall and Stanford. The former remained at a perfect attention stance, and the latter seemed surprisingly nervous for a senior squadron commander.

"I assume command of SFG-001," Kyle informed the Flight Group. "We still have flight crews and deck personnel aboard *Sphinx and Chipmunk* who will be reporting aboard today. Our starfighters will be coming over sometime tomorrow, so everyone should expect a busy day."

He glanced around his people, and gestured for the Flight Commanders to attend him.

"Flight Group, dismissed!"

#

After the collected personnel had cleared the deck, Kyle found himself standing with his six squadron commanders and Senior Chief Hammond.

"Chief, can you have someone take care of our gear?" he asked the Deck Chief, gesturing at the duffel bags he, Mendez and Zhao had brought with them.

"Of course sir," the NCO replied, moving away to police up someone junior to deal with the luggage.

Kyle turned back to the Flight Commanders. "All right," he began briskly. "I need to meet with Captain Blair in short order, but we have some time. I presume most of you have duties to be taking care of," he hinted, "but if someone can give me an abbreviated tour of the Flight Deck, I'd appreciate it."

"Of course, sir," Randall answered immediately, living down to Kyle's expectations of the most senior Flight Commander. "I can show you around while Commanders Mendez and Zhao get themselves settled in."

Kyle turned to the two officers he'd brought with him. "I want you two to do a more detailed sweep than I'll have time for," he instructed them quietly. "Check where your flight crews will be berthed; make sure you're on hand as our people arrive."

A pair of salutes answered him, and the two officers from *Alamo* allowed themselves to be guided away, leaving Kyle standing with Randall and Stanford.

As soon as they were alone, Randall turned to the other Flight Commander. "I'm delegating the ready squadron to you, Stanford," he said brusquely. "Don't scratch my paint."

"Sir," the pale man confirmed stiffly, and then stalked away towards what Kyle presumed to be a ready room.

"Don't mind Stanford too much," Randall advised Kyle after a moment of watching the other officer walk away. "He has a stick up his ass, but he's a decent pilot."

"I see," the Wing Commander replied noncommittally. "Your squadron is the ready one?"

"Yeah," the Flight Commander confirmed. "My flight crews at least. We moved most of the starfighters over to the Reserve Flotilla's guard station, so we only have a single squadron of *Badgers* aboard. We're trading off which squadron's personnel are on-call to man them though."

"*Badgers*," Kyle repeated slowly. "This ship is still flying *Badgers*."

The *Badger*-type fighter had been the last product of the wartime crash development programs, deployed to the Navy eighteen months after peace was declared – twenty years ago now.

"I thought *Avalon* was assigned *Typhoons*," he continued. The *Typhoon* type was ten years old, two generations behind the brand new *Falcon*, but still at least a usable fighter.

"She carried *Typhoons* when she arrived," Randall agreed. "At some point, those ships were pulled to fill out a sale to an ally, and we got the *Badgers* in trade. We're all looking forward to seeing the new ships you're supposed to be bringing, sir."

While they'd talked, Randall had guided his new superior from the side-portion of the bay set aside for shuttles to an observation railing from which they could view Kyle's new domain. *Avalon*'s main flight deck was thirty meters tall, eighty meters across, and stretched four hundred meters deep into the carrier's hull.

Right now it was an echoing, empty, space. Equipment designed to service and move five-thousand-ton ships was neatly stored away against the sides. A handful of crewmen were rolling up the hoses they'd used to quickly refuel the shuttle from the *Sphinx and Chipmunk*. From the observation deck, Kyle could make out four hatches, sized to take starfighters, spaced evenly along the opposite side.

"We have four launch tubes per side," Randall explained, pointing them out. "We kept the *Badger*s aboard in the tubes – they'll be easy to deploy out that way once the new birds are aboard. With a full deck load, we can load new birds into the launch tubes every forty seconds."

The pilot sounded proud of that, and given the age of the equipment they had to work with he was probably right to be. A forty second turn-around on the launch tubes meant a total of over three minutes to put the entirety of SFG-001 into space – three times the design requirement for a modern carrier to deploy its even larger fighter group.

"That... isn't fast if we have an emergency," Kyle observed.

Randall nodded.

"I guess they didn't realize how important rapid launches would be when they built her," he agreed. "They did retrofit in an alternative, but I'd be terrified to use it."

"What's the alternative?"

"There's mass manipulators mounted all along the deck," Randall explained. "All carriers have them to catch the returning birds, but ours are also wired so they can run in reverse – theoretically, we can turn the center twenty meters of the deck into a single massive launch tube and blow the entire Group into space in one shot."

Kyle shook his head, eyeing the deck askance. The ability to blast everything on his flight deck into space at the push of a button wasn't entirely appealing to him, though he'd prefer it over having to wait three minutes to put his fighters into space in an emergency.

"Any other old tricks I should know about?" he asked.

The Flight Commander shook his head with a grin.

"That's the thing about *Avalon*, sir," he replied. "I'm not sure any of us know *all* of her tricks."

CHAPTER 2

New Amazon System, Castle Federation
20:20, July 5, 2735 Earth Standard Meridian Date/Time
DSC-001 Avalon – *Captain's Office*

"Enter," the Captain's voice ordered through the door after Kyle had pushed the announcer key. The Wing Commander had presumed, based on the Captain's instruction to stop by, that Blair would be in his office even though it was late evening by the standardized time all spaceships and space stations adhered to.

The door caught the verbal instruction and slid open, allowing Kyle to step into the Captain's office and salute crisply.

"At ease, CAG," Blair ordered. The military, tradition-bound as it always was, had dug up the ancient acronym for 'Commander, Air Group' as the nickname for the commander of a Deep Space Carrier's fighter group almost as soon as the concept of the carrier had been re-invented.

"Have a seat – and lose the jacket," the Captain continued, gesturing at the chair in front of his desk. "I thought I told you to lose that already?"

"I haven't been by my quarters yet," Kyle admitted as he sat down in the chair. The seat quickly contoured to him as he glanced around the room, taking in the semi-spartan appearance of the office. The desk was Castle Federation Space Navy standard, a hunk of plastic and metal familiar to any officer in uniform. Behind the desk was *Avalon*'s commissioning seal – a gold circle around a hand rising from waves, with the hull number DSC-001 at the top and the ship's name at the bottom. On the left wall, some long ago artist had painted a mural of the Battle of Trinity – the arrowhead of *Avalon* flanked by two Alliance battleships as the Commonwealth shipyards burned behind her. The mural was worn, but the artist's skill still showed the fire of one the greatest battles of the last war.

"I didn't intend to invoke Captain's priority," Blair observed. "We are, after all, in a holding orbit with giant holes in my hull where I should have guns."

"When the Captain says 'stop by my office,' you stop by," Kyle replied with a small smile.

"It is good to see some alacrity around here, I'll admit," the Captain answered. "Welcome aboard *Avalon*," he continued. "How's the Flight Deck?"

"Lacking in anything resembling modern starfighters, but clear, clean and ready to receive the new birds," Kyle answered. More than that would take time.

"Any impressions of your crew yet?" the Captain asked. "First thoughts, I suppose."

Kyle shook his head. "Nothing concrete, sir."

Blair nodded, as if that was the answer he expected, and then stood and crossed to stand in front of the mural of *Avalon*'s greatest victory, his hands clasped behind his back.

"I owe you an apology," he said calmly. "I prefer not to interfere in the operations of the Space Force personnel aboard my ships, but it became necessary for myself and the Ship's Marshal to arrest several of your people. I've arranged for them to be replaced from the Reserve Flotilla Defense Group, but it will have an impact on the morale of your people."

"What were the charges?" Blair didn't strike Kyle as a martinet, but if he'd been arresting Flight Group officers and crew before the new CAG was even aboard, there'd better have been a good reason!

"This ship had a problem with things leaving and arriving that shouldn't," Blair said. "Flotilla guardship is a punishment detail, so there's a lot of it I was willing to ignore – but one group was smuggling parts *off* the ship. And another was smuggling Euphoria chips *on*."

Kyle's fists clenched involuntarily at the mention of Euphoria chips. One of the pilots aboard *Alamo* had ended up addicted to the better-than-reality virtual sims – which were ten times more addictive for someone with a starfighter pilot's additional implants – and had committed suicide when Kyle had tried to force him to go off the habit.

"You had evidence." It wasn't a question. "How many?"

"Eight of your people," Blair said quietly. "Between that and a few other things we've dug up, I've also arrested over *fifty* Navy crew and officers."

"I'll deal with the morale issues," the Wing Commander said grimly. "Better that than *Euphoria* amidst my pilots."

"I'd hoped that would be your opinion," the Captain told him, continuing to gaze at the mural. "It's only a symptom though, Wing Commander.

"The whole ship is like this mural," he explained. "A faded memory of past glory. The name *Avalon* conjures prestige, honor, history – but everyone important knew she was half-way into the Reserve. Captain Riddle hadn't even so much as *tested the engines* in two years.

"SFG-001 and SFG-279 were so intermingled, I'm not even sure Vice Commodore Larson knew which one he was supposed to be commanding before I turfed him off of my ship," Blair continued.

Oscar Larson was the Vice Commodore in charge of SFG-279, the Starfighter Group assigned to defend the New Amazon Reserve Flotilla.

"There is rot through the entire ship," he concluded. "Some of it is drugs, alcohol, and misbehavior fueled by being stuck on a punishment detail – that I think we can ignore if it stops.

"Some, like stealing parts and smuggling *dangerous* drugs, we can't," Blair said flatly. "The Marshal hasn't had a chance to solidly investigate the Flight Deck – I'm leaving that to you."

"That isn't going to help me improve morale," Kyle observed, considering the task before him. The last thing he wanted to start off his new command with was a witch hunt.

"There is a real core of good people on this ship," the Captain replied. "Some are incompetents with too much political influence to keep out of uniform, so they stuck them here to make it look good. Some pissed off the wrong person, and we need to salvage them.

"And some need to crash and burn, or we can't risk taking this ship into battle. Are you a family man, Wing Commander?" Blair asked.

Kyle shifted uncomfortably.

"Not in the sense you mean it, sir," he said simply. "I have a son, but I haven't seen him in years."

The Captain turned to facing Kyle, shaking his head.

"You should," he said strictly. "But that's not the point," he shrugged. "This ship's crew is like a child – massive potential, but they've gone a little astray.

"For good or ill, the Joint Chiefs have put us in charge of them. We need to find the problems that need to be removed, and remove them. Others, we can ignore if they fix themselves. Do you understand me?"

"Sir," Kyle said flatly. "I will run my Flight Deck as I see fit." And his own life as he saw fit, as well. His job was to deliver Blair a combat-ready starfighter group when it was needed, and tradition said that how he did his job was his own concern.

"Of course," the Captain agreed. "I want to make sure we are on the same page, that's all," he added quickly. "I have reason to believe there are problems in the Flight Group that haven't been revealed yet. I think Larson was covering up more than just parts and drug smuggling, and it's as important to you as to me if he was!"

The Wing Commander relaxed slightly. His over-reaction had been as much about the Captain's comment on his son as anything else; that situation wasn't anyone's business.

"Do we have any idea what he was hiding?" he asked.

"If I knew, I'd have more guidance to give you," Blair replied, his voice frustrated. "I know that I haven't been able to confirm how many fighters they moved over to the Flotilla Defense Station. Even on this crap a detail, though, I can't imagine he was selling his *starfighters*."

"I'll keep my eyes open, sir," Kyle promised. "If I need support..."

"Any requests you have of SFG-279, the Flotilla Defense Station, my people, or of JAG will have my full support unless I know you're wrong,"

Blair promised in turn. "I've arranged so that you have the records of the flight crews Larson took with him as well. If you want to switch some of those he left behind with those he kept, I'll sign off on the orders."

"Understood," Kyle accepted. He stood and started to leave, but turned back to meet his new Captain's eyes. "Sir, this is *Avalon*," he said quietly. "Is it really this bad?"

For the first time, he realized how tired Blair looked. Bags hung under the Captain's eyes and it looked as though new lines had cut their way into his face.

"It might be worse," the Captain said bluntly. "But however bad it is, CAG, it's *our* job to turn this ship back into a warship of the Castle Federation Space Navy!"

New Amazon System, Castle Federation
00:10, July 6, 2735 Earth Standard Meridian Date/Time
DSC-001 Avalon – *Flight Group Commander's Office*

Kyle was, like the vast majority of military officers throughout history, not a fan of paperwork. Actual paper was rarely involved anymore, formal command orders being one of the few exceptions, but the various branches of the Castle Federation's military forces required their officers to fill in a vast quantity of forms and reports. Once complete, those forms and reports were transmitted via quantum entanglement to Joint Command on Castle – a flagrant abuse, in Kyle's opinion, of mankind's mastery of one of the great mysteries of creation.

He preferred, of course, to know how many munitions he had for his starfighters, how many starfighters he had, and how reliably he could repair said starfighters. That required detailed inventories, logs – and forms and reports. He'd made his peace with paperwork a long time ago and learned to use the summaries the ship's computers could prepare for him as a tool.

Two hours into reviewing those summaries for *Avalon*, he'd sent a request over the Q-com to Joint Command for a number of records. Comparing them was... illuminating.

First, and perhaps most terrifying, was that SFG-001's squadrons shouldn't have been flying *Badgers*. There was no record at Joint Command of the switch Randall had described. Central's records had been the source of his understanding that the ship's squadrons were equipped with *Typhoons* – and those records hadn't changed since then.

It was possible the starfighters had been switched with SFG-279's squadrons aboard the Flotilla station, but he couldn't tell. The station's computers had bounced him when he'd queried them for the status of the squadrons aboard. It was certainly within Vice Commodore Larson's authority to restrict that information – if nothing else, he was senior to Kyle in rank – but it was odd.

Missing starfighters were the most glaring concern, but not the only one the records contained. So far, he'd only skimmed the files on his squadron commanders, and they were everything Blair had warned him. Randall was the nephew of a Federal Senator, but his command evaluations suggested he shouldn't have been given a single fighter, let alone a *squadron*. Stanford, on the other hand, had a sterling command record with glowing reviews – and a black mark involving a 'borrowed' shuttle and the daughters of *two* separate admirals that had brought his career to a complete halt.

Rokos' record seemed as solid as the man himself, but all of his previous postings had been to planetary and reserve flotilla defense groups. A fluke of the Space Force that would still leave any commander wondering *why* he'd never served aboard a carrier.

Lancet's record was the cleanest of all four of the Flight Commanders leading his new squadrons, with no clear reason why she was aboard *Avalon* – except that Kyle knew the reputation of the Admiral whose flag her last carrier had flown, and could read between the lines.

Two of his officers were definitely solid. The other two he wasn't sure of their competence or judgment, but he would reserve his opinion until he'd run training exercises. Zhao and Mendez he knew well and could lean on, but he knew that favoritism would only weaken the weapon he needed to forge.

It was hard to put his finger on what worried him. The replaced starfighters were a big deal, but the general level of completeness of the paperwork was off too. He *expected* a certain degree of missing paperwork, or of pieces that weren't filled out right. All of the Group's paperwork was marked as in and complete – Larson either had never sent anything back to his Commanders and Chiefs, or had simply signed off on *everything*.

The answer to most of his questions, Kyle knew, would be with the Chiefs themselves. He pulled up the first of their records – Senior Chief Petty Officer Marshall Hammond of the Castle Federation Space Force. He wasn't surprised to realize that the man on Deck duty when the new Commander, Flight Group, came aboard had been the most senior Space Force NCO on the ship.

Hammond had come to *Avalon* some years back from the battlecruiser *Thermopylae,* accompanied by one of the worst reviews Kyle had seen that wasn't attached to a demotion. It looked like the Chief had barely dodged being cashiered for disobeying orders and insubordination to *Thermopylae*'s CAG.

Thermopylae was a ship that Kyle knew, though. She was the first ship of the *Last Stand* class, a sister ship to his old *Alamo* – and the Marine Gunnery Sergeant assigned to Flight Deck security aboard *Alamo* had come to her from the older ship. She had in fact, unless Kyle had the dates wrong, served aboard at the same time as Chief Hammond.

He checked the date. Unless the schedule had changed in the last week since he'd left, Gunnery Sergeant Peng Wa would have the night duty. Kyle tapped a series of commands on the flat screen that served as his desktop and computer screen.

"Duty officer," he said calmly as the junior officer holding down the carrier's communications center in the middle of the midnight shift appeared on his screen. "I need a Q-com link to *Alamo*, attention Gunnery Sergeant Peng Wa. She should be on duty."

"Of course, sir," the very young-looking Ensign replied. As CAG, Kyle was one of the three officers with full authority for use of the quantum entanglement communications array. "Please hold on one moment."

Deep in the bowels of the ship, a number of tiny bits were carefully changed. Their entangled pairs, light years away in the Castle system, changed in turn. A routing code told the computers on that end to connect to *Alamo*, and the data transmitted from *Avalon* was dutifully and automatically loaded onto the tiny bits in the relay station that linked to *Alamo*. A re-invention of the ancient concept of the 'switchboard' allowed what was, unavoidably, a two-point communications network to reach anywhere and anyone in the Federation.

A few minutes passed, presumably as the Ensign spoke to a similarly junior officer on the battlecruiser, and then the youth re-appeared on Kyle's screen.

"We have Gunnery Sergeant Peng for you sir," he reported. "I'm connecting you now."

The delicately petite features of the hardest-minded and -bodied woman Kyle had ever met appeared on the screen.

"CAG, it's good to hear from you," she said cheerfully.

"Gunny, how's the ship?" Kyle asked. "Remember, I'm not your CAG anymore."

"And I'm not your Gunny," Peng Wa replied. "*Alamo* is holding together just fine. How's the Navy's Old Lady?"

Kyle considered for a moment and shrugged. "She's old," he said bluntly. "Listen Peng, I need a favor."

"I still owe you for the *Gulf*," she replied. "Shoot."

The Wing Commander shook his head. "That was my job," he observed, "but I'll abuse your goodwill regardless. Did you know a Chief Marshall Hammond aboard *Thermopylae*?"

Peng's smile actually managed to widen. He wasn't quite sure how a woman so small could have a smile so broad – or how a smile so bright could be so shark-like.

"Wait, you've got *Hammond*?" she asked.

"He's my senior Deck Chief, and there are issues with the Group," Kyle explained. "I need to know if I can trust him. His last report from *Thermopylae* was the worst I've seen."

"Permission to speak freely, sir?"

Kyle blinked at that. He'd never known Peng to need permission. "Granted," he answered after a moment.

"Wing Commander Oshawa was an ass," she explained bluntly. "He ordered Hammond to clear three starfighters he'd down-checked so they could fly an op, rather than waiting to cycle three birds that had just returned.

"Hammond refused. He's no respecter of rank without brains, so he wasn't exactly *polite* about it – hence the insubordination."

"Was he right?" Kyle asked quietly.

"I don't know sir," Peng admitted. The petite Marine shrugged. "I break heads and shoot pirates, sir, I'm not qualified to judge the flightworthiness of a starfighter."

"That's fair, Gunny," the pilot agreed. "Thank you."

"I will say though, sir," the Marine told him, "that when we threw Hammond's farewell party? The flight crews of those three birds picked up the tab for *everyone*. They felt they owed him something."

New Amazon System, Castle Federation
08:15, July 6, 2735 Earth Standard Meridian Date/Time
DSC-001 Avalon *– Flight Deck*

With all the starfighters aboard loaded into the launch tubes, *Avalon*'s Flight Deck was disturbingly empty to Kyle. The old carrier's Deck wasn't much bigger than the Flight Deck aboard his old battlecruiser had been, and his instincts said the entire Deck should be a buzzing hive of activity. SFG-279 aboard the New Amazon Reserve Flotilla Station had the patrol duty for the system, though, and the *Falcons* that had arrived with the new Wing Commander weren't scheduled to come aboard for another few hours.

He tracked Hammond down by finding the one part of the two hundred meter long deck that *did* have activity. A cluster of Spacemen and Petty Officers was gathered around the Deck Control Office, where Hammond was giving directions for final preparations of the deck.

"MacArthur! I want your team to check berths seventeen through thirty-two – make sure the new adaptors for power and fuel are set up!" the Senior Chief snapped. "Abdul! Your team can take thirty-three through forty-eight."

People scattered away from the Chief in clusters, and Hammond turned to a young man who was waiting politely to speak to him. The youth had two silver carets above a set of wings on his collar, marking him as a Junior Space Force Lieutenant, and one of the starfighter pilots.

"Chief, the simulators in the pilot room are down," the Lieutenant told Hammond. "When are we going to get someone to look at them?"

"They're not *down*, Lieutenant Kovalchick," Hammond said patiently. "They're *turned off* – there's a slight difference. There isn't much point in you boys and girls flying simulators programmed for *Typhoons* and *Cobras* when we're bringing aboard a full group's worth of *Falcons*."

"That's just programming, isn't it?" the Lieutenant asked.

"That's what I would have thought, until Chief Ambrose nearly blew one up," the Deck Chief replied. "We'll have the simulators running by the end of the day Kovalchick," he promised. "Try reading the tech specs on the *Falcons* – they're enough different from the *Badger* you'll need the review!"

"That's not a bad suggestion," Kyle told Kovalchick, joining the conversation. The dark-haired youth almost leapt out of his skin at realizing his commander was listening in. "*I'll* need to review the tech manuals before I jack into one of the *Falcons*," he continued, "I flew a *Cobra* aboard *Alamo*. The Chief'll have the simulators up soon, right?" he glanced at Hammond.

"Like I said, Ambrose is working on it," the Deck Chief confirmed. "I think our simulators are older than the software was coded for, so we'll need to build in a work-around."

"Of course, sir, chief," Kovalchick stammered. He flushed darkly as he threw a quick salute and evaporated from the Flight Deck.

Kyle turned his gaze on Hammond, who was quietly chuckling.

"Something funny, Chief?" he asked.

"Just that Kovalchick is off-duty," the Chief replied. "He's bothering me to make it possible for him to do *more* work. He's a good kid."

"Situational awareness needs work," Kyle observed cheerfully. "Otherwise, sounds promising. Do you have a few minutes for me, Chief?"

"From the moment you read that parchment yesterday until one of us dies, quits, or is promoted off *Avalon*, you own my life, sir," Hammond told him. "Plus, the new birds don't start coming aboard for another two hours, so all I have to do is bark at kids to make sure we don't hook a fifteen year old adaptor up to a brand new starfighter."

Kyle glanced around the Deck, and then gestured to the Deck Control Office behind Hammond. From there, they could see the entire Deck and control most things from the consoles, but no-one would be able to hear them. The same soundproofing designed to allow someone to control the Deck from the office also made it impossible to hear anything inside the office unless the intercom was turned on.

Hammond led the way in and shut the door behind them. "Coffee, sir?" he asked, offering Kyle a cup. Once the Wing Commander had taken it, the Senior Chief met his gaze. "What's up, sir?"

"Trying to get a sense of my most senior Chief, Chief," Kyle told him quietly. "You served aboard *Thermopylae*, right? Why were you transferred here?"

"You saw the record," Hammond said flatly. It wasn't a question. "Insubordination, disobedience to orders. If the CAG had pushed it to a Board, he might have been able to kick me out, so the Captain put a black mark in my file and hustled me off to a backwater posting to soothe the man's ego."

"What did you do?" Kyle asked.

"We were responsible for security for a Senatorial visit to Phoenix," Hammond began, waiting for Kyle to nod understanding.

Phoenix was the largest and most important of the single-system polities that made up about a third of the Alliance of Free Stars, a binary star system with three worlds and twelve billion souls. That made her, after the Coraline Imperium and the Castle Federation itself, the third-most important member of the Alliance, and the source of the third largest fleet. The Federation would send any high level government mission on a warship, and that ship had to keep in perfect trim.

"We had six two-ship flights out at all times, flying Area Space Patrol," Hammond continued. "But Oshawa forgot to build an allowance for escorting the Senators to and from their meeting – with those trips, we had no safety margin. We had to send out new birds as soon as the current flight came aboard.

"Three of our starfighters had picked up defective parts somewhere along the line, and were showing a frequency mis-harmonic in the mass manipulators," the Chief continued. "It was within tolerances, but it was a *constructive interference* – my judgment was that it would progress to being actively dangerous to the ships in under an hour of flight time."

Kyle shivered. Mass manipulators in close proximity to each other had major issues with frequency interference. It took careful balancing to keep a fighter operating efficiently and safely. A growing mis-harmonic like the one Chief was suggesting would at *best* leave the fighter stranded without fuel as the manipulators became unable to reduce the ship's weight to reduce its fuel use. At worst, the mass manipulators would fail to compensate for the starfighters acceleration – a result that was scientifically referred to as 'spaghettification.'

"And Oshawa?" he asked in the silence Hammond left for the danger to sink in.

"If we didn't launch those three birds, we'd be down two ASP flights, basically," the Chief replied carefully. "In front of the Phoenix Space Navy, we'd look like we weren't able to maintain our own squadrons – or that our CAG was incompetent and couldn't set up an ASP he could maintain while meeting his other mission reqs, which was the truth. The Captain would have ripped him a new one.

"So he *ordered* me to remove the grounding and clear the starfighters for action," Hammond finished, with a shrug. "My response was, well, rude."

"He want you to clear starfighters to fly that would have been actively dangerous to their crews," Kyle repeated, wanting to clarify.

"That is correct, sir," Hammond said flatly.

"Chief, if I ever order you to do that, you have my permission – hell, my *order* – to be rude in response," Kyle told his senior non-com softly. Peng's impression of the man seemed on target – it took a lot of nerve to calmly explain to your new boss why your old boss wanted you off their ship.

"Don't need your permission, sir," the Chief told him. "I will *not* put kids like Kovalchick in danger to make us look good in front of an *ally*. If we need the birds to stop a Commonwealth fighter strike from killing the ship? I'll launch 'em any day – that's the cost we all signed on for."

"Indeed," the Wing Commander agreed softly. "Thank you, Chief. I know what I needed to about you now."

"And what's that, sir?"

"That I can trust you with the lives of the men and women under my command," Kyle stated flatly. "Now, Chief, I need to ask you a question, and I want an honest answer from you."

"Can't guarantee you'll like my answers sir, I'm not one for sugar-coating."

"Wouldn't want coating on this, Chief," Kyle told him. "Ambrose and Miller," – the other two Space Force Senior Chiefs aboard *Avalon* – "what's your opinion of them?"

Hammond looked down into his coffee cup for a long moment. Finally, he took a sip and looked back up at Kyle.

"They're both solid non-coms, good techs," he said firmly.

"Good," Kyle answered. "Would you trust them with the sacred honor of the Force?"

He *watched* the flippant response die on Hammond's tongue as he caught the dead-serious tone. The Chief considered for another long moment, and then drained his coffee cup.

"Yeah," he said quietly. "I would. What's this about, CAG?"

"The starfighters should all be aboard by twenty-one hundred hours?" Kyle asked. Hammond nodded. "I'm calling a meeting with all three of you then," he told the Chief. "Make sure all three of you make it."

He glanced out at the Flight Deck.

"This ship deserves the best we can give it," Kyle said quietly. "If you

three work with me, I think we can all be worthy of her."

Glynn Stewart

Chapter 3

"Bravo Lead to *Avalon* Flight Control, my board is green," Flight Commander Michael Stanford reported into the radio, leaning back and connecting the wires from the old starfighter to the dataport on his neck. With a deep inhalation, he allowed his implants to interface with the spaceship.

"Bravo Lead, *Avalon* Flight," the Control center replied. "Your flight plan is on file and your fuel tanks show thirty percent. Bravo Squadron is go for launch on your order."

Stanford re-ran his mental checks on the starfighter. Everything checked out.

"*Avalon* Control. Launch the Squadron," he ordered.

A moment later, acceleration slammed him back into his seat. Even with the entirety of the starfighter's incredible ability to manipulate mass and gravity set to compensate for acceleration, a fraction of a percent of the thousand gravity launch made it through. It lasted mere seconds though, and then Stanford was out in space.

All eight ships had launched simultaneously, and he passed a quick order for the squadron to form on him, eyeing the obsolete ships on his scanners as they gathered around.

The *Badger* was an older design, a forty-five meter long cylinder with four missile pylons mounted equidistantly around her circumference - the *Badger* had been the last pylon-based design before they'd moved to internally mounted magazines. For this flight, a transfer from *Avalon* to the Reserve Flotilla Station, the four pylons were empty and the fuel tanks were only partially filled.

None of the eight ships in his squadron had their full flight crews. Since everyone who flew over to the Station would have to be shuttled back, Stanford had ordered his gunners and flight engineers to remain behind. If some disaster required Bravo Squadron to engage the enemy with their twenty-five kiloton-per-second popguns, the pilots could handle those weapons themselves.

The New Amazon Reserve Flotilla orbited the massive hydrogen gas giant Rio Grande, forty-seven light minutes away from the blazing F4 furnace of New Amazon. Given the orbits, they were currently over fifty light minutes from Nuevo Salvador, the system's sole inhabited planet.

Avalon, technically the Flotilla's guardship until she left on her new tour of duty, orbited slightly outside and behind the Flotilla, which put her almost four hundred thousand kilometers from the spindly structure of the Flotilla Station. Two battleships, six cruisers and four deep space carriers orbited with the station, an entire navy for a single system star nation – a *rich* single system.

These ships were all old, laid down at the end of the war. They'd served dutifully in peace, and then been laid into mothballs, ready for the war that the Federation was afraid would resume at any moment. Four Reserve Flotillas were scattered across the Federation, combined equalling two thirds of the active hulls of the Federation Space Navy, – a security blanket for a nation and its allies all too afraid of the looming behemoth of the Terran Commonwealth.

Shaking his head to scatter the wool he was gathering, Stanford confirmed his squadron was clear of both the deep space carrier and the massive refit and supply ship *Sphinx and Chipmunk* that hovered 'above' her.

With a silent command to his pilots, the zero point cells were spun up, positrons drawn off and fed into the engine nacelles. Eight blasts of matter-antimatter annihilation threw the old starfighters towards their final home.

At the barely four hundred gravities the old *Badgers* were limited to, it still only took them ten minutes to cross the distance to the massive cross-shaped structure of the Flotilla Station. Four flight decks, each the size of *Avalon's* flight deck and capable of storing six eight-fighter squadrons, defined the shape of the station. Habitat modules, repair gantries and storage containers were linked to the flight decks by personnel tubes and more gantries.

Like any of the Reserve Flotilla Stations, the New Amazon one had been assembled from hundreds of separate pre-fabricated modules, and it showed in the haphazard nature of its construction. The only thing Stanford knew to be certain was that the access to the flight decks was clear.

As the starfighters approached Station, Stanford inched ahead of his squadron by delaying his deceleration by a fraction of a second.

"New Amazon Flotilla Station, this is SFG-001 Bravo Lead," he reported over the radio. "We are on approach to Flight Deck C, requesting clearance to land."

"The trap is armed, the deck-center is clear, you have the call Commander," the Flight Controller replied.

A mental command flicked the full details of his starfighter's approach vector to the station. Moments later, a tiny adjustment from the side thrusters had aligned the *Badger* with the center of Flight Deck C, and a burst of thrust from his main engines sent him drifting forward at a handful of meters per second.

Passing through the end of the flight deck, his ship trembled beneath him as the gravity trap caught him. Designed for starfighters arriving at emergency combat speeds, the trap smothered his velocity almost instantly. A second later, the ship trembled again as he passed into the carefully contained atmosphere of the Deck.

"Computer interface engaged," Flight Control reported, and Stanford disengaged the jack connecting him to the ship. Tiny, perfectly controlled jets from his thrusters delivered the ship into a waiting crane.

A minute after making the call, his ship was tucked into one of the handful of remaining empty spots on the deck. Stepping out of the craft, he surveyed the neat rows of *Badgers*. There were empty spots remaining for the rest of his squadron, but then the deck would be full of the obsolete fighters.

"Your shuttle is waiting at Bay Two," a familiarly gruff voice told him, and Stanford looked up at the shaven-headed form of Space Force Senior Chief Kawika Liago. Liago was a massive, dark-skinned man with a shaven head – and he was also Vice Commodore Larson's right hand man.

"Your flight isn't for forty minutes," the Chief continued, "and Commodore Larson wants to speak with you."

For a moment, Stanford considered refusing. Larson was no longer in his chain of command, and he doubted that the Vice Commodore had anything to say that he wanted to hear. Then Liago's massive hand descended on his shoulder, and he reflected on the fact that the non-com was capable of breaking him in half with one hand.

"Lead on, Chief," he said timidly.

New Amazon System, Castle Federation
12:30 July 6, 2735 Earth Standard Meridian Date/Time
New Amazon Reserve Flotilla Station, Station Commander's Office

Stanford knew he was a small man, and that it was not particularly difficult to be physically intimidating to him. Liago managed it with ease, but the big man was physically imposing and intimidating to almost everyone.

He could never quite explain why Oscar Larson terrified him.

The Vice Commodore, the most senior Space Force officer in the system even now, was a tall, lanky whited-haired man who looked like a stiff wind would blow him away. He wasn't known for sitting still, and was pacing by the display screen taking up the entire back wall of his office when Stanford entered.

Centered in the display screen was *Avalon*. Behind her, the twin battleships *Judgment* and *Retribution* orbited above Rio Grande, their black bulk an intimidating backdrop to the old carrier. Next to

GLYNN STEWART

the carrier, the massive cylinder of the *Sphinx and Chipmunk* refit and supply ship hovered. The extended arms connecting the freighter to the carrier were almost invisible at this distance. The starfighters being carefully transported across the space between the ships *were* invisible, even eight of the thirty meter ships barely a dot.

"I'm glad you could take time from your busy day to meet me," Larson said snidely, returning Stanford's salute briskly and walking around his desk to stare down at him. "I'm sure ingratiating yourself with your new boss is taking up your time."

Stanford didn't answer, quailing somewhat as he looked up at the Vice Commodore and trying not to show it.

"Please, Commander, sit, have a drink," Larson told him, gesturing towards the chair in front of the desk as he walked back to stare at *Avalon* on the viewscreen.

Stanford sat, aware that Liago hadn't left the room. The massive Chief Petty Officer had taken up a stance next to the door, wordlessly suggesting that leaving without permission would be a bad idea.

"I hear that Roberts and Blair are busily turning over stones and arresting chipheads," the Vice Commodore told Stanford. "It must be getting warm over there."

The Flight Commander flushed, with a quick glance back at Liago. He'd known the CPO had been aware of his own alcohol smuggling, but he hadn't been sure if Larson hadn't known – or simply hadn't *cared*.

"Suffice to say, I can prove your activities," Larson continued, stepping from the screen to his desk and swiping a command on the desk. Overlaid on the image of *Avalon*, a dozen tiny screens appeared, each playing a different video of Stanford.

"But there's no need for us to get confrontational," the Vice Commodore continued, a second swipe clearing the videos. He walked around the desk, to look down at Stanford's sitting form again.

"I just want you to remember that I still have friends aboard *Avalon*," he said quietly, directly into Stanford's ear. "And if you're thinking this pair of martinets are making the right time to bring up old history, I want you to remember that – and remember that Lieutenant Williams is assigned *here*."

The flush was gone now. Stanford knew his face was white, and he did his best to maintain some composure instead of completely cracking under Larson's pressure.

The Vice Commodore was suddenly gone, back behind his desk and fiddling with controls.

"Give my greetings to my old crewmates," he finished, suddenly cheerful as he began to bring up his paperwork. "Enjoy your flight."

Liago didn't even move, but somehow he was looming heavily over Stanford. He couldn't get out of the office fast enough.

Glynn Stewart

Chapter 4

New Amazon System, Castle Federation
21:00 July 6, 2735 Earth Standard Meridian Date/Time
DSC-001 Avalon – *CAG's Office*

From the window of the Flight Group Commander's office, Kyle Roberts watched the last 'eight-pack' of starfighters slowly maneuver its way onto his Flight Deck. A metallic framework strapped to a set of rockets, the eight-pack carried its payload of starfighters stacked vertically in neat ranks of two – two fighters across, four fighters on top of each other. Given the size and mass of the *Falcon*, that made for an assembly over sixty meters long, sixty meters wide, and fifteen meters tall that massed well over fifty thousand tons after the framework's own mass was accounted for.

Even with the gravity of *Avalon*'s Flight Deck under extremely careful control, the slightest error or misjudgment could result in damage to the ships, even the complete destruction of the eighty billion Federation Stellars worth of starfighters – or worse, injury or death to his people.

This was the sixth and last pack of fighters, however, and his deck crews had handled each with aplomb and confidence. They'd taken a bit longer than he'd expected, but they'd managed the job without injuries or more than a handful of scratches on the *Falcon*s.

The chime for his door sounded a couple of minutes after the hour rolled around, and he checked the status of his Petty Officers on his implant. Chief Petty Officer Harvey Carlisle, the most senior of his non-Senior Chiefs, had the deck, which meant Hammond, Ambrose and Miller were free.

"Enter," he instructed.

The doors slid open and the three most senior non-commissioned Castle Federation Space Force personnel aboard *Avalon* entered in a pack. Kyle gestured them to the three chairs in front of his desk while he continued to watch the Flight Deck through the window.

"Any issues with the loading?" he asked the men and woman behind him.

"None," Hammond replied tersely. "We'll see if they picked up any issues in transit over the next few days as we test them out and let the flyboys stretch their wings, but the *Falcons* are supposed to be solid birds."

Kyle nodded and ordered the screen over the window to the Flight Deck to close. After a moment, the room dimmed slightly as the stark lighting of the Deck faded, and he turned to face his Senior Chief Petty Officers.

Marshall Hammond was as much a known quantity as Kyle had on the ship. The grizzled older man looked perfectly relaxed; leaning back in the chair he'd been offered.

Harj Ambrose was a dark-skinned man of medium height with close-cropped black hair and sharp black eyes. He'd settled into the offered chair with his hands crossed in his lap, eyeing his new boss pensively.

Petitia Miller was the last of his Senior Chiefs, a frail-boned woman with ice-blue eyes that contrasted sharply with her darker skin and hair. She was perched on the edge of her seat, but her body language suggested a greater willingness to attack than to flee.

"Chiefs, thank you for meeting with me," Kyle said quietly. "We don't know each other well yet, though I know that will have to change. Hammond here comes highly recommended by an old friend, and he recommends you two. I hope to trust you, because we have a problem."

"I know the Captain broke a Euphoria chip smuggling ring aboard this ship," he continued grimly. "This is a punishment station; I *know* there are drugs and alcohol being smuggled aboard. In the end, if that stops, I do not care," he finished bluntly. "If someone's drug or alcohol habit is a problem, I expect you and the Flight Commanders to make sure it *stops* being a problem before I learn about it."

He met their gazes and all three nodded slowly as the message sank home. The informal discipline that would stop problems before the Wing Commander brought the hammer down came from the Chiefs and Senior Chiefs – often even when dealing with junior officers.

"Those things I can ignore," he repeated, "but there are offenses which are crash and burn in the Force. I *know* some of those were going on here too. Abuse. Intimidation. Theft. I don't trust *any* of the paperwork," he finished, gesturing to his desk.

"Most of the Force crew are good people," Ambrose said softly, but Hammond interrupted, shaking his head.

"That and fifty Stellars will buy you an expensive latte," he said bluntly. "We all know there're some real bad apples on this ship."

"There are," Kyle accepted softly. "And I want them off. Understand me, Chiefs – I can and *will* transfer crew and pilots to SFG-279 on the word of three Senior Chiefs. I'll settle for getting them off of our ship."

"If you want me to hand someone over to JAG, I need evidence. Something we can take to a court martial."

The three chiefs exchanged looks, and then Miller shrugged.

"The Captain got the worst of the drugs," she said quietly. "There're some bullies and abusers – nothing criminal, but getting them off of the ship is all we really need."

"You three can give me names?" Kyle asked. "I'll also take recommendations for replacements from Two-Seventy-Nine. We're not planning on giving Larson much choice in these transfers. Nothing worse?"

"Don't get your hopes up," Ambrose admitted with a sigh, and looked to Hammond. "Tell him about Randall."

The Senior Chief hesitated, and looked over to Miller. The frail-looking woman nodded firmly, and Hammond sighed and met Kyle's eyes.

"Flight Commander Randall is my most senior officer," Kyle said quietly. "Technically, if not for Larson busy-bodying around, he commanded SFG-001 until I arrived. He's an ass-kisser, but I didn't suspect more."

"Flight Commander Randall," Hammond replied, "is a bully, and a thug. You've seen him abuse Stanford, dump work on him?"

The Wing Commander nodded.

"That's only the start. He does that for everything," the Senior Chief told him. "You can always tell when something fishy is going on, because Randall *hasn't* delegated it to someone else."

"What kind of fishy?"

"Nothing we can prove," Miller said softly. "I run the parts inventories – I *know* stuff has gone missing, but I can't track the thefts."

"Randall might be the only one I can't even transfer without some kind of crime to hang on him," Kyle said. "Abuse and over-delegation don't count."

Hammond glanced at Miller and Ambrose, both of whom nodded to him. With a sigh, the big Chief pulled a data chip out of one of his pockets and laid it on Kyle's desk.

"There's a long story here," he started, "but it begins with a crime we *can* prove – Flight Commander James Randall raped Flight Lieutenant Michelle Williams, an officer under his command."

The words dropped into the quiet of the austere office like anvils.

"You can prove this," Kyle stated flatly. Rape was a crash and burn offense. There was no mercy if it could be proven. No excuses. It would be a long time before Randall saw the light of day if it was true.

"This chip contains all of the details of Flight Commander Stanford's investigation," Hammond replied. "Williams was in his Bravo squadron, before she was grounded and transferred to the Reserve Station by Larson."

"Stanford buried this?" Kyle demanded in a low, dangerous voice. Anyone who covered for a rape would crash and burn along with the rapist if he had a say – and as the Commanding Officer of *Avalon*'s Flight Group, he did.

"I don't know, sir," the Chief admitted. "I know he completed his investigation – pulled together witness statements, medical records, enough proof to satisfy a court martial – and reported it to the Vice Commodore. I never heard anything after that, but you won't find that report in the ship's computers – and it definitely never made it to JAG. I, um, stole a copy to be sure it was never lost."

"I need to review this," Kyle told them, his eyes on the innocent looking data chip. "Please tell me this is the worst."

"It's the worst we can prove," Ambrose told him. "We'll give you names of others, pilots, gunners, engineers and deck crew we need off the ship. If we trade them out for the best of the Two-Seventy-Ninth, we can deliver you a solid crew."

"But the rot has to be cut out first," Wing Commander Kyle Roberts said grimly, and picked up the data chip. "I thank you for trusting me with this, Chiefs. I swear to you, upon the sacred honor of the Space Force, this report will not go astray again."

"Justice will be done."

#

Kyle read the report. It took him over an hour, and then he read the report again, to be certain. By the end, a deep weariness and a queasy unease filled him. Stanford's report was detailed, supported, and complete. The report from the doctor who'd examined Williams was included. Video footage of the examination of the scene was included. Security tracking records showing where both Randall and Williams had been, and that Randall's tracker had been disabled during the attack.

There was enough verifiable evidence in Stanford's report that there'd be no need for further investigation – the Flight Commander had assembled enough evidence to justify charges against – and likely convict – his superior.

And other than the version he'd been handed on a chip, he could find no trace of the report in the system. Most of the evidence had vanished from the records as well – the only copies were in the report.

Kyle Roberts was not a perfect man, or even, in his opinion, a particularly good one. He had abandoned his high school girlfriend when she got pregnant and fled to the Navy, and had never gone home. His only contact with his son was through his mother, who had let Kyle's ex move in and helped take care of them.

He was pretty sure he was the worst father in the Federation's fourteen systems, but that was a... petty failure compared to the evil that he was looking at.

Randall had systematically stalked, cornered, and raped an officer under his command.

Another officer had proven it, to an extraordinary level.

And that proof had disappeared.

There was no trace, anywhere in *Avalon*'s systems, of Stanford's report.

Somewhere between Stanford completing the report and it being delivered to the Federation's Judge Advocate General, it had disappeared. The Flight Commander had allowed this.

Kyle couldn't reconcile the detail and completeness of the report with the willingness to let Randall walk away – and to continue serving under his command.

The mystery could wait, however. Regardless of what had happened to the report before, he had it now – and his duty was clear.

He triggered a command in his implant.

"Blair," the Captain's voice replied several moments later as the intercom channel opened.

"Captain, it's Roberts," Kyle told him. The Captain's implants *should* have told him that, but Kyle knew his own implants – part of being a fighter pilot – were vastly more powerful than most people's, and *he* could miss data sometimes.

"It's well after twenty-two hundred ship-time, Wing Commander," Blair said, a soft chuckle underlying his words. "What was so important it couldn't wait until morning?"

"I found one of those problems that need to be removed," Kyle told him flatly. "I need to meet with you and the Ship's Marshal immediately."

All humor dropped from the Captain's voice.

"My office, ten minutes," Blair ordered. "I'll page Khadem."

Blair was waiting when Kyle arrived in his office. From the look of the papers and empty coffee cups shoved off to one corner of the spartan, Navy-Issue, surface, he'd been working when Kyle had paged him. Now, the gaunt man was leaning back in his chair looking at a physical picture frame with his biological eye.

"What was so important that it couldn't until tomorrow?" the Captain asked.

"We should probably wait until the Marshal is here," Kyle told him.

"Fair," Blair agreed. "He'll be a few minutes, I woke him up. Have a seat," he continued, gesturing to one of the two chairs in front of the desk in the small office.

Kyle took a seat, glancing at the painting of the Battle of Trinity on the wall. He spent a moment studying it, looking to see if they showed the Marine transports often forgotten in images of the battle. Like so many others, though, this picture only showed the three capital ships that had spearheaded the strike into Commonwealth space.

Blair put the picture he'd been looking at down where Kyle could see it, revealing an image of the Captain, a dark-skinned woman of Blair's height with a stately grace to her, and two dusky-skinned, blond-haired, girls.

"My wife and daughters," the Captain explained. "The girls are ten and twenty – I'm missing the younger's school theater play tomorrow, or so her latest letter informs me."

"They're back on Castle?" Kyle asked politely.

"Yeah, they're in New Cardiff, just outside Joint Command," Blair confirmed. "It was convenient when I was in Planning, but then Admiral Kane convinced me to take this command. What about your boy?"

Kyle shifted uncomfortably.

"His mother and I don't speak," he admitted. "I haven't seen the boy in years."

He didn't like to admit that he'd *never* seen his son. He wouldn't pretend to himself that he hadn't run away from Lisa and Jacob, but his *Captain* didn't need to know the details.

"I'm surprised," Blair said quietly. "Your file has you paying the highest voluntary child support the Space Force will allow."

The Wing Commander twitched. He wasn't aware that datum was *in* the file his Captain could see.

"The Force takes care of most my needs," he said carefully. "My ex is still in school – she's studying for a medical specialization in neural augmentation and neurosurgery. She lives with my mom, and I help make sure the boy is taken care of. It's the least I owe them."

"Becoming a father was the happiest moment of my life," Blair said quietly, his hand on the picture of his daughters. "I can't imagine missing more than a decade of their lives."

Kyle was saved, thankfully, by the arrival of Lieutenant-Major Ahmed Khadem from having to respond to *that* comment. He gratefully accepted the opportunity to talk about safe topics like a rapist under his command, rather than his family situation.

"Captain, Wing Commander," Khadem greeted them as he entered the office. The Lieutenant-Major – roughly equivalent to one of Kyle's Flight Commanders – was the senior member of the Federation Marines serving as Military Police aboard *Avalon*. Even once they embarked the short battalion of Marines they were taking on their tour with them, Khadem would still stand apart from those troops as the Ship's Marshal.

"I don't know about you two, but I do actually sleep at night," the MP, a dark-skinned man with jet-black eyes and hair, told them dryly. "I intended to stop by your office tomorrow to pay my respects, Commander Roberts, but I'm guessing something more urgent came up?"

"Take a look at this," Kyle told him, passing the chip Hammond had given him to the MP. "I've made sure there are copies of this in the system," he continued. "It seems to have gone astray the last time it was handed over."

GLYNN STEWART

"There's a reason Lieutenant-Major Khadem came aboard with me," Blair said grimly as he brought up the executive summary of the report. Speed-reading it, the Captain cursed aloud. "And this went *missing*?"

"I haven't had a chance to pin down Stanford about it," Kyle admitted. "I'd prefer to grill him over it myself before we get official – he drafted this report, after all, and that makes me willing to extend him some credit."

"Is there proof of these accusations?" Khadem asked, eyeing the terse text of the summary Blair's computer was throwing on the wall.

"The appendices include camera footage locating Randall, security tracker records, and the report of the ship's doctor on Lieutenant Williams' injuries," Kyle said quietly. "All of them checked out as legitimate Navy records. And equivalent time stamps and index numbers are missing from *Avalon*'s records."

"That is almost as terrifying as the allegation that one of our senior officers raped an officer aboard this ship," Blair said flatly. "Marshal – I want you to look into *how* this report vanished from our systems in detail, is that clear?"

"As crystal, sir," Khadem said flatly.

"And Randall?" Kyle asked softly.

"You have the authority to sign his arrest order yourself," Blair pointed out.

"He's my second in command," Kyle replied. "I want both of our authorizations on the order. Mine is already in the system," he told Khadem.

The Captain nodded, blinking rapidly as he accessed *Avalon*'s computer, clearly adding his approval before he turned to the ship's senior Military Policeman.

"Marshal Khadem, arrest Flight Commander James Randall," the Captain ordered.

The Marine grinned and bowed slightly.

"*Insha'Allah*," he said quietly. "With pleasure, sir."

#

Kyle accompanied Khadem and his Military Police to Randall's quarters. It was tradition that the MPs didn't enter Flight Country without an escort of a senior Space Force officer, mostly to remind the MPs that in this section of the ship, even the Captain's authority had to go through the CAG.

Khadem had called ahead and had a team of three MPs, probably half of the police awake on the ship as it approached midnight, meet them at the entrance to section set aside for the senior Space Force officers aboard. All three were in full uniform, including black shell body armor and stunners.

This was his territory, and Kyle led the way to Randall's quarters without hesitation. One of the many advantages of the high-bandwidth neural interfaces used by starfighter flight crews was the ability to download and follow a map without anyone around you being able to tell.

"Ready?" he asked the MPs as they halted outside the Flight Commander's door. The Marshal and his men drew their stunners and nodded grimly, and Kyle flipped an override code from his implant to the door lock.

The door slid quietly open and the MPs charged in. Kyle could fault neither Randall's reflexes nor his paranoia. From the speed he was moving, he'd clearly had some kind of alarm programmed into his implants in case the door opened unexpectedly, and he had a gun to hand, readily reached from his bed.

The pistol barked once in the humming quiet of a starship at midnight. One of the MPs stumbled backwards, breathing sharply, but it was the only shot Randall fired. Even as he pulled the trigger, the stunners opened up, sparking electron lasers that left the Flight Commander spasming in agony as electricity coursed through his body.

"You okay Stef?" Khadem quickly asked the shot MP. She flashed him a thumbs up, rubbing a gloved hand over the visible dent in her body armor. The Marshal then turned to Randall, who was had fallen from his bed and was now twitching on the floor.

"Flight Commander James Randall," he said formally, "you are under arrest. You have the right to remain silent – anything you say will be recorded by police implants and may be used in your court martial. You have the right to military counsel provided by the Federation. Do you understand these rights?"

Randall's only response was to whimper against the pain of the stunner blast.

CHAPTER 5

His late night wearing on him, Kyle had settled a massive coffee and several donuts on his desk to work his way through before diving back into the records and paperwork of his new command. He'd only taken a single bite of the first donut, however, before Stanford barged into his office.

"One generally knocks when entering their boss's office, Commander," Kyle observed calmly, as he put the donut back on the plate.

"You arrested Randall," Stanford said flatly. He had apparently barely thrown his shipsuit on, and the uniform outfit wasn't sealed correctly. His blond hair was an uncombed mess, and he seemed unable to stand still.

"Yes," the Wing Commander confirmed. "Congratulations, you are now my senior squadron commander. Assuming," he said sharply, leaning forward across his desk to capture the agitated officer's gaze, "you have an acceptable explanation for how your report about Lieutenant Williams' rape went missing."

He'd expected that dart to land home. Stanford's reaction was not what he expected. The Flight Commander shook his head.

"You couldn't have asked me that *before* you loosed the bull in the china shop?" the pale-skinned officer demanded, his blue eyes even more watery than normal. "If I'd known you were willing to move this quickly, we could have acted to protect the Lieutenant, rather than putting her in danger."

"What do you mean?" Kyle demanded.

"I was warned, *yesterday*, that if that history was dredged up there would be no witnesses to testify," Stanford told him stiffly. "I needed *time* Commander – time to be sure I could trust you. Time to be sure we could *protect* Williams. Now..."

"Who threatened you?" Kyle was on his feet now, but his voice was quiet – so quiet he worried for a moment that Stanford hadn't heard him, as the man did not reply.

"*Who*, Commander?" he repeated.

"Vice Commodore Larson," the older officer admitted in a quiet voice. "The first time, in *this very office*, after telling me that all copies of my report had been destroyed. He told me then that he would destroy what was left of my career and *bury* Williams.

"Then yesterday," he repeated. "Sir, *please* – we have to do something."

Kyle was already in the system, slamming an override code into the communications center to give him a direct line to the New Amazon Reserve Flotilla Station.

"Get me Major Neilson," he said sharply into the empty air, his implant turning on his computer and linking him through to the commander of the Station's MPs.

Part of his wall turned into a video screen, the image of the Major's shaven-headed face appearing on it.

"Wing Commander Roberts," he said calmly. "I wasn't expecting to see an emergency override code from you.

"Major Neilson," Kyle greeted him. "This is urgent. I need you to take Flight Lieutenant Michelle Williams into immediate protective custody." He glanced over at Stanford, the smaller man starting to sag in relief. "I have reasonable grounds to believe her life is danger."

He paused.

"I need the station locked down, Major," he said finally. "I'll get you the authorization from Captain Blair as senior Navy officer in the system as soon as I can, but you need to make sure no one leaves the Station until he confirms otherwise."

The Major blinked.

"I'll have Williams taken in immediately," he confirmed. "I can't lock the station without Blair's order, though, and I'll need reinforcements," he said. Kyle met his gaze calmly, and the Major shrugged. "Hell, I knew your father, Commander. Get me Blair's order ASAP – I'll make sure nobody leaves. You damn well better get me reinforcements," he concluded, "I'm not sure how many of my own men I can trust if the rocket is going up."

The video cut, and Kyle turned to Stanford.

"I'm going to need you to tell the Marshal everything you told me," he said quietly. "If Larson tried to cover for Randall, then by the Honor of the Space Force, he will burn right next to him."

New Amazon System, Castle Federation
08:30 July 6, 2735 Earth Standard Meridian Date/Time
New Amazon Reserve Flotilla Station

Flight Lieutenant Michelle Williams had problems. Jumping at loud noises. Flashbacks. Nightmares. Worst of all, a doctor who refused to admit these existed, since diagnosing her with Post Traumatic Stress Disorder would require him to admit what had happened.

She knew she looked like crap as she half-stumbled towards her quarters from yet another waste of time medical appointment. Her black hair was far past regulation length, matted and unkempt from a lack of brushing. Her eyes were bloodshot and her shipsuit wasn't properly sealed. Her superiors in Flight Control kept threatening to write her up, but they didn't *get* it.

Michelle Williams was a *pilot*, equipped with neural implants ninety-eight percent of humans couldn't even handle. Flying had been her escape from home, only to turn to ashes in her mouth – and then be *stolen* from her to protect her attacker.

Between modern therapy, drugs and nanites, even PTSD could be treated. In the aftermath of the attack, even as she had been panicking, terrified and hurt, she'd *known* the Space Force would take care of her.

The thought that a senior officer could bury that she'd been attacked – could in many ways bury *her* – hadn't even occurred to her.

A year of neglect and betrayal left her wandering half-lost through the corridors of the Flotilla Station, lost, unkempt, and jumping at every tiny noise.

The grinding noise of an improperly maintained door sliding open had her skittering away from the door like a terrified rabbit. Shaking herself and feeling silly, Michelle turned to face the door to see who had entered the hallway.

Her attempt at finding calm shuddered and she swallowed hard at the sight of Senior Chief Kawika Liago, Vice Commodore Larson's right hand man. Only one man at Rio Grande had the power, if not the authority, to force her doctor to ignore her issues – and that man was Larson.

"Ms. Williams," the massive shaven-headed petty officer rumbled. "I am truly sorry about this."

"About wh–" Williams began, and then she saw the weapon Liago was drawing. She didn't wait to see what it was before she turned to run.

She triggered an emergency alert in her implant as she began to run, but that was all she did before the dart-gun barked twice. Her shipsuit was unarmoured, unable to prevent the darts from delivering their load of nanites into her system.

Her run continued for about a dozen more steps and then every muscle in her body froze and her implants shut down as the various nanites took effect.

Michelle went down face first, able to *feel* her nose break as she smashed into the metal decking, but unable to move or respond in any way, even through her implants.

Liago picked her up with ease, slinging her over his shoulder like a sack of potatoes. Part of her mind was wondering when she'd lost so much weight, even as the rest of her was panicking and trying to access her implants.

Her eyes were paralyzed open. She couldn't even not watch at Liago carried her away from her quarters, in the direction of the flight decks. It wasn't until they turned off from the main corridors, into a maintenance section that Michelle knew linked to a set of airlocks, that she realized what was going to happen.

She was going to die. They were going to make it look like a suicide, and that would be all too believable to everyone around her. The doctor might have refused to acknowledge her condition, but everyone around her knew *something* was wrong. If she appeared to commit suicide by airlock, everyone would believe it.

Whatever else may have happened since, Michelle Williams had joined the Federation Space Force because she was a fighter. She tried to struggle, tried to get even a tiny amount of motion, even enough control back to retrigger her implant's emergency signal.

Her body betrayed her. The nanites were blocking nerve signals throughout her body and had disabled her implants. There was nothing she could do as Liago calmly carried her towards the outside of the ship.

Slung backwards over Liago's shoulder, though, she saw the MPs arrive before he did, and realized her emergency signal had got out before her implants had been disabled. Even if she could have warned Liago, she wouldn't have.

Four Military Policemen, in body armor and carrying stunners, came around the corner behind them at a trot. At the sight of her and Liago, they broke into a run. They closed half of the distance to Liago before the Chief heard them, and turned back to face them.

"Chief Liago, please put Lieutenant Williams down," the lead MP asked politely. Michelle could no longer see what was going on, as Liago's broad back was between her and the MPs.

"She seems to have broken into the liquor early," Liago rumbled. "I found her near the airlocks, I was going to take her back to her quarters."

It sounded reasonable to Michelle. Liago was senior to the four men who'd intercepted her – and was known to have the ear of the Vice Commodore. She was doomed.

"Chief Liago, put her down," the MP ordered flatly. "We will take care of her."

It might have been Michelle's imagination, but she was sure she heard the distinctive humming of stunners being charged.

"I've got her, Corporal," Liago replied, his voice grumpy. "There's no need for concern."

"Lieutenant Williams is to be placed in protective custody and transferred to *Avalon* for her protection," the MP told him flatly. "You will put her down and step away from her or we will fire."

Liago dropped Williams roughly, her limp body crumpling to the metal floor and her head thumping against the wall. Despite the pain, she was unable to even blink through the paralyzing nanites, and could see the entire scene with the big Chief and the four armored MPs.

She saw him pull the gun out from his shipsuit pocket before the MPs did, and tried to shout a warning. The nanites still kept her frozen, and she watched in horror as Liago spun, far faster than she ever expected the big man to move, and fired.

The body armor of the lead cop exploded into two red splotches as the big pistol barked loudly.

The MPs responded instantly. The sparking noise of stunners answered the pistol's crash as invisible beams slashed across the corridor. Liago jerked as the first beams struck home, but remained standing.

Whatever body armor or inhuman endurance the Senior Chief had, however, didn't help him when the MPs overcharged the stunners and fired again.

Michelle had always been vaguely aware that the electron laser of a Navy stunner could be turned up far past the 'shock' setting, but watching it happen was an entirely different experience. The air smelled vaguely burnt as three *visible* lightning bolts blasted across the hallway.

Kawika Liago stood frozen for a moment as a new smell of burnt meat filled the hallway, and then, slowly, collapsed.

"I thought I told you to be debriefed by Marshal Khadem," Wing Commander Roberts' voice came over Stanford's in-head link. "I don't recall ordering you to assign yourself to fly Major Neilson's reinforcements over to the Station."

"The Lieutenant-Major is leading the team himself," Stanford offered timidly, checking the controls of the shuttle as he began to decelerate towards the Station. "We figured it would be more efficient if he kept me under his eye."

"Right," Roberts replied dryly. Stanford noted that his new superior made no mention of the two *Falcon* starfighters Stanford had ordered to escort the shuttle.

"I have news from Neilson," the Wing Commander continued. "Williams is safe – she's in the Station Infirmary now, being treated for a dose of paralytic nanites. Neilson has his most trusted men guarding her."

"Paralytics?" the pilot hissed. Even subvocalized, he drew the attention of his co-pilot, but he waved them off with a gesture towards his ear that every human with a neural implant would recognize.

Paralytic nanotechnology had been invented in the Commonwealth over a century earlier, as an attempt at a more 'elegant' solution to disabling someone non-lethally than the variety of methods currently available, most of which involved delivering an incapacitating electric shock. Paralytics blocked conscious nerve signaling, and could also disable neural implants.

Unfortunately, blocking conscious nerve signaling turned out to also often block *un*conscious nerve signaling. The chance of heart attack, suffocation, and similar fatalities was *worse* with a paralytic nanite than it was with a proper electric shock weapon, so scientists had gone back to the drawing board.

Paralytic nanites were still the favorite of kidnappers and assassins, people who didn't overly care if their victim lived or died – mostly because the nanites could be ordered *out* of the victim when you were done, leaving no traces.

"Is she okay?" Stanford demanded.

"She's fine," Roberts told him. "But she was being kidnapped by Chief Liago. He drew on the Station MPs and killed one. They fried him. He's dead."

Stanford was silent for a long moment, considering and watching the station grow in his screens.

"If Liago was involved, Larson was in this up to his neck," he said quietly.

"We already knew that," his boss told him. "But with this, Blair is entirely on-side. You and Lieutenant-Major Khadem are to proceed *immediately* to Vice Commodore Larson's office and place him under arrest."

Stanford glanced back at *Avalon*'s top MP, who had dropped himself into the spare seat at the back of the cockpit. The MP flashed him a thumbs up, confirming that he was on the call as well.

"Understood, sir."

Stanford quickly checked in with his co-pilot to confirm they were clear to dock, and took the shuttle slowly, carefully, into the Station Flight Deck Alpha. As the gravity trap caught them, Stanford looked down the neat rows of *Badgers* lining the Deck – another six squadrons to go with the six they'd brought from *Avalon* and stored in Deck C.

"CAG," he said distractedly, checking that the line was still open to Roberts, "quick question for you."

"What is it, Commander?" Roberts asked in a sharp voice.

"How many *Badgers* are supposed to be on the Station?" the Flight Commander asked, eyeing the nearly fifty obsolete starfighters.

"SFG-279 had six squadrons assigned to them," Roberts replied immediately. "I assumed those were the ones that ended up on *Avalon*."

"Between yesterday and today, sir, I've seen twelve squadrons worth," Stanford said quietly. "Shouldn't there be at least some *Typhoons* aboard?"

Silence answered him for a long moment, and the pilot unstrapped himself from his seat and turned back to face Khadem before Roberts finally answered.

"Pin Larson down, Commander, Major," he said quietly. "I think we have more questions for him than we thought."

New Amazon System, Castle Federation
12:30 July 6, 2735 Earth Standard Meridian Date/Time
New Amazon Reserve Flotilla Station, Station Commander's Office

Stanford really had no business accompanying Marshal Khadem's MPs to Larson's office, and both he and the Marshal knew it. Khadem had still said nothing as the pilot joined the six MPs they'd brought to the station in drawing a stunner from the shuttle racks, and allowed Stanford to lead his team through the Station.

"Where are the station MPs?" he asked Khadem after a few minutes. He'd half-expected them to be joined by some of Neilson's men.

"Neilson doesn't have enough of them he trusts," the dusky Marine replied grimly. "He's keeping them busy and out of our way. Once we've seized Larson, we'll probably have to take him back to *Avalon*."

Further discussion ended as they reached the Station Commander's office, where Larson exercised his command of the New Amazon Reserve Flotilla's defenders. It was a relatively plain door, tucked away less than a minute's walk from the Station Combat Information Center, where the Vice Commodore would exercise command of his squadrons in an emergency.

"Open it," Khadem instructed one of his men. He drew his own stunner up to the ready position and hit the 'charge' button on its grip.

Stanford imitated the Marshal and felt a reassuring hum from the weapon as it cycled up its charge chamber.

The selected MP stepped up next to the door and hit the panel that should have opened it. The security door failed to respond. The MP turned his gaze towards it, focusing on it for a moment, and then turned back to Khadem.

"Standard overrides aren't working, sir," he told his boss. "It's locked down under the Commodore's personal code."

The Lieutenant-Major nodded grimly, stepping up to the panel and tapping the golden badge of his office, a layered block of molecular circuitry that could override almost any lock in the Navy, against it.

The panel flashed bright red, and then slowly conceded to the police override. The door slid silently open, revealing the last sight that Stanford had been expecting to see.

The office was the same as it had been when Larson had threatened him. The viewscreen behind the desk still showed *Avalon* – only now it was spattered with blood.

Larson was sitting in the chair at his desk, the retractable monitors extended around him for what looked like daily paperwork. A service automatic, the standard seven millimeter caseless high-velocity sidearm issued to every officer, was in his right hand, and his brains had been blasted all over the wall-screen behind him.

"Stop," Khadem ordered as Stanford started forward. "No offense, Flight Commander, but you have no idea what to do at a crime scene. My men have forensics training."

The Marshal waved his MPs forward around Stanford, each carefully stowing their stunners and pulling out white gloves to cover their hands.

Stanford, standing back out of the way, contacted Roberts over the com. He made sure Khadem was copied in, in case the MP had something to add.

"Larson's dead," he said flatly. "Looks like he committed suicide."

"What the fuck," Roberts replied, his voice just as flat. "He shouldn't even have known you were coming – and he sure as hell didn't strike me as the type."

"He wasn't," Khadem interjected grimly. "Looks like we showed up faster than someone was expecting – this was a botched job."

"Botched job?" Roberts asked over the channel.

"I'll flip you both visual," the MP replied. "I don't want Stanford getting his boots in this mess."

The image that flipped up on Stanford's optic nerves almost made him throw up. Khadem was looking very closely at the shattered back of Larson's head.

"Looks like he blew his brains out to me," the pilot muttered.

"It's meant to, but the man pulling the trigger was in a hurry and botched his angles," the MP explained. "See these wounds up here?" Khadem, apparently oblivious to the gore and mess, pointed to a set of smaller holes, just above the gaping wound where the hollowpoint had exited. "Those are *entrance* wounds, gentlemen – someone shot him in the back of the head with a needler. Once he was dead, they started positioning him to make it look like a suicide – only they realized we were on our way and rushed it."

"If they'd got the angle right, the first wounds would have been obliterated, and we would probably have written it off as a suicide," the Marine finished. "But someone botched it – I'd say an amateur with a professional's tool and game plan."

"Liago's tool, Liago's plan?" Roberts asked quietly. "That would explain the amateur."

"Possible," Khadem replied. "I'll need more time to examine the scene, see if the station's internal sensors picked up anything that wasn't wiped."

"I think we're missing a question here," Stanford said slowly, wiping the horrifying image of his old boss, the man who'd made his life living hell for two years, from his implants. "I thought whatever the hell was going on here had Larson in charge. But if Larson was running things, who shot him?

"And why?"

CHAPTER 6

New Amazon System, Castle Federation
09:00 July 7, 2735 Earth Standard Meridian Date/Time
DSC-001 Avalon – *Captain's Break-out Room*

It was a small staff meeting. In the aftermath of Larson's death and the questions it raised, Blair had ordered the ship's senior officers to convene to discuss everything they'd dug up. Kyle had brought Stanford, now his senior Flight Commander, with him.

Blair had been joined by Ship's Marshal Lieutenant-Major Khadem, who'd been running the investigation, and a tall blond woman he didn't recognize.

"Wing Commander Roberts, this is my executive officer, Senior Fleet Commander Caroline Kleiner," Blair introduced the woman. "We've had an exciting few days since you arrived, or I'm sure you'd have met already."

Kleiner extended her hand for a perfunctory handshake, and Kyle felt like he was being carefully measured – and not necessarily judged to measure up.

"Everyone here is aware of what's transpired over the last few days, leading up to Larson's murder," Blair continued once all five of them were seated in the tiny table in his break-out room. The little meeting room, directly next to the Captain's office, was even less decorated than the office. A small Navy-standard table occupied the center, and the only decoration on the wall was a duplicate of *Avalon*'s commissioning seal from the office next door.

"How is Lieutenant Williams?" Kyle asked. "I haven't heard anything since Stanford brought her aboard."

"Doctor Pinochet assures me she will recover," Blair answered. "The nanites inflicted some nasty internal damage, though, and the Doctor won't clear her for service until she's had a chance to assess her mental state."

"She deserves everything we can do," Kyle said softly. "I don't think the Space Force has ever failed one of our own so badly."

"I agree, Commander," the Captain told him. "She's under guard now, and Dr. Pinochet is one of the best I've ever known. She will be as safe as we can make her, and we *will* make this right."

Kyle nodded, satisfied for the moment, though he resolved to check in on the Flight Lieutenant himself later.

"Ahmed, if you can fill us in on what you and Major Neilson have discovered since Larson's death," Blair instructed the Marshal after a moment of quiet.

"Mostly, what we've discovered is that whoever did it was better at covering their tracks than committing the crime," Khadem told the others. "All security cameras and scanners in the station section that Larson's office is in were disabled for a seventy-six minute period by a short-out in the wiring. It looks natural, but we're assuming sabotage as the timing is too convenient.

"Currently, we have about four hundred and twenty people who were in the zone at the time," he continued. "None should have had access to a needler, but a large fraction would, theoretically, have known how to trigger the wiring short-out."

"Can we search their quarters for the weapon?" Kleiner asked.

"Even on a military base, that wide a search would require a warrant," the Marshal replied. "We could get it, but it would be a waste of time: I know what happened to the gun. One of the waste disposal units in that section reported a spike in high density materials during the recording blackout. The gun was incinerated before we even found Larson's body.

"Neilson is still digging through everything he can find of Liago and Larson's movements, trying to see if we can track down someone who would have had a motive for this, but in the absence of further information it doesn't look like we'll be able to identify the killer," Khadem concluded.

"What about Larson's actions?" Blair asked.

"Most of those have fallen into my area," Kyle interjected. Khadem gestured for him to continue, and the bulky Wing Commander flicked a command from his implant to the projectors hidden in one of the blank walls.

"When Commander Stanford boarded the station to deliver the Lieutenant-Major and his MPs, he drew my attention to something odd," Kyle explained. The screens warmed up, showing four images of flight decks with rows of fighters, all almost identical.

"These are images of Flight Decks Alpha through Delta on the Flotilla Station – all taken late last night," the Wing Commander continued. "Over the last two days, Michael has landed on both Alpha and Charlie," the two images flashed. "He noticed that both bays were full of *Badger*-type starfighters, equivalent to those we'd taken off of *Avalon*, and asked how many there were supposed to be."

Kyle gestured, and the other two images flashed.

"As you'll note, Bravo and Delta also only contain one type of starfighter – all *Badger*-type."

"Is this supposed to mean something to me, Commander?" Kleiner asked.

"The *Badger* starfighter design dates back to the end of the War, ma'am," Kyle told her politely. "The design is twenty-one years old, and the Space Force hasn't purchased any for twelve. They are a Class Two export, and the design, less the positron lance, was recently released for civilian design and manufacture.

"In short, the *Badger* is utterly obsolete," he concluded. "Because this station is an utter backwater, Starfighter Group Two-Seventy-Nine was assigned fully half of the *Badger*s still in service."

"So we have forty-eight squadrons of these ships in service?" Kleiner asked. "That seems excessive if they're as obsolete as you claim."

"No, Commander," Kyle said quietly. "The Force currently, officially, has twelve squadrons of *Badger*s in service. There are twice as many

*Badger*s on the New Amazon station as we're supposed to have *in the entire Space Force*."

As that sank in, the CAG looked over at Captain Blair.

"When we first discussed the issues on *Avalon*, you said you didn't think things had fallen so far as to worry about starfighters being stolen," he reminded him. "It looks like you were wrong.

"*Avalon* should have had six squadrons of *Typhoon*s aboard – a Class One Export, restricted to our allies, and still in service in secondary duties throughout the Navy and Space Force," he continued. "SFG-Two-Seventy-Nine should have had six squadrons of *Badger*s, yes – and ten of *Typhoon*s and two squadrons of *Cobra*s, our current frontline starfighter."

"We are missing an entire modern carrier's fighter group, eighteen *squadrons*, of frontline and last-generation starfighters," Kyle explained to a silent room. "That is what Larson was blackmailing Randall to protect. That's why Larson was killed – because he sure as hell didn't sell a hundred and eight starfighters and replace them with obsolete junk without help."

Silence filled the room.

"How?" Kleiner finally asked. "Shouldn't the pilots and squadron commanders have noticed when their ships were sold out from under them?"

"A posting like this turns over its people a lot, except for those shoved here as a punishment," Stanford told her, his voice soft. "If they were careful and co-opted some of those officers posted here as long-standing punishment, they could hide a lot from us. I know my squadron was fully equipped with *Badger*s when I arrived."

"And no one except another Vice Commodore or a Navy Captain could override Larson's security lockouts to see the records," Kyle reminded them. "And why would someone check the records for what ships were on station according to the station, versus what Joint Command recorded?"

"With Larson dead, do we have any way of learning what was going on?" Blair asked.

"Randall," Kyle said reluctantly. "With everything going on, we can pin treason on him as well as rape. Both are firing squad offenses, and both would be open-and-shut cases. We can offer clemency if he comes clean on everything that happened – offer life in a JD-Justice penitentiary rather than a bullet."

"I *really* want to see that fucker hang," Kleiner snapped. It was the first fully human moment she'd shown so far and Kyle suddenly liked her a lot more.

"You're his CO, Kyle," Blair said. "Can I trust you to handle it?"

Kyle nodded grimly, and then tilted his head as a message came through his implant.

"I've just been advised by Doctor Pinochet that Lieutenant Williams is awake," he told the others. "If you'll excuse me, I think I have a new pilot I need to welcome aboard."

New Amazon System, Castle Federation
09:25 July 7, 2735 Earth Standard Meridian Date/Time
DSC-001 Avalon *– Main Infirmary*

It took Michelle a minute or so to even begin to orient herself when she woke up. The last thing she remembered was the burnt pork smell of Liago falling beside her, and then darkness. Now, at first all she could recognize was pain. Her entire body ached.

After a moment, she realized that the pain, while pervasive, was muted. She recognized the sensation of pain medication, and slowly opened her eyes to confirm that she was in a Navy infirmary. That realization had her unconsciously pressing further into the bed, away from the wall.

Dr. Donner, the senior physician on the New Amazon station, was *not* her friend – he'd repeatedly signed off on the evaluations that said there was nothing wrong with her.

Her motion caught the attention of the nurse in the room, a cute brunette whose insignia labeled her as a Federation Space Navy Nurse-Lieutenant. She wasn't familiar to Michelle, and she had a perfect heart-shaped face that sent a half-forgotten tremor through Michelle's body.

"Lieutenant Williams," the nurse spoke to her quietly. "You're awake. How do you feel?"

"I hurt," Michelle managed to croak, and the nurse nodded slowly, clearly checking something in her implants.

"We reduced your pain medication to bring you out of the induced coma," she said softly, still keeping her voice low as if she knew about the headache slamming Michelle's skull. Given the scanners available in a Navy medical facility, she possibly did.

"I'm going to fetch Dr. Pinochet," the nurse continued. "Please, don't move until she's had a chance to check you over – you still have quite a bit of damage."

Michelle barely had time to wonder what had happened to her and who 'Dr. Pinochet' was before a short, dumpy woman appeared, with close-cropped red hair and the two gold circles and snake staff collar insignia of a Fleet Surgeon-Commander.

The sight of a completely different doctor caused Michelle to try and push herself away, her breathing coming short and sharp as she tried.

"Please Lieutenant, calm down," Pinochet said. Like the nurse she spoke quietly, but her tone was fierce. "I swear to you, upon the honor of the Navy, that you are safe."

Michelle found herself shaking her head and pressed against the wall, but the Surgeon met her gaze and held it, with an intensity she couldn't turn away from.

"You are in the main infirmary aboard *Avalon*," Pinochet continued. She gestured towards the door out of the private room. "There are two armed military policewomen outside that door, who've been in this star system less than five weeks between them, with orders not to let *anyone* in this room without the explicit permission of myself or Wing Commander Roberts. At no point in the sixteen hours since you came aboard have there been less than three Space Force officers or senior non-coms sitting in the waiting room, *glaring* at anyone who even made too much noise near your room.

"No one, and I mean *no one*, is getting into this room to hurt you," the Doctor finished. "Please, Michelle, we *understand* how badly we have failed you. We *will* protect you. I won't ask to trust us, not yet – but please, relax."

The sheer fierce protectiveness of this dumpy, motherly, doctor managed to break through Michelle's defenses. Suddenly, unexpectedly, she was crying. Pinochet was there in a moment, holding her gently and getting her settled back into the bed.

"What happened?" Michelle finally managed to ask, cleaning her face as gently as she could with a tissue.

"What do you remember?" the Doctor asked.

"Liago grabbed me after yet another waste of time appointment with Donner," she said fiercely. "Paralyzed me somehow – I *knew* he was going to throw me out an airlock." Michelle shivered at the memory of the sheer helplessness. "Then, there were MPs, and he was shot. After that, nothing."

Pinochet nodded briskly, pulling a chair up next to Michelle's bed. As she spoke, she began going through the readouts of the bed and the scanners attached to it.

"Yesterday morning, Wing Commander Roberts arrested Randall for your attack," she explained quietly. "The *original* medical reports, before the edits and deletions started sneaking in, have been forwarded to me. Liago apparently believed that killing you would help protect Randall."

"Flight Commander Stanford somehow knew you were in danger though, so they put out an order for the MPs to take you into protective custody," Pinochet continued. "They found you and Liago, and drew the correct conclusion."

"When Liago *died*, however, his implant sent a garbled message that the nanites in your body had no idea how to translate. They went crazy and starting shutting down and overloading neural pathways at random."

"The MPs rushed you to the New Amazon Station infirmary – where Doctor Donner apparently finally remembered how to *be* a damned doctor. He saved your life," *Avalon's* doctor told Michelle. "Then he called me and confessed everything. I ordered you transferred here immediately, in case anyone *else* on that damned station was insane."

Michelle blinked slowly, trying to take all of this in.

"Dr. Donner told you?" she said softly. "That he kept telling me nothing was wrong?"

"Dr. Donner has a damned Euphoria chip habit," Pinochet said flatly. "Larson held that over him to get him to ignore your condition, as it would end his career.

"Well, now Donner's career is over, but Larson is dead – and he seems to think that's a fair trade."

"Larson's *dead*?" Michelle asked, horrified.

The door behind Pinochet slid open before she could say more to reveal a large, red-haired man unfamiliar to Michelle. His collar bore two gold circles flanking a set of golden wings – a pilot-track Wing Commander, presumably the Roberts that Pinochet had mentioned.

"I suspect that's a question I should field, Doctor," he rumbled. "Is Flight Lieutenant Williams up to a conversation?"

"Yes. She's not cleared for anything *else*, though," the dumpy Surgeon-Commander made clear, glaring fiercely at the Wing Commander. "I'll need a few more days of assessment before I can even begin to say when she'll return to active duty."

"That's fair," Roberts told her with a nod. "May I speak with her in private?"

"I'll be watching her vitals from outside," Pinochet warned. "I will cut you off if it's starting to strain her – she is still in quite a lot of pain."

The big Wing Commander nodded his acceptance and stood aside, allowing Pinochet to leave the room. When the door slid shut behind the doctor, he remained leaning against the wall and turned his gaze back to Michelle.

"I'm planning on staying against the wall over here," he said quietly. "Seems that's about as unthreatening as I can be."

"I'm Wing Commander Roberts," he continued. "Your new commanding officer – the paperwork to transfer you back to SFG-001 was processed last night. Welcome aboard *Avalon*."

Michelle watched him carefully. Despite his imposing size and authority, Roberts didn't scare her. Something about the way he stood and held himself suggested that anyone trying to hurt her was going to have to go *through* him – and they wouldn't enjoy the attempt.

"I know Pinochet gave you some of the details, but here's the high-level," he continued. "I've arrested Randall for assaulting you. That's an open-and-shut case. Liago tried to murder you and was killed resisting arrest. Based on his involvement and other evidence, we attempted to arrest Vice Commodore Larson. Someone *else*, currently unknown, murdered Larson to keep his other activities quiet."

"What other activities?" she asked.

Roberts seemed to think for a moment, and then shrugged.

"This Station is missing about sixteen squadrons of modern starfighters," he told her. "We think Larson sold them, but everyone we know is involved is dead – except Randall."

Michelle didn't like where this was going.

"I really, *really*, want to shoot the bastard," Roberts continued. "I'm afraid he's the only one who could break open a conspiracy running to the highest levels of the Joint Department of Logistics."

He shifted a bit, holding Michelle's gaze.

"He attacked an officer under his command," the CAG said flatly. "If you say the word, there's no deal, Lieutenant. We'll sweat him, but we won't offer clemency. I can make certain he faces the firing squad for what he did to you."

Nothing in Michelle's life had ever tempted her so much as to say 'just shoot him,' but she was also a soldier and a pilot. Sixteen squadrons of modern starfighters was a force that could conquer entire *star systems* given the right support and transport.

"The same conspiracy that let him cover up that attack," she said quietly. "Without that conspiracy, he'd have hung months ago, wouldn't he?"

Roberts simply nodded.

"He won't walk free?"

"He's had anagathics," Roberts said quietly. "He might still be alive to walk out after sixty or seventy years."

The image of Randall, the arrogant, dandified son of one of the Federation's wealthiest families, in a Joint Department of Military Justice penitentiary for the rest of his life had a certain appeal. Especially once the other men and women in the prison learned who he was and what he'd done.

"Break him, Commander," she told Roberts. "Rip open that conspiracy before they hurt anyone else."

The Wing Commander nodded. He removed a datapad from inside his uniform jacket and laid it on the table beside him.

"So forget Randall," he told her. "What are your plans?"

"My plans are the Force's plans," Michelle told him automatically. Even after being betrayed, jerked around and treated like shit for the last year, she was still an officer of the Castle Federation Space Force.

"The Space Force failed you," her new CO said bluntly. "Doctor Pinochet is a brilliant doctor, and I have every confidence in her ability to restore you to active duty status. That said, given what has happened, she and I have the authority to sign off on an Article Seventeen discharge."

An Article Seventeen discharge was an 'honorable separation due to major injuries incurred in service of the Federation.' She would receive the same pension she'd have got after twenty years' service, and a courtesy promotion that would bring that pension up to roughly her active duty salary. The Navy would still cover her treatment, but she'd be away from the carrier where she'd been attacked.

"Sir, I refuse to be defined by what *he* did to *me*," she said quietly, and continued more fiercely.

"I am a pilot and an officer of the Castle Federation Space Force," Flight Lieutenant Michelle Williams told her CAG. "Give me a fighter and an enemy, and I will do my duty."

With Larson's murder, the brig detail aboard *Avalon* was on high alert. As Kyle understood it, the entire Military Police detachment aboard the old carrier had been replaced when Blair had come aboard, which at least gave Khadem some men and women he could utterly rely on.

Two MPs were standing outside the brig, and checked Kyle's implant ID before they allowed him in. Four more were standing guard in the waiting area, under the command of a hard-faced, shaven-headed woman with Staff Sergeant stripes and a shotgun Kyle suspected might be a portable gateway to hell.

"You're clear, sir," she said crisply after running his implant ID against her approved list. "We've got the brig locked down tight. No-one is getting at Randall unless we let them. Hell, we've even taken the brig onto independent life support."

That was potentially extreme, in Kyle's opinion, but given that someone had murdered the officer in charge of an entire Reserve Flotilla Station and its defending squadrons, he wasn't prepared to tell Khadem's people they were going too far.

"Where is he?"

"Cell Six," the Sergeant replied, gesturing to one of the monitors showing the occupants of *Avalon*'s cells.

Kyle glanced at the monitor. James Randall was sitting on the bunk of his cell, a hardware book reader to hand but apparently being ignored as the disgraced Flight Commander stared at the wall. He seemed in shock.

"Have you had any problems?" Kyle asked.

"Not since he shot Stef," the Sergeant replied. "Being shot with a stunner takes the fight out of most people."

"Can you inform Marshal Khadem that I'm going into speak with the prisoner?" Kyle requested. "He's aware of it."

"Yes, sir." The woman paused for a moment, blinking aside in the familiar way of someone communicating through a neural implant. A few seconds passed, and then she returned her attention to Kyle. "He says 'go ahead, but try not to break anything important,' sir."

"Thank you Sergeant," Kyle told her, and headed for Cell Six.

As he entered, Randall looked up at him from the bed and shrugged his shoulders.

"Welcome to what appears to be my new quarters, sir," he said calmly. "I'd offer you a seat, but I seem to have a shortage of amenities."

Wordlessly, Kyle closed the door behind him and leaned against it. He could unlock it with his implant at any time, but for the moment, the room was sealed.

"It's an impressive hole you've dug for yourself, Randall," he finally said, his voice cheerful. "I think we might be up to three separate capital charges now."

"Three?" the prisoner replied, sounding surprised. "I thought this was all over the ridiculous accusations that girl made?"

For a long moment, Kyle said nothing, simply holding Randall's gaze. The other officer caved quickly, glancing aside and losing some of the stiffness in his posture.

"Suffice to say that I have plenty of proof of that one," Kyle told Randall quietly. "Enough proof that were we at war, the Captain and I would have convened a summary court martial this morning – and a firing squad this afternoon."

What little starch remained in Randall seemed to leak out of him in a long sigh, and he looked back up at Kyle with weary eyes.

"So what, you're here to gloat? To laugh at seeing one of the Randalls dragged down into the dirt with the commoners?" he asked.

"No," Kyle admitted. "I'm here because Larson and Liago are dead, and I think you know enough about what they were doing to tell me why."

James Randall froze. One moment, he was slouching, weary, and the next he was an unmoving caricature of a man.

"Larson is dead," he said flatly.

"Shot in the back of the head, then someone tried to make it look like a suicide," Kyle confirmed. "That, along with a hundred-odd missing modern starfighters, doesn't look good for anyone. You came here in command of a squadron of *Cobras*, Randall. What happened to them?"

Randall looked around the cell, his eyes darting like a caged animal.

"I refuse to say anything further without a JDMJ advocate present," he said calmly. "I know my rights."

"You have the right to a speedy and fair trial," Kyle reminded him. "Given the proof of the assault on Lieutenant Williams and that we can prove there is no way you *didn't* know when Larson sold your squadron out from underneath you, I think JDMJ will fast-pace it. Your best case is that they'll execute you within six months. Might be as little as three.

"Plus, given Larson's fate, I could just have Khadem cut the security on your cell back to normal," he continued. "It would be an interesting experiment in the reach of this conspiracy, and might help us unlock more clues."

Randall looked away, focusing on the wall at the far end of the cell.

"What are you offering?" he said finally. "You wouldn't be here if you didn't have a deal."

"I can take the firing squad off the table, and guarantee you'll live to see trial and have your story heard," the Wing Commander said flatly. "More than that, I'm not sure you even deserve."

The tiny cell was silent for a long minute.

"Fine," Randall finally said. "Get Khadem in here – I'm only going to go through this mess once, and you'll want it all on record."

#

Khadem quickly relocated them to the brig's solitary interrogation room, where the dark-haired MP fiddled with a recorder setup until he was satisfied.

The room was even more spartan than the rest of the ship. A single table was welded to the floor, and three flimsy plastic chairs that Kyle wasn't even sure would hold under his weight were the only mobile pieces of furniture.

Unwilling to risk the chairs, Kyle remained standing by the door, watching Randall and Khadem face each other across the table.

"Everything is being recorded," Khadem told the prisoner. "Please state for the record that this is of your own free will."

"I'm doing this for clemency, not because I *want* to," Randall told him with a rude gesture. "But yeah, you haven't tortured me, I haven't seen any truth drugs, whatever constitutional right you're worried about hasn't been violated."

"All right," the MP said with a pained glance back at Kyle. "Why don't you start at the beginning? You came aboard the New Amazon Station three years ago in command of a squadron of *Cobra* type starfighters. How did Larson convince you to sell them?"

"Money," Randall said with a shrug. "At first, it was just money. Later on, he came to rely on me to help scheme out how to sneak out the ships, but at the beginning he just put a pile of cash on the table and asked if I wanted it.

"The Space Force never did me any favors," he continued. "My family's influence barely balanced the jealousy the commoners always feel for the Federation's First Families – and Larson was being paid a two *billion* stellar chunk of each sale. Put two hundred mil in front of either of you, see if you don't think about it."

"Where did the money come from?" Khadem asked.

"It turns out Excelsior Armaments gets a lot of quiet queries, asking if they can sell Class One or even front-line fighter models 'under the table' to folk we don't normally sell birds to," Randall told them. "Some of the offers are a *lot* more than the Federation pays for even a Falcon. It was enough money that even a giant interstellar corporation got tempted."

Excelsior Armaments was one of the few companies authorized to sell Federation export military technology outside its borders. They were a big player in the Federation, one of the top suppliers of starfighter and aircraft munitions, but they'd never managed to field an acceptable starfighter prototype. They were, however, cleared to buy Space Force surplus starfighters and export them to approved trading partners.

The rules around that export were strict, though. *Badgers* were a Class Two military export, with a relatively loose list – Excelsior couldn't sell them to the Commonwealth, or to any system or star nation currently on a watch list. Class Ones were for sale to allies only. The *Typhoon*, the current Class One export ship, was still a perfectly functional starfighter for being ten years out of date. Excelsior was only permitted to sell *Typhoons* to members of the Alliance. *Cobras*, being the Federation's current front-line starfighter, weren't cleared for sale to *anyone* without direct Senate sign off.

"I don't know what Excelsior was making off a sale," Randall said, "but Larson's chunk of each was enough to buy me, Liago, and a bunch of other guys," he shrugged. "We controlled *Avalon*'s MPs, the surveillance systems, everything."

"How did you hide the starfighters going missing from the flight crews?" Kyle asked, curious. Every flight crew he'd ever known was obsessed with their ships.

"I guess the 'hero of *Ansem Gulf*' never served on a backwater posting like this, have you?" Randall asked bitterly. "We had new flight crews coming in every week, old flight crews going out even more often. We always had an extra squadron of birds, and an excuse to re-arrange squadrons. A little bit of switching people between flight decks and squadrons, and no one notices that starfighters are being replaced."

"You couldn't hold this façade up forever though," Kyle noted. "Sooner or later, an inspector would come through, or *Avalon* would be either called up or scrapped – or, hell, just Larson being replaced would have brought all of this out."

"Thought the same thing myself," Randall admitted. "It took a year before Larson let me in on his endgame – if it ever came out, or after we ran out of real ships to sell, the plan was to steal *Avalon*. Captain Riddle was a non-entity, and we owned the MPs and the armory. Anytime we wanted, we'd seize the ship and fly off."

Kyle couldn't help but stare at the Commander in shock. The sheer brazen audacity of the plan was mind-boggling. Even old and obsolete as *Avalon* was, she was still a Federation Deep Space Carrier, which put her light years beyond the ships available if they'd taken her, say, further rimward from the Federation.

"We were out of starfighters other than *Badgers* and were about ready to run when Larson learned about the refit plan," Randall told them. "He wanted the new guns, the new fighters – and he wanted the refit ship."

"With the old *Avalon*, we could have made ourselves the supreme mercenaries in rimward space," the prisoner continued, a fiery enthusiasm lifting his voice. "With the refitted carrier, the *Falcons*, and a refit ship to give us the core of a new industry? Larson meant to found a new *empire*, and Liago and I would have stood at his right hand."

With a sigh, Randall slumped.

"Then Blair came in like the goddamn Inquisition," he said quietly. "Arrested half of our people for other offenses – transferred the other half out-system. Suddenly, we had no manpower. Larson was on the station, where we barely trusted anyone. Some of the folks we'd been bribing were getting nervous. Some of the folks we'd been threatening or blackmailing were getting hopeful."

"Once you arrested me," Randall shrugged. "Larson had to act on his threat to Stanford, or the whole house of cards would come tumbling down as people called his bluff. Of course, that's what happened *anyway*, and he ate a bullet for his troubles."

"I'm going to need names, Randall," Khadem told him firmly. "Who you were dealing with at Excelsior. Who's left of your little conspiracy on the ship. Everyone involved in this mess."

"If you're really co-operative," Kyle reminded him cheerily, "we might even say enough nice things to the Court Martial to get your sentence under half a century."

Randall glared at him.

"You're an asshole, Roberts," he said resignedly. "I'll give you what you want, I don't want a bullet 'tween the eyes. Hell, I can even give you

Larson's blackmail files – see who you can nail of those guys.

"You've killed *my* dreams of wealth and empire, and I'm enough of a bastard to want to kill a whole bunch of other folks' dreams on my way down."

CHAPTER 7

New Amazon System, Castle Federation
11:15 August 4, 2735 Earth Standard Meridian Date/Time
DSC-001 Avalon *– Main Infirmary*

"Well, Flight Lieutenant, I have good news," Surgeon-Commander Pinochet said cheerfully.

Michelle Williams was back in uniform and feeling better than she had in over a year. She'd been back on *Avalon* for four weeks now, seeing Pinochet for counseling sessions every day, and she'd even managed to get a haircut. Her black hair now hung to her shoulders, a neat, functional, cut that could be easily worn under a helmet and pushed aside to allow access to the datajack under her left ear.

"What's the news, Doctor?" she asked softly.

"I met with Wing Commander Roberts and Flight Commander Stanford this morning," Pinochet told her. "As of the end of this meeting, you are officially reinstated to active duty. These sessions have gone well and you've got back on an even keel far faster than I expected, especially given how long everything was neglected."

The pilot didn't leap to her feet in joy, but it was a struggle for a moment. During her exile aboard the Reserve Flotilla Station, she'd barely spent any time in space. Finding out, on her return to *Avalon*, that she was grounded until she got her issues squared away had been frustrating.

"You *will*," Pinochet continued, her tone sharper, "still be required to meet with me for twice weekly sessions. We've made immense progress, my dear, but your mind and heart aren't healed yet. Do you understand me, young miss?"

"Yes, ma'am," Michelle replied crisply. "Thank you," she continued, more quietly. "I was starting to think, well, that I was going crazy."

"My dear, if it takes me *four weeks* of chemical, nanite, and talk therapy to get your head back on straight, you *were* going crazy," Pinochet told her bluntly. "We're done with the first two, thank God, but let me know if you have any issues or concerns, all right? We're booked in for your next appointment in four days, but you're on a priority list that the ship will let through to me at any time of day or night. If you need me, do *not* hesitate. Understand?"

"Yes, ma'am," the younger woman repeated. "When do I get back to work?"

"You have a meeting with Stanford in his office at noon," Pinochet told her. "Your implants should be updating with your new schedule now."

As the doctor was speaking, Michelle 'heard' the soft ping she'd long ago associated with a data update to her in-head computer. A quick skim of the data, in a blink of an eye, confirmed that she was back on active flight duty, and assigned to Stanford's squadron. The meeting with the Flight Commander was on her schedule, but nothing later that that.

"We're done here," Pinochet continued. "I'll see you in a few days. Good luck, Michelle." The doctor offered her hand.

Flight Lieutenant Michelle Williams took it with a smile.

#

Williams was early for her appointment with Commander Stanford, arriving easily ten minutes before she was supposed to be meeting with *Avalon*'s senior squadron commander. Nonetheless, as soon as she arrived at the door to his office, it slid open for her and the pale-haired officer waved her in.

She hadn't been in Stanford's office since returning the carrier, and was surprised to realize that it was the same office he'd been in before. Being the senior squadron commander, Stanford should have been able to move into Randall's old office, which was much larger.

This office, though, seemed to fit her new commander like a well-worn glove. The Flight Commander had served on *Avalon* for two years now, and the office showed it in the peculiar organization of the files and screens. Nothing was *quite* the way regulation would have it, with desk screens forsaken in favor of using the entire wall-screen as a working space.

As Williams entered the office, she caught a glimpse of what looked like her file on the wall, then Stanford wiped the wall to a view of outside *Avalon* with a sweep of his hand. Turning to her, he offered his hand.

Michelle returned the gesture with a firm handshake and nod, wondering once again how short the Commander was – she'd forgotten over the last year that she over-topped Stanford by an easy fifteen centimeters.

"Please, Flight Lieutenant, have a seat," he instructed. He watched her carefully as she obeyed, clearly taking in her cleaned up appearance and ease of motion. "It's good to see you looking better," he said softly. "I'm sorry."

"It wasn't your fault, boss," Williams told him. "They say I owe you my life."

Stanford made a throwaway gesture. "A *lot* of people were involved in that," he said quietly. "I should have acted a year ago, and to hell with Randall or Larson."

The younger pilot shook her head. "Without someone *other* than those two on station, I don't think that would have ended well for either of us," she told him. "Let's leave the past in the past, Commander," she continued. "We have a job to do."

Stanford visibly shook himself.

"So we do," he agreed. "The CAG has shaken up the squadrons quite a bit," he told her. "I've taken charge of Alpha Squadron, and about a third of my personnel are from the two squadrons Roberts brought from *Alamo*. You've been slotted into my squadron structure since we did the reorganization."

"You're assigned as the pilot for Alpha Six," he concluded. "You'll be in our second flight, flying under Flight Lieutenant Pritchard. I know you're senior enough for your own flight," Stanford told her, "but you'll forgive us for wanting to ease you in at least a little bit."

"I understand, sir," Williams said calmly. She hadn't been senior enough to lead a four ship flight – the combat sub-unit of a fighter squadron – before her exile to the Reserve Station. She hadn't even considered the possibility of commanding one on her return to active duty – and now she did consider it, she was glad she was being 'eased back in'.

"In that case, let's introduce you to your crew," Stanford told her. His eyes made the small sideways flicker of someone accessing implant data, and then he smiled at her. "They actually just arrived, their timing is perfect."

Behind Michelle, the door slid open and a man and woman, both with the two silver carets of Junior Lieutenants. The woman's carets were over a silver cannon, marking her as Michelle's gunner, where the man's were over a wrench, marking him as their engineer.

"Flight Lieutenant Williams, meet Junior Lieutenants Hans Garnet and Christine Devereaux," Stanford introduced them.

Michelle eyed them for a moment. Garnet was a black man of her own height with a shaven head and a physical pudginess not *quite* at the limit of regulation. Devereaux, on the other hand, was taller than Michelle and whipcord thin, with blond hair and a feminine athleticism that would have intrigued her were the woman not her subordinate.

"Mr. Garnet, Ms. Devereaux," Michelle greeted them. "I look forward to working with you."

"I suggest you take some time and get to know each other," Stanford told them. "You are booked for an all-squadrons drill at thirteen hundred hours."

Williams glared first at her squadron commander, and then at her implant clock.

"In that case, sir, as you say – we should take some time."

In forty five minutes, after all, she was going to have to lead this pair into simulated combat in front of the entire flight group.

There weren't enough simulators aboard *Avalon* for all forty-eight of her starfighter crews to be in them simultaneously – an oversight corrected in later designs, but there'd never been enough space to retrofit any more into the first carrier.

Fortunately for the ability of the carrier's fighter group to train as one body, the starfighters themselves could be used as simulators. Stanford watched from the deck next to his own *Falcon* as the crews climbed into their ships.

He spotted Michelle at her fighter's dock, only five away from his own Alpha One, and made a point of picking out the other squadron commanders. He did not, however, see Wing Commander Roberts anywhere.

At least, not until his giant of a CO slapped a meaty hand on his shoulder.

"How you feeling this morning, Michael?" Roberts demanded cheerfully.

"Good, sir," Stanford replied hesitantly. "The Group is shaping up well."

"I agree," the big Commander told him. "Which means it's time to start throwing wrinkles into the mix."

"Sir?"

"My crew and I will be taking over the OpFor for this exercise," Roberts told Stanford. "Unless I misread my chain of command this morning, that puts *you* in command of SFG-001."

"Good luck," the Wing Commander finished with a wicked grin.

With another boisterous clap on Stanford's shoulder, Roberts walked off towards *Avalon*'s Starfighter Control Center.

Stanford looked after him for a long moment, then turned back to the ladder, meeting his gunner's gaze.

"What do we do, boss?" the younger man asked.

"Get in and jack in," Stanford ordered. "Then we show the CAG we've been paying attention in school.

New Amazon System, Castle Federation
13:10 August 4, 2735 Earth Standard Meridian Date/Time
SFG-001 Alpha Six – Falcon-*type starfighter*

For the first time in months, Michelle took her seat at the center of the small cockpit of a starfighter. Behind her, Deveraux sat on her right and Garnet was on her left. All three of the seats were recliners, easily set to whatever was most comfortable – once jacked into the neural interface, you weren't very aware of your body. While the starfighter had a small bunkroom and kitchenette for long flights, combat could require as many as five or six hours jacked in – and completely unmoving.

After a fight or intense simulation, that reclining function was often the only reason starfighter crews could walk.

"You know, Lieutenant," Deveraux said quietly as they all reclined back, "if you're feeling rusty, I can fly us. I've been checking out on the simulator, I almost have the hours to apply for a switch to pilot track."

Michelle pursed her lips, knowing the gunner couldn't see her. The offer was probably genuine, but it was also a subtle undercut to her authority – after all, if the gunner could fly the fighter, why was the pilot in command.

"How many simulator hours do you have?" she asked after a moment.

"Two hundred and eighty-three," Deveraux answered with pride, and Michelle smiled.

The gunner was telling the truth – with three hundred simulator hours in under a year, she *could* apply for a transfer to pilot, and it might even be granted. For now, though...

"I have four hundred in the last six weeks," Flight Lieutenant Michelle Williams told her subordinate gently. "Over four *thousand* total, and fifteen hundred live flight hours. Your offer is appreciated, but unnecessary."

"Jack in," she ordered.

As the chair's systems extended the leads that connected to her flight suit, Michelle smiled to herself. From the moment she'd been brought aboard *Avalon* she'd scraped every hour of simulator time her 'invalid' status would allow her. She was grateful for the practice, as it made the *Falcon* feel like a familiar warm blanket as the leads jacked home, and her mind slipped into the computers.

"Garnet, check the simulator interlocks," she ordered over the starfighter's internal net. She could feel the flight deck around her, the *Falcon*'s sensors feeding directly to her brain.

"The Deck Techs should have done that," the Junior Lieutenant complained, though the net told her she was obeying.

"Do you want to be the fighter that accidentally fires the engines or – stars forbid – the positron lance because the simulator lock-outs failed?" she asked rhetorically. Firing the starfighter's antimatter engines for even a fraction of a second would make a mess of the flight deck – firing the fifty-kiloton-a-second main gun would *gut* the carrier.

Of course, with the fighter's zero point cells disabled and the little ship running on ship-fed power, that *shouldn't* be possible. But it *had* happened. Once. That was more than enough.

"Interlocks confirmed," Garnet responded after a few seconds. "All systems are disabled, control input is feeding to the simulation. We are cleared to enter the sim."

A single thought-command from Williams later, the starfighter was suddenly in deep space. The other forty-seven fighters of Starfighter Group Zero Zero One surrounded them, but beyond the starfighters, local space was empty.

They weren't the last into the sim, she noted, watching as more ships lit up slightly on one of her mental displays. Easily twenty seconds passed after Alpha Six's arrival until the entire Group was fully jacked in.

"All right everyone, this is Wing Commander Roberts," a voice said directly in her ear. "Flight Commander Stanford will be leading the group for today's exercise. I am commanding the Opposing Force, which will be arriving... now."

A massive burst of blue Cherenkov radiation announced the arrival of a starship exiting Alcubierre-Stetson drive, and then Michelle swore aloud.

Emerging from the blue starburst was the massive bulk of a Commonwealth *Resolute*-class *battleship*.

CHAPTER 8

New Amazon System, Castle Federation
13:12 August 4, 2735 Earth Standard Meridian Date/Time
SFG-001 Alpha Actual – Falcon-*type starfighter*

Stanford stared at the immense bulk of the battleship for a long moment. The warship was a thousand meters from her rounded prow to the flat edge of her engines, with the smooth lines of her oval hull swelling to a three hundred meter bulk at her center of mass.

She'd been designed so that no matter where his squadron approached from, they'd be facing roughly half of the battleship's guns – easily thirty ninety-kiloton-per-second anti-starfighter guns backing up the nine megaton-per-second positron lances of her main battery.

The ship's deflectors were also much more powerful than his *Falcons*, which meant that Wing Commander Roberts could start picking them off from almost twice the range at which their own main guns could hit the starship's hull.

If *Avalon* had been present in the scenario, the battleship could likely have ended the entire battle in a single salvo of her main guns – though the old carrier's new arsenal would probably have put enough antimatter and missiles in space to ruin the Commonwealth commander's day.

Missiles. Even as Stanford finished his first gasp of shock at the presence of the battleship, a plan popped into his head.

"All right everyone, you see the big boy," he told the Group over the radio. "Wedge formation, Echo Squadron on point. All ships, fire a full missile salvo on the battleship. Interface your AIs, get me maximum vector dispersals – I want a shield, people, not a spear."

Of the other four squadron commanders, Stanford knew at least two would have objected to his order putting them in the brunt of the fire. Rokos simply grunted as the starfighters sprang into action around Stanford. Every one of the forty-eight ships fired four Starfire XI missiles. Even as the *Falcons* began to blaze forward at five hundred gravities, the missiles shot forward at just over a thousand.

"Echo Squadron, Foxtrot Squadron," Stanford continued as the assault began. "You're the ECM shield. Keep their sensors distracted – and as you're doing it, keep throwing missiles at them."

"Once Echo and Foxtrot are bingo on missiles, Charlie and Delta will move up to cover us all," he ordered. "Once you're bingo, Alpha and Bravo will move up – that should get us to one fifty kilos."

The warbook in his computer insisted that at one hundred and fifty thousand kilometers, the *Falcon*'s fifty kiloton-per-second positron lances would burn through the *Resolute*'s magnetic deflectors. He hoped they were right, because he wasn't sure how many ships he'd have left by that point.

"Go," he murmured softly, knowing the computers would carry his words to everyone in SFG-001's tactical net.

They'd been en-route for sixty seconds, and barely begun to close the range even at five kilometers per second squared, when the first positron beams started to flicker out from the battleship. Between the electronic counter-measures being thrown out by the missiles themselves, plus Rokos' squadron's support, all of the missiles and fighters survived.

That, Stanford knew, wouldn't last.

"Random-walk, people," he ordered. "Keep them guessing!"

Roberts had to be using AI routines to run most of the battleship's weapons, even in a simulated environment. That meant a little human randomness would throw them off, possibly carry a few more of them through.

By ninety seconds in, the *Resolute* had shredded more than fifty missiles. Echo and Foxtrot squadron fired again, adding another sixty to the shield bearing down on the battleship – a threat the warship's defenses could handle, but also one it had to respect.

Eighty second later, the first ships died as more missiles fell – and positron lances began to smash into the front wave fighters. Echo and Foxtrot held under fire for another ten seconds, salvoing more missiles to continue covering the Group's advance, and then fell back as Charlie and Delta swept forward. For a moment four squadrons worth of counter-measures filled the space around SFG-001 and even Stanford couldn't make out his ships.

When the chaff cleared, the exchange was over – two fresh squadrons spearheaded the charge, and the eleven surviving fighters of Echo and Foxtrot's sixteen fell back inside the cone held by Alpha and Bravo.

Charlie and Delta weren't as lucky. Stanford watched, as calmly as he could, as Lancet and Zhao's squadrons writhed in the battleship's defensive fire. Their deflectors brushed away *most* of the light positron lances – but enough hit home to wipe away half of both squadrons by the time they were running out of missiles.

Then a lucky hit from the main guns took out Lancet's ship, and Charlie squadron's tactical network collapsed. It took precious seconds to restore – seconds that Wing Commander Roberts didn't give his people.

"Alpha and Bravo, moved forward to pick up the slack," Stanford ordered sharply. "Echo and Foxtrot, support us with countermeasures. Full missile salvo – everything we've got left!"

Not a single ship of Charlie squadron remained as twenty-seven other starfighters surged forward. Only two of Delta's eight starfighters remained, and Stanford watched grimly as the intimidating bulk of the battleship lunged towards them.

Missiles blasted out from his remaining ships, a hundred-plus bird salvo that the battleship *had* to acknowledge.

"AI, link to all missiles for remote detonation," Stanford ordered silently as his fighters charged forward behind their missile shield. Now they were close enough that the deflectors were failing to stop *any* direct hit from the battleship's positron lances.

"*Now*," he snapped, and the computer obeyed.

Scattered across the two hundred thousand kilometers between his Starfighter Group and the *Resolute*, the ninety-three surviving one-gigaton antimatter warheads detonated. Space descended into a hash of radio waves and radiation, his starfighter computers showing an extrapolation of where the ships would be.

For a battleship, a kilometer long and rated for two hundred gravities of acceleration, that extrapolation could allow hits. For a starfighter, *thirty* meters long and rated for *five* hundred gravities, it reduced the hit chance to almost nothing.

"Blast through and *hit him!*" Stanford snapped over the channel, hoping that the com system's lasers would get through.

Moments later, his ship blasted clear of enough of the cloud to target the battleship – only one hundred and forty thousand kilometers away!

The little starfighter jerked as the simulated zero point cells opened up their antimatter capacitors. A stream of positrons, skimmed from the quantum froth underlying reality, blasted away from the *Falcon* at ninety-nine percent of the speed of light.

Other beams joined his, ripping into the battleship and turning its mighty armor into explosives that tore themselves apart. The positron lances tore deep into the warship, shredding machinery, systems – and zero point cells.

Moments later, antimatter capacitors ruptured under the barrage and the battleship disappeared in a sharply white explosion.

Nine of SFG-001's starfighters survived the final round of counter-fire to watch the battleship die. Alpha Actual wasn't one of them.

New Amazon System, Castle Federation
14:00 August 4, 2735 Earth Standard Meridian Date/Time
DSC-001 Avalon *– Flight Group Briefing Room*

Roberts watched as all one hundred and forty-odd of Starfighter Group 001's pilots, gunners and flight engineers filed into the briefing room. Unlike many other aspects of the old carrier, *Avalon*'s briefing room had been designed to hold the entire fighter group crew when the ship had been laid down.

"All right people," he said cheerfully. "Today, you killed a battleship. Not bad. Of course, if that had been a *real* battleship, Flight Commander Stanford and I would have been writing a lot of 'Dear Mrs. Johnson' letters tonight, so let's go over what *didn't* go right."

"You sent us up against a fucking *battleship*," a voice snapped from the back. "How the hell was that a fair fight?!"

Kyle's implant identified the speaker as a Gunner from Zhao's Charlie Squadron. The loss of their tac-net had shredded that squadron, so he expected some bitterness from them. Enough so that he'd overlook the insubordination. Mostly.

"You're right," he agreed cheerfully. "That wasn't a realistic scenario – Commonwealth doctrine would call for a battleship like the *Resolute* to be accompanied by a carrier. A hundred or so *Scimitars* or *Darkswords* would have rendered the entire strike by our group moot, don't you think?"

The *Scimitar* was the Terran Commonwealth's current front-line fighter, roughly equivalent to the Federation's *Cobras*. *Darkswords* were older, a slightly better starfighter than the Federation's *Tempests*. Rumor had it that they had a seventh generation fighter like the *Falcon* in development, but hadn't deployed any yet.

"For that matter," Roberts continued, his smile warmer than his words, "the appropriate counter-tactic to Commander Stanford's missile shield is to use heavy missiles as area effect weapons against us."

"Given those two caveats, however, deploying the Group against a battleship is hardly 'unfair.' *Avalon* and her fighter group have *thirty-six* capital ship kills to our credit. SFG-001 has killed battleships before – and I want us ready to do it again."

"Nine of forty-eight came home," Kyle told his people softly. "From the perspective of the Joint Chiefs, thirty-nine starfighters for a battleship is a fair trade. One hundred and twenty lives and eighty billion Stellars of Federation hardware, trade for approximately twenty-five *hundred* lives and sixty *trillion* Stellars of starship."

He let the numbers sink in.

"There is no theoretical reason why a carrier or battleship can't be built for starfighter accelerations, people," he reminded them. "The fuel cost would be outrageous, which is why we don't, but it would be doable. A battleship or cruiser's positron lances and missiles are vastly more powerful and longer ranged than those on a starfighter."

"But even the mightiest battleship in the era of antimatter weapons is an eggshell armed with a sledgehammer. And a fifty trillion Stellar warship *isn't* expendable."

"A two billion Stellar starfighter is," Wing Commander Roberts finished bluntly. "Our role is to be expended, and to protect our carrier in the process."

"*My* job is to make sure as few of us are expended as possible. I do not like 'Dear Mrs. Johnson' letters. If we ever have to fight a battleship, I want to bring more than twenty-seven of you home!"

"So, given that as a starting point, let's look at how we did – and what we can do *better*."

New Amazon System, Castle Federation
17:00 August 4, 2735 Earth Standard Meridian Date/Time
DSC-001 Avalon *– CAG's Office*

"Have a seat, Michael," Kyle told his subordinate with a smile as they entered his office. The last four weeks had been too busy to do much to customize the Space Force Standard furniture and decoration, but he *had* installed a mini-fridge. New Amazon had some amazing breweries, and he pulled a pair of beers from the fridge, sliding one across the table to Stanford.

The Flight Commander grabbed the bottle carefully, and gave his Wing Commander a dark look.

"A beer is supposed to make up for that three hour grilling you just gave me?" he asked.

"Ha, no," Roberts replied. "If I'd spent three hours grilling you, you probably wouldn't be *getting* the beer. Only about forty minutes of that was on *your* performance."

"Point," Stanford accepted, cracking open the bottle. "We are still on duty," he observed.

"My Deck, my rules," Kyle ordered. "For not expecting me to dump wing command in your lap and probably expecting a more generous scenario – like some of our pilots – I'm actually impressed you manage to take down the *Resolute*."

"Would have been nice had I *lived*," Stanford pointed out mildly. "You'd have been writing 'Dear Mrs. Stanford' to my *mother*."

Kyle shivered, and it wasn't entirely feigned.

"Mothers suck," he admitted softly. "*None* of those letters are fun, but telling my pilots' moms they aren't coming home is second only to telling their *kids*."

He knew from Stanford's record that the junior man had never had to write the family of a fallen officer. Not many officers in the peacetime Federation had.

"*Gulf*?" Stanford asked quietly.

"The *Gulf* and a few suicides," Kyle confirmed softly. He'd been promoted to Wing Commander after leading the strike on the *Ansem Gulf* – a passenger liner boarded and captured by pirates. The pirates had waited for the Castle Federation Marines to board, and then revealed they'd used the two weeks it had taken the Navy to catch them to *arm* the civilian starship.

Of the *Alamo*'s forty-eight starfighters, seven had died in the first salvo – including Wing Commander Rani Desai. By the time Kyle had managed to re-organize the fighter group and disable the weapons mounts, fifteen starfighters – and forty five crew-men and -women – were gone, along with a third of Peng Wa's Marines.

Most of the Navy and the Space Force figured that most other commanders would have fallen back – potentially saving more of the squadron, but abandoning six hundred Marines and fifteen *thousand* civilians. Kyle had counter-attacked.

The promotion, accolades, and the knowledge of fifteen thousand saved lives had been a frail shield against those forty-five letters.

"Hence kicking the shit out of the squadron in sims?" Stanford asked timidly after a moment.

Kyle shook himself and nodded. "I figure the more I kill our people in simulations, the less likely it is some coked up pirate with a sixty year old mass driver or, God forbid, an actual Commonwealth attack, will kill them."

"Speaking of our people, how did Williams do?" he asked, taking a long sip of his own beer. He wasn't inclined to play favorites, but if anyone in the group *deserved* a little extra attention, it was the one brave enough to turn down a legitimate Article Seventeen discharge because they *wanted* to serve.

"We gave her less than an hour to get to know her new crew," Stanford replied slowly, considering. "She didn't survive – but she outlasted *me* by three quarters of a second."

"She's *good*, boss, and I'm glad to have her back aboard," he continued. "That's our last empty slot filled – with Williams back on active duty, we have a full flight group. Any word on when we ship out?"

"The last of the holes are patched in the ship," Kyle told him. "Our Group is a little rustier than I'd like, but we can run sims while under A-S drive. I know the Navy-side was running full power drills on the new main battery while we were debriefing our people, and my implant tells me they fully checked out."

The Wing Commander checked his implants for the note he expected to find, and nodded cheerfully as he saw the quick heads up from the Captain.

"Captain is still checking in with Joint Command," he told Stanford, "but he's expecting to ship out at nineteen hundred hours tomorrow. There'll be a formal notice, but you can pass a quiet word to the Chiefs."

"Can do," the Flight Commander confirmed. "It'll be good to see the Old Lady move again. It's been too long for her."

"Hell, Commander, it's been too long for *me*," Roberts told his subordinate with a chuckle, "and I've only been sitting dead in space

for a month!"

Glynn Stewart

CHAPTER 9

New Amazon System, Castle Federation
05:00 August 6, 2735 Earth Standard Meridian Date/Time
DSC-001 Avalon – *Bridge*

The bridge of a twenty-eighth century warship is an inherently calm, quiet, place. Most of the scurrying and conversations took place either in specialized departments hidden away in *Avalon*'s hull, or entirely inside the ship's network.

An even dozen reclining chairs, easily conformed to a user's personal taste, formed two semi-circles around the center dais. Each chair had a pair of medium sized screens, adjustable to show whatever the occupant desired, but the real working connection was the cyber-jack at the back of each of the seats.

Kyle was certain that the wall-screens that wrapped the entire room in a perfect replica of the space outside the carrier were there entirely for the eight observer seats at the back of the bridge. With the carrier about to make her first Alcubierre-Stetson voyage in ten years, he'd expected the seats to be full, but only five had been taken.

Avalon had been under way for ten hours now, having left the New Amazon station behind in a flare of superheated exhaust. The ship's immense mass manipulators reduced her mass exponentially, allowing immense matter-antimatter thrusters to propel her twelve million tons with a reaction that, at least theoretically, mirrored the rockets mankind had first touched the stars with.

Now, however, they were clearing the gravitational safety zones around the various planets, stations, asteroid belts and other miscellanea that made up a star system, and about to leap to the stars. It was a sight Kyle never grew tired of.

"Navigation, please confirm that we have cleared all detectable gravity zones," Captain Blair requested aloud. For all of the instant data transfer available to the crew, tradition demanded certain orders and requests be spoken aloud.

Like the bubble of stars surrounding the bridge crew, it was probably for the observer.

"All identified gravitational objects are beyond effect range," the navigator reported from her couch. "Current gravitational force is beneath one pico-meter per second squared. We are prepared to warp space on your command."

"Engineering, please confirm status of Class One mass manipulators," Blair ordered.

The *Avalon* had dozens of Class Two and Class Three mass manipulators throughout her hull, even discounting those aboard her parasite craft like Roberts' fighters. Under the power of those devices' ability to generate and manipulate mass and gravity, she could fly and fight – but it took something more to outspeed light.

"All five Class One's are at ninety-nine-plus percent," the junior engineer on the bridge reported aloud. "Engineering reports prepared to warp space."

The Class One mass manipulators were an order of magnitude larger and more powerful than any others of their kind. In some ways they were the simplest, and had been the first built, but their sheer scale made them an immense undertaking. *Avalon*'s five Class Ones represented over sixty percent of the original cost of her construction. Four were required to warp space, with the fifth standing by in case there was a problem.

"All hands, prepare for Alcubierre drive," the Captain ordered. He let several moments pass. "Navigation, please initiate interior Stetson stabilization fields."

A faint haze settled over the screens surrounding the bridge as hundreds of small emitters across *Avalon*'s hull woke to life, stretching a field of electromagnetic and gravitational energy around the ship. Useless in any other circumstance, the only purpose of the Stetson field was to protect the ship from the immense forces it was about to unleash.

"Interior Stetson field active," the Navigator reported. "Exterior field on standby, mass manipulators on standby."

"Lieutenant-Commander Pendez," Blair said softly. "You may initiate space warp at your discretion."

"Yes, sir!" the younger woman agreed enthusiastically. Moments later, the ship shivered slightly, and the bubble showing the space outside the ship distorted.

Kyle's practiced eye picked out the four sets of distortion, the perfectly scaled singularities *Avalon* was generating sucking in all light that passed by them.

"We have singularity formation," Pendez reported. "Exterior Stetson field is active, no containment issues. Initiating warp bubble… now."

Avalon's immense arrays of zero point cells flared to life, and the power feeding to the Class One manipulators increased a thousand-fold. The distortions seemed to move, and the space beyond the carrier wavered in their influence for a long second.

Then a bright flash of blue light encapsulated the ship, and the New Amazon system was gone, replaced by a flickering and chaotic glow of Cherenkov radiation.

"Warp bubble established," Pendez confirmed. "We are under way."

Kyle exhaled softly. After having hundreds of the Navy's best people swarming over the carrier for a month, he hadn't *expected* any issues, but it had been ten years since *Avalon* had last gone faster than light.

Before he could get up to leave, his implants picked up a ping from Blair. Softly, so as not to distract the men and women plugged into the starship around him, he approached the central chair.

The Captain blinked and disconnected, turning towards Kyle.

"That went smoothly," he said quietly so only the Wing Commander could hear. "How's the fighter group?"

"Solid," Kyle allowed. "Don't tell any of them I said that, though," he warned. "I still have my stick out, and the more they think *I* think they're not making the grade, the harder they'll work."

Blair chuckled and shook his head. "That only works for so long, Commander," he replied. "Sooner or later, you have to admit they're doing okay."

"I will," the Wing Commander said cheerfully. "Sooner or later."

"We have our final flight plan from Joint Command," Blair told him, changing the subject. "I'd like to go over it with most of the senior staff. Are you and Stanford free for a staff meeting at ten hundred hours?"

Kyle blinked, checking his and Stanford's schedule in an instant. By the time he'd finished blinking, he'd confirmed that he was free, and moved a meeting between Stanford and Senior Chief Miller back three hours.

"We are now," he confirmed.

"All right," the Captain accepted with another chuckle. "It's time to walk everyone through what our lords and masters intend for us."

Under Alcubierre Drive, Castle Federation Space
10:00 August 6, 2735 Earth Standard Meridian Date/Time
DSC-001 Avalon – *Main Conference Room*

The back wall of the main conference room on *Avalon*'s bridge deck was taken up by a screen showing the exterior of the ship – currently a faintly glowing maelstrom of Cherenkov radiation and strange lightning.

The light from the screen mixed with the room's overhead lighting to cast strange patterns of shadow across the glossy faux marble surface of the bog-standard Navy conference table at the center of the room. The room could hold as many as forty people, but for this staff meeting it held only the carrier's senior officers.

Roberts and Stanford took seats halfway along the table, almost at the back of the small gathering of people, facing the screen where Kleiner and Blair stood surveying their crew.

"Good morning everyone," Blair finally announced once the officers were seated. "Now that we are underway and all of our systems fully checked out, Joint Command has provided me the final updated version of our orders."

A holographic image of the galaxy appeared above the conference table, and then rapidly zoomed in on the area around the Castle Federation, some four hundred light years towards the galactic rim from Earth. Once at the level where individual stars could be distinguished, colored carets snapped into view around them: fourteen bright green markers for the Castle Federation itself; twelve dark blue markers for the Coraline Imperium, the next largest member of the Alliance; and thirty-six lighter blue markers for the other Allied systems. The three dimensional image was focused on Castle and their allies, but a dozen red-gold carets marked systems closer to Earth – border systems of the Terran Commonwealth.

"We are currently on route to the Phoenix system," Blair informed any member of the staff who hadn't been keeping up with the daily electronic briefings. A pair of stars with a single caret flashed bright purple, marking their current destination. "It will take us about seven days to travel those fourteen light years."

"This is our final shake-down for this refit," Blair concluded. "Phoenix's yards will be able to repair any issues we encounter on the way there, but once we leave Phoenix we won't be visiting many systems with full shipyards." A wholly unnecessary gesture on Blair's part highlighted fifteen more systems in purple. All were single-system star nations on the Commonwealth side of Alliance space.

"Our next destination is Hessian, twenty-one light years from Phoenix," the Captain continued. "From there, we complete an arc across the Commonwealth border, averaging a bit over one week's transit between systems. We should return to Castle just before Christmas."

"I have been informed that barring absolute disaster, we are *required* to be in Castle for the New Year's celebrations," he told everyone. "I am told that we will hold pride of place in the annual Fleet Review."

Smiles and nods rippled through the conference. Kyle shared a bright grin with his senior subordinate. He would have to have SFG-001 practice their parade formation flying, though with over four months to work with, he'd have lots of time to whip them into a shape that wouldn't embarrass them.

Blair waited calmly for the commotion to die down.

"That, unfortunately, is accompanied by a piece of bad news," he warned them. "We will hold pride of place in the Fleet Review on January First – and we will deliver *Avalon* to the Merlin Yards for decommissioning on January Sixth."

Dead silence fell over the room.

"I am sure we all suspected that this would be *Avalon*'s final voyage," Captain Malcolm Blair informed his people sadly, "but Joint Command has now confirmed that. We will show the flag on the frontier, and then we will bring the Grand Old Lady home to lay her to rest."

"I would prefer that this information not leave this room," he said. "We've only just got morale aboard this ship up to something I would regard as acceptable. I do want you to consider it in your department planning and – especially – in your personnel reviews. The new *Avalon* will commission shortly after we deliver the Old Lady to Merlin. They will be looking to us and our crew to man her with personnel that understand the legend of *Avalon*."

"Our job over the next four months is to remind the galaxy of that legend," Blair told them. "When we return to Castle, we will return having shown that *Avalon* and her crew are still worthy."

Kyle nodded firmly in response to Blair's words. Serving on *Avalon*'s last voyage could be either a waste of time – or a career-making feather in one's cap.

Which one would depend on how hard they worked.

CHAPTER 10

Under Alcubierre Drive, Castle Federation Space
14:15 August 8, 2735 Earth Standard Meridian Date/Time
DSC-001 Avalon – *Flight Deck*

Shouting from the Flight Deck drew Kyle's attention as he headed towards the flight control center. He stopped, then changed direction towards the commotion. A number of the fighter bays were currently under repairs due to a repeating short, but that shouldn't have been causing issues.

He reached the edge of Bay 18 and was about to turn the corner towards the commotion when he finally recognized the voices involved.

"This is an absolutely *unacceptable* state for a warship of the Federation Navy," Senior Fleet Commander Caroline Kleiner bellowed. "Get this crap stowed away before there's an accident."

"Ma'am," Kyle heard Chief Hammond start, only to be cut off by the XO.

"I'm not interested in excuses, Chief," she snapped. "Get this crap off the Flight Deck *now*."

That was enough.

Kyle stepped around the edge of Bay 18 and surveyed the situation. Bays 19 through 23 had been shut down by an electric short, resulting in a small-scale electromagnetic pulse in Bay 20. Hammond's crew had moved everything except the starfighters themselves out of the bays to allow them to fix the damage without risking more unshielded hardware.

This had left neat stacks of pallets and several mid-sized pieces of machinery sitting in the middle of the Flight Deck – right where a shuttle would have to land if the carrier weren't in deep space under Alcubierre drive.

Kleiner stood next to the pile of gear, facing Senior Chief Marshall Hammond down while a dozen technicians who *should* have been repairing the damage to the fighter bays hovered like lost children pretending not to hear anything.

"Commander Kleiner," Roberts snapped as he approached. He caught the glance of relief Hammond sent him, but focused his gaze on the XO.

"You're here," she sneered. "Now maybe you can get the Chief to do his job."

"Commander Kleiner," he repeated, his voice flat. "My office. Now."

She stared at him in shock. His tone clearly hadn't registered when he'd first spoken, and now he nodded his head back towards the exit from the Flight Deck. With a firm nod to Senior Chief Hammond, he turned on his heel and left the scene, not checking to see if the XO was following him.

Thankfully, she did. From the way she moved, though, he was certain that she would have slammed the door to his office if the automatically sliding portal would have allowed it.

"What is the meaning of this?" she demanded as he took a seat at his desk and turned to face her. "Where do you get off undercutting me in front of your people like that?!"

"Because they are my people, Commander Kleiner, not yours," Roberts told her flatly. "And because you were making a fool of yourself."

"You seem to have forgotten," he continued, cutting off her angry sputtering, "that you are *not* part of Senior Chief Hammond or his people's chain of command. You, in fact, have *no* authority on the Flight Deck of this ship except that provided by the respect due to your rank – a respect you were happily pissing away."

She opened her mouth again, and he raised his hand. "If you have an issue with the Flight Deck, Senior Fleet Commander, you bring it to me. That way, I can do things like tell you that five fighter bays have been downchecked for a wiring short, and that I explicitly authorized them to remove the contents of those bays to expedite repairs."

"It was a bloody safety hazard," Kleiner finally snapped.

"Yes," Kyle allowed. "One that my Senior Chiefs and I had carefully considered and decided was worth it to enable us to get five fighter bays working without risking the loss of several dozen million Stellars worth of equipment."

"Your Chief was actively insubordinate," she replied. "I demand that he be disciplined!"

"No," Kyle said simply. "You do *not* berate *my* Senior Chiefs on *my* Deck," he snapped. "I will *not* permit it, do I make myself clear?"

Avalon's Executive Officer stared at him in plain shock. She had no authority over Kyle – or his people – and had just tried to use that nonexistent authority to interfere with the workings of his Deck. His sympathy was minimal.

"Where was this paternal instinct when you had a son?" she snapped.

She knew the words were a mistake as soon as they left her mouth. Kyle could see it in her eyes, even as he slammed his fist into his desk and rose to his feet. The normally cheerful Wing Commander said nothing, didn't even lean towards her, but looked down on her from his six inch height advantage.

"Get. Off. My. Deck," he ground out. "Now."

That, she finally listened to.

Under Alcubierre Drive, Castle Federation Space
17:05 August 8, 2735 Earth Standard Meridian Date/Time
DSC-001 Avalon – *CAG's quarters*

Kyle cursed under his breath as the asteroid next to his fighter flight's patrol route suddenly disintegrated. Obviously pre-placed explosions shattered the rock into a dozen pieces, and four Commonwealth *Scimitar* fighters erupted from behind it, missiles blasting towards the three ships accompanying his own *Falcon*.

The range was barely fifty thousand kilometers – knife fighting range, even for starfighters – and the Commonwealth went for lighter, faster, missiles than the Federation. Two of his wingmen died in balls of antimatter fire before they could even bring their ECM online.

Kyle's own ECM was online seconds before the simulation computer judged any of his wingmen to have activated theirs, and the missiles aimed at him and the fighter closest to him went astray, detonating against illusions their onboard computers insisted were real.

"Keep them busy," he ordered, "full salvo, straight into the pack." Eight missiles erupted into space, four from each of the surviving Federation fighters. Even as the missiles launched, Kyle started random-walking his starfighter, blasts of matter-antimatter annihilation twisting his course into an unpredictable corkscrew.

Moments later, the nose of his fighter aligned with one of the *Scimitars* for less than half a second. A thought took even less than that, and a blast of antimatter flashed out from the positron lance in the nose of his ship.

It connected for barely a tenth of a second, but that turned the side armor of the starfighter into a five kiloton bomb. The *Scimitar* flashed into nothingness, and its compatriots began to return fire.

Six lances, each *much* weaker than the single weapon on the *Falcons*, blasted out into space. The Commonwealth ships were co-ordinating their fire, sweeping entire regions of space that the two Federation starfighters might random-walk into.

A lance passed within meters of Kyle's starfighter as he jinked it up and to the left. Even as he started to react to that and return fire, though, the co-ordinated pattern saw fruit – his last remaining wingman came apart in a ball of fire as a beam cut into his hull and detonated the ship in a flash of matter-antimatter annihilation.

Continuing to random-walk the starfighter, Kyle did something he would never have done with a live crew, and took control of the seven surviving missiles away from his starfighter's gunner. Even most starfighter pilots couldn't have handled that data bandwidth, but Kyle had been pulled out of a class of Navy enlistees for the Space Force due to his high neural bandwidth capacity.

The Commonwealth ECM was good enough that the missiles were starting to drop out – he lost two even as he assumed control of the salvo – and he didn't think he was going to get direct hits. With the one-gigaton warhead of a Federation missile, though, he didn't need them.

He mass-detonated the four surviving missiles in the middle of the Commonwealth formation. The closest fighter was barely two kilometers away, and was completely destroyed by the blast wave. A second fighter, five kilometers away, would have survived if it hadn't had to reset systems from the radiation wave – a pause in their random-walking that allowed Kyle to line them up for his positron lance.

The last fighter was clear of the explosion and salvoing his own missiles at Kyle, using them to try and herd the Federation ship into the line of his positron lances. The Wing Commander smiled grimly and launched his own missiles, ready to try and turn the game around.

Then the entire simulation paused as a warning he'd previously set up triggered, informing him he was receiving a message from the Captain.

Kyle took a moment breathing to reduce his adrenaline levels, then removed the sim helmet that was jacked into his implants. Without the physical controls he would use in actual cockpit to augment his mental commands, it wasn't a complete simulation, but it still served a purpose in keeping his skills sharp.

"Roberts," he acknowledged over his implant, accepting the call from the Captain.

"Kyle, it's Malcolm," Blair told him unnecessarily. "Can I see you in my office please?"

"Yes sir," the Wing Commander replied with a sigh he filtered out of the transmission. It appeared that his confrontation with Kleiner wasn't resolved just yet.

Under Alcubierre Drive, Castle Federation Space
17:45 August 8, 2735 Earth Standard Meridian Date/Time
DSC-001 Avalon – *Captain's Office*

Kyle wasn't surprised to find Commander Kleiner in Captain Blair's office when he arrived. He was surprised by just how tired she looked at even a casual glance. The rigid precision he was used to seeing in the woman had faded away into a slouched posture, only accented by the surprisingly visible redness to her eyes.

"Commander Roberts," she said quietly, before Blair could even gesture Kyle to a seat, "I owe you an apology."

That was *not* what he'd been expecting. He took the seat the Captain gestured him to, as much to allow himself to gather his thoughts as anything else.

"I had some very bad news this morning, and it affected my judgment significantly more than I thought it had," the XO continued. "I crossed both professional and personal lines that I should not have."

She met his gaze levelly, and Kyle realized he'd underestimated how red her eyes were. He wasn't much of a judge of these things, but he was pretty sure she'd been crying. Their clash this morning was more in line with his image of the Commander than this apologetic wreck.

"I won't say it was nothing," he said quietly. She'd mashed his personal berserk button pretty hard, and come within millimeters of being physically evicted from his office. Kleiner finally glanced aside, and he noticed that her left hand was missing the plain gold band she'd worn since she came aboard. A horrible suspicion of just what her 'bad news' had been hit him, and he forced something akin to a smile.

"I won't say it was nothing," he repeated, "but we all have our weak spots that can compromise our judgment, don't we?"

There was a flash of anger in her pose, then the XO relaxed and took a deep breath.

"I'm not used to it," she admitted.

Kyle looked at Blair for help. He knew how to counsel men and women younger than him under his command. He wasn't sure he had *any* idea how to deal with an older superior who'd just been 'Dear Jane'd.

The Captain shook his head.

"Can I rely on your both to put this aside as a momentary lapse of good judgment?" he asked calmly. "Or am I going to have to treat you like teenagers and separate you?"

Blair's tone made it a joke, to which Kleiner mustered a weak smile, but there was a rod of iron down the middle of the words.

"I would ask that you apologize to Senior Chief Hammond," Kyle told Kleiner. "Your only authority over my Chiefs is moral, and if you don't apologize after today, you'll never get that back."

"He's not the only one," she admitted. "Hell of a fucking day."

"Kyle's right, Caroline," Blair told her. "It's time for you to start digging *up*."

CHAPTER 11

Under Alcubierre Drive, Castle Federation Space
9:00 August 9, 2735 Earth Standard Meridian Date/Time
DSC-001 Avalon *– Main Infirmary*

Michelle traded shy smiles with the nurse outside Surgeon-Commander Pinochet's office. She was the same brunette that had been taking care of her when she'd been in the ward, a young lady named Angela.

"Doctor Pinochet is waiting for you," Angela told Michelle, her smile seeming to widen at the sight of the Flight Lieutenant. "She said to send you right on in."

"Thanks, Angela," Michelle told her, returning the smile. The two women held each other's gaze for a moment longer, and then Angela glanced aside, flushing slightly as she returned her attention to the patient she was checking in on.

The small incident kept a smile on the Flight Lieutenant's face as she entered Pinochet's office. The motherly doctor gestured her to a seat in front of her desk and leaned on her steepled hands, looking her over carefully.

"How are you doing, Michelle?" she asked, her eyes holding Michelle's.

"Good," the pilot replied automatically. She met the doctor's gaze levelly. "Surprisingly good. Getting back in the cockpit has been fantastic."

"So the note I have from Commander Stanford says," Pinochet told her, leaning back and relaxing. "He's extremely pleased to have you back on active duty, though he did question how you managed to sneak so much simulator time in."

Michelle flushed. She hadn't been supposed to be spending *nearly* as much time in the simulator as she had. Pinochet hadn't quite ordered her not to be working at all, but it had been strongly recommended.

"I'd lost my edge," she replied honestly. "I needed to get it back if I wanted to get back into the cockpit at all."

"I don't argue with results, Lieutenant," Pinochet told her, looking her up and down. "You look good, and you sound good. How are the nightmares?"

The sudden segue threw Michelle for a moment, then she slowly shook her head. "Not... good," she admitted. "Better – not every night anymore – but still not good."

Unlike most of the last year, she now had more than *one* nightmare – the one about Randall and now a new one about Liago. She'd also picked up one that combined the worst elements of *both* – the paralysis of Liago's attack with the violation of Randall's.

"Not surprising," Pinochet reminded her. "They're a necessary part of the healing process, unfortunately, especially with a cyber-memory ready to play whenever you hit the wrong reference."

The pilot shivered. With Pinochet's help, she'd finally inserted a code lock on the recorded memory in her implant of the attacks. Without it, any time her brain tried to flashback to the events, her implant obediently supplied a video-perfect recording of the attack.

There was a *reason* code locks were the first things doctors treating PTSD implemented – and it was something Doctor Donner hadn't even touched for her.

"I'm dealing," she told the doctor. "It's still not easy, but I *can* deal now."

"Good," Pinochet replied. "I'll put a note in the system to have you issued some sleep meds. I *don't* want you taking them regularly, but if you're having a bad night with the dreams, they will help."

"Thank you," Michelle said, bowing her head in acceptance.

The doctor smiled and launched into her next question.

#

After an hour session with the Doctor, Michelle felt utterly wrung out. It was never comfortable to dig that deeply into one's own psyche, however necessary it was, and she suspected doing it on a twice weekly basis was going to be a drain. It would help her recover, but it was going to be a drain.

She was focusing so much on the thought she almost ran directly into Angela. The nurse half-squeaked as she dodged backwards, spilling half a tray of hypo-spray injectors onto the floor.

"I'm sorry!" Michelle exclaimed. Angela flashed her a harried smile, and started collecting the 'sprays.

"It's all right, I should have been watching where I was going," the nurse said.

With a shake of her head, Michelle joined Angela on the ground, helping collect up the sprays. That earned her a brighter, less harried, smile that set her heart to pounding. As they stood up again, she realized how close she was to the nurse and hoped that Angela couldn't hear her.

"Give me a sec?" the nurse asked quickly, stepping back slightly. She slotted the tray into its home and turned back to Michelle. "Sorry, wanted to talk to you," she told the pilot. "Got a second?"

Michelle nodded, curious now – and realizing that the nurse *had* to be able to hear her pounding heart. Angela led her out into the hallway outside the infirmary, away from prying ears, and turned to face her.

"I know what you're being treated for," she started hesitantly, "so I'll understand if you say no, but do you want to go for a drink at the end of my shift?"

For a moment, all Michelle could do was look at the gorgeous nurse in shock. For all of the smiles, she hadn't figured the woman to be her type.

"Sorry, I didn't mean to push," Angela continued after a moment of silence, but Michelle held up a hand and smiled.

"You just took me by surprise," she admitted. "I don't know where things can go," she continued honestly. She was still twitchy about being *touched*, after all. "That said, I would *love* to go for a drink with you."

Angela smiled back with a tiny sigh. "Deck Six officers' lounge at nineteen hundred?" she asked.

"It's a date."

Under Alcubierre Drive, Castle Federation Space
21:00 August 9, 2735 Earth Standard Meridian Date/Time
DSC-001 Avalon – *Deck Six Officers' Lounge*

Flight Commander Michael Stanford did not, generally, admit to being a soft heart or having favorites among his squadron's personnel. After everything Williams had gone through, though, he'd found himself keeping a careful, surprisingly paternal, eye on the woman.

"If you keep watching that pair, I'm going to think I'm doing something wrong," his companion told him half-jokingly.

He laughed softly, and turned back to his date. There were only two Officers' Lounges on *Avalon*, but it was still pure chance that his date with Fleet Commander Kelly Mason had brought him to the same one that Williams was in.

The lounge wasn't large, a two-tiered affair that bordered on the carrier's main atrium to allow it a wall of real greenery. The furniture was a slightly better than usual grade of Navy standard issue, and the food was identical to that served in every mess on the ship, but it did allow a quiet oasis of peace and faux luxury on the warship. A similar, larger, 'restaurant' along the longer side of the atrium provided the same service to the enlisted crew.

From the balcony where Stanford had cracked open a bottle of wine from his personal stash to share with Mason, he could easily see the table next to the window where Michelle and Angela had been sitting, heads together like a pair of naughty schoolgirls, since they arrived.

As her commander, he was aware of Michelle's inclinations – and he assumed that the ship's nurse was equally aware. That meant the scene was hopeful and heart-warming for him.

But, as Mason said, he was here for something else. He turned his practiced smile back on the voluptuous blond who, as *Avalon*'s Tactical Officer, controlled enough firepower to wreck a small world.

"My apologies," he offered gracefully. "I was checking to see if I needed a 'dad with shotgun' moment."

The Tactical Officer chuckled, a sound that ran over his nerves like a warm bath. "Don't give my boss ideas," she murmured. "She may have kissed and made up with *your* boss, but Kleiner knows what got you exiled to *Avalon*."

"I am reformed," Stanford told her expansively, holding his hand to his heart. "Reformed, and wounded by your disregard."

She chuckled again, and smiled wickedly.

"Not *too* reformed, one hopes," she murmured.

Chapter 12

It was a smaller group that gathered in the conference room on arrival in Phoenix. The big wall-screen was now focused on the pair of F-class stars whose intricate and eternal dance around each other provided light and life to the three habitable planets of the Phoenix system.

Kyle joined the Captain, Kleiner, and the ship's next two senior Navy officers – Fleet Commander Mason, the ship's Tactical Officer, and Fleet Commander Alistair Wong, the ship's Chief Engineer.

The holo-projector currently showed the carrier itself, with *Avalon's* truncated arrowhead hull translucent to allow sections of the interior to be highlighted. Kyle noticed that even as the Captain surveyed his senior officers, his cyborg eye stayed focused on the hologram.

"So, we've had a week in Alcubierre drive and we tested everything before we left New Amazon," Blair said calmly. "Where are we actually at?"

Kyle glanced around the table, following the Captain's eye, and watched Mason shrug and lean forward. Instead of using her implants, the Tactical Officer tapped at a keyboard in front of her for a moment, and several systems in the hologram of the carrier lit up in orange.

"Of our twelve one-point-two megaton-per-second guns, seven were out of alignment on install," she reported. "My people, working with Commander Wong's team, have six fully to specification." One of the positron lances flashed. "Lance B-2, however, is still out of alignment due to a warped magnetic coil. This wasn't a replacement we could do under A-S drive, but it's only a twelve hour job in a proper yard slip."

"Two of our missile launchers, all of Broadside C, are also down-checked due to part issues. We *could* fire C-2 in an emergency, but C-1 is completely out," she continued. "Both of those repairs are also difficult with on-board resources, but again are simple repairs in a proper slip."

"Otherwise, all of *Avalon*'s weapons fully check out," she finished. "Big guns aside, we're no battlecruiser or battleship, but anyone who gets in range of my lances is going to know they've been touched."

"My understanding is that we will have that yard slip," Blair told her, then switched his glance to Kyle.

The Wing Commander smiled. With a flicker of thought to his implant, he added his forty-eight fighters to the hologram in neat ranks in front of the carrier.

"The *Falcons* are impressive ships," he told the other officers, "but like any brand new technology, they are temperamental. We've had exactly five birds that *haven't* had some kind of issue, but it's all been repairable out of onboard resources."

"We're down to two starfighters trying to be hangar queens," Roberts concluded, highlighting those two with a thought, "but my Senior Chiefs assure me both will be online inside of forty-eight hours. We could use a load of replacement spare parts, given those we've used up getting the Wing online, but we are ready to go. I've prepared a schedule for a four fighter carrier space patrol for the extent of our stay in Phoenix."

"Shouldn't be needed, but I trust your judgment, Commander," Blair allowed before turning to Wong. "Commander Wong, how's the rest of the ship?"

The Chief Engineer was a tall and skinny Asian man with a shaved head that gleamed in the light of the hologram as he leaned forward, studying the image of the ship. Under his study, multiple systems turned faint shades of orange.

"We've had a number of minor issues," he reported, his voice clipped. "One of our life support plants seems unable to run at full capacity. The lights in Deck 16 keep burning out in under fourteen hours. One of the fighter bays on the Flight Deck started producing localized EMP fields."

"As with the Fighter Group, these have mainly been repaired out of on-board resources," Wong continued. "We need updated replacement parts. If possible, Life Support Plant Seven should be replaced. A number of the exotic matter coils in the Class One Mass Manipulators will be due for replacement prior to our expected decommissioning date. I can maintain and repair, but we should increase our stockpile of replacement coils."

"I also want to take advantage of the opportunity to fully assess the calibration of our Stetson stabilizer emitters while we are in Phoenix," the Engineer finished. "We identified a small mis-harmonic, currently non-dangerous. It's a low risk, but one I want to address."

"Thank you, Commander," Blair replied. "I agree – the last thing we want is an issue with the stabilizers!"

Without the stabilizers, the best case was that *Avalon*'s interior would be awash with the ultra-intense radiation created inside the warp bubble, killing everyone. The worst case was that the *exterior* stabilization field failed – dumping that radiation in front of the ship was predicted by some of the original math. That could easily sterilize half a star system.

"We have been given permission to dock at McKeon Station," the Captain continued. "My understanding is that we are slotted for a repair slip, as everyone expected the refit to have some teething problems, but I will make sure before we arrive."

"I am also informed that the battlecruiser *Dauntless*, flagship of the Royal Phoenix Navy, is also at the station," he told them. "Commander Kleiner, Commander Roberts – you and I have been invited to join Sub-Admiral Blackbourne and Captain Campbell for dinner tomorrow evening, after our arrival at McKeon station."

"*Dauntless* is a ship with a long legacy; the third of her name fought alongside *Avalon* in the war," Blair explained. "Consider this a state dinner – dress blacks, *with* medals."

Roberts sighed. He hated wearing medals.

Phoenix System, Kingdom of Phoenix
17:50 August 14, 2735 Earth Standard Meridian Date/Time
DSC-001 Avalon *Shuttle Six*

This time, Kyle was trying to be good and had taken his seat in the main compartment of the shuttle with the other passengers while the two Flight Lieutenants from his wing flew the shuttle over to *Dauntless*. Like Kleiner and Blair, he wore his dress uniform jacket over the shipsuit that was the base for all Federation uniforms.

The jackets of the two Navy officers were identical to his, but with gold piping compared to his dark blue. Kleiner's jacket had the usual peacetime officer's collection of qualification ribbons and badges, but Blair's medals were impressive. His included the qualification ribbons, but also had a top row that held two purple hearts and seven awards for valor, ending in the tiny gold icon of the Federation Star of Heroism.

Blair's was only the fourth uniform that Kyle had seen that star on other than his own. He lacked the older officer's collection of other valor awards, though, and other than the peacetime ribbonry, his only other decoration was the Space Force Combat Badge – earned with the Star at *Ansem Gulf*.

Most of Kyle's attention was tied up in his implants, as he piggy-backed onto the shuttle's optical sensors to view their surroundings. Behind them, *Avalon* was nestled into the immense network of girders and personnel tubes that made up one of McKeon Station's many repair slips. 'Beneath' the shuttle stretched the immense bulk of the Royal Phoenix Navy's primary shipyard and repair facility.

The Station put the Reserve Flotilla station in New Amazon to shame. It had grown haphazardly over the last fifty years, from the single starship construction yard the RPN had maintained before the war, to an immense structure capable of refitting half of the RPN's twenty capital ships at once.

"The Queen is worried," Kyle murmured, his gaze running along the length of the station.

"What makes you say that?" Kleiner asked. "Get an email from her?"

"Check the exterior cameras," he told her. "All four ships of their reserve are in for refit, and they've got all six construction yards working."

An Alcubierre-capable capital ship cost some fifty trillion Stellars to construct, a measurable percentage of a healthy system's Gross System Product. Even with three worlds and eight billion souls to draw on, the construction of *six* capital ships simultaneously was a noticeable fraction of the Kingdom's national GDP, let alone the government's budget.

The Senate had, the last Kyle had heard, just approved a building program of twelve new warships across the Castle Federation's *fourteen* star systems. Whatever had made that august body nervous was clearly being felt in the smaller Alliance members as well.

"We're all worried," Blair said softly, confirming Kyle's thoughts. "*Avalon* is on this tour due to an increase in piracy – and I don't think anyone in the Alliance really believes in space pirates."

Kyle nodded silently, his attention on the ships around them. Even a 'small' interstellar freighter was the size of *Avalon* and an important contributor to its home system's economy. Some starship theft happened – but most 'piracy' was done with in-system ships and stealth. An uptick across multiple systems suggested something more – usually another interstellar power stirring the pot.

Someone like the Terran Commonwealth.

"There she is," Blair pointed out, and Kyle sensed that the Captain was now in the system with him. He followed the other man's attention and spotted *Dauntless* coming out from behind McKeon Station. The flagship of the Royal Phoenix Navy and one of her sister ships, a heavy carrier from the look of her, orbited fifty thousand kilometers away from McKeon Station. Black watchdogs, guarding an immobile flock.

Dauntless was an even-sided diamond, fifteen hundred meters long and a quarter kilometer across at her widest beam. Each of her eight 'broadsides' bristled with positron lances and missile launchers, flanking launch tubes for her starfighters.

"Two years old, fourteen and a half million tons," Blair murmured aloud. "Second of the class, eighth of the name *Dauntless*. I'm a carrier man, but that is one hell of a battlecruiser."

Phoenix System, Kingdom of Phoenix
18:30 August 14, 2735 Earth Standard Meridian Date/Time
BC-067 Dauntless *– Flag Mess*

Kyle admitted that Sub-Admiral Patrice Blackbourne put on a fantastic meal. The one star admiral commanding *Dauntless* and the carrier *Adamant* had clearly convinced his staff and chef to go all out on behalf of the three Federation officers.

While Blackbourne only commanded a pair of warships, *Dauntless* was intended to be the lead unit of any major formation the RPN took to war, so her flag facilities were impressive. Among them was a flag mess designed to hold almost sixty people.

The three black-uniformed *Avalon* officers were heavily outnumbered by the senior officers of Blackbourne's staff and the two ships under his command. The Phoenix officers wore almost identical black shipsuits as the base of their uniform, but their dress uniform jackets were much flashier than the subdued garments Castle issued its officers.

The Navy officers wore dark blue jackets with short tails, gold braid at the shoulders, and embroidery down the sleeves. The small number of Royal Phoenix Space Force officers, Kyle's counterparts, wore similar jackets in a dark burgundy.

The entire flag mess had been covered in drapery in the same dark blue and burgundy colors, and only vast quantities of bright lighting kept the dark colors from sobering the mood.

All three Castle officers had sat together, at Sub-Admiral Blackbourne's right hand, through the meal. Once the excellent food had been cleared away, Captain Blair had become consumed in a conversation with Admiral Blackbourne and Captain Campbell of the *Dauntless*, gesturing for Kleiner and Roberts to 'go mingle.'

Kyle proceeded to find the bar and the dessert buffet, in that order, and then took up part of the wall with a glass of wine and a decadently good brownie. He could seek out company, but as one of the guests of honor, he knew he wouldn't be standing alone for long.

He was approached almost immediately, as it turned out, by a woman with short-cropped hair the color of burnished copper and the dark burgundy jacket of an RPSF officer. She had the lithe body of a consummate athlete, and moved with a panther's grace that caught his eye as she approached.

Her shoulder boards carried four narrow brands of gold braid, marking her as a Sub-Colonel – equivalent to his own rank. His implant provided the memory of being introduced – her first name was Jenaveve, but someone had coughed at the wrong moment and he hadn't caught her name or whether she served aboard *Dauntless* or *Adamant*.

"Sub-Colonel," he greeted her with an inclination of the head and an extended hand. "I'll confess that the introductions were a complete blur to me," he told her with a grin. "If you'll do me the favor of re-introducing yourself?"

She returned the smile, slightly, and shook his hand firmly.

"I am Sub-Colonel Jenaveve LaCroix," she told him. "I command *Dauntless'* Demons – the fighter wing."

While Phoenix fighter wings did have numbers, they were also assigned names when they were established. Unlike the Federation's Starfighter Groups, those names were the main reference.

"I am impressed by *Dauntless* herself," Kyle admitted. "I can't help but assume that her fighter wing is to match."

"My men are the best," LaCroix replied with a small smile. "Our *Chevaliers* are no *Falcons*, of course, but that will change in time."

"Of course," Kyle agreed. "I heard the *Templar* was supposed to enter flight trials shortly?"

The *Templar* was the Kingdom's seventh generation starfighter, supposed to be a fraction less-heavily armed than the *Falcon* but with matching speed and an even more powerful electronic warfare suite.

LaCroix winced. "It did," she said shortly. "There were... interference issues with the mass manipulators. Six flight crew died."

Kyle shared her wince, and offered his glass in toast to the fallen flyers.

"*Per ardua ad astra*," he said quietly.

LaCroix drank and nodded her agreement.

"How is the *Falcon* to fly?" she asked after they'd let a silent moment pass.

"A dream," Kyle told her. "I haven't spent as much time in real space in one as I'd like, but I swear the engineers worked some magic with the compensators and gimbals. I've never flown anything as smooth."

"The pilot makes all the difference," the Phoenix officer observed. "I heard *Avalon*'s wing had issues?"

Kyle took a sip of his drink and raised an eyebrow at her over the glass. That wasn't exactly polite to point out to an ally. He shrugged.

"She's been off front-line duty for a while," he admitted. "SFG One took some molding to get back up to grade, but they're starting to live up to my standards."

"Are they now?" LaCroix murmured, eyeing him. "Care to put your money where your mouth is, Wing Commander Roberts?"

"Oh?" he asked cautiously.

"Exercising against other Phoenix wings only gets us so far," she told him. "They have the same doctrine, same tactics, as we do. It stops becoming a stretch for anyone after a while. I would *love* to put my Demons up against *Avalon*'s wing – see if their extra experience can offset your people's superior fighters."

"My people *are* making my grade now," Kyle warned, and the Sub-Colonel grinned brightly at him.

"You know that, and *I* know that – but my people don't. Either they listen when I tell them that, and make up the difference with teamwork, or they learn a valuable life lessons," she told him.

"Losing wing buys the beer – and losing *commander* buys the other dinner," LaCroix proposed. "Sound like a bet, Wing Commander?"

Kyle returned her grin.

"I'll take that wager," he told her.

CHAPTER 13

Phoenix System, Kingdom of Phoenix
9:30 August 15, 2735 Earth Standard Meridian Date/Time
SFG-001 Alpha Actual – Falcon-*type starfighter*

"So boss, I heard about your side bet," Stanford told Kyle over a private channel.

"The one where if we win, they have to buy the entire wing drinks?" the Wing Commander asked dryly. He'd made *that* one clear to everyone, Stanford knew.

"Nah, the one where if we lose you buy LaCroix dinner," the Flight Commander replied. "So, boss, should we lose so you get a date?"

"Ha!" Roberts barked. "Somehow, I don't think the entire Flight Group would be willing to trade buying drinks for the Demons, even for getting the CAG laid."

"You'd be surprised," Michael muttered, knowing perfectly well that Roberts would hear him over the mental link.

"Play nice, Flight Commander," was all his boss told him. "I have LaCroix on another channel, we should be clear to link the simulations in a couple of minutes."

As soon as Kyle signed off of the channel, Stanford flipped to a second private channel with the other Flight Commanders.

"He didn't go for it," he reported. "Told you."

"Does he really expect to win this?" Shannon Lancet asked quietly. "The Demons are the Kingdom's *best* and we're..."

"Good," Mendez interrupted, to the shock of the Flight Commanders from the original SFG-001. The two Flight Commanders from *Alamo* had always seemed a cut above to Stanford and his compatriots. "Better than our people think they are – better than *your* lack of faith deserves."

"Hell, I was willing to go for it just to get the man *laid*," Rokos told the others. "I'm with Mendez," he continued. "The Group is good – one *hell* of a lot better than we were. But we could use Roberts laying off the men, too."

Zhao laughed, a melodic peal from the tall and elegant woman.

"I'm not sure the man has got laid while I've known him," she told the others. "And even if he did, I don't think it would make him lay off the Flight Group. But kicking the Demons' butt? *That* will get him to give the crews some slack."

"Some slack they'll have *earned* – and he knows, like we all do if we're paying attention, that we can do it."

All of the squadron commanders were silent for a moment, then the Wing Commander linked them into *his* circuit.

"All right people," Roberts told them, presumably unaware of their prior discussion. "We are syncing with *Dauntless'* simulation computers in sixty seconds. I'm downloading the formation I want your squadrons to assume now."

A moment of silence passed as the squadron leaders reviewed them.

"These intervals are garbage!" Lancet declared. "Half of them are too close, half of them are too far. The only squadron with a decent formation is Alpha, and you've got Foxtrot and Echo intermingled with them. What is this?"

"It's what a rookie reserve wing would do," Rokos observed quietly.

"It's what the wing the Demons *think* we are would do," Stanford agreed, his mental attention turning to Roberts.

"Exactly," the CAG told them, his mental voice tinged with pride. "This is what we're going to do..."

In reality, Kyle's six thousand ton command starfighter – which traded out the fourth missile in one of its launchers for dramatically expanded computer support – rested in its maintenance cradle in the bay on *Avalon's* Flight Deck.

In the simulated world conjured by the synchronized computers of two carriers and almost a hundred starfighters, the ship sat slightly to the left of the central part of the chaotic-looking arrangement he'd provided his people.

The scenario he and LaCroix had agreed to was straightforward, negating most of the tricks that could be played with starfighters. The two fighter groups had each assumed formations in front of what was referred to in training design as 'nominal carriers' – wireframes of the motherships with no ability to influence the engagement except as targets.

The Demons' formation, he noted was just about perfect. Their intervals were all randomized, but with a clean synchronization set up to allow each ship a clear field of fire at every moment in the cycle.

His own formation was neater than it looked – the fields of fire were clear eighty-five percent of the time, and the excessive drifting he'd built in worked better for defense most of the time. More than anything though, it *looked* unprofessional.

"Here they come," Rokos announced over the command network.

Kyle nodded to himself and switched to an all-hands channel. "All right folks, let's go meet Phoenix's best," he told them. "Keep your EW suites in intel-gather mode until I tell you otherwise," he continued, "and play lame duck. Let's see how sloppy we can convince them to get."

That got a few chuckles on his command net, and the CAG smiled to himself as he sent his own starfighter spiraling forward at five hundred gravities. If his people could carry this sim – if they could even hold their own – it would do wonders for his people's morale.

"Landon," he said quietly, linking to his ship's gunner. "Most of the data from everyone's electronic warfare suites is going to be dumping into our systems. You know what you're looking for – let me know when you've got it."

The *Chevaliers* were similar to the *Falcons* in base design, thirty meter long wedge-shaped ships. The Phoenix fighters were just as fast as the newer Federation ships, but narrower, and hence lighter and more lightly armed.

The two clouds of starfighters closed at almost ten kilometers per second squared, and the hundreds of thousands of kilometers between them began to evaporate far too quickly.

"Their ECM is good," Landon reported after a minute. "I'm not getting much of a read on them."

Kyle considered. He needed a reaction, but he couldn't waste missiles – not yet.

"All ships," he said softly, opening a channel to all of his people. "Give them a two second blast of positrons."

"We're not going to hit *anything* at this range," Lancet objected.

"I know," he agreed. "So let them think we're useless – I want to see how they react."

A few seconds later, obedient to his orders, lightspeed simulated antimatter blasted out from the fronts of his starfighters. Enough firepower to level a good sized city hurtled through space at the Phoenix ships – and missed them by as much as hundreds of kilometers as magnetic deflectors threw the charged particles aside.

But the target formation shifted. Intervals tightened slightly, allowing the deflectors to reinforce each other so as to throw any other long range attacks aside harmlessly. And the change to the formation meant orders had to be given...

"I've got them!" Landon announced over the ship's internal net. Eight of the *Chevaliers* were suddenly highlighted in bright red on Kyle's display: squadron command ships.

"Sloppy," Kyle murmured. "Sloppy indeed." The Demons, 'knowing' they were facing inferior opposition, had been relying on the passive security on the internal networks. Active security would have bounced and re-bounced the messages as well as encrypting them, preventing him from identifying the command ships – but also requiring the direct attention of at least one officer in each squadron.

"Download targets to Alpha and Bravo squadrons," he ordered Landon. "Set up the parameters for Snicker-Snack and download to everyone."

At their closing velocity, missile range was half a million kilometers, which they would reach... now.

"All ships, fire as per download," he ordered.

Forty-eight ships each fired four missiles each, a single salvo from every one of their launchers. One hundred and ninety-two Starfire missiles, each carrying a one-gigaton antimatter warhead – enough to kill a starship, let alone a starfighter – blasted away from his ship's at one thousand gravities.

The bright white light of his people's missiles were the only activity between the two fighter groups for thirty seconds as the Demons waited for a better targeting solution. Then ninety-six missiles blasted away from the *Chevaliers*, heading for Kyle's people.

A timer popped up in his mental screens. It started at one hundred and thirty seconds – twenty seconds before his missiles would reach the Phoenix fighters, roughly when they would start trying to take the missiles out.

Given the apparently disorganized swarm of missiles his people had launched, he was sure LaCroix's pilots and gunners were sure they would easily handle the salvo, and then gut his people.

Another thirty seconds passed, and a second salvo blasted away from the Demons. At ninety seconds from impact, a second salvo blasted away from his own ships. The virtual space between the two wings was now filled with antimatter fire and intelligent missiles seeking self-immolation.

"Stand by," he murmured into the all-hands channel when the counter hit fifteen. He was sure his pilots were on tenterhooks and hardly needed the warning.

"*Now*," he snapped as the timer hit zero. "Execute Snicker-Snack!"

Whether or not any of his people were familiar with the old poem about the Jabberwock and the vorpal sword, they understood *perfectly* what he wanted of them.

He'd timed the launch and execution perfectly. At his command, the formations around him suddenly snapped into place – intervals opening and shortening to clear *every* ship's line of fire.

Every ECM system on forty-eight starfighters blasted to full strength at the same time, and a seventh generation starfighter's systems made the five-year-old *Chevaliers* look like children shouting into tin cans. He *knew* their scans of his group had just turned to garbage.

Then his people opened fire. Positron lances ripped out at the speed of light, bracketing starfighters, herding those that evaded.

As antimatter flashed across space, the missiles had their own part to play. The execution command that flashed out ordered a third of them to detonate in place, sending blast waves of radiation rippling out in front of their compatriots.

However co-ordinated the strike was, however perfect the timing, there was no way that Kyle's people could take out *all* of LaCroix's fighters in a single missile salvo.

But with everything combined, they could easily take out eight.

The Demons tactical network came crashing down as *every* squadron commander, including LaCroix herself, 'died' in hammer blows of fire.

"Rokos, Zhao, co-ordinate missile defense," Kyle ordered. The Demons salvo was still inbound, after all.

"Everyone else... *hit them!*"

Phoenix System, Kingdom of Phoenix
19:00 August 15, 2735 Earth Standard Meridian Date/Time
McKeon Station – Dancing Starcat bar

The Demons, Stanford reflected, took losing surprisingly well.

'Buying the drinks' was one thing. What the Demons had actually done was more along the lines of 'rent the entire lounge and pay for an open bar.' Two entire fighter groups, almost three hundred men and women in the uniforms of two different nations, had descended on the Dancing Starcat in full force.

That worthy, a domestic housecat with a starry night sky for a coat, adorned much of the restaurant. It had even been etched onto the pint glasses the bartender was filling up two at a time for the swarming pilots

The two CAGs were nowhere to be seen, the slight Flight Commander noted, making him the senior officer of the chaotic crowd. There were seven Phoenix Space Force Majors around somewhere, but the two he'd seen were leading the way in terms of getting drunk.

Stanford himself was dealing with a not-entirely-newfound sense of responsibility. Roberts had yet to ask or even make much of a point as to how he'd ended up as one of the most senior active duty Flight Commanders in the Space Force, and he found himself wanting to live up to the faith his new boss had put in him.

Right now, that was manifesting itself by picking a table in a corner of the bar and moderating his drinking while keeping an eye on their people.

He was about to get up and collect his third beer of the evening when a shadow fell across his table. He looked up – and then further up! – at a mountain of a man looming over him. The bar lights reflected off the man's shaven skull in a way that reminded Stanford of Liago and sent tremors of fear through him.

"You're in my table," the mountain rumbled. "Move it, little man."

"The bar is closed for a private function," Stanford told him, but he could *hear* his voice tremble. The massive man grinned.

"Don't matter," he pronounced. "This is Argo's table, no one sits here."

"I was just leaving," Stanford muttered, sliding out of the table. His attempt to defuse conflict apparently failed, as the collar of his jacket was suddenly grabbed up in a fist the size of a dinner plate.

"Might've been," Argo growled. "But you sat in Argo's seat. Gonna teach a lesson."

Before Stanford could try anything, a distinctive and familiar hum cut through the hubbub of the bar. Argo's head turned, tracking the noise like a turret, to find a pair of women, both in the black and burgundy uniforms of the Phoenix Space Force – and both training fully charged stunners on the giant.

"I *know* the management has warned you about muscling your way in when the bar is closed," the closest of the women, a petite but curvy blond, told Argo calmly. "No one is going to blink twice if Rachel and I taze your ass and dump you for the Station cops."

The lithe brunette behind the speaker simply grinned and made a 'move-along' gesture with the barrel of the electro-laser.

Argo stared at the two women, as if unable to comprehend that a pair that he outweighed would actually threaten him.

"Put the Commander down, Mister Argo, and walk out," the speaker continued. "Or we shoot you, apologize to Commander Stanford for the aura effect, and dump you with the cops with charges of trespassing and assault."

Stanford hit the ground as Argo released him, managing to land mostly balanced as the giant growled wordlessly and started forward. Both of the stunners stayed locked on him and he apparently changed his mind, walking past the women and down towards the exit.

Shaking her head, the blond officer holstered her weapon and offered her hand to Stanford.

"Major Sherry Wills," she introduced herself. "This is Sub-Major Rachel Parks," she continued, indicating the woman behind her who grinned at Stanford and winked.

Delicately, Stanford took Sherry's hand and kissed the back of it.

"Enchanted, Major," he greeted her with a smile. "Your timing was impeccable!"

"Our pleasure," Rachel told him, the brunette slipping into one side of his table. With a smile and a gentle, easily-resisted, push, Sherry slid Stanford back into the table, and herself in on the other side of him.

"We were coming over to introduce ourselves," Sherry told him as he found himself sandwiched between the two women. "Argo just gave us a chance to do so with *flair*."

He laughed, and smiled at them.

"That he did," he agreed. "That he did."

Nobody was that reformed.

Sub-Colonel Jenaveve LaCroix made an excellent hostess, Kyle realized, and one who knew the ins and outs of McKeon Station with a flair and comfort that helped put him at ease. The restaurant she picked was a higher-class establishment, with soft music playing in the background and woven tapestries covering the station's bare metal walls.

Kyle didn't feel particularly out of place in the Green Line Lounge in his dress uniform without his medals, but LaCroix had dressed up for the evening in a knee-length red dress that clung frankly to every muscular curve, leaving very little of her frame to his imagination.

They'd spent the excellent dinner talking shop. She seemed more amused than angered by his suckering her flight crews into overconfidence, and told a story of an exercise where she'd conspired with a cruiser Captain to bring an overweening carrier commander down a few pegs.

Then the conversation had drifted to *Ansem Gulf*, and how Kyle had earned his valor decoration.

"The news made it sound like the pirates had turned the *Gulf* into some kind of Q-ship," he explained softly as she refilled his wine. "In truth, it was a bunch of pre-war mass drivers and pulse lasers. The only real guns in the whole bunch were on a half-dozen third-generation junk starfighters from the Stellar League."

The Stellar League was a loose coalition of systems, roughly the size of the Alliance, to the south and corewards of the Terran Commonwealth. While their technology was patchwork, it wasn't too far behind the Commonwealth or the Alliance – otherwise, the Commonwealth would have swallowed them up years ago.

That said, even a League third-generation starfighter dated from before the end of the war.

"Nothing they had would have been more than a passing threat to a cruiser or carrier," he told LaCroix. "We had starfighters and boarding shuttles, and they took us by surprise."

He shrugged.

"Honestly? Once we survived the first salvo, they never stood a chance. But it was a near-run thing regardless."

"I think you give yourself too little credit," the Sub-Colonel told him. "What you just did to my Demons is pretty demonstrative of what *normally* happens when someone takes out the leadership of a fighter group. You held your people together and carried the day – we're not impressed for nothing, Kyle."

"Touché," he admitted, inclining his glass towards her.

She leaned forward, brushing her arm against his and smiling at him.

"I was impressed *before* you managed to show my people a badly needed lesson in not underestimating your enemies," she continued. "And at this point, I've done just about everything short of hit you over the head with a club and drag you back to my quarters, and I *don't* think you're that oblivious. What gives, Kyle?"

He sighed, and leaned back away from her.

"I have a son," he said quietly.

"You're not married," she pointed out. "I'm not pushing, Kyle. Though I'll admit I'm not used to rejection!"

Kyle made a throwaway gesture.

"Believe me, Jenaveve," he said quietly, "it is not you. Were circumstances different, you'd be more successful. But I promised myself a long time ago I'd never leave anyone else behind."

"I wasn't exactly looking for wedding bells here, Commander Roberts," she pointed out. "You're a dear, but your duty will take you a long way away."

"What you want isn't my style, Jenaveve," Kyle told her. "I don't think I even *could* do a quick fling."

"I won't begrudge anyone their choices," she replied with a shake of her head. "You don't know what you're missing!" she finished with a lascivious wink.

"I don't," he agreed, raising his glass to her in a silent toast. "But I've enough regrets, and wouldn't want to miss you."

She laughed.

"In that case, Commander Kyle Roberts, you'd better plan on splitting a few more bottles with me," she told him. "If I can't bed you, I *will* by the stars get you relaxed another way!"

CHAPTER 14

The atrium aboard every Castle Federation warship was considered an essential part of the life support system by Castle designers, and an effete luxury even by many of the Federation's allies.

Michelle Williams, like many officers and crew of the Federation's military, found it a place of quiet sanctuary amidst the inevitable bustle and rush of a starship under way. Six days and eighteen light years out of Phoenix, the raven-haired pilot was enjoying a moment of quiet peace with Angela amidst the squat trees.

Here, away from prying eyes, the pair held hands carefully. Their relationship had yet to progress past a light peck on the lips, and Michelle was unspeakably grateful for the nurse's patience. With a small smile, the pilot leaned her head against the other woman's shoulder and activated a program via her implants.

For the next fifteen or so minutes, she'd get a warning buzzer if anyone came near this, very concealed, corner of the pseudo-wild forest *Avalon* carried in her heart.

Gently, ever so gently, Michelle ran her fingers up Angela's shoulder and into the nurse's long brown hair. Taking the other woman's contented sigh as permission, she laced her fingers into Angela's hair and drew her gently around to kiss her softly.

Slowly, hesitantly, their kisses grew more passionate. Then, with a moment of sudden decision, Michelle pulled Angela down to the soft moss on the ground. For a minute, they continued to kiss.

Then a momentary misjudgment of an angle brought Angela's full, if slight, weight down on top of Michelle and suddenly she wasn't seeing the gentle face of the lovely woman she'd come here to spend time with. She saw another face, one with paler hair and a far uglier expression.

With a gasp of fear, Michelle threw Angela off her, rolling away into a combative stance before she even knew what she was doing.

She crouched there, hyper-ventilating and trying to control her breathing as Angela slowly rose to her own knees and met her gaze.

"I'm sorry," Michelle gasped. "I'm sorry."

"You weren't ready," Angela told her aloud, but Michelle saw the hurt in her eyes. "Give it time."

"I'm *sick* of giving it time," the pilot spat. "The Doc says I'm fit for duty – I'm a *fighter*, dammit, not some weak-willed *civilian*."

Angela twisted her lips into a figment of a smile.

"That's what makes it harder for you," she said quietly. "There are wounds even now that only time can heal."

The nurse gripped Michelle's shoulder tightly, but from a distance – giving her both the space her panicked psyche needed in that moment and the warmth her heart needed always.

"I can be patient, dear one," she told the pilot. "I thought you knew you were ready – I was shocked."

Michelle looked up at her through the tears in her eyes and could see Angela trying.

"I thought I knew I was ready," she whispered. "When will I be?"

"When you are," Angela told her. "And I will be here."

Thorn System
17:00 August 26, 2735 Earth Standard Meridian Date/Time
SFG-001 Actual – Falcon-C type command starfighter

Theoretically, flying a normal combat space patrol in an allied system was not part of the CAG's job. After sitting around McKeon Station for days, and then spending six days in transit, Kyle had been bored out of his skull – and desperately missing the feel of deep space around him.

His wedge-shaped command starfighter swept towards Rose, the sole habitable planet of the Thorn system. Thorn was one of over thirty single system star nations scattered around the Castle Federation and Coraline Imperium that had signed on with the Alliance during the war against the Commonwealth.

Thorn was wealthier than some of those systems, with three capital ships in their fleet, and a massive industrial presence scattered throughout the entire star system. They were still poor compared to Phoenix, or even most Federation systems, but they were secure against most threats.

Three other *Falcon*s accompanied him, drawn from Stanford's Alpha squadron, including Lieutenant Williams' ship. The young pilot had seemed distracted when they'd prepped for the flight, but it hadn't shown up in her flying or her link into the network. He wasn't going to go interfering with his people's lives unless invited.

The CSP was well ahead of *Avalon* herself, closing with the planet at two and a half times the old carrier's acceleration. Their course carefully shaped away from most of the industry and in-system shipping, so it took longer than it should have for Kyle to notice the ships heading their way.

"Landon," he said quietly over the starfighter's internal net. "Vector twenty-six by forty. What do you make of it?"

A moment of silence passed, but the net told him that the gunner was focusing the passive scanners on that region of space.

"Three ships," the junior officer reported. "Warbook calls them *Stardust*-class heavy gunships. One hundred sixty meters long, four hundred thousand tons mass, main armament is twelve one-hundred-kiloton lances with a narrow forward firing arc. Rated for two-fifty gravities acceleration."

"Guardships," Kyle observed quietly, watching the three sublight warships blasting towards *Avalon*. "I wouldn't want to get in front of them, but I'd be more scared if the things were actually rated for Tier Three acceleration."

The various factors tied into fuel efficiency of a ship using an antimatter thruster combined with mass manipulators were a complex multi-factorial calculation with a number of 'plateaus' – or tiers. Each tier was significantly less fuel efficient than the tier below it. A Tier One ship used almost no fuel, but even with modern technology could accelerate at perhaps sixty gravities.

Only missiles could afford the fuel to mass expenditure of Tier Four acceleration, but starfighters and their five hundred gravity accelerations were rated for Tier Three – and were approximately one percent as efficient as a capital ship running at Tier Two.

The gunships approaching them were probably newer than *Avalon*, and might have as much as thirty or forty gravities advantage over the carrier. Kyle's starfighters, however, could outfly them drunk and blindfolded.

"They're pushing hard," Kyle continued, his mental voice still soft. "I *know* Captain Blair notified Thorn before we left Phoenix, and when we arrived."

His four ships weren't *much* of a threat to the three much larger ships, but SFG-001 could shred them with ease. Picking a fight with a Castle Federation Deep Space Carrier was suicide for those ships – so what the hell were they *doing*?"

"Lyla, ping them with a Q-com request," he ordered his ship's engineer. "And spin the zero point cells to full power. Just in case."

Without the proper ID codes, Kyle could contact *Castle* – some fifty light years away – with less time lag than he could talk to the *Stardust*s two light minutes away. A Q-com request was a radio ping communicating the code required to tell the massive switchboard array in Castle orbit to transfer any communication to the bits entangled with his starfighter. That code, however, had to travel at lightspeed.

A little over two minutes later, the starfighters AI informed him of an incoming communication.

"Starfighter flight, identify yourselves," a harsh female voice ordered.

"This is Wing Commander Kyle Roberts of *Avalon*'s flight group," Kyle responded. "We are flying a CSP as per the Alliance Treaty of

Mutual Defense, Section Five Sub-Section Three. Please advise of the intentions of your squadron."

"This is Commander Adele Richards of the Thorn Defense Force," the woman replied. "Please transit your authentication code."

"Commander, you are contacting me via a military-only quantum entanglement channel," the Federation officer reminded her. "I am transmitting my authentication, but you owe me a *damned* good explanation."

The TDF officer waited for a long moment – probably validating his codes with Federation Command, which seemed excessive to Kyle but was consistent with the paranoia.

"Your codes check out, Commander," she admitted with an audible sigh of relief. "I apologize for the paranoia. I presume, then, that the Alcubierre emergence we detected was *Avalon*?"

"We are on schedule and Captain Blair informed you when we arrived in-system, Commander Richards," Kyle said slowly. "I'm waiting on that explanation."

"We've had issues lately, Wing Commander," Richards told him. "Scheduled and properly IFFed arrivals – that then proceeded to blow away or capture civilian shipping. We're missing a bunch of freighters that were supposed to arrive in the last six months – and we *know* one of them was taken right on our doorstep."

"Pirates?"

"It's that or Commonwealth," the Thorn officer told him. She let that hang for a long moment. "What evidence we have looks like retro-fitted freighters and *maybe* some junk fighters from the war. I know Alliance Command thinks it's pirates."

"That's my mission brief," Kyle replied. "That's why we're out here, after all."

Of Thorn's three capital ships, one was off supporting an Alliance nodal force sixty light years away. Thorn Defense Force Command would hesitate to uncover their system with either of the remaining ships, and Kyle doubted they had a much higher opinion of their gunships than he did.

"My Captain and I will want to co-ordinate with TDF Command," he continued. "Assuming that no one tries to shoot us down before we make orbit."

"My orders from Command were to meet you and escort you in if you *were Avalon*," she replied. "But given the recent events, we couldn't even take the Q-com confirmations as solid. We'll see you safely to Thorn."

Thorn System
08:00 August 27, 2735 Earth Standard Meridian Date/Time
TDF Command Station, Briefing Room Gaiman

The Thorn Defense Force centered its operations from a massive, half-kilometer across, space station in orbit around their home planet. Kyle had amused himself on the shuttle flight over to the station by counting launch and flight bays.

Unless they had a noticeably different number of starfighters assigned to those features than the Castle Federation used, the TDF station was home to roughly two hundred of the little ships. A cruiser, carrying another fifty starfighters, orbited Thorn exactly opposite the station. The other cruiser was currently playing nursemaid to the mining platforms in the system's asteroid belt – a reasonable precaution, given Commander Richards' description of the recent incident.

Kyle, Captain Blair and Commander Kleiner had been invited aboard the station to consult with TDF command, then been guided through the bulk of the installation by a cheerful young woman in a gold uniform with black shoulders.

She delivered them to a briefing room with two men and three women in it. The uniforms were unfamiliar to Kyle and he found himself consulting the database in his implant to identify it.

According to his files, the red torsos of the two-toned jackets all five officers wore marked them as command- or flag-ranked officers. The tiny gold pips on their collars designated their exact ranks. All five Thorn officers had four gold pips on the black collars, marking them as Admirals.

His database also concluded that the TDF only *had* seven officers of flag rank, and didn't sub-divide their ranks the way Castle or Coraline would. All five of the Admirals were technically equal, with authority decided by seniority and specialty.

"Please, be seated," the oldest-looking of the three women, a slim officer with iron-gray hair, asked. "I am Admiral Emily Maybourne, the Chief Defense Officer of the Thorn Defense Force. My companions are Admirals Josephine Heart, Angelina Wong, Harold O'Brien and Chris Riker. Admiral Janeway is busy being a security blanket in the asteroid belt, and Admiral Nguyen is aboard *Floss Silk* with Alliance Task Force Thirty-Four."

"You honor us, Admiral," Captain Blair told the TDF's senior officer as Kyle and Kleiner sat. "I did not expect to be greeted by the entire TDF admiralty."

"The last time *Avalon* was here, we were negotiating our entry into the Alliance, Captain," Maybourne told them, taking her own seat. "She helped stand off a Commonwealth Battle Group that hadn't received the memo that we weren't interested in annexation. Your ship is remembered fondly here."

"She's an old ship, but still a good one," Blair allowed. "I don't expect we'll make as much of an impression this visit, but we're still intending to do some good."

"You've been briefed on the situation out here, I assume?" Maybourne asked.

"Of course," Blair replied. "But there's a vast gap between the viewpoint of a thirty year old analyst, however gifted or well-intentioned, who's never seen war and is sixty light years from the danger; and the viewpoint of the people at the scene."

The old Admiral nodded thoughtfully, then gestured to Admiral Heart. "Admiral Heart is our head of Defensive Intelligence. She can brief you."

Heart was a petite woman with golden-blond hair and a soft face. Something about her eyes, though, suggested to Kyle that taking this woman as mere decoration could easily be a fatal mistake.

"Thorn is one of the key interface points between the Alliance and the Commonwealth from an economic standpoint," she said softly. "While our annexation was prevented by an Alliance task force, there was no blood actually shed. We remain on good terms with the Commonwealth, so much of the trade into our region of space comes through here."

"This results in us seeing between eight and fourteen star freighters a month," Heart continued, and Kyle pursed his lips in a silent whistle. Castle saw almost twice that, but even the average Federation system would normally only see half a dozen of the massive Alcubierre drive civilian starships in any given month.

"As we are linked into both Alliance and Commonwealth Q-com networks, almost all of our arrivals are scheduled weeks or months in advance. In a normal year, about a dozen of those schedules are broken or revised without us being made aware, but we can usually sort that out quickly."

"In the last twelve months, *nineteen* ships haven't made their scheduled arrivals," Heart said grimly. "We have only confirmed the safety of ten of them. Given the normal nature of a missed arrival, we figure three or four of those are probably around somewhere, but that leaves at least five ships – interstellar freighters – gone missing."

"And there was *Santana*," Maybourne pointed out. Heart nodded, making a small 'I was getting to that' gesture with her hand.

"*Santana* is the reason we didn't just assume we were having issues tracking people down," the tiny Admiral told the Federation officers. "She was an Imperial-flagged ship carrying, among other things, fifteen hundred zero point cells destined for here."

Fifteen hundred zero point cells was the entire annual production of a factory. A *large* factory. From one basic cell, a manufacturer could build a power plant, an engine... or a military grade positron lance.

"We believe someone knew what she was carrying and where," Heart continued. "She arrived on schedule – and a second arrival, appeared an hour later. The second ship was scheduled and flying the proper codes for her origin.

"Instead of heading in-system, however, the ship rendezvoused with *Santana*. Shortly after she did so, *both* ships turned around and left the system. *Santana* hasn't been seen since," she concluded grimly. "We only have long range scans of the event, but the ship appears to have been a regular freighter. We *did,* however, confirm the presence of starfighters when they rendezvoused."

"Any details on the starfighters?" Kyle asked, leaning forward across the table to face Admiral Heart and speaking for the first time. "That might give us some ideas of what we're facing."

"The nearest ship was almost three light minutes away, Wing Commander," Heart told him. "We're lucky we managed to detect the starfighters at all, let alone identify them."

"We've been discussing with other members of the Alliance," Maybourne added, with Heart's briefing seemingly over. "All told, we have *confirmed* the theft or destruction of eight interstellar freighters, and there are at least twelve more no-one can locate."

"These aren't small or cheap ships, people," she continued. "Even for your Federation, a star freighter requires a partnership of independent operators, massive financial cartels and the government to ever get built. *Twenty* of these ships, ignoring their cargo, is a forty percent of Thorn's annual GSP. The impact to their home systems cannot be underestimated."

"These pirates are well on their way to triggering massive economic depression in half a dozen systems or more," Maybourne concluded. "Thorn is one of the best defended systems impacted, but the only ship we can spare is with Task Force Thirty-Four. Most of the other systems have a single capital ship, or even only guardships and fighters."

"That's why they sent us," Blair said confidently. "*Avalon* is old, but we have a reputation to uphold. Q-ship carriers and pirate fighters are no match for my people."

"Space pirates just seem so... improbable," Kleiner said sharply. "These ships are ten *trillion* Stellars apiece – who the hell can they fence these too?"

"The probability of an event that has occurred approaches unity, Commander," Heart replied harshly. "There are systems rimwards of the Alliance without the resources to build such ships that would still pay the equivalent of hundreds of billions of Stellars for them – and stolen goods are never sold at a loss."

Kleiner made an apologetic gesture. "You misunderstand me, Admiral – I do not doubt what has occurred. I just wonder if there is another actor behind those we see – a *Terran* actor."

The room was silent for a moment as everyone considered her words. Kyle had been thinking the same thing – Commander Richards had outright stated that fear. He could see that, despite what they might say, the Admirals of the Thorn Defense Force had the same worry.

"What would they gain?" O'Brien finally asked. "Even the value of all of these ships is just a blip to the Commonwealth."

"Six depressed systems," Kleiner pointed out. "Systems in economic depressions don't build new ships. Don't upgrade their weapons. Aren't prepared to defend themselves. These pirates, regardless of whether the Commonwealth backs them, are making us vulnerable."

"My President has made it very clear," Maybourne said slowly, "that my government does not believe the Commonwealth is behind this. I fear," she continued, her voice quiet, "that this is because the Alliance is not ready for a renewed war."

"Regardless of their backers, we must deal with these pirates," Blair said firmly. "We can't prove it's the Commonwealth – and no one is going to start a war over suspicions."

"I'd appreciate it if you can forward all of your available intelligence to *Avalon*," he continued. "We're here for another day, and then we're heading to the Hessian system. If we can identify potential targets or bases, I may detour from our schedule."

"In the absence of a target, however, the best we can do is remind these scum that the Alliance is watching – and that no-one out here stands alone!"

Glynn Stewart

CHAPTER 15

Hessian System
11:05 September 4, 2735 Earth Standard Meridian Date/Time
DSC-001 Avalon *– Main Conference Room*

When Kyle made it into the conference room to join Kleiner and Blair for the daily update, he knew he was late. An overcharge in one of *Avalon*'s older circuits had managed to overload half of the circuits in his starfighter, and he'd spent the morning wrapped in a cocoon of extra shielding as he ran through system checks with Lyla and Chief Hammond.

His shipsuit was askew and he was pretty sure he had some kind of engine oil smeared across his face. He had yet to be late for one of these meetings, and he was hardly looking forward to Kleiner's snide commentary.

To his surprise, however, Blair was alone in the conference room. The Captain was pouring coffee into three cups, mixing each carefully. He glanced up as Kyle entered the room.

"Two sugars, no cream, right, Commander?" he asked.

"Yes, sir," Kyle said slowly, finally allowing himself to take a breath.

"Caroline just stepped out, she'll be back in a moment."

"Thank you, sir," Kyle said gratefully, taking the warm cup in hands shivering slightly from over-exertion.

"Catch, Commander," a voice said from behind him. Kyle turned to find Kleiner behind him. He put down the coffee cup just in time to catch the warm damp cloth she tossed him.

"Hammond said you'd caught an oil spill," the XO explained with a smile. "Figured you'd be more comfortable *without* that on your face in the meeting."

Shaking his head at the difference in reaction from what he'd been expecting, Kyle nodded his thanks and applied the cloth to the smear on his face. With that dealt with, he gulped half of the cup of coffee, then looked up at the other members of *Avalon*'s senior command crew.

Both were grinning at him.

"Thank you," he said quietly. It wasn't just for the coffee and facecloth, and all of them knew it.

"If Wing Commander Roberts is feeling more human, we should get started," Blair told them. Behind him, the screen lit up with the view from *Avalon*'s bow cameras, showing the entire Hessian system.

"We've been in the Hessian system for two hours," Kleiner began. "We've communicated with System Control and they've advised me that they don't have a free docking port for us."

"I didn't think Hessian was that busy?" Kyle asked.

"They're not normally," the XO agreed. "Of course, that means that Hessian Orbital has a grand total of *two* docking ports. One is occupied by *Jäger*, Hessian's Imperium-built strike cruiser. The other one is occupied by a Federation-flagged star freighter – and they have a second star freighter, flying Stellar League codes orbiting just behind the station."

"Four starships in orbit at once when we arrive," Blair observed. "Is that a record for them?"

"The last time Hessian had more than four starships here was the *Battle* of Hessian," Kyle replied, checking the database in his implant. "A five ship Alliance Task Force under Imperial command ambushed and destroyed a four ship Commonwealth Battle Group trying to seize the system. Normally, they have *Jäger* and maybe one freighter."

"We've been assigned an orbit," Kleiner confirmed. "I've also received a request for us to send a senior officer to Hessian Orbital to set up a meeting – not sure why we can't do that over Q-com."

"Hessians don't do anything important electronically if they can avoid it," Blair told her. "They attach a great importance to being able to look a man or woman in the eyes when you speak with them, and video isn't enough." He shrugged. "For the same reason, you'll need to go over to negotiate re-supply on food and consumables," he told the XO. "It should be straightforward enough. Have they said who they want us to meet?"

"No," she replied. "I don't like it."

"The Hessians are an odd bunch," Blair admitted. "But they're solid members of the Alliance, I wouldn't worry."

"Very well, Captain," Kleiner conceded. "I'll have a shuttle prepped to take me over when we arrive."

"I'll set up the CSP and make sure we have a couple of fighters to escort the shuttle," Kyle told them. His implant was running the numbers on the local defenses and he wasn't liking what he saw. "No insult to the Hessians, but I'm only seeing two squadrons of fifth-generation fighters – *Typhoons* we sold them. The rest of their defensive craft are fourth-generation ships – it looks like a slightly upgraded *Badger*."

"The *Jäger* is a formidable ship," Blair allowed, "but yes, I'm seeing the same data. Keep your people's eyes open, both of you. This ship represents more firepower than the entire system defense force."

"And, Kyle?" Blair continued softly after a pause. "You are *not* going to be flying the CSP yourself. I trust the Hessians, but I've got an itch between my shoulder blades. Keep the Group at Readiness Two."

Readiness Two meant that the starfighters' missile magazines were loaded and fuel tanks were full, with a full squadron in the launch tubes. At least one squadron of flight crews would be on duty and in their ships at all times. Draining as it would be on Kyle's people, it also gave them a ready reaction force – and cut the time for full scramble on the old ship by at least a minute.

"Yes, sir," he acknowledged. "We'll keep your itch scratched."

Hessian System

12:30 September 4, 2735 Earth Standard Meridian Date/Time

DSC-001 Avalon – *Fleet Commander Kelly Mason's Quarters*

The ship's clock might have shown it as the middle of the day, but both Stanford and Mason were off-duty and had been so for over four hours.

The Flight Commander hadn't *meant* to end up spending the 'night'. Mason had been chilly to him after Phoenix, and he hadn't been sure his offer to cook her a 'breakfast dinner' this morning would be accepted.

His culinary offerings had been accepted, however, which led to a rude awakening several hours later when his implant starting pinging a priority communication.

Unwilling to extricate himself from the shapely Fleet Commander, he accepted it as a purely implant call.

"Stanford, it's Roberts," his CO said briskly. "*Don't* tell me where you are – I just stopped by your quarters – but I've called a Squadron Commanders' briefing in thirty minutes. Be there."

The click in his head of the channel closing left him sighing aloud as he glanced over Kelly Mason's slowly waking person.

"Go back to sleep," he told her. "Duty calls, and such as we are *never* off-duty."

The blond Navy officer swung herself around to allow him to rise, and sat up herself, stretching in a way that threatened Stanford's ability to make it to the briefing.

"Didn't expect you to sleep over," she said muggily. "Was nice, but seems out of character, no?"

Half-way into his shipsuit, Stanford paused as her words sunk in. He looked back at Kelly to see that she'd leveled her calm blue gaze on him and smiled. His heart, not one for dramatics, found itself going 'pitter-pat.'

Flight Commander Stanford swallowed, and returned the smile.

"It was, wasn't it?" he said softly. "I've got to go!"

He stole a quick goodbye kiss and slipped out of Mason's quarters to head towards the Flight Bay.

It took him a good two minutes to realize he was whistling.

Hessian System
13:00 September 4, 2735 Earth Standard Meridian Date/Time
DSC-001 Avalon – *Flight Group Briefing Room*

Flight Commander Michael Stanford was still more than a little distracted as he joined *Avalon's* other five squadron commanders in the briefing room, waiting to hear what emergency had caused Roberts to wake him up. Part of that he could easily mark up to having been awoken in the middle of his off-shift, but the remainder was definitely something else – something unfamiliar to him.

Confusion over a woman was *definitely* not his style, and it kept him distracted enough that he missed Roberts stepping up to the podium and clearing his throat.

"Ladies, gentlemen – as of now, we are at Readiness Condition Two," the Wing Commander said calmly.

Stanford's attention finally snapped to the here and now, and he stared at *Avalon's* CAG.

"What's going on?" Rokos asked.

"Neither Captain Blair nor I can put our fingers on it," Roberts admitted, "but both of us have an itchy feeling between our shoulders. With the pirate attacks, and Hessian's weak defenses, we may be feeling paranoid – but I'll remind you that paranoids have real enemies."

"The whole affair stinks," Rokos said bluntly. "I *hope* some of the pirates try something – the scum are a waste of oxygen."

"I'm with Commander Rokos," Stanford agreed. He doubted Roberts disagreed, for that matter. Stanford had seen the footage of *Ansem Gulf* after *Alamo's* marines had finally boarded. The Wing Commander had *been* there. "Give us something to shoot at and we'll make hash of it, CAG."

"I'm counting on it," Roberts replied with a grin. "I'm also hoping we don't find *anything*. Rokos – your Echo squadron is in the tubes as soon as we're done here. We cycle the squadrons – four hours in the tubes, then two hours per flight of combat space patrol.

"This system may be a member of the Alliance, but *Jäger* is old, and their planetary defense fighter wing are no spring chickens either," the CAG explained. "If the shit hits the fan, it will be up to Avalon to sort it out.

"So, yes," he finished, with his teeth bared in what could be called a smile, "I am hoping the pirates try something while we're here."

Hessian System
09:00 September 5, 2735 Earth Standard Meridian Date/Time
SFG-001 Alpha Six – Falcon-*type starfighter*

Michelle yawned and stretched in the cockpit of her starfighter. For all that most of her awareness was wrapped up in her implant and the semi-artificial world it was projecting to her optical nerves, she could still feel the simple pleasure of the stretch in her muscles.

"Are we keeping you up, boss?" Deveraux asked over the net, her mental voice carrying an overtone of gentle amusement.

"Waking me up early, more like," the Flight Lieutenant replied. As she spoke, she automatically rechecked the positions of the ships around her – most especially, Senior Fleet Commander Kleiner's shuttle.

"And for baby-sitting duty at that," Garnet interjected. The engineer's tone was grumpy. He sounded like he'd needed more beauty sleep.

"The Cap'n and the CAG are worried," Michelle told her flight crew, glancing across the other ships. Two more *Falcons*, the remainder of the current CSP, orbited roughly a thousand kilometers forward of *Avalon*. *Jäger,* the old ex-Imperial battlecruiser, was nestled against the main orbital station, opposite the freighter that was causing everyone's navigational headache.

On the edge of her mental screen, the second star freighter slowly drifted forwards. Her orbit would bring her barely ten thousand kilometers from Hessian Orbital, though over fifteen times that from *Avalon.*

Almost unconsciously, Michelle tagged the freighter for the starfighter's computer to watch. She didn't expect trouble, but the

Stellar League ship was also the only major vessel moving around in orbit. The only other ships she could see were sublight schooners, a hundred thousand tons at most.

"Kayla, does your crew see anything odd?" she sent to the other starfighter escorting the XO's shuttle.

"Not a peep," Flight Lieutenant Kayla Morgaurd replied. "Hell, this place is missing a bunch of ships that *should* be here."

"This isn't Castle," Michelle said quietly, but she had the same feeling. It wasn't that the system was being quiet, or anyone was hiding – the system was just dirt-poor. Most systems could build better vessels for in-system shipping than the schooners she was watching. At least two of the small ships were using *ion* thrusters – and had no mass manipulators aboard at all!

"The Commonwealth took out most of their extra-planetary industry during the war," Garnet said quietly, interrupting Michelle's thoughts. "A hundred and forty years of investment and about thirty million people – a war crime, but it's not like anyone from that battle group ever made it home to be held accountable."

Michelle shook her head silently. For all of her dislike of the behemoth that had tried to conquer her home, even she had to admit that the Terran Commonwealth *usually* fought its wars cleanly. The exceptions, though, tended towards the utterly horrifying.

"Escort-Alpha, this *Avalon* Two," the shuttle hailing her interrupted the depressing conversation. "We are entering approach now and are under Hessian Orbital's guns. Commander Kleiner says thanks for riding shotgun, and you're clear to return to CSP."

"Pass on my regards to the Commander," Michelle replied. "Gentle docking."

She and Morgaurd slowly decelerated their fighters, curving in an arc that would take them back to *Avalon*, passing right under the Stellar League ship.

"Check your vector," she ordered Morgaurd after glancing over the course plot for the other starfighter. "We don't want to get that close to the freighter – League ships tend to be uncomfortable around other people's starfighters."

Morgaurd acknowledged with a wordless click, and the vector shifted further away. With the two tiny ships' scanners stretched to maximum, it wasn't like they needed to be *that* close to *Avalon* to keep an eye on everyone.

The scanner macro that she had set up on Kleiner's shuttle informed her that the transport was docked with Hessian Orbital and locked down. According to her brief, the shuttle would remain aboard until Kleiner was done with her meetings.

For all of the jitters and 'itchy shoulders' that seemed to be spreading through *Avalon*'s crew, Hessian was quiet – dirt-poor, but harmless.

Then another scanner macro pinged. It took Michelle a good second to realize it was the one she'd set on the Stellar League freighter.

Her starfighter had just passed 'behind' the ship, into the ionized path left behind by the freighter's station-keeping engines, and the macro was bleeping a higher than expected level of radiation.

Even linked into her implants, Michelle wasn't sure what the system was telling her. Elevated levels of radiation at the five hundred eleven kilo-electron-volt level?

Her implants then happily told her the meaning of that energy level, and her heart stopped as it resolved the separate point sources.

A hundred zero point cells?

She hit the Q-com activation sequence.

"Vampire! Vampire! Vampire!" she snapped. "The League ship is a pirate!"

Even as the words left her lips, her starfighter's sensors – now focused on the raider – saw paneling eject away from her hull. Missiles blasted away from the freighter's hull, targeted on *Avalon,* followed by dozens of starfighters.

All of that paled in Michelle's mind though, as four half-megaton-per-second positron lances ripped out from behind concealed panels. Two hit *Jäger,* ripping through her unprotected hull and shattering the battlecruiser before she could even move. One hit the Federation freighter, blasting the civilian ship into pieces.

The last hit Hessian Orbital dead center, ripping its way through the hydrogen fuel tanks in a flash of annihilating matter that tore the station apart in a ball of white flame.

CHAPTER 16

Hessian System
09:26 September 5, 2735 Earth Standard Meridian Date/Time
SFG-001 Alpha Six – Falcon-*type starfighter*

It felt like Michelle stared at the small sun that had been forty thousand human beings for an eternity. Their course had brought them behind the pirate in time to provide mere seconds of warning – hardly enough to save an immobile station from weapons that moved at the speed of light.

The missiles targeted on *Avalon*, however, were *not* moving at the speed of light. They were accelerating at ten kilometers per second squared, rapidly shrinking the distance to the old carrier.

"Dump our missiles at the pirate," she ordered Deveraux. "Keep the lance spun up – we're going after *their* missiles."

With every mass manipulator thrown to full power and the antimatter thrusters opened *all* the way, the impact of the *Falcon* rapid-firing all twelve of her missiles at the enemy ship barely rocked the six thousand ton ship.

"Williams, this is Rokos," Echo Squadron's commander broke into her channel. "We're launching from *Avalon* now – can you get a bead on those missiles and starfighters?"

"Garnet?" Michelle asked. "What have you got the Commander?"

"Twelve missiles, look like Starfires," the engineer reported. "Their range will suck, but they're small and easy to hide."

"Forty starfighters, mix of origins," he continued, then paused. "Boss – ten of them are *Cobras*."

"Fuck," Rokos swore on the channel. "I'll let the CAG know. Watch those starfighters, but take those missiles from behind – you sweep, we'll mop up."

"Clear, sir," Michelle replied. A second channel flipped open to Kayla Morgaurd, confirming the other starfighter's location.

Morgaurd's *Falcon* swung in line with Michelle's ship, five hundred kilometers off her starboard bow as both of them opened their engines up at full power.

It didn't take them long to get a clear shot at the missiles and open fire. Glittering beams of positrons swept through space, tracking the smart weapons, each of which tried to dodge in turn.

She quickly realized Garnet was right. Real capital ship missiles were much bigger and carried more ECM to fill her targeting systems with static. Even more so, though, real capital ship missiles were *smarter*.

Michelle and Morgaurd's beams swept the missile salvo into an ever-tightening spiral in space – and then Echo Squadron cleared their own weapons. Twelve seconds later, every missile was dust.

"Yes!" Kayla bellowed over the channel. "Suck *that* you pira–!"

For a moment, the other pilot forgot the random-walking that needed to be second-nature to a pilot in a combat zone. A moment was all the closing pirate starfighters needed – and Kayla Morgaurd and her crew died as three thirty-five kiloton positron lances intercepted her fighter at once.

Michelle was alone in space, with forty pirate fighters behind her, and only the eight friendly ships of Rokos's Echo Squadron heading towards her.

Where was the rest of the wing?!

Hessian System
09:30 September 5, 2735 Earth Standard Meridian Date/Time
DSC-001 Avalon – Flight Deck

Kyle made it onto the Flight Deck just as Rokos' squadron blasted into space from the launch tubes. He saw Senior Chief Hammond forcing order on the chaos that was reigning across the Deck, directing flight crews to their fighters and getting the next set of fighters moving toward the launch tubes.

Only half of his attention was on the here and now, however, and he'd linked his implant into the ship's communications. As he dodged his way across the deck towards his own starfighter, he was linked into Flight Lieutenant Williams' comms with Rokos.

"*Cobras*?" he demanded as he heard the report.

"Wait, what?" he heard Stanford shout, and turned more of his attention back to where he stood. The senior Flight Commander had been coming up behind him, heading towards his own ship. "What about *Cobras*?"

"We have forty fighters inbound," Kyle told him shortly. Stanford, like the rest of his pilots, scored very high on the bell curve for implant compatibility, but Kyle scored as much higher than them as they did over the average. Most of his people couldn't interface while doing other tasks as well as he could. "Ten of them are *Cobras*."

"I can guess their serial numbers," Stanford replied grimly. "Forty ships versus ten isn't a winning combination, boss, even if our birds are twice as good."

"I know," the Wing Commander admitted, looking out over the chaos of the Flight Deck. He trusted Rokos to deal with the missiles, but the starfighters were too much for a single squadron.

Foxtrot squadron was about to slide into the launch tubes when Kayla Morgaurd and her crew died, and Kyle made his decision.

"Hammond," he barked, linking his words to the other mans' implant. "Belay loading the launch tubes."

"Sir?" the Chief asked, somewhere between confused and horrified. "But Rokos' squadron..."

"One more squadron won't save him or *Avalon*," Kyle snapped. "Pull back Foxtrot and clear the center deck.

"Have all hands stand by for a full deck launch."

"We've *never* tested that," Hammond objected.

"I know you, Chief," Kyle told him quietly. "You've checked the gear. You know it works. It's just a question of whether or not the *idea* works at all – but in three minutes, those *Cobras* will be in range of *Avalon*."

"You're insane, boss," the non-com replied. "Get the hell into your fighter, then. We'll blow the deck in ninety seconds."

#

"Clear the Main Deck. Full deck launch in thirty seconds."

Hammond's voice echoed across the deck and through the implants of every starfighter pilot, gunner and engineer in SFG-001. Kyle was glad for his implants, as the main cabin of his starfighter was still packed with the shielding cocoon they'd put in for the testing earlier. It had been awkward at first, but once he was linked to the ship he barely noticed.

"Zero gravity in ten seconds, clear the Deck," Hammond repeated.

The seconds ticked by, and Kyle sank deeply into the symbiosis with his starfighter. Every missile checked out. The engines checked out. The zero point cells that provided fuel for the engines and ammunition for the main positron lance checked out.

"Zero gravity, I repeat, zero gravity. Starfighters assume launch positions."

Outside, Rokos' wing was starting to engage the pirate fighters, and *Avalon* herself was trading blows with the pirate freighter. Kyle's implants reported the ship had massively powerful deflectors, reducing the range of *Avalon*'s secondary weapons well below the current gap between the two ships – and with the planet so close by, Blair wasn't going to fire up the main battery.

Time was precious. Every second that passed risked the lives of Kyle's men and women. But the positions of the starfighters in the deck had to be *perfect*.

His starfighter slid upward in the zero gravity, tiny bursts of thrust from the maneuvering thrusters drifting the *Falcon-C* command fighter into the center of the deck. Around him, the other thirty-seven remaining ships slotted into the positions mandated by a launch plan thirty years old.

He winced as his implants reported the death of one of Rokos' ships as the starfighters slotted into position. Then another. Half a dozen of the pirate ships were debris along with them, but he'd lost three fighters already.

"All ships in position," Hammond's voice reported. "Hold on people, this is gonna kick like one hell of a mule."

"Full deck launch. Now."

A *Falcon*'s mass manipulators were rated to absorb five hundred times the gravity of Earth. That was, however, with other mass manipulators dedicated to manipulating the mass of both the starfighter and its fuel. There was, as with everything else, an efficiency curve. With every mass manipulator set to counter acceleration, the ship could completely absorb two thousand gravities and reduce the next thousand by ninety-nine percent – and would consume *every* mass manipulator and erg of energy the spacecraft had.

The mass manipulators in the walls of *Avalon*'s flight deck left absorbing inertia to the starfighters themselves. They spun up to reduce the mass of everything in the center zone by a factor of roughly fifty thousand. Then a series of massive electromagnets charged up, and turned the core of *Avalon*'s Main Flight Deck into a giant railgun.

Ten gravities of acceleration made it through, slamming every member of the starfighters' flight crews back into their couches like the fist of an angry god.

Thirty-nine starfighters blasted clear of *Avalon*'s bay, bearing down on the remaining pirate ships. Kyle bared his teeth in a hunting grin as he switched the *Falcon*'s systems back to normal, and the little ship shot forward at five hundred gravities.

"Charlie, Delta, Foxtrot Squadrons," Kyle snapped, linking to the all-hands channel for the three squadrons as he spoke. "Reinforce Echo, drive those starfighters back. See if you can take a *Cobra* intact, but keep them off *Avalon*."

"Alpha, Bravo Squadrons," he continued, switching to the channels for those wings. "You're on me – we're picking up Alpha Six – and then we've got a pirate to kill!"

The Starfighter Group split smoothly, fourteen fighters forming on him as Lancet, Zhao, and Wolter – the pilot he'd promoted to command Foxtrot after Randall's arrest – took their twenty-four to pull Rokos's chestnuts out of the fire.

For the first time in over a decade, it was time for *Avalon*'s fighters to dance.

Hessian System
09:31 September 5, 2735 Earth Standard Meridian Date/Time
SFG-001 Alpha Six – Falcon-*type Starfighter*

The first salvo of missiles Michelle had loosed at the pirate 'freighter' hadn't done much. It was a truism of modern space combat that even a ship like *Avalon*, with old-style neutronium armor, couldn't withstand a single solid hit from an antimatter warhead.

Whoever had retrofitted the pirate had been very aware of that truism. More hull plating had been blasted away as the missiles approached, revealing a *very* modern laser missile defense system. Salvos of four missiles apiece were child's play for a system like that.

And it wasn't as if she or Deveraux had the time to babysit the missiles all the way in, either. Caught in the space between two rapidly closing starfighter groups, Michelle spent half of her time random-walking to avoid enemy fire – and the other half trying desperately to keep up with the targeting data Echo Squadron was feeding over encrypted laser-coms to avoid friendly fire!

She had enough warning to keep dodging their positron lances, but being stuck between the two combatants meant she didn't have enough time to engage herself.

"Keep your eyes open, Deveraux," she ordered. "I'm going to try something, and if you get a bead on any of those bastards, light them the hell up."

Deveraux didn't verbally acknowledge, but Michelle felt the other woman take control of the positron lance through her implants.

Even as the pilot took a deep breath to steady her nerves and updated her download of Echo Squadron's firing patterns, another one of *Avalon*'s starfighters came apart. A lagging missile from a salvo fired by the pirates missed the defensive sweep that caught its compatriots and hit Jean Canard's fighter head on.

As the third of Echo Squadron's ships died, Michelle flipped her *Falcon* up ninety degrees. Up to now, she'd been focusing on trying to either join up with Echo Squadron or reach *Avalon*. That was looking more and more like suicide – and the pirate freighter was doing *far* too good a job of heading away from the carrier.

She blasted away from the 'dogfight' and set her sights on the freighter itself.

"Take a look at *that*," Garnet's voice suddenly cut into her thoughts. She took half a second to be sure the starfighter continued to random-walk, and then followed the engineer's mental pointer.

Avalon had turned. The eight hundred meter long arrowhead of the old carrier now pointed *directly* at the enemy fighters. The pirates weren't in range for the anti-fighter guns to penetrate even the weak deflectors the small ships carried, so Michelle wondered for half a moment what was going on.

Then the electromagnetic and boson detectors on her *Falcon* went wild, and she watched in awe as five entire squadrons of starfighters blasted into space in a perfect formation.

The pirates didn't seem to know what to make of it, and seemed to almost pause in space as three of those squadrons charged directly at them.

The other fifteen ships began an arc that would bring them swinging by Michelle – on their way to the pirate ship.

"Hold up your horses for a moment, pilot," Wing Commander Roberts' ever-cheerful voice sounded in her starfighter's cabin. "I don't know about you, Lieutenant Williams, but *I* think you need some friends to take on an entire pirate starship!"

#

A few minutes of careful maneuvers slotted Michelle's starfighter into position amidst the two squadrons of ships heading for the pirate carrier. 'Beneath' them, the battle between the rest of *Avalon's* starfighter group and the pirate ships had begun to take on a less frantic tone with the pirates shifting course to stay out of the radius of the carrier's anti-fighter guns.

With the Wing Commander's command starfighter added to Alpha Squadron, the two squadrons were back at full strength despite Morgaurd's death – though Michelle was out of missiles, so she wasn't sure how much value to place on her own ship.

The pirate ship had been on a vector away from *Avalon* when she'd opened fire, and had promptly demonstrated that she was rated for the same tier two acceleration plateau as the old carrier. She was accelerating away at two hundred and ten gravities, slowly but surely adding to her velocity away from the pursuing Federation ship.

"*Avalon* is not going to catch her," Kyle told his people grimly. "The Captain tells me that by the time the bandit is clear enough of Hessian for them to be comfortable using the main guns, she'll be far enough away that her demonstrated deflectors will be enough to stand off even our new batteries."

"So we get no support from the old girl?" Mendez asked. "Typical Navy."

"Hardly, Commander," Kyle said sharply. "We'll co-ordinate a mass missile strike – *Avalon* will fire once the target is two hundred thousand kilometers from the planet."

That made perfect sense to Michelle – if she'd thought about it, she probably shouldn't have fired her own short-range missiles this close to Hessian. A one-gigaton explosion in even a middle orbit could cause havoc with the satellite network and planetary communications.

"Conveniently, those birds will pass us just as we hit a hundred thousand kilometers – which is what my starfighter is telling me is the range of our missiles under these conditions," he continued. "Watch your sixes and keep your eyes peeled – I don't trust those other buggers to stay tied up with Rokos and the others!"

Michelle focused on the scanners showing space around them. With a missile strike as the main attack plan, covering everyone else who still *had* missiles seemed like their best plan.

"Deveraux," she said quietly. "Keep our sensors trained on the starfighters. Looks like we default to the backdoor."

"They look busy to me, boss," the gunner replied.

"Let's keep an eye on them anyway," Michelle told her. "Unless you want to explain to the CAG how some two-bit pirate snuck up on us?"

Hessian System
09:42 September 5, 2735 Earth Standard Meridian Date/Time
SFG-001 Actual – Falcon-C *type Command Starfighter*

His implants gave Kyle a nearly god-like view of the battlespace. Every starfighter's sensors were linked back to *Avalon* via tightbeam laser-coms, and the carrier itself was linked to his command starfighter by a Q-com link.

That link carried the sensor data from every one of his forty-plus starfighters, plus the take from the carrier's own powerful sensors. In a battle with a larger scope, the carrier would deploy some of her scant supply of Q-com equipped drones to provide a real-time view of part of the entire star system.

Four of his squadrons were engaged with the pirate starfighters. Echo Squadron had lost four of their number before the other squadrons engaged, but the pirates were down ten ships – including three of the stolen *Cobras*.

The remainder of his force was burning hard after the pirate ship. Part of him still found it hard to believe such a thing existed, but there was *something* going on. There were enough manufacturing and storage facilities in Hessian orbit to make blowing away the station profitable – but it still seemed excessive to Kyle.

"SFG One Actual, this is *Avalon* Guns," Kelly Mason interrupted his thoughts. "We show Bandit One clear of Hessian. Launching in ten, watch your scopes."

Moments after she'd finished speaking, the sensor feed from *Avalon* reported the launch of eight heavy capital ship missiles.

The Starfires carried by his starfighter massed twenty tons apiece and were powerful, terrifying weapons. The Jackhammer missiles carried by Federation capital ships massed two *hundred* tons. Their endurance was measured in hours, and their terminal velocity from rest in percentages of lightspeed. The Jackhammer's ECM and ECCM were better and their onboard computers were smarter.

For all that, the two missiles shared an identical warhead. If allowed an hour of flight time, *any* warhead on the Jackhammer was redundant – and even *Avalon*'s neutronium armor wouldn't withstand a gigaton-range antimatter explosion.

The missiles had twice the acceleration of his starfighters, and crossed the distance to his squadron at a terrifying pace. Even *knowing* that the missiles were smart enough to avoid hitting his own people, they were scary.

"Watch that pirate's guns," he ordered his people, putting action to his words and beginning to random-walk. "Stand by to fire missiles in concert with *Avalon*'s birds."

He suspected that somewhere, in one of the many hundreds of treaties that defined the relationships between star nations, there was something that required him to demand the surrender of the ship that had destroyed Hessian Orbital before he blew them to hell.

Kyle didn't bother to look it up. He spent the time instead calculating the exact moment his people had to fire to co-ordinate the time on target salvo.

They were close enough now that the pirate ship began to open fire. Positron lances swept through space, the ninety kiloton-per-second guns the Commonwealth and many others used as anti-fighter weapons.

He smiled coldly as one of Stanford's pilots missed their random-walk and crossed into the path of one of the beams – to be saved by her deflectors. The Federation had heavily upgraded the electromagnetic deflectors mounted on the *Falcons* over the last generation of starfighters, and the pirates had overestimated the range they could hit his people at.

"Alpha, Bravo, all ships," he said aloud, letting the computer open the channels once more. "Launch full salvo on my mark... Mark!"

Fourteen ships each fired four missiles apiece. Fifty-six Starfire missiles leapt into space, on vectors that would bring them to the target within seconds of *Avalon*'s heavy missiles.

"Flight Engineers, cover them with your ECM," Kyle continued. "Gunners, ride them in. Pilots – don't let that bastard touch you!"

Missiles and starfighters shot through space, and more and more beams of positrons began to glitter between the stars. Kyle's ships were still well out of their own range, but they were rapidly approaching the distance at which the raider's guns could touch them, deflectors or no.

Unlike the Jackhammers, his missiles *needed* to be covered by the fighters' electronic counter measures and guided by the fighters' computers. He couldn't pull his people out, even though he knew some wouldn't survive the attack.

Even as he twisted his starfighter through a series of random maneuvers intended to throw off the pirates' targeting software, he watched his people with pride. Their formation might have looked like a chaotic mess to an outsider, but there was purpose to it.

They really had learned everything he had set out to teach them, and now it was making the difference between life and death.

The pirate ship was growing closer, and the seconds were ticking down. Positron lances flickered closer and closer, trying to box in his starfighters – and mostly failing, as his people random-walked out of the boxes with practiced skill.

Their luck could only last so long. A starfighter died. Then another. A third – and Kyle knew the pirate was doomed. Even if they somehow stopped the missiles, they couldn't stop the starfighters either – and the *Falcons'* positron lances would rip her to shreds.

The missiles crossed some invisible line in space, and the pirate's positron lances started targeting them – leaving the fighters for the more immediate threat. As soon as they did, Kyle triggered a command in the heavy Jackhammer missiles.

The entire battlespace around the missiles disintegrated into a hash of jamming even on his screens. Focused electromagnetic pulses blasted forward from the heavy missiles, and massively powerful transmitters sent out immense quantities of static.

His people's missiles couldn't duplicate the sheer power of the Jackhammers, but they added their own contribution, turning the pirate's defensive efforts into a disorganized mess.

It was a testament to the people who'd retrofitted the ship that they *still* stopped almost all of the Starfires.

Only two Starfires and four Jackhammers made it through. Six one-gigaton warheads went off as one, wiping the pirate ship from the face of the Hessian system.

CHAPTER 17

Hessian System
09:55 September 5, 2735 Earth Standard Meridian Date/Time
SFG-001 Actual – Falcon-C *type Command Starfighter*

With the pirate freighter gone, Kyle turned his attention back towards his other four squadrons going after the pirate starfighters. Even with the feed from every one of the ships feeding through *Avalon*'s computers, the battlespace around the rest of the Starfighter Group was a mess of jamming and radiation.

Most of the jamming was originating from his people's *Falcons*, which were demonstrating the superiority of their electronic warfare suites over the older starfighters. Even the *Cobras*, solid sixth generation fighters, were outmatched by the *seventh* generation *Falcons*.

What was clear even through the jamming, though, was that the pirate wing had had enough. Only four of the original ten *Cobras* remained, and fourteen of the other thirty ships had gone down with them. Half of the pirate's numbers were debris, and they were turning tail.

All of the ships, despite their varying ages and origins, had been retrofitted to match the *Cobras*' four hundred and fifty gravity acceleration. With their carrier gone, all twenty remaining ships were blazing for the outer system with every ounce of thrust they had.

"This is Rokos," Echo Squadron's commander's voice came over Kyle's communicator. The other man sounded tired, but eager – the best you could hope for after losing half of your squadron. "The bastards are making a run for it. Permission to pursue?"

"Negative, Flight Commander," Kyle told him, running the vectors through his implant. "Let them go, but follow them. Give them a two hundred gee advantage."

"Why the hell would I let them go?" his junior demanded. "They can't outrun us!"

"We've taken enough losses for today, Russell," Kyle said quietly. "Let's consolidate the Group before we run them down – we've got a fifty gravity edge, and we've got thirty-eight fighters to their twenty. One clean pass and it's over – I won't risk people when I can spend *time*."

There was silence for a moment, then a crisp and apologetic "Understood, sir."

"Don't worry, Commander. They have nowhere to run," the CAG reminded Rokos. "Without their carrier, their only hope is to find somewhere to hide – so don't let up on them.

"Just stay the hell out of range."

Hessian System
11:00 September 5, 2735 Earth Standard Meridian Date/Time
SFG-001 Actual – Falcon-C type Command Starfighter

It took Kyle's two squadrons just over an hour of maneuvering at their full five hundred gravities to catch up to and match vectors with the pursuing squadrons. As the fighters slotted into their usual twisted multi-dimensional 'formation,' he raised Rokos again.

"I assume tactical command, Flight Commander Rokos," he said calmly and formally.

"You have command, sir," Rokos accepted.

"How are you holding up?" Kyle asked softly. The channel was only between them.

"I will feel better once we have turned these cowardly scum into ashes," the other officer said grimly.

"We want at least some alive," Kyle warned. "I am going to demand their surrender – hell, I'm surprised they *haven't* surrendered already."

"They're heading for Hessian IV's Trojan cluster," Rokos pointed out. "If they get there far enough ahead of us, they can hide in the debris field. Lock to a rock and go cold, we might miss them even knowing where they are."

Kyle checked. The trailing Trojan cluster – asteroids gathered in a point of low gravity created by the interaction between Hessian IV, a massive gas giant, and its sun – was roughly fifty light minutes away from the inhabited planet. Even with the head start the pirates had, they should bring the starfighters into range in a little over four and half hours – and still a million kilometers short of the cluster.

"If that was their plan, then luck was not on their side today," he said grimly. "And I intend to make damn sure of it."

"With you all the way, CAG. Let's finish them."

Hessian System
13:00 September 5, 2735 Earth Standard Meridian Date/Time
SFG-001 Alpha Actual – Falcon-*type Starfighter*

Michael Stanford watched the pirate starfighters flee before *Avalon*'s fighter group with a distinct sense of unease. The whole stunt didn't make any sense to him – why had they blown away the entire space station with a Federation carrier *right there*?

Unless...

"They knew everything we were *supposed* to be," he said aloud.

"Sorry, boss?" his gunner asked. For all that most communication went through the network, his gunner's station was only about three meters away from him.

"If we'd had the fighter wing we had *before* the refit, what would have happened when those pirates hit us?" Michael asked softly.

"That bunch against our old *Badgers*? They'd have ripped us to pieces!" the gunner replied.

"And eaten *Avalon* for breakfast," Stanford finished. "These pirates *knew* what fighters we were supposed to have – they would never have risked killing the station and *Jäger* if they didn't."

The other man in the cockpit was silent, but Stanford's brain ran in rapid circles.

The pirates had the fighters that Vice Commodore Larson had sold. They'd known what Larson's ship was meant to have been carrying in terms of fighters and weapons – they'd been wrong, but their intel had only been a few months out of date.

Randall had said it was governments and corporations buying the starfighters, not pirates, but he could have been wrong – and Larson could have sold intelligence as well, figuring knowledge of *Avalon* was a harmless bit of profit.

Stanford looked at the image of the system his implant was laying out in his mind. These pirates were smart and capable – they had managed to acquire top-line starfighters and detailed intelligence. They could do the math on whether they'd reach the cluster before the Federation fighters caught up with them.

If they couldn't hide, what did they expect to gain from running?

With their carrier gone, the pirates could only escape by ditching their ships and sneaking out on civilian transit or meeting another ship to pick them up.

That thought echoed in Stanford's head as he looked at Hessian's trailing Trojans. It was a denser cluster of asteroids than most, with a high heavy metal content that was making a mess of the Starfighter Group's long-range sensors. If the pirates made it to the cluster, they could shut down and hide with ease. An entire starship could hide in that mess.

And the pirates needed to leave the system.

"CAG, we have a problem," Stanford snapped into a channel that linked him directly to Roberts. "They're not running *from* us – they're running *to* someone. A friend – a friend with a real ship hiding in that cluster of heavy metal rocks."

There was a long pause on the channel, an unusual one for the Wing Commander, then Kyle responded.

"Damn," he said softly. "Didn't even cross my mind. *Well* done, Michael – I'll have *Avalon* pulse them with the shipboard array."

Avalon's immense radar arrays were orders of magnitude more powerful than the active sensors on the *Falcons*. The high powered pulse that followed scrambled Stanford's sensors for a second as it washed over them.

Then the return rippled back through the squadron. Each individual fighter's sensors were weak, but networked together the starfighter's computers could collate and synthesize the data – resolving even small or concealed signatures with a powerful enough pulse to identify them.

It took longer than *Avalon's* computers would, but *Avalon* was light minutes behind them now. Michael waited patiently as the networked squadrons ground through the data.

Then his breath caught in his throat as the computers emotionlessly drew in the smooth oval shape of a Commonwealth battlecruiser.

CHAPTER 18

Hessian System

13:05 September 5, 2735 Earth Standard Meridian Date/Time

SFG-001 Actual – Falcon-C *type Command Starfighter*

Kyle looked at the shape of the warship with trepidation. He'd thought he'd been chasing twenty mostly obsolete fighters with almost forty super-modern ones. He hadn't even replenished his ship's munitions, and his implant computer happily pulled up the data to tell him most of the *Falcons* had a single four-missile salvo left. Some, like Williams' Alpha Six or his own command ship with its reduced magazines, were completely empty.

The ship in the asteroid cluster was even bigger than the *Resolute* he liked to use in exercises. Eleven hundred meters long and sixteen million tons, the warbook was happily informing him it was almost certainly a *Hercules*-class battlecruiser.

That made their lurker one of the Commonwealth's newest and most powerful warships, but at least gave Kyle and his people one distinct advantage: the *Hercules-class* were unabashedly optimized as *shipkillers*. Their heavy armament, in missile batteries and heavy positron lances, was only somewhat reduced from the last generation of *battleships*, and their fighter complement and anti-fighter armament was weaker than most carriers or even regular cruisers.

"They know we're here," Stanford reported.

Kyle saw what his senior commander meant immediately. The massive radar pulse had been unmistakable, and the battlecruiser's captain clearly knew what it meant. Zero point cells flared to life throughout the massive hull, and the radiation and boson detectors started to go nuts as the ship's engines followed.

"Damn," Kyle said softly. The battlecruiser was more than twice *Avalon's* size – and should *not* have been here.

"Lyla," he continued calmly, addressing his engineer. "Record for transmission to that cruiser."

A ping popped in his implant a moment later, letting him know she was ready.

"Commonwealth vessel," the CAG said flatly. "You are in violation of the sovereign space of the Hessian system and are interfering with the pursuit of identified pirates responsible for the destruction of Hessian Orbital.

"As per the Section One of the Alliance Treaty of Mutual Defense, we will defend the territorial integrity of the Hessian system. Stand down and withdraw, or your presence will be taken as an act of war."

He swallowed, hard, then sent the transmission from his implant.

"All crews," he said softly, activating the channel. "We are approaching a Commonwealth battlecruiser. She shouldn't be here – and our pirates are running to her."

"I have demanded that they stand down and withdraw," he paused. "I do not expect them to comply. It looks like we're about to fire the first shots of a new war."

"Watch each other's backs, maintain your random-walks, and stand by for further orders," Wing Commander Kyle Roberts told his people. "Whatever happens, today will be a date that will live in infamy. Let it be said that we did our duty."

The channel was silent. Thirty-eight starfighters tore through space, their speed ever-increasing as they closed on the pirates and the unexpected intruder.

"There's your answer, boss," Landon suddenly interjected on the fighter's internal net. "They're launching!"

The battlecruiser was moving. Engines and mass manipulators flickered to full power, and the massive Terran ship began to move towards SFG-001 at two hundred and thirty gravities.

And as she moved, she fired. Twenty missiles ripped free from the warship's hull, followed moments later by ten starfighters.

Fifteen seconds later, a second starfighter squadron shot into space. Fifteen seconds after that, a third followed. Thirty starfighters shook out their formation, and then dove for SFG-001 at five hundred gravities.

In front of them, twenty missiles blazed the trail.

#

Prioritization came first.

The battlecruiser's second salvo of missiles was launched two minutes after the first, as the first began to close the distance to Kyle's crew.

Both waves of capital missiles were going to pass by SFG-001 before the Commonwealth fighters entered missile range of the Federation starfighters. If they kept up the 'slow and steady' rate of fire, a third wave would arrive as the two fighter wings exchanged fire.

Kyle's implant database suggested that the Commonwealth's heavy capital ship missiles were similar to the Federation's. These would accelerate at a thousand gravities for three hours. Since *Avalon* was tens of millions of kilometers behind his ships, the missiles would have to go ballistic in the middle.

If they were half as smart as the Jackhammers the Federation used, that meant that any of them that made it past his fighters would only be visible to *Avalon* in their terminal attack mode. If SFG-001 didn't stop the missiles, *Avalon* was in danger.

"Track those missiles, target them with your lances," he ordered calmly. "Hold your Starfires until I give the order – be ready to use them on those starfighters."

"What about the battlecruiser?" Lancet demanded. "We need our missiles for her!"

"The battlecruiser won't matter if those starfighters kill us," Kyle told her grimly. "They'll expect us to think that – so I want a mass salvo, straight down their throats as they close.

"We'll have to take the cruiser with lances," he continued. "We're way out of range for *Avalon* to provide fire support, but we're also closing *damn* quickly. Rip her in half, but try and leave big enough pieces for Intel to pick over.

"I want to know why she's here," Kyle concluded grimly. "And at a quarter cee closing? It's a risk we can afford."

After four hours of accelerating at full power, his ships were rapidly creeping up on twenty-five percent of the speed of light, their theoretical maximum safe velocity. At that speed, it was only going to take them twenty minutes to close the range with the cruiser.

His squadron commanders passed on his orders, and the Federation starfighters spread out, opening up more vectors for lances and sensors on the missiles. His implant started to throw up timers in his head – time to the first missile salvo. Time to the second missile salvo. Time to missile range of the fighters, and time to the third salvo.

He tried to stretch to release tension, only to smash his fingers against the shielding in the cockpit and curse. Losing himself in his implants had helped distract him from the cocoon he was wrapped in, but he knew he was going to regret the time spent locked into it later.

"There goes their ECM," Landon murmured over the net, and Kyle watched as the battlespace disintegrated into hash as the missiles came closer to his starfighters.

The CAG smiled grimly, adjusting his own course to sweep the nose of the fighter with its fifty-kiloton-a-second positron emitter across the region of space he knew contained the missiles. Pulses of pure antimatter blasted into space, and electronic-counter-counter-measures strove to resolve their targets.

The *Falcon*'s ECCM gear, the newest the Federation had, won the electronic duel. Not every missile appeared at once, but as each one appeared, it was blasted into oblivion by watching starfighters. Unlike starships or even starfighters, the weapons had no electromagnetic deflectors to reduce positron lance range – their only defense was not to be targeted at all.

The first salvo died well short of SFG-001, but the second set of twenty missiles was right on its heels, and the battlespace was filled with radiation from the first salvo.

The last missile of the second salvo died in the middle of Kyle's formation, thankfully still hundreds of kilometers away from any of the Federation starfighters.

Kyle watched the distance to the Commonwealth starfighter wing carefully. Now they were closer, his warbook happily identified them for him – *Scimitar* class ships, the Commonwealth's latest sixth generation ship. They were narrow cylinders, quite unlike the wedge shape of the *Falcons*, and carried multiple smaller positron lances against the *Falcon's* single lance.

The *Scimitar* was the offset to the *Hercules*-class battlecruiser – unquestionably optimized to kill starfighters. Commonwealth doctrine only saw the starfighter as a defensive unit, used to hold off Alliance starfighters while capital ships made the kill.

Kyle grinned coldly as the timer ticked down.

It was time to show them the flaws in their doctrine.

"Full jamming, full ECM, full missile salvo – *now!*"

Hessian System
13:25 September 5, 2735 Earth Standard Meridian Date/Time
SFG-001 Alpha Six – Falcon-type Starfighter

All around Michelle's starfighter, the other starfighters of SFG-001 launched their missiles. A handful of the fighters from Rokos' Echo Squadron were as empty on missiles as she was, but the Federation starfighters still threw over a hundred Starfire missiles into space.

She ignored the missiles, knowing that Deveraux would take care of adding their ECM to the wave of jamming and chaos helping shield the missile strike. Her focus was on the heavy capital ship missiles fired by the Commonwealth battlecruiser.

The latest salvo of those missiles passed through their own fighters at the same time as they fired their own missiles. The battlecruiser's missiles were closing far faster and were the immediate threat.

The Federation missiles were still thirty seconds away from impact, and the Commonwealth fighter missiles thirty seconds behind that, when Michelle drew a bead on the first capital ship missile and fired. She missed, the missile's heavy ECM fooling her targeting sensors, but swept the positron beam across space to catch it a second later.

Without the CAG's ridiculous implant bandwidth compatibility, Michelle could only focus on so many things going on in space at once. With no missiles of her own in the offensive salvo, she focused on shooting down the capital ship missiles.

A second blew apart under her fire, then a third.

Then her entire sensor array blacked out in a burst of overwhelming static as her comrades' missiles struck home. Over a hundred gigatons of antimatter explosions filled space with radiation and the natural jamming of matter-antimatter annihilation.

For a long moment, Michelle couldn't see *anything* more than a few hundred meters from her starfighter, and she waited grimly for the chaos to clear. She hadn't been the only one shooting down missiles, but she *knew* at least two were left.

The radiation wave slowly began to clear, and her scanners were pushing hard to pick out those last missiles – *there.*

She spun her fighter in space, acceleration leaking through to press her against the side of her chair as she turned the *Falcon* ninety degrees in a fraction of a second to track the missile about to pass through the Federation formation at thousands of kilometers a second.

The fighter aligned with where the missile would be for half a second, and Flight Lieutenant Michelle Williams sent a beam of pure antimatter out into space to intercept it.

Then, and *only* then, did her computer flip up the projected course of the command starfighter that the *Falcon*'s sensors had just resolved from the radiation.

She watched in horror as her beam ripped through the missile and detonated its one-gigaton payload of antimatter – less than eight hundred meters from Wing Commander Kyle Roberts' starfighter.

Hessian System
13:28 September 5, 2735 Earth Standard Meridian Date/Time
SFG-001 Alpha Actual – Falcon-type Starfighter

"Yes!" Kyle's exuberant shout echoed over the command channel linking him to Michael Stanford and the other squadron commanders. "That's gutted them – now clean them up and let's get ready to— "

The command channel was silent for a long moment.

"CAG?" Lancet asked. "CAG, what are your orders?"

"I'm not seeing Zero-One-Actual on my scopes," Zhao replied. "He was..."

"Right next to that last missile," Rokos said grimly. Even as the Echo Squadron commander spoke aloud over the channel, a blinking text message appeared in the mental viewscreen of Michael's implant.

You're senior. Make the call.

He was senior. Randall had been senior before, had actually technically been the commander of SFG-001. With Roberts' arrival and Randall's arrest, Stanford had taken over the second in command role along with command of Alpha Squadron.

Running back through the scanners, he could see what Rokos had seen. A one in a million shot in several senses had taken out the last missile, a lucky shot that might easily have saved *Avalon* – but fluke had put the CAG's starfighter right there.

The lethal radius of a one-gigaton antimatter warhead against a starfighter was estimated at just over one kilometer. Kyle Roberts was *gone*, which put one Flight Commander Michael Stanford in command.

If he could hack it.

Roberts' strategy for taking out the battlecruiser was *insane* – relying on calculated shock and aggression over normal tactics. Stanford wasn't sure he had the gumption to carry it all the way through.

On the other hand, he realized with a steadying breath, he *also* had inherited command of a starfighter group hurtling towards a battlecruiser at a quarter of the speed of light. Not following through on Kyle's plan wasn't an option.

"This is Stanford," he said into the silence of the channel, surprised at how steady his voice is. "We can all read the numbers on that missile. I am declaring Commander Roberts MIA and assuming command of SFG-001."

"Acknowledged," Rokos replied immediately. Seconds passed, and Stanford was prayerfully grateful for the near-complete annihilation of the Commonwealth fighters.

The other Commanders slowly acknowledged, even as SFG-001 swept into positron lance range of the handful of remaining *Scimitars*. The pilots and gunners didn't need further direction, and the outnumbered Commonwealth ships died in moments, their weaker lances failing to penetrate the *Falcons'* deflectors.

"We need that battlecruiser in retrievable chunks," Stanford told his newly inherited fighter group as calmly as he could with his heart pounding in his chest. "On my mark, begin full deceleration. Target all lances on the engines – let's take enough of the bitch intact to know why they were here."

He paused. "Let's do Commander Roberts proud, people."

Hessian System
13:30 September 5, 2735 Earth Standard Meridian Date/Time
SFG-001 Alpha Six – Falcon-type Starfighter

She'd killed the CAG.

The thought echoed in Michelle's head to the point where she barely heard Stanford's commands. She'd had her sensors trained on the point in space where the missile had detonated, and even now she was straining to detect the command ship.

Her computer gave her the likely impulse provided by the explosion. It also informed her that the starfighter was likely intact – and she thoroughly ignored the next datum that everyone aboard was already dead of radiation poisoning.

Without thinking, Michelle adjusted her course, ignoring the battle around her as she vectored towards the line her calculations showed the *Falcon-C* had to have followed.

"All fighters, decelerate on my mark!" Stanford's voice echoed in her ears, and she ignored him as her mental fingers danced through calculations.

"What are we doing, sir?" Deveraux asked, able to follow the pilot in the system.

"We're going after the CAG," Williams whispered softly. "There's a chance he's alive."

"He was too damned close! The rest of the group is decelerating – we can't break off like this!"

Almost as Deveraux spoke, a direct channel opened up.

"Alpha Six, what the hell are you doing?" Stanford demanded.

"I'm going after the CAG, sir," Michelle replied firmly. "We'll hit the battlecruiser as we pass, but if *someone* doesn't stay on his vector, we'll *never* get them back."

"We've got them dialed in, Lieutenant," her squadron commander said gently. "We can pick up the bodies later, but we *need* every ship we can get for this strike! Get back in formation!"

"If any of them are alive, they need help now, not later," Michelle said sadly. "I'm sorry sir, but I can't obey that order."

She cut the channel before Stanford could continue.

"Ready the lance, Deveraux," she ordered, her voice far calmer than she'd expect for having just, technically, committed mutiny. "We're going by first, and we're going by fast – don't try and hit the bastard, just fuck his sensors."

"And what will you being doing?" her gunner asked, something in her voice suggesting that at least *one* other person understood.

"I'll be finding the CAG. Now hang on!"

Hessian System
13:35 September 5, 2735 Earth Standard Meridian Date/Time
SFG-001 Alpha Actual – Falcon-type Starfighter

For all that Michael was giving serious thought to permanently grounding Lieutenant Williams when they all returned to *Avalon*, her decision not to decelerate with the rest of the starfighters gave them all a tiny, ever-so-slight, advantage.

Her arcing course took her around the limits of the battlecruiser's range roughly five seconds before the remainder of the Federation fighters headed straight into it. The brilliant pulses of her positron lance flickered through space.

At that range, over a hundred thousand kilometers, a *Falcon's* fifty-kiloton-a-second lance couldn't penetrate the powerful electromagnetic deflectors that scattered charged particles away from battlecruiser's hull, protecting her from positron beams.

She hadn't tried. She'd launched a 'dazzler' attack – swinging the beam of her positron lance around the target in a spiral that scattered positrons throughout the field of the electromagnetic deflectors. For a few precious fractions of a second, the space around the Commonwealth warship was filled with radiation and charged antimatter, blinding her sensors.

Those fractions were enough for Starfighter Group Zero Zero One to cross half the distance from the hundred and twenty thousand kilometer effective range of the battlecruiser's ninety-kiloton-a-second lances against *their* deflectors to their own sixty thousand kilometer range.

Their own jammers, and dazzler strikes from several squadrons, took them the rest of the way. Over sixty positron lances ripped out into space from the battlecruiser, each capable of ripping one of the tiny starfighters to shreds.

Two struck home before the Federation ship's reached their range.

Then it was their turn.

Thirty-four beams tore through space. The battlecruiser's deflectors still threw aside some. Others missed outright, computers fooled by the Commonwealth warship's ECM.

Uncountable millions of charged positrons made it through, colliding with the Terran ship's hull. Positrons met their regular matter counterparts and annihilated in bursts of pure energy and five hundred and eleven kilovolt radiation.

No armor, however mighty, could withstand its own component material exploding. The beams cut through the back half of the cruiser, ripping apart machinery, tearing open fuel lines and destroying power lines.

One of those beams of pure antimatter ripped open the containment on the ship's main containment tank, and her own stock of antimatter added to the chaos.

It took just over three seconds for SFG-001 to pass into and out of the battlecruiser's weapon range. Four starfighters didn't survive the pass.

The battlecruiser was left in three powerless pieces, illuminated by the explosions of ejected zero point cores and her shattered engines.

CHAPTER 19

Hessian System
13:50 September 5, 2735 Earth Standard Meridian Date/Time
SFG-001 Alpha Six – Falcon-*type Starfighter*

Michelle had been right. The other starfighters of SFG-001 hadn't been close enough to nail down a vector for Roberts' spinning and disabled starfighter, and were too far away to localize it once they'd decelerated to destroy the Commonwealth battlecruiser.

For fifteen long minutes, she'd thought she'd thrown away her career for nothing when she hadn't found anything. Deveraux and Garnet were starting to make noises about returning. Then, a tiny blip pinged the sensors.

"Focus on that, Garnet!" she ordered, straining her eyes and implants to try and resolve it. The engineer obeyed her order, and the image suddenly cleared up.

It was unquestionably a *Falcon* starfighter. Dark and without power, it looked like a floating tomb.

"I have no power signatures, nothing," Garnet said softly. "They're gone, sir."

"A *Falcon* is armored enough to conceal a suit signature," Michelle replied stubbornly, even as her heart died a little inside her.

Ten minutes later, even that tiny hope was gone. As the starfighter closed distance and velocity with the wreck, they soon passed the line where they should have detected life-signs or any remaining power.

"We came this far," the Flight Lieutenant said sadly. "We may as well lock on and bring them home."

If nothing else, a six thousand ton mass moving at a quarter of the speed of light was a navigation hazard.

As they closed, she forced herself to tune out the sensors and focus on the finicky task of matching the vector and rotation of the uncontrolled wreck. She matched velocities to within a few hundred meters per second, slowly closing the remaining distance.

A thousand kilometers. A hundred. Carefully, she matched the spin of her own ship to the command starfighter, a dizzying sensation for herself and her crew.

Five kilometers.

"Sir, I'm getting something odd," Garnet said quietly.

"This is *not* as easy as it looks," Michelle replied, her voice strained as she tried to balance three dimensional vectors to match an object given motion by an explosion.

"Yeah, well you might want to be even more careful," Deveraux told her sharply. "There was some extra shielding in the cockpit that messed up our sensors at a distance."

"What do you mean?" Michelle demanded, locking the ships at two kilometers apart.

"Someone's alive over there," Garnet confirmed. "But I wouldn't be pausing if I were you, boss – whoever's left is fading *fast*."

Hessian System
03:00 September 6, 2735 Earth Standard Meridian Date/Time
DSC-001 Avalon *– Flight Deck*

There was a medical team already standing by when Michelle slowly and carefully lowered her starfighter to the landing deck. The 'medical facilities' aboard a *Falcon* were limited, but the auto-doc had managed to pump Wing Commander Roberts full of enough drugs and tubes to keep him alive for the achingly slow trip back to the carrier.

She'd passed two of *Avalon's* Search and Rescue shuttles going the other way, searching out the time-delayed beacons of starfighter auto-eject pods. The other four remained in orbit around Hessian, continuing to hunt down the scattered survivors of Hessian Orbital.

Combined with the local small craft and freighters, there were fifty or so ships scouring the debris field for anyone who might have survived. The odds weren't good, but Michelle wouldn't begrudge anyone the search.

According to the auto-doc, though, they'd had less than twenty minutes before the radiation damage to the Wing Commander would have been fatal. If she hadn't disobeyed orders, Commander Roberts would have died.

With a sigh, Michelle exited her starfighter behind the medics, nodding for her crew to return to their quarters while turning to face the control center she knew would contain her acting CO.

She didn't make it six steps before said acting CO intercepted her.

"I'm pretty sure regulations say I should court martial you," Michael Stanford's quiet, drained, voice said from behind her. He had apparently snuck up from the other side of her ship while she was focused on carrying herself to her doom.

"On the other hand, I have Dr. Pinochet's professional assessment of the auto-doc's readouts," he continued. "According to her, the computer *over*estimated the Commander's chances. There were minutes to spare before you got him hooked up. Potentially seconds.

"Saving the life of a comrade at risk to one's own life is usually worth a medal," the Flight Commander concluded, his eyes unreadable as he looked towards the exit the stretcher was leaving. "You're not getting one," he said dryly. "But the record will show that I ordered you to pursue Commander Roberts' fighter. Do you understand me, Flight Lieutenant Williams?"

With every bone and muscle in her body, Michelle drew herself up to attention and saluted.

"Sir, yes, sir," she replied as crisply as she could.

"The prognosis still isn't good," Stanford told her quietly. "We'll know more in the morning – get some sleep, Lieutenant."

Michelle turned to walk away, then paused and looked back at the squadron commander.

"What about yourself, sir?"

"Someone has to co-ordinate S and R," he told her. "We have the best gear in the system – if we couldn't save their station, helping save as many as we can is the best we can do."

Michelle waited a moment longer, remembering her mission when all of this began.

"Any word on Commander Kleiner's shuttle, sir?" she asked.

Stanford shook his head.

"Her docking port was less than two hundred meters from the fuel tank, Michelle," he said gently. "There's a thousand techs on the surface scanning every frame of every video and scanner we have, but it looks like Kleiner and her crew were completely vaporized.

"Get some sleep," he repeated after a long moment of silence. "I will make it an order, Flight Lieutenant."

"Yes, sir," she accepted wearily.

Hessian System
05:00 September 6, 2735 Earth Standard Meridian Date/Time
DSC-001 Avalon *– Flight Control Center*

"*Bessarabia*, we need you in sector 74-CT-9," Stanford told the tiny schooner cutting its way through the debris field. "One of our probes picked up a heat signature, might be a fragment large enough to keep power and atmo."

"*Jawohl, Avalon*," the captain replied. Moments later, the ship on the control screens surrounding Michael changed course. The half-dozen schooners in Hessian atmosphere, with their relatively low-powered ion drives, could move through the debris field without the risk of radiation and other issues larger ships would have.

Around Michael, a new shift of Federation Space Navy officers and ratings were filing in, replacing the night shift. Twenty hours and two shift changes had passed, but the personnel in *Avalon*'s Flight Control Center were as determined to find any survivors as they had always been.

"How's the search, Flight Commander?" a quiet voice asked behind Michael.

With a start, he turned to find Captain Blair standing at his shoulder, the man's cybernetic eye spinning slightly too quickly for his peace of mind as the Captain surveyed the FCC.

"Slow," Michael admitted. "I think we'd found most of those we were going to find before I got back. We're up to two hundred and eighty-five."

Blair winced, and Michael nodded his grim agreement. According to Hessian, there had been forty-two thousand, seven hundred and fifty-five men, women and children aboard Hessian Orbital. Seven survival pods had launched, and been retrieved, but now it was up to the fluke of fate to have saved anyone left.

The more time passed, the lower their chances got.

"What about our people?" Blair asked. "All of the emergency beacons should be up now."

"We pulled four survival capsules out of orbit," Stanford told him. "The SAR shuttles have confirmed they've picked up three more out where we fought the *Hercules* and they expect to bring them aboard inside the hour."

A starfighter's crew segment was a tiny fraction of its multi-thousand ton mass. The ships were designed so that if the onboard AI had enough warning of the starfighter's destruction, it could eject the entire compartment as a survival pod to save the crew.

Seven pods launched out of twelve fighters lost was a *very* good ratio. They'd been lucky – and still lost at least seventeen people, including the two confirmed dead on Commander Roberts' fighter.

"We've also pulled in about fifteen from the Commonwealth squadrons – but none from the pirates," Stanford concluded. "Any word on the cruiser itself?"

"Major Crystal will be attempting to board the various fragments shortly," Blair replied. "Kyle's decision to go after them with lances looks like it's going to pay a huge dividend – we might get a damned clue as to what the *hell* Terra thinks they're doing."

Michael glanced away, surveying the screens and the sensor data showing orbit.

"How is he, sir?"

"Alive," Blair confirmed. "Beyond that, I don't know. Dr. Pinochet has had him in intensive care since he arrived, and young Miss Angela made it very clear that, Captain or no Captain, I have no place in the surgery ward during the aftermath of a battle."

The Captain sighed, and laid his frail hand on Stanford's shoulder.

"I talked to Joint Command," he said after a long moment. With a gentle pull, he got Michael to turn and see the paired gold circles of the insignia in his hand.

"They have confirmed your promotion to Wing Commander," Blair said softly. "Until such time as Kyle can return to active duty, you are officially *Avalon*'s CAG."

"I can't take this, sir!" Michael protested. "*Kyle* is this ship's CAG."

"And he still will be, when and if he returns to active duty," Blair confirmed. "He remains senior to you by a significant time in grade, *Wing* Commander Stanford."

"But for now, I need to make sure someone is in the slot and able to put this ship's fighter group back together," the Captain continued grimly. "We've taken a gut-punch, Michael, and I fear what we'll find on that battlecruiser.

"I need to know my fighters can go to war if we have to. That's now your job, CAG."

Michael stared down at the insignia that had somehow ended up in his hand.

"Yes, sir," he acknowledged slowly.

"First, though, I recommend you get some sleep," Blair told him. "Captain's orders."

CHAPTER 20

Hessian System
12:00 September 8, 2735 Earth Standard Meridian Date/Time
DSC-001 Avalon – *Main Infirmary*

Kyle woke up slowly. Nothing felt quite right. His entire body *hurt*, a weakness and fiery ache that seemed to saturate every inch of his being. His eyes hurt and *itched*, his eyelids were heavy and sandy.

Keeping his eyes closed against the strange feeling, he tried to query his implant for where he was and what time it was.

There was no response.

His eyes snapped open to darkness, and he realized he had *no* idea where he was or how he'd got there. He knew who *he* was... but his memory was foggy, fuzzy. Everything seemed a little uncertain, and lacking the sharp clarity he now only vaguely recalled.

He tried to query his implant again. Time. Location. Self-check routines. Nothing. His implant was silent – it was like the molecular circuitry installed in his head was gone.

That thought had him bolt upright in the bed. The motion tugged along the tubes and sensors connected to him, scattering a tray of scanners across the floor with a metallic clatter as he realized that he was naked under the smart blanket.

Light filled the room in response as the door opened and a young brunette woman rushed in. Kyle was *sure* he knew her, but he couldn't put a name to the face. He should have looked at her and remembered everything he knew about her, and been able to access her Navy service record with a thought.

"Commander, please don't move," she told him. "We're still running a lot of meds and nanites into and out of your body. Losing one of those tubes could be dangerous."

"My implant..." he choked out, finding his mouth as dry and sandy as his eyelids. How long had he been sleeping?

"Your implant was damaged," the nurse told him. "It's been disabled until we've dealt with the gross physical injuries."

"Water," he got out, and she nodded quickly.

"Of course, Commander," she replied. She had a glass of water into his hand before she'd finished speaking, and ever so gently helped him drink it – slowly.

He gave her a grateful smile, knowing it wouldn't be misconstrued. It was funny what he remembered without his implant – he couldn't remember the woman's *name*, but he knew that she was in a relationship with one of his female pilots.

"Lie back down," she instructed. "I'll fetch Dr. Pinochet."

Slowly, somewhat unwillingly, Kyle obeyed. The woman fussed over him, making sure all of the tubes – some connected in *very* sensitive places! – were still connected and flowing correctly. Once that was done, she swept out of the room.

Thankfully, she turned the lights in the private room on low. Kyle was at least not left alone in the dark, even if he was left alone with his thoughts.

He remembered a battle. A Commonwealth warship. He wasn't even sure what that *meant* – his memory, his knowledge, everything was so foggy without his implant. Had they won the battle? Were his people okay?

It was a few minutes before the dumpy, red-haired, and reassuringly familiar form of Doctor Alison Pinochet entered the room. She softly keyed the door to close behind her and walked to the side of his bed, crossing her arms and looking down at him.

"You've left me a fine mess to fix, haven't you?" she said quietly, a catch in her throat that Kyle didn't recognize.

"There was a battle," he said softly. "I remember that much. How bad?"

"Horrific, but not for us," she told him. "Twenty-four of your people either didn't eject or died of injuries before we got to them. We're still totaling the Commonwealth's butcher bill – and Hessian's."

"The station," Kyle remembered with a flinch.

"Between the station, the freighter and *Jäger*, the Hessians are estimating over fifty thousand dead," she told him, and he flinched back from her.

"How long was I out?" he asked. "My implant is disabled."

Pinochet shook her head. "A little over two days," she said quietly. "And I'm afraid that Miss Alverez engaged in a little white lie."

Kyle met her gaze calmly. Somehow, he could guess what was coming.

"We didn't disable your implant, Commander," the doctor said softly. "It was too badly damaged – we *removed* it."

"I can't remember anything without it," Kyle admittedly softly, swallowing hard against the burn of fear inside his chest. "I can't remember Alverez's *name.*"

"Your first implant was installed when you were *four*, Commander," Pinochet reminded him. "You've had a *military grade* implant since you were eighteen. Your organic memory is badly atrophied."

"Can you... put it back?" he asked, hating how much his voice sounded like he was begging.

"As soon as the physical damage from the radiation is fully repaired," she assured him quickly. "You have a full backup on file from before you launched, so we'll probably be able to run the builder nanites tonight. You should have your implant back by tomorrow morning."

Something in her tone caught his ear, and he looked the doctor directly in the eye.

"What's the catch, Alison?" he asked, very, very softly.

"NSIID," she answered bluntly, and the ground fell out from underneath Kyle.

Neural Scarification Induced Interface Degradation. He somehow still remembered that. Nanotech could rebuild the molecular circuitry inside his skull, but damaged neurons still healed in their own way and at their own pace. If the damage to his implant had hit the wrong way, his ability to interface with an implant could be damaged – even completely destroyed.

"How bad?"

"I won't know until we start hooking you up again," the doctor replied. "But your implant was *completely* overloaded by radiation and EMP. You could be looking at a complete loss of bandwidth."

Kyle had an unusually high level of compatibility with the brain implant technology. That was why, twelve years before, the Federation Space Force had drafted a much younger Spaceman Recruit Kyle Roberts out of a Federation Space Navy recruitment class.

To even *be* a pilot, you had to be in the ninety-ninth percentile of the human race with regards to implant bandwidth. Kyle was in the ninetieth percentile of that ninety-ninth percentile. But NSIID could render even him unable to fly.

And twenty-four of his people had just died in the first battle of a war that could easily consume his home.

Hessian System
17:00 September 8, 2735 Earth Standard Meridian Date/Time
DSC-001 Avalon *– Flight Country*

Angela slipped into Michelle's quarters with a noticeable grin on her face. Despite being busy setting up candles on the desk she'd detached from the wall to serve as a table, the Lieutenant couldn't not notice.

"What canary did you eat on the way down?"

"It seems I'm not the only one sneaking around Flight Country tonight," the nurse told her. "I almost physically ran into Commander Mason slipping into Commander Stanford's quarters."

"Oh gods," Michelle replied, with a choked giggle. "What did she *say*?"

"Shh!" Angela quoted, putting a finger to her lips. She looked over the 'table' with its candles and covered plates. "Where'd you get all of this?"

"One of the mess ratings owed me a favor," Michelle explained, setting a small 'smoke control' box on the end of the desk to keep the candle flame from setting off alerts. "Seemed a good time for it."

"But seriously," she continued, "Michael and Kelly? Damn."

"You didn't know?" Angela asked. "Their relationship is only a slightly better kept secret than *ours*."

A warm flutter ran through Michelle at Angela's description of them as a 'relationship.'

"Why keep it a secret?" she asked quietly. "There's no chain of command issues." For that matter, she and Angela *weren't* keeping theirs a secret.

"Yeah, but if Stanford ends up CAG, it looks bad," Angela pointed out.

"That won't happen, right?" Michelle asked hopefully, her voice small. "We *got* the CAG back."

The nurse went silent, looking at the other woman with suddenly sad eyes.

"I can't say anything," she said quietly. "You know that. Already said too much."

A chill fell over the cabin, and Michelle found herself looking at the empty second bunk in the room. Kayla Morgaurd's fighter had *not* been one of the ones where the survival pods had worked.

"There's a lot of empty bunks in Flight Country," she said quietly, changing the subject if not really improving it. "I didn't want to be alone tonight."

She saw Angela hesitate in indecision, and took the decision into her own hands. The other woman came willingly into her embrace.

In the end, even the carefully sealed covers weren't enough to keep the food warm for them.

Despite knowing his new implant wouldn't be turned on until Dr. Pinochet was there to check on everything, Kyle tried to access it as soon as he woke up.

The complete lack of response was no less disconcerting than it had been before, though at least he knew the reason now. His memories remained fuzzy, with only a few clear-ish memories and faces. He recognized Dr. Pinochet, thankfully, and he *thought* the nurse was Angela Alverez.

He also remembered his ex and his son – and he remembered enough that the fact he remembered surprised him. Even with most of his memory committed to silicon and currently missing, Lisa Kerensky's face was still perfectly clear in his mind – as was what he *thought* was the latest photo his mother had sent of Jacob.

Kyle was mulling over just what that meant, in the limited context of his currently atrophied memories, when Dr. Pinochet and a dark-skinned blond Senior Surgeon-Lieutenant he really didn't think he knew came into the room.

"Good morning, Wing Commander," Pinochet told him. "This is Doctor Xue Carstairs, our cybernetic specialist. She'll be helping me with your implant activation."

"Everything went okay?" he asked.

"That is what we are to establish," Carstairs told him in a clipped voice – *not* a native Castle accent. Somehow, despite his shattered memory, he placed it as from 'Anjing'.

Of course, without his implant, he knew *nothing* about Anjing.

"We have scans to complete before activation," she continued. "Lay back."

Once Kyle was on his back, with his head immobile, the cyberneticist placed a U-shaped sensor around his skull. It had no leads or displays from what little he could see, and presumably she was running it from her implant.

She made a few non-committal sounds and left the sensor in place for five minutes without giving any sign of a further plan.

"What do you see, Doc?" Kyle eventually asked.

"The implant growth was smooth," she replied. "Some synaptic linking issues. Can't tell the impact until we turn it on."

"Does the hat come off?"

"No. Hold still, activating."

That *hurt*.

It had been twelve years since the last time Kyle had an implant booted from scratch, and that had been due to a careful upgrade, implemented in stages over two days. There had been no damaged connectors, no neurons that would literally *snap* at the first attempt to run impulses through the connector.

Carstairs had clearly been expecting his reaction. The doctor's hand had been sitting on the end of the sensor, and as she activated his implant she'd moved to place it on his breastbone. As he tried to convulse in pain, that delicate long-fingered hand held him down with a grip of iron.

"We can't know what links will break until activation," she said calmly as a fire burned inside Kyle's head. "It won't last long."

It probably didn't last more than thirty seconds, but those thirty seconds took a small eternity to pass. When it finally did, Kyle's head slowly cleared. His memories came clearly now, but slowly.

He was right – he didn't know Carstairs. He *did* know Angela Alverez, the young nurse who'd been taking care of the previous day – and she was dating his Flight Lieutenant Williams.

And there had been a battle. The battle's details were still foggy, more than he'd remembered before but more clinical than the rest of the memories from the backup.

"We assembled a partial memory of the battle from the data you downloaded to *Avalon*, but the backup was from the night before launch," Pinochet told him quietly.

"What happened to me?" he asked. He'd been too uncertain before, too foggy on his thoughts and memories, to ask.

"One of the battlecruiser's missiles detonated seven hundred and fourteen meters from your starfighter," Pinochet explained as Carstairs continued to poke at the sensor wrapped around his skull.

"That's *inside* the lethal radius," Kyle replied. "How?!"

"You were apparently testing circuits prior to the flight and had additional shielding layered around yourself," the doctor said. "Must have been uncomfortable as hell, but it saved your life."

"Landon? Lyla?" Kyle asked.

"They weren't as lucky," she replied grimly. "Flight Lieutenant Williams boarded your fighter and retrieved you and their bodies, but there was nothing she could do for them – she barely saved you!"

At seven hundred meters, the radiation burst from a one-gigaton antimatter explosion should have killed everyone aboard the starfighter. 'Lucky' barely began to cover it.

"Commander, try to access a database," Carstairs ordered sharply. "Any of the Navy's."

Shrugging, Kyle told his implant to flip up Carstairs' service record. The result surprised him – normally, when he queried a database he just *knew* the data. Technically, he was 'reading' it, but at a speed so fast he barely registered the process of learning the information.

Now... now her record popped up in front of his eyes via the implant, and he had to consciously review it. It felt... clunky. Slow.

"This isn't right," he said slowly.

"The implant adapts, Commander," Carstairs told him. "Shows you data the most efficient way."

The sensor suddenly moved away. Kyle stretched his neck, trying to get a feeling for the new speed of his implant. It was all wrong. Even as a child, without a military grade implant, he'd been able to access the implant's internal databases and network links instantly. The knowledge in his databases might as well be in his silicon-enhanced memory for the time it took him to access it.

Now he had to bring up virtual data screens and effectively *read* the data. He knew he was still 'reading' faster than he could read on a page, but not by much.

"Dr. Carstairs?" Pinochet asked, her voice gentle.

"Could be worse," the junior doctor said bluntly. "Scans rate sixty-fourth percentile. He can function."

Kyle's head spun. Sixty-fourth percentile?

"Thank you, Dr. Carstairs," Pinochet replied. Kyle was only vaguely aware of her escorting the junior doctor out and closing the door behind her. He stared at the roof, refusing to ask his implant databases the question his regularly enhanced memory already knew the answer to.

"I'm sorry, Wing Commander." Pinochet was suddenly sitting on the bed right next to him, looking down at him with concerned eyes. "You're still above average for interface capability, but... that's an eighty-two reduction in your personal bandwidth."

"Everything is so slow," he whispered.

"Welcome to the world the rest of us live in," she told him. "I'm only sixty-fifth percentile myself. I honestly have no idea what you've lost, so I won't waste your time with platitudes."

"Can I fly?" he asked aloud. He couldn't help it – he *knew* the answer. Without consulting databases or the doctor, he *knew*.

"No," Pinochet replied softly. "Above average or not, your current rating is barely a third of the minimum interface bandwidth necessary for starfighter service."

"I'm sorry, Kyle," she repeated. "It's theoretically possible that your brain will heal over time, and you will eventually get that bandwidth back, but for now..."

"I've placed an indefinite medical ground on your file," she concluded. "Barring a miracle, you will never fly a starfighter again."

CHAPTER 21

Hessian System
14:00 September 9, 2735 Earth Standard Meridian Date/Time
DSC-001 Avalon – *Main Infirmary*

Six hours wasn't enough time to adjust to the entire foundation of how your brain works being torn out from under you.

After about two hours, Kyle asked Angela for a datapad. The thin, somewhat flexible, data display devices were utterly ubiquitous in modern life, but he'd never been much of one for them. He could organize data faster and more cleanly in his head, after all.

He found it easier, though, to link his implant to the datapad and actually physically *look* at the information than to use the pseudo-visual interface his implant had defaulted to now that it couldn't rapidly download data into his brain anymore.

He was working on the letter to Kayla Morgaurd's family when Captain Blair knocked on the door of his private infirmary room.

"It's Blair," the Captain told him through the door.

"Come in," Kyle instructed. He laid the datapad aside as *Avalon's* Captain stepped into the room, but he saw the older man's gaze follow it.

"The Doc said you still had some interface capability," he said, questioningly.

"Yeah, but its running differently than I'm used to," Kyle replied. "The 'pad helps."

The Captain nodded slowly, pulling a chair up next to Kyle's bed.

"How are you holding up? NSIID is a nasty hammer blow."

"I've known for six hours, skipper," the pilot said quietly. "I don't know if it's even sunk in yet."

"I know," Blair agreed. "And I hate to ask you to make decisions so quickly, but I suspect I'm going to be looking at a tight deadline pretty quickly here."

"Not just a social call then, boss?" Kyle asked.

"I needed to see you were all right with my own eyes," Blair allowed. "Dr. Pinochet says she'll probably clear you out of here in the morning, but she wanted twenty four hours of observation."

"I hear you made Stanford CAG," Kyle said quietly. "I'm not even sure where I'll go when she does clear me out."

"It's a temporary appointment for now," the Captain told him. "The promotion is permanent though – given that I used the recommendation *you* wrote to argue for it, I doubt that's a surprise."

"No," the Wing Commander admitted. "It was time – past time, to tell the truth. Even Admirals should be able to accept that their daughters will do as they please, after all."

"That's true enough," Blair agreed. "Though I'll admit to *some* sympathy."

"If I'm grounded, you'll need to make Stanford's role permanent," Kyle told him. "You can't have an interim CAG, not with a wrecked Commonwealth battlecruiser floating around."

"That's what we need to discuss, isn't it?" Blair replied. He pulled a datapad out of his uniform jacket packet and laid it down next to Kyle.

"What's that?"

"Your Article Seventeen discharge, if you want it."

Kyle looked at the plastic and silicon device as if it was a snake and swallowed. He remembered being on the other side of this conversation with Lieutenant Williams. It felt like yesterday, for all that it had been weeks ago.

"NSIID of this caliber qualifies you for a full medical discharge, with pension," Blair continued into the silence. "Your promotion to Vice Commodore was already in the works, so your discharge promotion would be all the way to Commodore.

"You retire *and* get a raise," the Captain observed dryly. "A lot of people would love that option."

"I am a soldier of the Federation," Kyle said quietly. "My life belongs to the service."

"We generally let people go on that one after we fry half their brain, Commander," Blair snapped.

"We blew up a Commonwealth warship, Captain. On the eve of war, do you really expect me to walk away?"

"No," the Captain admitted with a sad smile. "Though part of me thinks I should make you, make sure your son gets to at least *meet* his father before the war kills you."

Kyle physically flinched. The thought of going home and facing Lisa and Jacob... wasn't as terrifying now, strangely. But it still wasn't comfortable.

"If you stay in the Space Force," Blair said after a long moment of silence, "I'll have to leave you in Hessian. A relief convoy is already on its way, they'll take you home. Then the Force will put you behind a desk – or, more likely, a teacher's lectern. Eventually you might command a planetary defense group, but barring a miracle, you'll never fly again."

"You're not exactly presenting the most glorious options here, skipper," Kyle replied dryly. "Go home in failure to the ex I abandoned or fly a desk for the rest of my life. You're setting me up for something, aren't you?"

"I see your sense of an ambush is still working," Blair said with a smile. "There is one more option. You no longer qualify for front-line *starfighter* service, but I've checked with the Doctor. What you were *left* with is more than half the officers in the Navy ever had."

"Due to your injuries, we've already fast-tracked your promotion to O-6," he continued. "I have confirmed with the Joint Chiefs of Staff that I have the authority to sign off on your transfer to the Castle Federation Space Navy with full rank and seniority."

"You'd be the only Senior Fleet Commander aboard, but, sadly, I have an opening for one," Blair concluded. "You're right, Kyle. We're on the eve of war – there's a team of five *hundred* analysts on the surface going over the data cores we pulled from that battlecruiser, and as many interrogating the prisoners."

"By tomorrow morning, I hope to know just what the Commonwealth was up to," he said quietly. "And then, I suspect, I will be taking *Avalon* to war."

"I could use you at my side when I do."

Kyle was silent for a long moment, regarding the Captain. He had never really thought about being a Navy officer. He'd enlisted in the Navy, originally, but the commission he'd been offered had been in the Space Force and he'd never looked back. He'd loved to fly, and he'd found a gift for tactics and command.

Now, though, he couldn't fly. The Space Force was no longer where he could best serve his country – but that same gift for leadership and tactics could still serve. He would still, in the end, be in much the same service even if he wore a different uniform.

"It's not how I planned to spend the rest of this tour," he finally said.

"I wasn't planning on losing Caroline," Blair said bluntly. "Or any of the other people we lost. I blame the Commonwealth. I suggest we prepare to levy payment upon them."

Kyle slowly nodded.

"Okay," he said with a deep breath. "If you want one battered ex-starfighter pilot for your XO, skipper, you've got him."

Hessian System
08:05 September 10, 2735 Earth Standard Meridian Date/Time
DSC-001 Avalon – CAG's Office

When Michael Stanford heard rummaging coming from Kyle's office when he walked by, he had a moment of hope that he'd dodged the bullet of being promoted to the slot. The sight of the other Wing Commander packing the handful of personal possessions he'd kept in the room into a stereotypically sterile cardboard box dashed that.

"Are you even supposed to be out of the infirmary yet?" he asked the younger man softly.

Kyle straightened and turned to face Michael with a familiar smile. He made a show of checking the time on a datapad sitting on the desk within his reach. He was dressed in full uniform, shipsuit and jacket, though there was something off about it Michael couldn't put his finger on.

"As of about five minutes ago, I am cleared for light duty," he replied. "Figured I'd spend it getting my things out of your way."

"Its official then," Michael said quietly. "I don't *want* the job, boss."

"You'll make a damn fine CAG," Kyle told him fiercely. "We both know it – you've been ready for the bump to Wing Commander for years."

"I sure as hell don't feel ready," the junior, if older, man replied. He stepped into the office, his implant telling the ship to close the door behind him as he took a seat on the desk. "I was *terrified* going up against that battlecruiser," he admitted.

"And?" Kyle put the box down on the desk and looked down at Michael. "So was everyone else. You took command when you needed to and led the strike."

"Anyone could have."

"No, not anyone," Kyle told him. "And you did. I call that one hell of a trial by fire to prove you can do the job. Besides," the big man shrugged, "I can't anymore."

Michael finally caught what was wrong with the uniform. Kyle's space-black shipsuit and jacket weren't piped along the seams with the blue of the Space Force – the uniform was piped in *gold*. The distinction was subtle, but his former boss wore the uniform of the Castle Federation Space *Navy* – and as he noticed the different coloring, he realized the insignia was different too.

Kyle had lost the gold wings of a senior pilot, but he'd gained a third gold circle where Michael's new promotion gave the junior man two.

"I'm sorry, sir," Michael said with a growing smile. "I missed your promotion, *Senior Fleet Commander*."

The big officer shook his head.

"And here we see the perception we require of our senior officers," he concluded. "The Captain asked me to step into Commander Kleiner's slot. It seemed a better idea than retirement – and means I can keep an eye on our new CAG. Make sure you don't get in *too* much trouble."

"You know me, sir," Michael replied. "If I get in enough trouble, do you think I can talk you into taking the second circle back?"

"You won't get in that much trouble, Michael," Kyle told him calmly. "You wouldn't be letting me down – you'd be letting down *your* people."

The new Wing Commander winced. *That* was a point that bore more than a little weight.

"When will the Captain tell everyone?"

"All of the senior officers will be at the briefing by the Hessian analysts at nine hundred hours," Kyle told him. "We plan on telling everyone then. I wanted to let you know in advance – and the Captain asked me to tell you you'll be formally confirmed as CAG at the same meeting."

Wing Commander Michael Stanford, Commander Air Group of the Castle Federation Deep Space Carrier *Avalon*, nodded slowly as he swallowed hard.

"Thank you, sir," he said softly. "Good luck, sir. I get the impression XOs need a lot of it."

Kyle offered his hand and Michael took it in a firm handshake. His own frail hand disappeared into the new XO's massive grip, but he drew strength from the confidence of his former commander.

"So do CAGs," Kyle told him. "But you'll need less than most – I've left you a *damn* good team."

CHAPTER 22

Hessian System
09:00 September 10, 2735 Earth Standard Meridian Date/Time
DSC-001 Avalon – *Main Conference Room*

Kyle joined Captain Blair in the main briefing room before any of the other officers arrived. A young woman in the uniform of a Hessian Security Service Colonel had taken a seat at the other end of the table from *Avalon's* two senior officers, but she simply gave Kyle a silent nod.

He found himself paying more attention to the department heads as they arrived than he had for any of the previous meetings. Before, as CAG, he had been effectively 'first among equals' of the carrier's department heads, reporting directly to the Captain. Now, as the ship's Executive Officer, all of the department leads reported to him.

Stanford arrived first, the new CAG having only been a few minutes behind Kyle. The slim blond officer traded a calm nod with Kyle, but his eyes showed his discomfort with his new role.

Next in was the ship's Operations Officer, Fleet Commander Rachel Armstrong. She was a tall and heavily built woman only a centimeter or so shorter than Kyle, with skin and hair as black as space. Armstrong would be Kyle's main deputy in handling the administration of the ship, and she picked up on his new uniform and insignia almost instantly.

"Congratulations, sir," she told him. "I look forward to working with you."

"Thank you, Commander Armstrong," Kyle replied. "I get the impression we're going to be busy," he added, glancing at the spook waiting patiently at the other end of the table.

Armstrong took her seat as Kelly Mason came in behind her. The voluptuous blond woman ran the carrier's heavy weapons, and they'd worked together closely. Her gaze, he noted, was solely for Wing Commander Stanford, and Kyle smothered what he knew was a patronizing smile at the pair's attempt to *not* be obvious.

Fleet Surgeon-Commander Pinochet entered alongside Fleet Commander Alistair Wong. The Chief Engineer, a stick-thin Asian man with a few centimeters of height on Kyle himself, took one look at the Hessian Colonel and promptly dropped into the chair next to Kyle – as far away from the spook as possible.

Last to arrive, technically late but by less than a minute, was Lieutenant-Commander Maria Pendez, the ship's Navigator. A small woman with a reputation for breaking hearts among the Marines and Space Force officers who were her only available 'prey,' she was dark-eyed and dusky-skinned, with curves seemingly designed to disable male brains at fifteen meters.

Once she had taken her seat, the door slid shut behind her at a silent command from the Captain, and Blair rose to face his department heads.

"Good morning everyone," he greeted them. "As I'm sure you can all guess from Colonel Karla Bach's presence, we had a significant breakthrough on the cores pulled from the Commonwealth ship we engaged. She came up this morning with a briefing packet for me, and I've asked her to share it with everyone."

"First, however, I'll take advantage of having all of the department heads together to make two announcements that will be spread to the rest of the ship this afternoon:

"Firstly, I have confirmed Wing Commander Michael Stanford's promotion with the Joint Chiefs," Blair told everyone, gesturing slightly to Stanford. "They have agreed with my decision to place him in command of SFG-001, making him *Avalon*'s new Commander Air Group."

A murmur of congratulations ran down the table, but as it died down Kyle noted that everyone was starting to look at *him*. Armstrong had noted the new uniform and insignia when she entered, and now the others were starting to notice it.

"Commander Stanford's promotion is unfortunately necessary as Commander Roberts' injuries have resulted in his medical grounding," Blair explained, the words hammers on Kyle's already taught nerves. "Since it is not to anyone's benefit for an officer of Commander Roberts' caliber to be sidelined, I consulted with Admiral Kane as soon as Dr. Pinochet made me aware of the situation."

"As of yesterday afternoon, Kyle has formally transferred to the Federation Space Navy, with the rank of Senior Fleet Commander. I have, with Admiral Kane's approval, offered the Commander the Executive Officer role aboard *Avalon*, and he has accepted."

Blair gestured for Kyle to speak, and he rose to his feet, quickly consulting his datapad for the remarks he'd prepared.

"We all know each other by now," he told them quietly. "While this wasn't where I planned on ending up, I am pleased to be working with all of you. I intend to sit down with each of you over the next day or so to go over your departments' status and needs."

"As you'll understand once Colonel Bach has completed her briefing, this is more important than you may think," Blair added. "We are going to be operating on very strict time limits – if there *anything* we need, let Commander Roberts know as soon as possible."

Kyle glanced around the table, meeting each of his new subordinates' gazes, and returned to his seat.

"Now," Blair continued, "I think we should stop burning Colonel Bach's time and let her get to her presentation."

The Hessian Security Service Officer was on her feet before the Captain had finished speaking. Standing, Kyle realized she was an astonishingly short woman – barely five feet tall. Combined with a slim build and long blond hair, she managed to give off the twin impressions of both fragility and carefully restrained energy.

"Thank you, Captain," she allowed. Touching a hidden key on the briefcase she'd put on the table, she linked it into the conference room's systems and threw a holographic image of a Commonwealth battlecruiser into the air above the conference table.

"This, Ladies, Gentlemen, was the Commonwealth battlecruiser TCNS *Achilles*, commanded by Commodore Patrick Riley," she said calmly. "Riley did not survive the destruction of his vessel at the hands of your starfighters. Neither did his Executive Officer, Tactical Officer, or Chief Engineer."

"Those are the only four people aboard a Commonwealth vessel with the ability to initiate an emergency purge of the vessel's data cores," she explained. "With their death in the first pass, and the focus of lance fire on the rear of the ship, your SAR shuttles retrieved *Achilles*' data cores intact, and unwiped."

"We were provided some of the best slicing software available to both the Castle Federation and the Coraline Imperium, and our own people are extremely skilled and had built highly effective tools of their own. I won't go into details," Bach said dryly, "but the combination of these software suites allowed us to break the encryption on the core in less than five days. It might be a new record."

Kyle shivered as he eyed the floating hologram of the starship that had nearly killed him.

"So what were they doing here?" he asked.

"It's called Operation Puppeteer," Bach answered. "Commonwealth Intelligence has never convinced their fleet commanders to stop using meaningful names, so that gives you an idea all on its own."

The battlecruiser shrank and slid to one side of the table, with a second ship joining it. This ship was smaller, more box-like – the appearance of a relatively standard Alcubierre-Stetson drive star freighter.

Blinking highlights rapidly added themselves to the design. Massive, battlecruiser-sized, positron lances. Fighter style rotary missile launchers. Electromagnetic deflectors and anti-missile lasers.

"*This* is a *Blackbeard*-class Q-ship," Bach told them. "Designed to be able to fool even a skilled boarding team. Alliance Joint Intelligence has suspected the existence of something like them for some time. Fitted with a collection of random starfighters acquired by a mix of means, they have faked being pirates all along the border. According to *Achilles'* files, there were eight of them, backed up by an equal number of battlecruisers, causing very specifically located havoc."

"The intention was to draw Alliance forces out of position – covering some systems, leaving others uncovered. Drawing down of the nodal force at Midori for pirate-hunting missions was a high priority."

"But why?" Mason asked. "Drawing our forces out of position? Reducing the nodal fleets? The only reason they'd want to do that if is…"

The two starships vanished, replaced by a three dimensional image of the space recognized as the 'border' between the Alliance and the Commonwealth. Despite the Castle Federation and Coraline Imperium providing the bulk of the Alliance's military might, neither actually directly bordered the Commonwealth. The 'border' consisted of a dozen systems like Hessian and Thorn, single-system polities with shaky economies and small fleets.

Three dimensional arrows marked fleet paths, moving out from four systems – the closest Commonwealth Navy bases – to half of the 'border' systems, and as many systems in the next layer.

"Is if they were about to launch a major assault," Bach finished the sentence for Mason. "Ten days, ladies and gentlemen. In ten days, the Terran Commonwealth plans to once again attempt to conquer the systems of the Alliance."

The room was dead silent for a long moment.

"Colonel Bach has provided a detailed briefing packet that I want each of you to review," Blair said quietly, "but I think we all needed to see it like this."

"I received confirmation just prior to this meeting that, based on this evidence, our Senate and the Coraline Imperator are activating Article One. A renewed Alliance High Command will be assembled over the coming weeks, but for the moment, our orders will continue to come from the Federation Joint Chiefs."

"They are reviewing the full data download from *Achilles*, and will have to re-deploy all available assets to hold back this assault," he continued. "We are one of those assets, and given the situation and the success of this 'Operation Puppeteer,' they will have no choice but to deploy us."

"Review your department status with your subordinates and with the XO," he ordered. "I expect to have movement orders inside of twelve hours – make *damned* sure that you're ready to go."

The room remained silent, but each of the department heads slowly nodded as Kyle looked around. Thirty years of peace were about to end in fire, but they'd all known it was possible. They'd all signed on knowing the Commonwealth's ambition to unify humanity would not wait forever.

It was time to learn whether they were truly worthy of their uniforms.

CHAPTER 23

Hessian System
10:00 September 10, 2735 Earth Standard Meridian Date/Time
DSC-001 Avalon – *Tactical Officer's Day Office*

Michael Stanford stopped Kelly in the corridor outside the conference room as the other officers dispersed to deal with clearing their departments for war.

"We need to talk," he told her quietly.

"Now is hardly the time," she replied sharply, glancing around the corridor to be sure no-one had heard.

"It's important, Kelly," he said. "In private."

"Fine!" she agreed. "Meet me in my office in five minutes."

The weight in his chest hardly lifted in those five minutes as he made his way through the ship by a circuitous route, though he knew his attempt to conceal what was going on barely rated as pro forma. Their relationship was an open secret – he *knew* Kyle knew about it.

He slipped through the door into Mason's office and triggered the privacy lock exactly five minutes to the second later, and faced his exasperated looking lover across her desk.

"Michael, the pair of us now control this ship's entire offensive capability between us," she told him fiercely. "We both *need* to get on making sure our areas are ready, especially if we're leaving tonight. What the hell is going on?"

"Exactly that," he said softly, hating himself for every word that left his lips. "*We* now control this carrier's firepower. I will be out in space with my pilots, and you'll be back here with *Avalon*'s guns and missiles. If one of us makes a mistake, *everyone* else will pay for it."

Kelly looked like she'd been punched in the gut. She knew exactly what he meant, but he had to say it – to clear the air to be *sure* she understood.

"We cannot afford to be emotionally compromised in the face of the enemy," he finished quietly. "I... we..."

"Damn you Michael Stanford," she choked out. "You could have cut this off when it was just a fling. We could have gone our separate ways, and neither of us would have cared any more than we did about the rest of our one night stands."

"But no," she told him, "you had to stick around. You had to be what I didn't expect – to offer breakfast, to stay the night. You weren't supposed to be *important*."

"This wasn't supposed to happen at all," he replied, his voice soft and his heart heavy. "Were we at peace, I'd make it work. Were we just completing a flag tour, and then scattering to new ships – I'd make it work."

"But we're going to war," Michael concluded. "My fighters *will* be in battle – and *will* need cover fire. The carrier *will* be in danger. Everyone around us needs to know we can do our jobs."

"We don't share a chain of command," she argued. "It's not against regs."

"Can we risk it?" he asked, and watched her eyes fall. "It's not just about us, Kelly. It's about what happens to our shipmates if one of us screws up. If one of us is emotionally compromised."

They were both silent, facing each other across the plain desk in the spartan office. Finally, she nodded.

"We both have jobs to do," she said sharply, the firmness of her words undermined by the tremble in her voice. "I think we should get to them."

"I'm sorry, Kelly," Michael told her softly.

Despite everything that had happened in the last week, Michelle came into the urgent briefing the newly-promoted Wing Commander Stanford had called with a smile on her lips. There was something to be said, she reflected, for the theory that one had to 'get back on the horse' after a misstep.

And Angela had been *ecstatic* to help her try every angle of 'on the horse' either of their fertile imaginations had been able to invent over their free time for the last several days.

So despite the battle, and despite her worries over the CAG, her mood was starting to look up.

The empty spots in the briefing room threw her equilibrium off, and she was grateful that both Deveraux and Garnet were with her. The Group had been lucky in whose survival pods had fired off, and every squadron except Alpha and Echo was effectively intact.

Alpha and Echo had nine flight crews left between them. Their sections of the briefing room felt empty, a ghost town of missing seats. Those holes were gaping wounds, and the entire Starfighter Group felt them, she knew.

Despite having a better idea than most of the extent of Commander Roberts' injuries – Angela had been appropriately silent on the matter, but Michelle had pulled his comatose body from the wreck of his ship – she was still disappointed when Commander Stanford stepped up to the podium without the CAG at his side.

"First and foremost folks, I have some simpler news," he said quietly. "As of this morning, I have been officially confirmed as *Avalon*'s CAG – SFG-001 is now under my command. Formal orders to that effect are being drafted, but it will some time before we rendezvous with them."

A ripple of conversation ran through the room, in varying degrees of anger and disappointment. Finally, one of Delta Squadron's gunners asked what most of the Starfighter Group's crews were thinking.

"What happened to Commander Roberts?!"

"People," Stanford told them, his voice sharp enough to cut glass, "I know we like to play games about how separate we are from the crew of the carrier that *happens* to deliver us to battle, but I would have hoped that at least *some* of you paid attention to the All Hands announcement this morning."

Michelle glanced away from the new CAG sheepishly. She'd been... otherwise occupied when the announcement had come through her implant, and hadn't checked into it after Angela had started her shift. From the shuffling around her, she was far from the only one who had missed it.

"For those of you who are not keeping up on shipboard affairs, *Senior Fleet Commander* Roberts has transferred to the Space Navy and accepted the position of Executive Officer of *Avalon*," Stanford told them. "As I think everyone can guess from that, his injuries are such that he is no longer qualified to pilot a starfighter."

"Now, that said," he continued briskly, "Commander Roberts is still this ship's XO, and I know he's going to be keeping an eye on us. So let's not disappoint him, shall we?"

Transferred to the Navy was a hell of a lot better ending for the former CAG that Michelle had hoped for when she'd shoved his charred body into her fighter's auto-doc. It wasn't, quite, dead after all.

"I know everyone was hoping for a quiet rest of the trip," Stanford said quietly once it was clear the flight crews had calmed down. "Unfortunately, it looks like we're having the exact opposite. You are all cleared for the information I am about to give you, but it remains classified Red-Four. Do *not* discuss it outside of this briefing room."

Red-Four was the lowest level of red classification. Red classification, however, was the level immediately beneath 'Top Secret.' Disclosure of Red classification information to an uncleared individual was grounds for ten years in a Federation penal colony.

"Thanks to *our* work in leaving enough of that battlecruiser intact for Intel to dig into, we now know that our worst fears around our recent upsurge in piracy failed to grasp the full depth of the threat."

"The pirates *were* a Commonwealth covert operation. What they were *not* doing was engaging in long-term economic warfare to weaken the Alliance border defenses," the CAG told them.

"They were engaging in an immediate operation to pull our forces out of position for an imminent invasion."

For a man who'd just dropped a verbal nuke, Michelle reflected as she stared at her new commander, Wing Commander Stanford looked surprisingly calm.

"In the face of a renewed war, *Avalon* will not be returning to Castle on schedule," Stanford told them. "Nor will we likely have time to wait for new flight crews or starfighters to be delivered."

"Thankfully, between our spare ships, spare parts, and the fact that Flight Lieutenant Williams retrieved Commander Roberts' fighter, we have enough starfighters to assemble five full squadrons. Conveniently, that's how many flight crews we have left."

"We will amalgamate Alpha and Echo Squadrons into a new Alpha Squadron under Flight Commander Rokos," Stanford continued. "Chief Hammond assures me that Roberts' command fighter will be cleared for duty within the week, and I will fly aboard her once she is ready."

"I need all of you to do what everyone else on this ship is going to be doing," he continued. "Go over your starfighters. Review your training. Run through virtual sims with your new squadron mates."

"I have no idea of the details beyond one thing – but that one thing is enough: we *will* be called to war. And ladies, gentlemen, *Avalon* will *not* be found wanting."

Chapter 24

Hessian System
21:00 September 10, 2735 Earth Standard Meridian Date/Time
DSC-001 Avalon – *Captain's Office*

"So how was your first day in the Navy, Commander?" Blair asked as he passed a steaming mug of tea across his desk to Kyle.

"As Dr. Pinochet *pointedly* reminded me when I met with her this afternoon, too busy for light duty," Kyle replied, gratefully taking the cup. "I got quite the lecture from her, though she at least understands that things are a *little* unusual right now."

"Don't overdo it, Kyle," Blair told him. "I need you – but I need you sane and functioning too. If the doc says to take it easy..."

"Sir, that is the *last* thing I want to do right now," Kyle admitted. "Left to my own devices, I'm going to brood over my implant and go nuts."

The Captain nodded and gestured his acceptance with his teacup.

"Very well, Commander, I'll trust your judgment for now," he said. "But if you need to slow down, or if you need help with any part of the XO's job that's out of your experience, let me know. I *have* done the job myself," he finished dryly. "Where are we at?"

"Well, like I said, Dr. Pinochet thinks I'm overdoing it," Kyle told him with a wide grin. "I think Commander Pendez is wondering whether seducing me will help her performance evaluation, though I *also* think she's smart enough not to try."

"Mason seems a bit out of sorts," he continued, "but I'm not familiar enough with her to be certain. She gave me a list of items we needed from Hessian – replacement missiles, mainly. Stanford gave me the equivalent for the SFG."

"Thankfully, it turns out Hessian has production plants for both capital and fighter missiles, both up to full Alliance standard. They've agreed to replenish our munitions from their planetside stores, and we should be fully loaded within the hour," Kyle concluded. While the various powers of the Alliance used different warship and starfighter designs, they'd decided early on to standardize missiles across the entire body.

"We're *damn* short on spare parts for the starfighters, and we don't have *any* spare birds left. Sadly, we can't do anything about that without waiting for some kind of delivery from the Federation."

"Which we likely won't have time to wait for," Blair finished for him. "Not bad for a first day on the job, Commander."

"I'd have *liked* a quieter start," Kyle admitted, "but the Commonwealth doesn't seem to be giving us much of a choice."

"No," Blair agreed. "We're going to have to make them regret that."

The ship's intercom pinged. Glancing upwards, Blair clearly activated it with his implant and responded.

"Blair. What is it?"

"This is Lieutenant Wilson, sir. We have a Q-com request from Castle for you – Priority Alpha One."

"Thank you Lieutenant," Blair replied calmly, which was more than Kyle thought he could have managed. Alpha One was reserved for either overriding orders or 'your position is about to come under attack'.

The wall of the office beside the two men flickered for a second, and then transformed from plain gray steel to a two-dimensional image of the formal seal of the Castle Federation: a stylized castle inside a circle of fourteen stars.

The seal occupied the screen for several seconds, and then faded into the image of a gray-haired woman in the Navy's blue-piped black uniform – with three gold stars on her collar.

"Fleet Admiral Blake," Blair greeted her with a moment of surprise Kyle shared fully.

Fleet Admiral Meredith Blake was the senior-most of the Federation's four Fleet Admirals, and the current Chairwoman of the Joint Chiefs of Staff – the uniformed commander of every branch of the Castle Federation's armed forces. She was *not* who Kyle had expected to be delivering their orders.

"Captain Blair, Commander Roberts," Blake returned the greeting. "As I'm sure you can guess, I have new orders for you. Given the magnitude of the situation and your own praiseworthy involvement in us knowing what's coming, I wanted to speak to you myself."

"Your capture of *Achilles'* data cores has given us a priceless forewarning of what is coming," she said calmly. "Commander Roberts' and Commander Stanford's promotions are only the beginning of the thanks I and my fellows intend to lay on *Avalon* for what you have done."

"Unfortunately, the first reward for a job well done is always another job."

"We are re-deploying units of the Allied Fleets as we speak, but we face the unfortunate reality that most of the forces along the border cannot be moved without creating new vulnerabilities that we are certain the Commonwealth will exploit."

"Reinforcements will be leaving Phoenix, the Federation, the Imperium, and the Trade Factor over the course of the next six hours, but we have only nine days," she concluded grimly. "In some cases, I fear that it will fall to those reinforcements to *retake* systems that will have already fallen."

"And there is one system that we have no ships in place to reinforce," she told them, and an image of the border appeared beside her, a single system highlighted.

The system was on the southern clockwards edge of the border between the Alliance and the Commonwealth, far away from the fronts of the last war or the centers of the Alliance's military might.

"Tranquility joined the Alliance after the war," Blake told them. "They've kept diplomatic and trade channels open all along – and no less than four major systems on the Commonwealth side of the border will suffer moderate, though unlikely dangerous, food shortages if the shipments from Tranquility stop."

"They've clearly decided to short-circuit this by seizing Tranquility. Unfortunately, Tranquility is twelve to fifteen days from any base or nodal force we can spare units from."

Kyle saw the reason she was speaking to them as soon as Blair did.

"We're fourteen light years from Tranquility ma'am. Seven days," the Captain said quietly. "But Hessian is defenseless if we leave."

"A relief force is already en route to Hessian and scheduled to arrive in five days," the Fleet Admiral told them. "Hessian is also not on their target list – the destruction of Hessian Orbital was intended to draw units there and out of the main fighting."

"Regardless, though, the simple fact is that *Avalon* is the only unit in position to reinforce Tranquility," she told them. "We're confirming the status of their fleet, but we know their only carrier is at Midori – and both of their cruisers are old.

"There are as many worlds in the Alliance who will suffer if the shipments from Tranquility stop as there are in the Commonwealth, gentlemen. Even if that was not the case, we promised them protection when they joined the Alliance. *Castle* did, specifically.

"The freedom of one of our allies and the honor of the Federation are at stake here, gentlemen. Is *Avalon* ready to fly?"

"We are, ma'am," Blair confirmed fiercely. "We can be underway within two hours."

"Then do so," she ordered flatly. "The very survival of our nation and our allies depends on the next ten days, and on every ship on the front.

"May the stars shield your path and light your way. Good luck."

Glynn Stewart

CHAPTER 25

En route out of Hessian System
08:00 September 11, 2735 Earth Standard Meridian Date/Time
DSC-001 Avalon – *Atrium*

Between the coma and his ensuing busy-ness, Kyle had almost missed the notifications about the memorial service for the crew and pilots who'd died, and for all of the people aboard Hessian Orbital and *Jäger*.

Blair made sure he didn't, thankfully, and he had struggled his way out of bed against the exhaustion that threatened to overwhelm him. Dressed in his brand new full uniform, he joined the Captain in the open clearing at the heart of the starship's atrium.

Every member of the crew who could fit in had joined them. The entire Starfighter Group was drawn up on one side of the clearing in neat, black-uniformed ranks. Facing them were hundreds of crew members – here to mourn Senior Fleet Commander Kleiner, the pilots, and the tens of thousands of dead.

The nature of space combat left few bodies behind. Caroline Kleiner's body would never be recovered, nor would most of the pilots'. The handful that *had* been retrieved were frozen in the ship's morgue, to be delivered to their families when *Avalon* returned home.

There were no caskets at the center of the silent formation gathered in the warship's green heart. An honor guard of Marines stood in a neat circle around a stone plinth, an obelisk of shining white marble three meters tall.

Bronze plaques marked the sides of that obelisk. Each was marked with names – exactly two hundred per plaque.

Many of those names were starfighter pilots, but that plinth had been taken from the shattered wreck of the battleship *Avalon* in 2692, a year before the current vessel had commissioned. That white stone and its plaques would be carried to any new ship that bore the name, as the living memory of every man and woman who had given their lives aboard the mighty vessel.

A tiny, spider-shaped, robot rested in Captain Blair's hands as he and Kyle approached the monolith. With perfect precision, the Marines stepped aside, allowing them to step up to the memorial.

Kyle stopped at the circle of Marines, giving the stone a textbook perfect salute that he held as the Captain reached it and softly placed the robot on the latest, half-empty, plaque.

"Spacers of the Castle Federation," Blair said aloud. "My brothers and sisters in arms.

"It is never easy to lose friends and comrades. Never easy to say goodbye. This memorial remembers for us, as if we would ever forget.

"We lost the least here in Hessian," he told his crew sadly. "Our losses pale into insignificance compared to the death toll aboard *Jäger* and Hessian Orbital. But that does not mean we feel our losses any less keenly.

"We remember," he repeated.

"We remember Senior Fleet Commander Caroline Kleiner," Blair continued, and the robot spun to life as he spoke, etching Kleiner's name into the bronze plaque – forever immortalizing her as part of *Avalon*'s sacrifices.

"We remember Flight Lieutenant Kayla Morgaurd."

And so it continued, as the Captain read off each name in turn, in decreasing order of rank, and the tiny robot continued to skitter its way across the bronze plaque, adding name after name to the roll of the fallen.

#

The Federation military, by and large, took most of its traditions from Castle, the first world of the Federation and still first among equals of the fourteen stars.

Glynn Stewart

Castle, in turn, had been colonized by a mix of people from dozens of regions and cultures intentionally looking to create a 'cultural mosaic.' This had more than a little to do with why a world with heavy Arthurian mythos woven into its names and traditions was ruled by a multi-person executive with more in common with the Roman Republic than any of Earth's governments at the time they'd left.

It also resulted in some traditions that even a native could occasionally find to be a peculiar mix. Bronze braziers scattered across the clearing spread the fragrant smoke of several varieties of incense, while paper lanterns floated overhead – lifted by electric heater-lights, not candles, aboard a starship.

Amidst the lanterns and incense were scattered tables loaded with food and – Kyle hoped! – non-alcoholic punch. Even he felt it was against the rules to not have alcohol at a Castle-style wake, but Navy regs restricted alcohol to the mess.

And it was now Kyle's job to enforce those regulations.

He sighed, shaking his head. Normally, he would be in the middle of the wake, living up the party while trying to shake off the grief. With his new role, though, he felt awkward and out of sorts. Before, only the pilots had been expected to look up to him. Now the entire *crew* was supposed to see him as an example.

Since Kyle wasn't sure what a good example *was*, he found himself on the edge of the wake with a glass of water, watching the party out of the corner of his eyes.

There was an underlying tension to the crowd he wasn't sure how to address. With his pilots, he'd have tried by getting them all drunk – and acting like an idiot himself. With three thousand crew instead of three hundred, he didn't think that would work quite as well.

A wake was supposed to honor the dead and encourage the living, but the crowd was quiet and subdued. Kyle figured most of them were considering the fact that they could easily be joining that list all too soon.

"I should have spiked the damn punch myself," he muttered. Having a third of the crew drunk for a shift would do less damage than the eroding morale he could sense around him.

"Does that mean you won't brig me if I admit I did?" a voice said from beside him. He glanced over to find Lieutenant-Commander Maria Pendez's dark eyes looking up at him with a dangerous sparkle.

"Only if I didn't hear you, and I swear my implant damage is causing my hearing to occasionally fritz out," he told her. "Nonetheless, Commander, *behave.*"

She graced him with a smile, stunningly white against her dusky skin.

"I confess to nothing," she told him. "But trying to get at least Mason and Stanford drunk was *damned* tempting."

Something about her tone made Kyle look around for that pair. To his surprise, they were *not* hovering around each other pretending not to make googly eyes as they'd been doing since just after Thorn. Stanford was in one corner with the Flight Commanders, sharing a drink and a joke with Commander Rokos. Mason was on the *precisely* opposite side of the party, engrossed in a conversation with one of her Lieutenants.

People didn't ignore each other that completely by accident.

"Shit," Kyle said softly.

"It ain't *my* job to watch ship morale – or morality, as everyone knows," Pendez said virtuously with a wink. "But that pair... something's up, and when I tried to lure Mason into 'girl talk' I got shut down so hard my ears still ring. You follow me, boss?"

"Thank you, Commander Pendez," Kyle told her. "I'll sort them out," he finished with a sigh. "As soon as I work out what exactly they *did.*"

"That's what Kleiner would do, so I figured it was your job," *Avalon's* Navigator told him cheerily. "My job, on the other hand, is to warp the very fabric of reality to take us all between the stars."

"Speaking of which, we're scheduled to initiate the Alcubierre drive at thirteen hundred. Unless I misread the schedule, that's about an hour into your first watch on the bridge."

She smiled toothily.

"Don't worry boss, I'll be gentle."

En route out of Hessian System
13:00 September 11, 2735 Earth Standard Meridian Date/Time
DSC-001 Avalon – *Bridge*

For the first time in his life, Kyle occupied the single chair on the raised dais in the center of a warship's bridge. Around him, *Avalon's* afternoon watch continued about their ordinary duties, pretending to be unaware that the current acting commander of their starship had been a Navy officer for a grand total of three days.

As he'd suspected for a long time, most of the screens around him were redundant. Even with his reduced implant capability, he'd managed to link into the bridge's network. Overlaid translucently on the walls and people around him was the view from *Avalon's* exterior, as if he wasn't surrounded by millions of tons of metal.

Of the ship's senior officers, only Pendez was on the bridge. A junior Lieutenant-Commander who looked far too young for the gold circle on his collar manned the Tactical station. The Senior Lieutenant at the Engineering station actually looked *older* than the man controlling the carrier's weapons.

Mixed in with the visual of the space outside the ship were multiple overlays of sensor data that would have been overwhelmingly complex if Kyle hadn't been a starfighter pilot. As it was, the amount of data was actually *less* than what he'd handled as a pilot. Unlike then, he had to consciously process the information instead of just *knowing* it, but he was still easily able to tell when the starship passed far enough away from Hessian to be clear activating the Alcubierre drives.

Kyle took a deep breath, and brought the procedures up on his datapad. He reviewed them carefully – a few minutes wasn't going to change their arrival time across a seven day voyage – and then looked over at Pendez.

The dusky-skinned Navigator was looking at him expectantly, and gave him a wink when she saw him look her way.

"Lieutenant-Commander Pendez, please confirm that we have cleared all detectable gravity zones," Kyle asked aloud, sending an electronic request along simultaneously. It looked clear to *him*, but Pendez was the one with the measurements for imitation of the Alcubierre-Stetson drive.

"All identified gravitational objects are beyond effect range," she replied, her voice crispy and formal. An electronic data packet flicked back to him in the network, a three dimensional model showing the source and magnitude of all gravitational forces on the carrier.

"Current gravitational force is beneath zero point seven picometers per second squared. We are prepared to warp space on your command."

"Senior Lieutenant Reid, please confirm status of Class One mass manipulators," Kyle asked the Engineering officer. He received the electronic download of the status of the massive exotic-matter-driven machines before he'd finished speaking, but waited for the verbal confirmation.

"All five Class Ones are at ninety-eight-plus percent," the junior engineer finally reported. "Engineering reports prepared to warp space."

Kyle triggered a prepared command on his datapad to open an all-hands channel to be heard across the ship.

"All hands, prepare for Alcubierre drive," he ordered, taking a tiny thrill in the fact that Blair was leaving this important, if simple, evolution entirely to him. He knew the Captain was in his office, less than twenty steps from the bridge, but the trust being extended was real regardless.

"Navigation, please initiate interior Stetson stabilization fields," Kyle ordered Pendez quietly after letting several moments pass.

The overlay of the exterior of the ship shimmered as the faint haze of the energy fields that would protect *Avalon* from the hellish interior of her bubble of warped space flashed into existence.

"Interior Stetson field active," Pendez reported softly as she flipped a more detailed report to Kyle. "Exterior field on standby, mass manipulators on standby."

There was a flicker showing on her report, a mild harmonic in the Stetson stabilization field, but the computer was sure it was within tolerance. Kyle made a mental note to speak to Wong about it later, and then turned his full attention to Maria Pendez.

"Lieutenant-Commander Pendez," Kyle said formally. "You may initiate space warp at your discretion."

All of the light around the carrier seemed to shiver and distort, warping around four separate points as four of *Avalon*'s five Class One mass manipulators spun gravitational singularities into existence – and a second Stetson stabilization field prevented those singularities from wrecking orbits across the Hessian system.

"We have singularity formation," Pendez reported. "Exterior Stetson field is active, no containment issues. Initiating warp bubble... now."

In the sensors and system reports feeding to Kyle, the entire ship strained as it dumped enough power to fuel half a world into the manipulators. A moment later, a bright flash of blue light encapsulated the ship, and the Hessian system was gone, replaced by a flickering and chaotic glow of Cherenkov radiation.

One battle was behind them – and they were on their way to another.

CHAPTER 26

Under Alcubierre Drive, near Hessian System
09:00 September 12, 2735 Earth Standard Meridian Date/Time
DSC-001 Avalon *– Captain's Office*

Scientists had never managed to modify the two-way link of a pair of quantum-entangled particles to allow any form of multi-point communication. Telecommunication engineers, however, had simply shrugged and resurrected the ancient concept of the switchboard.

Avalon's array of quantum-entangled bits were linked into three separate switchboard stations in Alliance space. Each of those station had its own arrays of entangled bits linked to other networks owned by Alliance powers, as well as many neutrals and even the Commonwealth itself.

This meant that the longest delay in the communication between the office Kyle was sharing with Captain Blair and the commander of Tranquility's defenses was the time it took the man's aide to confirm he was available for the scheduled call.

From Kyle joining his Captain in the office and placing the call, to the face of the First Admiral of the Tranquility Space Fleet appearing on the wall-screen, took about thirty seconds.

"Greetings, Captain, Commander," the extremely pale-skinned, shaven-headed, man in a burgundy uniform announced calmly, bowing with his hands clasped together before looking directly at the two Federation officers with dark eyes.

"I am First Admiral Sagacity Wu," he continued. "It is good to know that the Federation comes to our aid."

"I am Captain Malcolm Blair, and this is Senior Fleet Commander Kyle Roberts," Blair introduced themselves. "I appreciate you taking the time to speak with us this morning."

Wu inclined his head slightly, the action shading the heavy folds of his eyes into an almost sinister hue against the paleness of his skin.

"My world is in danger, and your Federation sends us all that they can," he said calmly and precisely. "One will always desire more ships, more aid, but I do not believe it is coincidence that brings *Avalon* to us once again, to honor the promises made upon the Flight Deck of your very vessel, Captain."

Kyle started to reach for his datapad to research *Avalon*'s role in the original treaty with Tranquility, only to stop himself – hopefully before the Admiral noticed! What would once have been an instant query of his implant's databanks would now actually take him time – and more importantly, be rude when dealing with the commander of an allied military.

"I wish we had more ships with us myself, Admiral," Blair admitted. "At least we will beat the Commonwealth there by at least two days."

Wu nodded sharply.

"Most likely, the Commonwealth forces have already left their bases," he told them. "We have received no declaration of war or other statement of their intentions, but my own personnel have reviewed the intelligence retrieved from the *Achilles*. The High Council has agreed with Alliance Intelligence's conclusions – the Commonwealth plans a sneak attack upon our world."

There wasn't much Kyle or Blair could say to that, and Kyle watched the Captain out of the corner of his eye to see how Blair responded.

"The Commonwealth believes the historical inevitability of their cause justifies much," the Captain murmured. "We will place ourselves at your disposal upon our arrival, First Admiral, but can you brief us on the status of your defenses?"

"With pleasure, Captain," Wu responded. He made no gesture or other visible command, but the screen suddenly split in two. On the left was the pale-skinned Admiral, and the right was an image of the Tranquility system itself.

Kyle realized quickly what made Tranquility unique – the planet was *huge*. He hadn't a chance to review the statistics before, but Wu's image of the system was rapidly overlaid with some of the basic statistics, and the planet was easily four times the diameter of Earth.

The planet's crust was extremely poor in heavy metals, giving it a surface gravity *lower* than Earth's, and extremely rich in phosphates, nitrates, and all of the other organic compounds useful for growing crops. Combined with a negligible axial tilt and near-circular orbit, something like seventy-five percent of the planet's surface land area had perfect growing cycles for most human food crops.

The size of the planet had also resulted in something else Kyle had never seen before on a habitable world – Tranquility had rings. Three, in fact, extending out to almost a full light second away from the world in loose-knit collections of ice and dust.

Most of the system's heavy industry was tied up in the asteroid belt, with a large complex tucked into the innermost of the four gas giants. A sixth world orbited halfway between Tranquility and its star, a fire-rock that held a few observatories and science stations, but nothing of real value.

"To begin with the most basic, the Tranquility Space Fleet commands three starships," Wu told them. "*Tranquility* herself was built to order five years ago in the Castle system and is equivalent to one of your *Victory* class carriers. *Sapanā* and *Mauna,* our two cruisers, are old Imperial ships bought when Coraline was decommissioning them. They've been heavily refitted, but are twenty-five years old.

"We also possess twenty-four guardships for home security, eight each of the *Śīlda, Abhibhāvaka* and *Rakshaka* classes," Wu continued. "I will have a data package on all of our ships forwarded to you once we are done."

"Our enemy has picked an excellent time from their perspective, I am afraid," the Tranquility First Admiral admitted. "Sufficiently so that I wonder about their intelligence.

"We use a modified form of your *Typhoon* type fighter, the *Hurricane*. Like our cruisers, it has been heavily updated over time and the *Hurricane-D* was one of the first seventh generation fighters deployed by an Alliance power.

"However, our entire current strength of the class is aboard *Tranquility*," he said calmly. "*Tranquility* is with the Alliance nodal fleet at Midori. Our cruisers and home defense squadrons are equipped entirely with the *Hurricane-C*, a rough equivalent to your *Cobra* design.

"The High Council gave us a choice between the budget to pay for *Mauna's* refit, and the budget to replace all of our fighters with the D model," Wu explained. "We chose *Mauna's* refit, which brings us to why the Commonwealth's timing is unfortunate."

"*Mauna* currently has no internal power," he said flatly. "Even if we could get her new reactors installed in time, half of her weapons are also being replaced. Without your vessel, Captain Blair, I would face an entire Commonwealth battle group with only the *Sapanā* and our guardships.

"I have faith in my men and women, but that is not a battle human courage and adherence to *dharma* can win for us," he said quietly. "Your ship may seem old and small, Captain, but I believe that she is enough to turn the tide.

"And I *know* that it is right and correct for her to be here."

#

Wu was as good as his word. Once they'd spent forty five minutes going through his plan to defend Tranquility, he'd sent over the full detailed specifications on every ship and starfighter the TSF had to defend their world with.

It was an odd mix.

Tranquility exported food to over fifty different star systems, and had money to burn. What they didn't have was heavy industry. Tranquility itself was unusually poor in metals of almost every kind, and the asteroid belt was the only source of raw materials.

They purchased all of their starships, freighters, cruisers, and carriers alike. Originally, they'd even purchased the starfighters to go aboard them, but eventually the High Council had agreed to fund the starfighter plant hidden on one of the moons of the innermost gas giant.

While most of the heavy industry was concentrated in the asteroid belt, close to where their materials were extracted, the gas giant's cloud scoops not only fed the fusion plants for the starfighter plant, but also ran the one facility in the system that produced the exotic matter necessary for mass manipulators.

That plant was only a few years older than the starfighter factory, and had been the real turning point in the existence of a local ship-building industry. Tranquility could, if they spent the effort, even build Class One manipulators now.

Mostly, though, they built the higher class devices that fueled a modern civilization – and allowed the local industry to build half-megaton schooners for in-system travel, and the half-megaton guardships of the Tranquility Space Fleet.

Kyle realized that at least two of the three classes of guardship Tranquility had built were better than most of their type. The *Abhibhāvaka* and *Rakshaka* – *Guardian* and *Defender*, if his datapad translated as well as his implant had – classes were designed as missile platforms, equipped with both Starfires and Jackhammers to engage at any range.

Wu's plan called for hiding the two missile-heavy classes of guardship in Tranquility's rings, where the dust and ice would shield them from most sensors while they pounded the Commonwealth squadrons.

The *Śīlda* – *Shield* – class ships were heavily armed with positron lances and anti-missile lasers, and rated for the same Tier 3 acceleration as starfighters. The plan called for them to go out *with* the starfighters, accompanied by a swarm of missiles launched by *Avalon*, *Sapanā* and the missile guardships.

If the Commonwealth forces made it through that, *Sapanā* would bear the brunt of the battle in orbit. She was old, but *Avalon* was even older, and the Tranquility ship had been just as heavily refitted.

"It looks solid to me," Kyle said quietly after he and Blair had each gone over the statistics for the Tranquility Space Fleet. "It's more defensive than I'd like, but that's what the situation calls for."

"Tell me, Commander, is *any* plan not more defensive than you'd like?" Blair asked dryly. "You are, after all, the man who took a fighter wing at a battlecruiser at a quarter of the speed of light."

"Aggression has its place," Kyle replied. "'Shock and awe' is a mainstay of tactics for a reason." He shrugged. "I'd like to think I've never taken an uncalculated risk, but I'd be lying. Hitting people hard throws them off, leaves them reacting. I'd rather be the one in control of the situation."

Which, as Kyle thought about it, explained some of why he'd ended up *in* the military. When Lisa had told him she was pregnant, he'd lost control of the situation. He'd panicked, and done something – *anything* – to give himself the illusion of control.

It was an... unwelcome insight.

"Commander?" Blair asked, arching his eyebrow at Kyle's sudden distraction.

"Nothing, sir," Kyle replied with a small shake of his head. "Personal insight, nothing important."

"Anything that can impact my officers *is* important, Kyle," the Captain replied. "You may want to consider that as XO – we don't want to pry into our people's personal issues, but when they start to affect their performance, we need to be aware of them."

Kyle nodded thoughtfully, considering Mason and Stanford. The pair were still being coolly correct with each other, and he wasn't entirely sure *what* had happened to the budding romance that had been softening hearts all over the ship.

"Everyone's on edge," he admitted aloud. "We're heading to war, after all."

"That's normal, but keep an eye on it," Blair instructed. "It filters up. The ratings will go to their petty officers, who will go their officers, who will go their department heads, who will go to you."

"If *you* have issues, you bring them to me," he finished. "Or, I suppose, Dr. Pinochet."

"In the end, however, we will arrive in six days. The Commonwealth will only be two days behind us – we *must* be ready to fight."

"We will be, sir," Kyle promised. "We'll all make sure of it."

Glynn Stewart

Chapter 27

Under Alcubierre Drive
19:00 September 12, 2735 Earth Standard Meridian Date/Time
DSC-001 Avalon *– Deck Six Officers' Lounge*

The officers' lounge was deathly quiet as Michelle poured wine into the two glasses Angela had snagged from the steward pulling waiter duty tonight. The two women had taken a table well back from the atrium today, tucked into a corner out of the main sitting area, and the pilot knew her lover was watching the subdued collection of officers behind them.

"They're all afraid," Angela said finally, her voice soft enough that no one else could hear it.

"And here is about the only place they can show it," Michelle murmured back. "Tradition says we officers show a brave face to the enlisted, even in the Space Force where we practically *outnumber* our enlisted."

Angela wordlessly flicked her fingers at the young man, a Steward Specialist Two, serving the tables.

"Tradition *also* allows for us to ignore that tradition in the mess, and hope that the trust extended to the Steward Division helps offset the realization of just how human the lot of us officers are," Michelle said dryly.

"*I'm* afraid," Angela admitted, laying her hand on Michelle's. "Starfighter crew is one of the most dangerous jobs we have. I don't want to lose you, my dear."

Michelle squeezed her lover's hand.

"I chose the uniform," she told Angela. "I chose the Space Force, I chose to go for my wings, I *chose* to fly a starfighter – and I wouldn't choose anything else."

"I know," the nurse said quietly. "And I wouldn't change who you are for an instant. But I know the odds, too, Michelle. I don't think there's *ever* been a fighter strike without losses."

"Our job is to keep *Avalon* intact," Michelle replied. "Which I, personally, see as a side benefit of keeping *you* safe."

Angela smiled softly, sadly, and Michelle squeezed her hand again. There wasn't much more she could say – when the Commonwealth attacked Tranquility, she would be out there with the rest of the pilots. Just as Angela would be in the infirmary, dealing with the inevitable injuries of combat.

That was their duty and nothing, not even love, could change that.

Under Alcubierre Drive
21:00 September 12, 2735 Earth Standard Meridian Date/Time
DSC-001 Avalon – *Executive Officer's Office*

No matter what uniform he wore, or what service he ended up in, it seemed that Kyle couldn't escape the never-ending curse of paperwork. His inability to run through the reports and approvals rapidly through his implant was coming back to haunt him as well, which led to him sitting in his office well after his watch was over, with a half-eaten donut and a datapad explaining why Fleet Commander Wong wanted to promote one of his petty officers.

The document on his pad was hardly stimulating enough to make him miss the admittance buzzer on his door. It took a moment for him to wake up enough to recognize what it *was*, but that wasn't the promotion request form's fault.

"Enter," he instructed.

To his surprise, Lieutenant-Commander Maria Pendez stepped through the door. As it slid shut behind her, she triggered the privacy mode that prevented anyone else from entering the room.

Since anyone above her in her chain of command, including Kyle, could override that privacy setting, he let this pass with a raised eyebrow.

"Come in, Lieutenant-Commander. Have a seat," he told her, gesturing to the pair of chairs on the other side of the desk. "I'm just catching up on paperwork – Kleiner was on top of it, but it breeds like rabbits."

His admittedly lame joke fell utterly flat as Pendez silently took one of the seats and faced him, her face far more drawn and tired looking than he was used to seeing from the cheerful Navigator.

"I have a problem, sir," she said finally. "It was easier to talk to Caroline about this, but she's gone. And it seems I can't deal with it myself."

Kyle waited for her to explain. Kleiner hadn't *planned* on being blown to hell, so it wasn't as if she'd left him a file labeled 'ongoing personnel counseling'. If she and Pendez had been discussing something, he had no information on it at all.

"I know I have a reputation as a man-eater," Pendez said bluntly. "It's... not without basis. I decided a long time ago I didn't want to marry or settle down with a military man. I also had *no* interest in being celibate – I am quite fond of men in many ways."

"I've always been up-front about the nature of the relationships I'm getting into," she continued. "Unfortunately, it appears that in at least one case that fell on deaf ears, and the gentleman in question is... unhappy about how things have progressed."

"I see," Kyle replied, hoping that he was wrong.

"He hasn't progressed to violence or anything like that," she assured him. "But he's been following me. Two nights ago he showed up outside my quarters. *Last* night he interrupted what was looking to be a *very* pleasant evening with one of the CIC shift supervisors. He started haranguing us until my date left. I *tried* to tell him it was unacceptable, that we were done and he needed to leave me alone – but it only made him madder."

"I see," Kyle repeated. "Should I be getting Lieutenant-Major Khadem in here?"

"No, sir!" Pendez replied quickly. "He's a good guy – I used to think so, anyway. He's just from Cauldron, and I should have looked up more about his homeworld before I jumped after a cute ass."

Kyle flipped up a summary of Cauldron on his datapad to make sure what he remembered was correct. Technically a Protectorate of the Commonwealth rather than an actual member world, Cauldron was a barely-inhabitable world orbiting a super-bright F-class star. With sixty percent of its surface desert, the planet had a small population, which seemed to be unified in their membership in a very old, very conservative, sect of Christianity.

"I'm surprised he was willing to sleep with you," Kyle admitted, glancing down the data fields.

"I'm not sure *what* he was thinking, but now he seems to think I'm committed to *marry* him," Pendez snapped. "And that any other man laying hands on me is 'sinning in the eyes of Jehovah'."

Kyle sighed and laid aside his datapad.

"And you don't want to press charges?" he asked, making certain.

"Not... yet," she admitted. "I know Commander Kleiner was going to try and talk to him. I don't know if she did, but I also suspect the twit will listen better to a man."

"Who is it?" Kyle finally asked. While it was unlikely that the man could have made it through the Academy if he was completely unable to listen to women, it still fell to the XO to put a stop to harassment. Regardless of said Exec's gender.

"Lieutenant-Commander James Russell, in Engineering," Pendez said in a rush. "I thought there was a good guy in there, but now his head is so far up his ass I'm not sure!"

"I will speak to him," Kyle said calmly. "But I need you to promise me one thing, Ms. Pendez."

"Yes, sir?" she asked hesitantly.

"If he harasses you again, you will page myself or the Ship's Marshal immediately," he ordered firmly. "What you describe from last night is already over the line, Maria. I will *not* permit it to be repeated, no matter how good a guy he is underneath. Understand?"

"Yes, sir," she said with a long sigh. "I understand, sir."

"Good. Now leave it with me for now," Kyle told her. "I will speak with Commander Russell."

CHAPTER 28

Under Alcubierre Drive
08:00 September 13, 2735 Earth Standard Meridian Date/Time
DSC-001 Avalon – *Main Engineering*

Kyle entered the central chamber of the Engineering Deck, the cavernous expanse holding the carrier's main zero point energy cells, with a strong sense of trepidation.

He'd had a chance since ushering Pendez out of his office the previous night to research Cauldron and the Church of the Final Advent in some detail. It seemed that somewhere between what he was sure had been an honest attempt on Maria Pendez's to be up-front about the nature of her approach and James Russell's cultural interpretations, there'd been a mis-communication.

The Church of the Final Advent was an odd conservative sect of Christianity born sometime in the first two centuries of the third millennium. It had an odd mix of cultural ideals and rituals, borrowed from a lot of different religions – not all of them Christian – but the one currently at play was simple. Cauldron's women chose their husband – that was their 'God-given right'.

Unfortunately, that choice was irrevocable once made – and it was formalized by the woman having sex with the man of her choice to mark the betrothal. Once a woman had 'given herself' to a man, tradition required the wedding to be within three months.

And regardless of whether betrothed or marriage, touching another man's woman was, as Pendez had quoted to him, 'a sin against Jehovah'. One that, according to the sociological article he'd found, written by one of the politicos who'd accompanied the original Federation humanitarian mission to the battered colony thirty years ago, Cauldron men were known to kill over.

Kyle was relying on the fact that Russell had managed make it through a Federation Academy, and all the culture shock that had to have come with that, to help him calm the man down.

It also made a good reason for him to visit the Engineering Deck for the first time since he'd set foot on *Avalon*. The central chamber was stunningly quiet. He *knew* just how much power the six massive zero point cells that surrounded him were pumping out – a single capital-ship-grade cell could power a large city.

"Commander Roberts," Wong greeted him, the Chief Engineer wiping his hands clean on a rag that had seen better days. "What brings you down the dungeon?"

"The dungeon, Commander Wong?" Kyle asked dryly. "I would have thought that was Marshal Khadem's domain."

"Nah, we keep our brigs well-lit," the engineer replied with a grin. "I can't say the same about every nook and cranny of the Engineering deck."

"You have robots for those parts," Kyle pointed out, only to be met with a shrug and another grin. "I need to speak to with Lieutenant-Commander James Russell," he said finally, concluding that the engineer was irrepressible.

"What's going on?" Wong asked slowly, stepping away from the controlled chaos of his domain. "Russell's a good man, though I'll admit he gets a bit strange around his religion some days."

"It's nothing major, yet," Kyle told him. "But he's earned himself a counseling session to try and keep it that way."

The engineer shook his head and sighed.

"I've had a chat or two with him myself," he admitted. "He's in Sector Four – he's running some robots checking into that damn flutter in the Stetson stabilizers. It's still within tolerance, but I won't rest easy until we *find* the damn thing."

"Will it cause issues if I pull him out for an hour or so?" Kyle asked. "I can find him at the end of his watch if you need me to."

"Nah, I'll just take it over myself," Wong replied. "Come on, I'll show you the way."

Kyle could think of three or four reasons why having the supervisor of someone he needed to counsel walk him in wasn't the best idea, but they all fell flat against the simple fact that he didn't know for sure where Sector Four of the Engineering Deck *was*.

He followed Wong through Engineering, trying to make sense of the chaos around him. It did fall into place after a moment or two – *that* collection of monitors and techs was showing the status of every zero point cell aboard the ship and controlling their power draw, while *this* collection was reviewing the interfacing fields of the Stetson stabilizers, and the *other* collection was moving positrons between capacitors to make sure none of them overloaded.

Of course, having no less than six major control stations in the same room caused an apparent degree of havoc, which was only exacerbated by the fact that the central chamber was also the main location where the various repair teams and drones crossed over to different sections of the ship.

Wong threaded his way through the chaos with practiced skill, leading Kyle into a side corridor that was, admittedly, noticeably more dimly lit than most of the ship. There were several doors opening off from it, but the Engineer lead him straight to a specific one, and opened it into the Sector Four Drone Control Center.

Kyle followed him into the room, which in many ways resembled the ship's bridge on a smaller scale. Three techs were sitting at consoles, using a combination of physical and neural interfaces to control the robots running repairs over a twelfth of the ship.

The central chair, from which an officer – in this case, Lieutenant-Commander James Russell – would oversee their work, was empty.

"Kricket," Wong said sharply, looking at a blond-haired women at one of the consoles. "Where's Russell?"

The tech looked up, blinking at the unexpected interruption, then glanced over at the center chair.

"He said he was stepping out to grab a coffee," she told the Chief Engineer. "That was... ten minutes ago?"

"Thank you, Senior Specialist," Wong said quietly.

By the time Wong had finished speaking, Kyle was back out in the quieter corridor linking Engineering's side chambers together. His datapad was out and he was already interrogating it for Russell's location.

His datapad promptly requested authorization. A second after that, it informed him that Lieutenant-Commander James Russell was on duty in Section Four Drone Control – and was physically in the Deck Eight Officers' Quarters.

The Engineering Deck was Deck Three. Russell was five decks and a quarter of the ship away from where he was supposed to be. But why...?

He ordered the datapad to give him *Pendez*'s location. It promptly informed him that Maria Pendez was off-duty and, barring a ship-wide alert, accessing her location represented a violation of her privacy.

With a snarl at the layers of authorization he'd normally have just flipped through on his implant, Kyle gave the portable computer his emergency override code.

Lieutenant-Commander Maria Pendez was in the quarters of one Senior Lieutenant Markus Antonio, Tactical Department. Unlike Commander Pendez's, however, Lieutenant Antonio's quarters were on Deck Eight.

They were, in fact, in the section that Lieutenant-Commander James Russell had just entered – and had no reason to be in.

"Wong," Kyle said sharply. "Call Marshal Khadem for me – have him meet me in Deck Eight Officers' Quarters."

The engineer looked at him in surprise.

"What's going on?" he demanded – but Kyle was already on his way.

Under Alcubierre Drive
08:30 September 13, 2735 Earth Standard Meridian Date/Time
DSC-001 Avalon – *Deck Eight Officers' Quarters*

Lieutenant-Major Khadem met Kyle just outside the hatch that led into the Deck Eight Officers' Quarters. The dark-skinned man's face was grim – and he was armed. He and both of the Marines he'd brought with him were in full black shell body armor, with the distinctive shapes of Federation-issue stunners in their hands and pistols on their belts.

"Wong filled me in as much as he knew," the Ship's Marshal, the Marine officer in charge of all security aboard *Avalon*, told Kyle. "We have a problem."

"I knew that," Kyle said bluntly. "I doubt Russell is hacking into Senior Lieutenant Antonio's quarters to congratulate his ex on her choice of partner."

"A worse problem," Khadem said flatly, gesturing his Marines to precede them through the door. "As in Lieutenant-Commander James Russell drew a Navy sidearm and four clips of frangible ammunition from the armory stocks last night."

Kyle stopped in mid-step. He hadn't expected Russell to be *armed*.

"How did he manage that?!"

"All Navy officers are *authorized* to carry a service sidearm on duty," Khadem pointed out calmly. "*Inshallah*, none of them will ever use one – and most don't even carry one unless ordered or specifically required by regs. But no poor Marine Lance Corporal is going to tell a Navy O-4 he can't draw a sidearm without a damned good reason."

"Damn," Kyle muttered. "All right, I'm still going to try to talk to him," he said grimly, "but you are authorized to stun him if you deem it necessary. Understood?"

"Yes, sir."

The two Marines led the way, but Kyle was barely a step behind them as they double-timed down the hallways, deserted an hour and a half into First Shift. Finally, they turned a corner and saw what Kyle presumed to be Senior Lieutenant Markus Antonio's quarters.

He made that presumption because the control panel next to the door had been removed and the electronic controls physically overridden. The door itself was closed, which made Kyle's heart beat far too quickly for his peace of mind.

"Marshal, override that door," he ordered.

Even with its electronic guts hanging down the wall, the door panel responded to the Marshal's override key. The door slid open, to reveal a frozen tableau out of the worst nightmares Kyle's imagination had been conjuring on the way up.

James Russell was a small man with pasty white skin and pitch black hair, close-cropped in a spacer's cut. He wore a partially unfastened shipsuit, and his eyes were wild as he waved the pistol in his hand at the room's other two occupants.

Maria Pendez was wrapped in the sheets, pressed back against the corner of the wall while Markus Antonio, a bronze-skinned athlete of a man whose completely naked form revealed at least two reasons the Navigator had gone for him, tried to stay between her and Russell.

"Russell, stand the *hell* down," Kyle snapped.

"I can't!" the young officer half-cried. "God demands it – she gave herself to *me*."

"I told you what was going on," Pendez replied, her voice surprisingly level. "It was just fun – you *knew* that."

"It wasn't to *me*," Russell replied, the gun wavering madly. There was no way Khadem could stun him without the pistol going off – which *might* miss Antonio. But might not.

"But you knew it was to her," Kyle said gently. "You *know* this isn't how things work in the Federation, James. Maria told you what you were getting into. Why this?"

He took a step towards James, only to freeze as the pistol waved in his direction. Unlike most of his fellow Navy and Space Force officers, Kyle knew perfectly well what frangible rounds did to a body. He'd seen it on the *Gulf* and had no desire to see it today.

"It doesn't make *sense*," James whispered, the gun now wavering back and forth between Antonio and Kyle. "Don always explained it to me, always made it fit with God's will! But this *is* God's will, and he can't explain how it's not!"

A puzzle piece fell into place in Kyle's mind, and he cursed the lack of his old implant capability. He would have run a search for other members of the Church of the Last Advent without even thinking before

– now he'd *had* to think, and he'd forgotten that Donald Indigo had also been a member.

Don Indigo had also been a Castle native, however, and used to adapting his religious views to other cultures. The older and more world-wise man had clearly taken Russell under his wing, helped him deal with the culture clash.

Unfortunately, Don Indigo had been a Space Force gunner – one who hadn't made it back from the strike that had killed *Achilles*. Without his friend to rely on as a translator, Russell had been even more lost than before.

Now he knew to look for it, Kyle could see the slightly glazed look in the Lieutenant-Commander's eyes. The twitch in the hand that held the gun, and the shivers running through the muscles of the man's legs.

"When did you last sleep, James?" Kyle asked quietly. "Not laid down in your rack and forced yourself to stay, but actually sleep."

The exhausted and half-mad engineer waved the gun at Pendez. "With *her*."

And the last pieces fell into place.

"James," Kyle said softly. "It's no-one's job here to fix you. It's not mine – and it's *certainly* not Maria's.

"But we can help you, if you let us," he continued. "Don wouldn't have wanted this. *God* wouldn't want this. What is the sixth commandment?"

For a long moment, Russell didn't seem to have heard him, then he whispered.

"Thou shalt not..." his voice choked off in a sob.

"Thou shalt not kill," Kyle finish for him. "I know everything's gone wrong, James, but I promise you – we can make it better. Just... give me the gun."

For a long, long, moment, Kyle wasn't sure if that was one push too far. Then, with one massive sob that wracked his entire frame, Russell handed Kyle the pistol and crumpled to the floor.

Kyle checked it, safetied it, and stepped to one side. He gestured to Khadem.

"Marshal Khadem," he said formally, his gaze. "Restrain Lieutenant-Commander Russell. Take him to the infirmary and play the recording of this... incident for Doctor Pinochet."

"Until I, Captain Blair, or Surgeon-Commander Pinochet say otherwise, he is in psychiatric detention," Kyle ordered.

He stood to one side as Khadem snapped a pair of handcuffs on Roberts and led the engineer, mostly gently, out of Antonio's quarters. The two Marines at the door braced to attention and saluted Kyle, then followed their commander out.

Finally, Kyle turned his attention back to the two remaining occupants of the room. Now the immediate crisis was past, Antonio was grabbing a pair of pants, a tell-tale shiver running through his muscles as the adrenaline started to come down.

Maria Pendez, however, still sat in the corner with a sheet wrapped around her and her eyes thoughtful.

"Let me make one thing clear, Lieutenant-Commander Pendez," Kyle told her. "This was not your fault. You did *everything* right, and you had no way of knowing how close to the edge James was."

"That poor man," she whispered, and Kyle shook his head gently at her.

"His reasons may be more sympathetic than I expected, but that does not change the fact that he stalked you and threatened you with a weapon," he said flatly. "While I will speak to Surgeon-Commander Pinochet before I make any charges myself, if either of you chooses to press them I will prefer them to JAG without hesitation."

"He waved a gun at you!" Antonio snapped. "What do you mean, 'that poor man'?"

"She means that our Navigator has a heart a few sizes too large," Kyle told the other man. "It's a virtue, in my opinion. One of her many hidden depths – she is much more than a pretty face."

From Maria's expression, she wasn't so sure that the same description applied to Markus Antonio anymore.

CHAPTER 29

Under Alcubierre Drive
12:00 September 13, 2735 Earth Standard Meridian Date/Time
DSC-001 Avalon – *Flight Group Briefing Room*

Stanford always found SFG-001's briefing room ominously large when the squadron commanders met there. The room, with its rows of chairs, was designed to hold every pilot, gunner, and flight engineer from six squadrons. The front 'stage,' however, could also double as a meeting room for the commanders of those squadrons, with the big holo-projector serving as an aid for tactics and logistics.

"How's the new organization shaping up for everyone?" *Avalon's* new CAG asked his squadron leads.

Alpha Squadron, now commanded by Flight Commander Rokos, had been assembled from the survivors of Alpha and Echo squadrons. The other four remaining squadrons hadn't been as bad, but deaths among those who'd successfully ejected and the loss of ships had required at least some consolidation in all five.

"Alpha is shaping up well," Rokos replied gruffly. "We lost a lot of good people, and morale is still crawling slowly out of the shitter, but they'll fly and they'll fight – and they'll do it as a team, too."

Michael glanced around the others. None of them spoke up for a minute, and he wondered if that was because they had no issues – or if they were still unsure of what to make of their new CAG.

Finally, Lancet shrugged. The slim blond women placed her hands on the table and glanced around the others.

"We're all in about the same boat as Russell," she said bluntly. "None of our squads got hit as badly as Echo or Alpha, but this 'Starfighter Group' is the size of a standard Wing. Everyone knows *everyone*. Almost thirty dead and Roberts grounded for life? People are starting to realize just what being a starfighter pilot at war means."

"They're afraid they won't go home," Mendez stated. "They all knew, intellectually at least, what being a starfighter pilot meant – but I don't think any of us really expected the war to renew on *our* watch."

The new CAG sighed, leaning back from the table and eyeing his commanders. He wasn't surprised by anything they were saying, but he wasn't sure he saw a solution, either.

"I've been too busy catching up on paperwork and the realities of being in command," he admitted. "How bad is it, people? Are we going to have a problem?"

"No," Wolter said sharply. The other four squadron commanders glanced at him quickly. Andrés Wolter had been promoted out of the New Amazon Reserve Flotilla's defending squadrons after Randall's arrest, and that few extra weeks still left him as 'the new guy'.

"I'm the most junior Flight Commander here," the sandy-haired pilot reminded everyone. "Two months ago, I was a Flight *Lieutenant*, and you'll forgive me for feeling I've a better feel for how some of our pilots and crew are feeling," he said bluntly.

"They're scared all right, no-one's pretending otherwise," he continued. "I don't think anyone with half a brain *ever* goes into battle without being scared – and the neural bandwidth capacity we require of starfighter crew corresponds pretty closely with above average intelligence.

"But don't forget, we all grew up in the shadow of the war. Most of us grew up in military families – and a *lot* of us knew a family where someone didn't come home.

"We signed up to be starfighter crews *knowing* the odds for survival in a fight. We all knew the war was coming – even if we all hoped it would be after our time in uniform.

"But we also knew – we *all* know, pilots and commanders alike," he gestured around the table, "that it wouldn't be the Alliance that started the war."

"And it wasn't," he concluded. "So yes, we've lost friends. We've been reminded of our mortality – and that's scary as hell."

"But I don't know about the rest of you, but *I* am pissed as hell at the Commonwealth," he finished. "And my squadron? They may be scared, but they'll take everything the Commonwealth throws at us."

Stanford grinned at his most junior squadron commander put his own thoughts into words, and glanced around the other commanders. Rokos looked just as grimly determined as ever, and Zhao and Lancet were calmly nodding.

Mendez looked more than a little taken aback, so it was him Stanford locked gazes with as he leaned in.

"Andrés is right," he reminded them. "Don't underestimate your people – don't underestimate their courage, and do *not* underestimate their anger. Our people thought they were on a cakewalk show-the-flag cruise – and those same people killed a goddamn *battlecruiser* for us."

"So yes, let's keep an eye on morale, but let's not expect them to curl up and die on us. They'll be willing to take on the Commonwealth for us – we need to make sure they're ready to."

Mendez finally met Michael's gaze and nodded.

"Now, as part of making sure our people are ready for anything," Wing Commander Michael Stanford continued with a smile, "I've had Senior Chief Hammond pull together a detailed simulation of a full deck launch for us. We pulled it off when we had to, but I think we can do it faster and we can do it cleaner."

"Don't you agree?"

Under Alcubierre Drive
13:00 September 13, 2735 Earth Standard Meridian Date/Time
DSC-001 Avalon – *Captain's Office*

"Well?"

"Well, what?" Kyle asked the Captain, glancing down the agenda on his datapad to see if there was anything specific the Captain was referring to. They'd just finished discussing the status of the positron capacitors that provided the ship's heavy beams with their extra punch, and next on the list was the recommended promotions in Engineering.

"I'm assuming Lieutenant-Commander Russell is *somewhere* on this detailed agenda of yours?" the captain asked dryly. "That situation seems a bit more top of mind than some standard time-in-grade and plays-well-with-others promotions, if you don't mind my saying."

Kyle sighed, and tapped the item in his agenda – at the very bottom. His report on the situation flipped up on his datapad.

"You've read the report," he said calmly.

"Yes. It was noticeably lacking in a long-term recommendation," the gaunt captain replied, his natural eye holding Kyle's gaze. "Psychiatric detention is all very well, but we do need to do something with that messed up young man."

"I am inclined to wait until we have Doctor Pinochet's report, and to see if Pendez or Antonio decide to press charges," Kyle said slowly. "I'll admit, my temptation is to dust off Article Thirty-Six though."

Article Thirty-Six was the portion of the Federations Articles of Military Justice that covered, among other things, 'aggravated assault on an officer.' None of the charges that could be laid under Article Thirty-Six could be sustained through shipboard administrative hearings, and none carried less than ten years in prison.

"You seemed to understand what was driving him pretty well," Blair observed. "I'm surprised you would be that harsh."

Something in the level gaze of the Captain's natural eye told Kyle he was being tested.

"At that moment in time, talking down Mister Russell without getting anyone hurt was the priority," the newly minted XO said bluntly. "Understanding and sympathizing with his grief and, well, near-insanity was necessary.

"However much I may understand what happened, and however much I may sympathize with his mental state at the time, the simple fact of the matter is that he stalked a fellow officer and threatened *two* fellow officers with a weapon.

"While it is possible that Doctor Pinochet's assessment of his mental state may be such that it would be... inappropriate to apply the full force of the Articles, under no circumstances do I feel it is appropriate to ask Lieutenant-Commander Pendez or Senior Lieutenant Antonio to serve on the same ship as the man who pointed a gun at them.

"Either he needs to be charged and face the consequences of his actions, or – at a minimum – he needs to be removed from this ship."

Blair nodded, releasing Kyle's eyes as he leaned back and smiled.

"Good," he said softly. "I'll admit, Kyle, that when your report lacked a recommendation on what to do with Mister Russell, I was concerned that I'd acquired a bleeding heart for an Executive Officer. Our job in cases like these is not to be fair, or even just. Our job is to maintain this ship as a weapon – a shield and a sword to defend the Federation."

"Especially now, sir," Kyle replied softly. "Too many of our people are afraid – adding the stress of sharing a mess with a man who tried to kill you?" He shook his head. "I'm not putting our people through that."

"I'm glad you agree with me, Mister Roberts," Blair told him with a grim smile. "I've already informed Doctor Pinochet and Lieutenant-Major Khadem that Russell is to remain under twenty-four hour security. We will give it more time before we decide what charges to press," he concluded, "but I will *not* have him wandering the corridors of my ship."

"Now, where were we on this lovely agenda you have prepared?"

CHAPTER 30

Under Alcubierre Drive
23:30 September 15, 2735 Earth Standard Meridian Date/Time
DSC-001 Avalon – *Outer Hull Observatory*

Almost every viewscreen and virtual 'window' aboard *Avalon*, when set to show the outside of the ship when under Alcubierre-Stetson drive, showed a simulation of what the stars around the starship's warp bubble would look like were the ship, somehow, traveling at its unimaginable speed without Doppler effects and gravitational warping.

Michael understood the reasoning for it. It was more useful than the actual exterior of the ship, if watching simulated stars pass by was useful at all. Perhaps more importantly, many people found the horrendously distorted bubble of light around a ship traveling faster than light disturbing.

He found it helped him think.

Fortunately for people like *Avalon*'s new CAG, the ship's designers had included a small observatory in the outer hull of the ship. In many senses, in fact, the observatory was *outside* the ship, built on top of the carrier's heavy neutronium armor.

From that tiny outer bubble of armored glass, Michael Stanford looked out on a universe seen through the strangest of lenses. Towards the front of the ship, where the warp bubble hurtled forward at two light years per day, decelerating towards the Tranquility system at an acceleration as mind-boggling as her speed, the light of the universe was red-shifted into a deep, pulsing, purple.

No star or other source of the light was visible. All of the universe was lost in the starship's speed and the incalculable gravitational distortion that forged the warp bubble in the first place, smeared into a single color of light.

Ripples of other colors were barely visible in that light, made of the deadly radiation trapped between the two layers of the ship's Stetson stabilizers. The purple faded towards a deep blue as you looked towards the side of the ship, but even there the warp bubble itself garbled any light from outside.

Behind them, the blue faded in a deep red reminiscent of blood. Smears of that red reached forward along the ship, and smears of the blues and purple reached backwards as well. The human brain couldn't process the impact of the red and blue shift of this velocity very well.

For a lot of people, just looking at the distorted bubble gave them a headache in seconds, or at least left them very uncomfortable. Michael simply sat cross-legged on a bench under the open observatory and watched it, drinking in the unfathomable energy of creation.

"I thought I'd find you here," a voice said softly behind him. "A bit out of the way, aren't you?" Kelly Mason asked as she stepped up next to the bench.

"I'm as off-duty as the CAG gets," Michael reminded her. He found his heart racing at her presence, and ordered it to slow down. "Not many people are going to be looking for me at ship's midnight."

"The Captain re-arranged the bridge shifts," Kelly told him, answering the unanswered question of why *she* wasn't on duty. "We wanted to keep Antonio busy enough to forget that someone was pointing a gun at him – *and* get him off the same shift as Pendez."

"How are they doing?" Michael asked softly. He'd been impressed by Kyle's handling of the situation. He hadn't met Senior Lieutenant Marcus Antonio at any point, but he quite liked what he'd seen of the ship's Navigator. Somehow, despite both of their tendencies, they'd never managed to get into trouble with each other.

"Pendez is... shaken up, but handling it pretty well," Mason said quietly. "Antonio... is more shocked that she kicked his overly pretty ass to the curb than anything else, I think. Splitting the two up kept them from causing issues."

Michael looked away from the glowing universe outside the ship to look at her. Kelly's gaze was locked on him.

"That's what I wanted to avoid with us," he admitted, acknowledging the point she was making.

"Did it work for you?" she asked bluntly. "Because it sure as fuck didn't work for me, Michael. You wanted to avoid being emotionally compromised? Well, breaking up *on the eve of a fucking war* sure as hell emotionally compromised us, didn't it?"

"Kelly, my job is to be expendable," he told her after a long, long pause. "The Federation can replace starfighters – and *starfighter pilots* – by the thousand for the cost of a single battleship or carrier. Our job – *my* job – is to fight and die at distances that keep everyone aboard the carrier alive."

"So? I hate to break it to you Michael, but whether or not I want to live with that risk is *my* choice, not yours," she replied. "Whether or not we're sleeping together isn't going to *stop* me worrying about you flying out there in a tinderbox with a gun strapped to it!"

Michael had to admit she had a point. He also had to admit, at least in the privacy of his own mind, that he'd been more scared for himself than anything else.

Kelly read his mind *far* more clearly than he wanted:

"What are you afraid of, Michael?" she asked. She slid onto the bench next to him and took his hands, unresistingly, into her own. "You weren't at all what I expected," she admitted, "and I was starting to think we really had something."

"So did I," he admitted aloud. "That's what I'm scared of. The last time I really fell for someone…" he shrugged. "Let's just say she got the posting we were competing for, and I got left in her dust. The only time since then I even came close," he smiled with bittersweet memory, "I wasn't doing so well at making my mind up between them, and, well, we all got ourselves in trouble. Hence, *Avalon*."

"Let me get this straight," Kelly said slowly. "You're worried I'm either going to use you for professional advancement; or steal a space shuttle with you to get you exiled again?"

He couldn't help himself. Her summary made him sound *ridiculous,* and he laughed aloud.

"That's what I thought," she said, and suddenly she was right next to him. Their hands were clasped, and she was inches away from him.

When they came up for air a minute later, he shook his head slowly.

"Okay, I can see when I'm out-maneuvered, out-logicked, and beat," he told her. "I concede."

"Oh good," she replied with a wicked grin. "Because it looks like we're both off-shift, and I think the bunk in my quarters is getting cold."

#

Once through the tiny door cut in the armor to allow access to the observatory, access to the remainder of the ship was by one of the long corridors that crossed each deck at regular intervals throughout the ship's length.

The observatory was on the same level, Deck Eight, as Kelly's quarters, and Michael found himself following the woman down the hall with far less hesitance than before. She was right, he knew. They were no less 'emotionally compromised' if they were together than if they'd separated, so they as may well get the *benefit* of the situation as well.

They were about fifteen meters in when the lights went out, followed a fraction of a second later by the artificial gravity.

Driven by the same mass manipulators that prevented the starship's acceleration from smashing the crew into mush and that drove her through space at faster than light speeds, the gravity should *never* fail.

Michael had his implant linked into the ship's emergency network before his feet had even left the ground. With a fighter pilots implants and bandwidth, he *knew* what was going on as soon as he was linked, the entire status report dumped into his brain in fractions of a second.

The Stetson stabilizers were failing. Failsafes had re-directed all power aboard the ship to maintaining the fields that stopped their warp bubble's radiation from killing everyone aboard *Avalon*, but the ship's computer calmly informed Michael that even with the extra power, the field would fail in four seconds.

With his implant at full speed, there was a lot Michael would *think* in four seconds – but not a lot he could *do*.

They were five meters from an emergency airlock door. With power re-directed, the doors wouldn't close in time to save them even if they made it through.

Avalon helpfully informed him that he was floating right next to the manual override lever. It would take two point five seconds to cycle the lock, and the radiation would not reach lethal levels for just under a second after the stabilizers failed.

All of this passed through his mind and implants in a quarter of a second, and it took even less time for him to make a decision.

Kelly had a Navy officer's implants and bandwidth – above average, but not the literally inhuman speed of a fighter pilot. Her eyes were starting to widen in horror at the status report as Michael issued an override command to his internal medical nanites.

He wasn't even supposed to know that command *existed*, but there were advantages to his misspent adulthood. Every muscle in his body was suddenly hit with the equivalent of a direct injection of adrenaline, and the pilot *moved*.

Michael grabbed Kelly, faster than she could react to without any warning, secured himself to the wall, and *threw* her. With no gravity to slow her or bring her to the ground, she cut a straight line towards the airlock door.

He spent the time. A quarter of a second. Half a second. It took a full second, but she passed the airlock and he *yanked* on the lever the ship's computer had directed him to. It resisted, but clicked into place as he threw every gram of his adrenaline-fueled body into the motion.

Emergency capacitors fired, and the airlock began to slide closed as he launched himself off. Time ticked off in fractions of a second as he hurtled through the air towards the lock. The door was moving quickly – but was it fast enough to save them?

The Stetson stabilizers failed as he passed through the airlock, entire sections of the ship flashing red as deadly radiation flooded the hull – but he was in the door! He was safe!

Then time crashed back to normal in a crescendo of pain as the airlock doors slammed just above his knees.

Deep Space
00:03 September 16, 2735 Earth Standard Meridian Date/Time
DSC-001 Avalon – *Executive Officer's Quarters*

The alarm ringing inside Kyle's skull clawed him awake in the middle of the night. His surprised motion launched him into the air, drifting away from his bunk along with the blankets in a complete lack of gravity.

That woke him the rest of the way up, and he finally requested a status update from the ship.

There was no response.

Blinking, concerned for his implant again, Kyle ran a quick self-test on the hardware. Everything *inside* his head checked out, and the internal log informed him that *Avalon* had transmitted an emergency alarm to all department heads and above for five point two seconds, after which it had terminated.

He pinged the emergency network, and inhaled sharply at the repeated lack of response. The momentum from *that* flung him into the wall.

Grabbing a hold of the frame of his bunk, Kyle considered the situation while he stabilized himself. If even the emergency network was down, *Avalon* had no power. At all.

He made his way, slowly and carefully, across his quarters to the emergency locker. Inputting a command code, he reviewed its contents, then removed two items – a pair of magnetic boots, and a standard seven millimeter Navy sidearm.

Once he had the mag-boots on, he could make at least an approximation of standing. Belting the pistol on carefully, he opened his implant up and sent out a general pulse on the officers' channel.

Glynn Stewart

"Anyone on this channel, please respond."

It wouldn't go *far* – there was enough metal in even *Avalon*'s internal hull to seriously mess with transmission if the optical network was down – but it should reach *someone*.

"This is Wong," the Chief Engineer replied. "Thank God you're up, Kyle."

"What the *hell* is happening?" Kyle demanded.

"I'll let you know as soon as I do," Wong told him. "All I know is that we're out of FTL and we have no power. I can't raise the bridge, I can't raise the Captain... you're the first senior officer on the channel."

"Can you get power back?"

"I'm on my way to Engineering now," the other man replied. "Unless Engineering is *gone*, I should be able to boot the secondary antimatter plants from the positron capacitors."

"Right now, we need power before anything else," Kyle admitted aloud. "How can I help?"

"I need someone on either the bridge or Secondary Control to provide override confirmations on the safeties I'm going to have to bypass if we want power fast," Wong told him. "I can just rip them out, but overrides are faster."

"I'm only a minute from Secondary Control," the XO answered. "Probably longer in mag-boots. I'll raise you again when I'm there."

"I'll be in Engineering by then," Wong promised. "Let's be about it, boss."

With a firm nod, entirely to reassure himself as Wong couldn't see him, Kyle carefully tested his balance on the mag-boots and then took off down the corridor.

CHAPTER 31

Deep Space
00:07 September 16, 2735 Earth Standard Meridian Date/Time
DSC-001 Avalon – *Secondary Control*

Avalon needed better emergency lighting.

Kyle had always been intellectually aware that the carrier had been a prototype, the first of her kind and never really intended to see action until all hell had broken loose on the frontier. That had never sunk in quite as clearly as it did while he made his way through the corridor to Secondary Control, dodging between the dim pools of light shed by the battery-powered emergency lighting.

Secondary Control, despite the emergency lighting, was a shadow filled nightmare house. Thankfully, it wasn't an *unoccupied* nightmare house, through the Ensign and two Petty Officers who'd been holding down the night shift looked utterly terrified.

"Thank God you're here, sir!" the Ensign exclaimed. She was a young, dark-skinned woman, whose name was Alison Li according to the service file Kyle's implant pulled.

"Ensign Li," he greeted her, glancing around the room. "Status report, please."

"I'm not... entirely sure, sir," she admitted.

"Ensign, all I know is that I was woken up by an emergency alert, we're out of FTL, and we have no power," Kyle told her dryly. "Anything you can tell me is helpful."

She took a deep breath and nodded, clearly trying to find some modicum of calm.

"We got an alert that the Stetson stabilizers were going into failsafe mode," she finally said. "Then they went into emergency failsafe mode and re-directed *all* power to try and sustain the stabilizer fields."

"It... didn't work," Li concluded, gesturing around. "Everything *should* have gone back to normal once we dropped out of FTL, but instead the entire network crashed. It's almost..."

"It's almost...?" Kyle repeated questioningly, and the Ensign – who couldn't have been more than twenty-one – blushed.

"Sorry, sir, thinking out loud."

"Finish the thought, Ensign," Kyle told her gently.

"I majored in computer systems, sir," Li told him. "It's almost like the main computer core took a direct EMP hit and then failed to reset. But the core is shielded – and it's right *beneath* the bridge."

A chill ran through Kyle's chest and he shivered.

"There are secondary emergency fiber optic links to the bridge and main engineering," he said slowly. "Have you heard anything from the bridge?"

"Last thing the Captain said was 'hold on,' right after the first failsafe warning came on. Nothing since," she said quietly.

A light and a buzzer on the main command console interrupted the conversation. It was the communications link to Engineering, and Kyle took a deep breath.

"I relieve you, Ensign Li," he said formally. "Don't go anywhere," he added, "I get the feeling I'm going to need every set of hands I can find."

He slipped into the central chair and activated the link.

"Roberts," he said simply.

"Roberts, it's Wong," the Chief Engineer told him. "Please tell me you've got power, an implant, and an override code."

"We're on battery power," Kyle replied. "Last I checked, this room is rated for forty-eight hours."

"Yeah, well, so's the bridge and I can't raise them," Wong said flatly. "I can't find or raise half my goddamn night shift, either."

That hung in the air for a long moment. If the stabilizers had failed before the Alcubierre drive had shut down, large parts of the ship would have been swept with devastating levels of radiation. The exact outer layers, in fact, where Wong's people would have been doing midnight maintenance work.

"What do we need to get power back up?" Kyle finally asked.

"Well, from the fact we're all still alive, I can confirm the positron capacitor failsafes are holding," Wong said calmly. "I'm going to manually feed Secondary Antimatter Three with hydrogen and positrons, but I'm going to need a bridge override to open the positron feed."

"I've been reading up," Kyle told him, as cheerfully as he could manage sitting in the shadows, "but somehow I didn't think I'd need to be overriding the safeties on our antimatter stores. You're going to have to walk me through that."

"Hold one," Wong told him. "Kellers, Anderson – are those feeds hooked up?" he shouted away from the microphone for the com link. Kyle couldn't hear the response, but the engineer 'hrmed' satisfiedly.

Kyle found himself waiting as he heard Wong walk away from the communicator. Every second that passed his fingers clenched harder on the arm of the chair. There was *nothing* he could do but trust the engineer, and every second they waited was one second less of air the carrier had.

Finally, Wong came back on the line.

"Okay, everything is hooked up," the engineer told him. "I'm flipping the override request to the main command console there. My code is in."

The single active screen on the console flickered slowly to full life, a flashing red 'emergency override request' occupying it. Slowly, carefully, Kyle typed in the nineteen-digit alphanumeric sequence of his bridge officer override code.

"Done," he told Wong.

"Hold on," the Chief Engineer replied. "But don't worry – if we've fucked this up, you'll never know."

Kyle found himself literally holding his breath for a long moment, until he heard *Wong* exhale heavily in relief.

"There she goes," he said aloud. "Secondary Three is online, XO. I'll hook it up to life support first, but we'll be able to start bringing the zero point cells online in ten minutes or so."

"How long to gravity?" Kyle asked.

"Thirty minutes, maybe more, maybe less," Wong admitted. "Without knowing what crashed everything, we have to double check as we go. Everything will take longer."

"Ensign Li said it looked like a hard computer crash, due to an EMP in the main core," Kyle told the Engineer.

Silence answered him for a moment.

"Yeah, combined with an emergency A-S shutdown, that could do it," Wong admitted. "It should have auto-reset, but then, the Stetson stabilizers shouldn't have failed."

"The manual reset is in the core, Commander," he continued. "If you can get there and confirm that's what happened, I can direct enough power there for you to boot her. That won't speed up gravity, but it'll give us a fighting chance to get the rest of the ship online."

"Understood," Kyle said grimly. "I'll check it out."

Standing, carefully to allow the mag-boots to lock on, Kyle turned to face his pitiful staff of three.

"There are mag-boots in the emergency locker," he told the floating Ensign. "Petty Officers Jackson, Sandel, you're our relay. Keep in touch with Commander Wong and anyone *else* who wakes up and gets in contact."

"Ensign Li," he continued. "You're with me. If you're right, we have a space carrier to reboot."

Deep Space
00:22 September 16, 2735 Earth Standard Meridian Date/Time
DSC-001 Avalon – *Main Computer Core*

Without his old implant bandwidth, Kyle had to pull out his datapad to find the access hatch for the vertical emergency access column leading up to the bridge. Ensign Li seemed impressed enough that he even knew they existed.

"Why don't they cover these in the Academy?" she asked as he slid the manual release to pop the door.

"The locations vary from ship to ship, even in the same class," he explained as he carefully maneuvered his mag-booted feet into the vertical tunnel. "Even a small re-arrangement of, say, a heavy positron lance, can require moving one of these five, ten meters. The location *should* have been covered in ship's orientation, but it's often forgotten." He shrugged. "In an age of zero point cells and antimatter reactors, who expects a starship not to have enough power to run an elevator?"

The young Ensign nodded slowly as she followed him into the spartan tube. There was a tiny ledge, barely large enough for one of them to stand on, next to a ladder that stretched from Deck One to Deck Ten along the center of the ship.

Kyle considered the ladder for about a second, and then turned off his mag-boots and used a ladder rung as a fulcrum to rotate himself and land on the wall. With his boots active, the wall was now the floor for his careful balancing act.

With his height and bulk, the access column was just wide enough to pull this off. Li managed it with significantly more space to spare, and he found himself silently envying her lack of centimeters.

Ducking slightly to dodge the ladder, he led the way up the ship. Unlike Li, apparently, as a Space Force Ensign his ship's crew had engaged in the 'sport' of column climbing. Walking along the tunnel like it was a hallway was *much* faster.

He popped the Deck Three hatch open onto another empty corridor, and felt a shiver run down his spine. It was the middle of the night. Most of the ship would be asleep, and only department heads would have gotten the alert he did.

It was still creepily silent throughout the ship. The silence from the Captain was starting to wear on him as well; Blair had been on the bridge. He should have been co-ordinating the effort to restore the ship – not Kyle and Wong.

"The door is secured," Li told him as she checked out the entrance to the main computer core. "No power at all, and this should have an emergency supply."

"That's... bad," Kyle said aloud. He clicked a channel open to Secondary Control. "Jackson? Relay me through to Wong."

"Yes, sir."

A moment later, the Chief Engineer was on the line.

"Roberts. What've you found?"

"Security to the core is sealed and has no power," Kyle told him. "Is that as bad as I think it is?"

"It's... not promising," the engineer said grimly. "Give me thirty seconds, we've got a second AM plant online and I'll re-direct power to that section. You'll need it to boot the core regardless."

"Thanks," Kyle said absently, eyeing the black control panel next to the door.

A few moments passed, then the panel lit up with its usual colors. The hallway lights followed a moment later.

"There you go," Wong told him. "You have lights, doors, and power to the core. You don't have gravity – I'm not turning a single mass manipulator on this ship on until we finish our survey of the Class Ones."

"How long is that going to take?" Kyle asked as he input his access code into the door panel.

"Get used to mag-boots," the engineer replied dryly. "And get that computer booted, that may help us bring gravity back sometime today."

The door slid open and Kyle gestured Li forward into the server room. The lights slowly flickered on around them, glittering across the solid black stalagmites of molecular circuitry that made up *Avalon*'s brain.

"There's a maintenance console," Li told him, pointing across the room. "I'll check it out."

Kyle nodded and gestured for her to get to work as he glanced around the room. Molecular computer cores were not his specialty, but even he knew there were supposed to be status lights on their bases. All of them were gone.

As he looked around the room and Li started to boot the maintenance console, he realized that several of the cores were *melted* – the tops had

264   GLYNN STEWART

begun to slag and run down as their fragile circuitry collapsed. A strong enough electromagnetic pulse could shut down the cores, but it would take *major* radiation to cause that kind of damage.

"It's all completely shut down," Li told him. "I can reboot it, but it's basically going to be core by core – there's too much damage to do anything else and I'll need to run self-check on each core as I start."

"How long will that take?" Kyle asked, looking over at the frazzled looking young Ensign.

She met his gaze uncertainly.

"At least an hour, sir," she admitted. "I'll have *some* computer support back up for Commander Wong inside of ten minutes, and I don't know if we'll get anything near a hundred percent capacity."

"The ship has a fifty percent computing reserve over its requirements," Kyle reminded her gently. "Get us over sixty percent online, and I'll put you in for a commendation."

The realization that she wasn't expected to perform miracles seemed to help, and the young woman relaxed, focusing on the computer.

Kyle glanced around the room, then up at the ceiling. They were on Deck Three. The bridge was immediately above them, on Deck Two. Above *that* was a consumable water storage tank, to provide an extra layer of protection for a bridge that was more exposed than most were comfortable with.

Each Deck of the ship had its own layers of radiation shielding. If enough had made it through to *here* to melt computer cores, what had happened on the bridge?

"I'm going to go check on the bridge," Kyle told Li with a mental sigh of acceptance.

"I might be able to boot some of the systems from there too," she replied. "Do you need me to come with?"

Kyle looked at the young woman at the maintenance console. Alison Li was twenty two years old, six months out of the Academy. She was a Navy officer, on a tactical track, but still in a field that would rarely require her to see death and horror first hand.

The man who'd walked into the slaughterhouse of *Ansem Gulf* couldn't take that officer – that *kid* – into what he suspected was waiting above them. There would be time for the war to show her those horrors yet – but not tonight.

"Nah," he told with the breezy cheer he'd mastered long ago. "I'll only slow you down here, and we'll need those computers."

Deep Space
00:30 September 16, 2735 Earth Standard Meridian Date/Time
DSC-001 Avalon *– Bridge*

The bridge was... about what Kyle had expected.

Even the emergency lights were out on Deck Two, burned out by the same EMP and radiation spike that had shut down the core, before it had passed through Deck Two's radiation shields. Kyle switched on the flashlight built into his pistol and used it to find his way to the open doorway into the bridge.

The smell warned him long before the light ever fell on anyone. A sizzled, burnt pork smell wafted out of the bridge, and he swallowed down nausea as he moved forward. Regardless of what awaited him, *someone* had to see it.

Someone had to stand witness.

The first body was hanging in zero gravity just inside the door. Kyle let the light rest on her for a long time. Chief Petty Officer Janet McKellen had at least tried to escape – slightly more resistant, maybe, to the immediate effect of the extreme radiation.

Her shipsuit looked melted, the complex polymers having run down her body in rivulets even as the radiation burned all of her exposed skin. If his memory of radiation damage was correct, she'd likely died of either heart failure or brain hemorrhaging.

At the level of radiation that would do that, it would at least have been quick.

Slowly, carefully, Kyle swallowed his urge to run and stepped forward over Janet's body. The light from his flashlight played over the night shift on the bridge. Seven other men and women were slumped over their consoles. Senior Lieutenant Antonio had been spared his shipmate's anger only to die here, his radiation-blasted corpse floating free between chairs.

It would take a medical team to confirm the definite cause of death and confirm individual identities. The crew's internal implants were as burnt out as the consoles that surrounded them.

Much as he wanted to run and leave the mausoleum *Avalon*'s bridge had become to that medical team, he had one duty he had to fulfill – both to the Navy and to himself.

His mag-boots clicked on the metal floor, echoingly loud, as he walked towards the raised dais in the center of the room, and shone the pistol flashlight on the occupant.

Malcolm Blair had been older than most of his crew, though that meant little in the twenty-eighth century, and his cybernetic eye meant he was more vulnerable to EMP than anyone else on the bridge. He appeared to have died instantly, still upright and locked into his chair with his natural eye open and staring.

Kyle looked at his Captain for a long, long, time. His implant was recording the footage, and the Navy's records would need it, but shock pinned him to the ground. He'd known – known from the moment he'd had to co-ordinate the repairs with Wong – what had to have happened.

It still was a shock to see the old man like this.

Slowly, gently, Kyle reached out and closed Blair's staring eye. It was all he could do for the man now.

#

Ensign Li was working away on the consoles when Kyle stepped back into the computer core. She looked up at his arrival, and something in his eyes must have told her something was up.

"Do we have any of the cores back up?" Kyle asked.

"Just one," she told him. "I'm just linking in to Engineering now."

"I need access, command override," he told her flatly.

"What's going on, Kyle?" Wong asked over the channel. "I *need* that computer. We're the only senior officers linked into the net, and we need the automatic damage assessment to tell us where to look for survivors!"

"We'll get to that next, but we need to take care of this first," Kyle replied quietly. "I wish we had at least Kelly or Pendez, but you'll have to stand witness on your own."

No one replied to that. Li looked confused, unsure what he meant. Wong was silent – he knew *exactly* what that had to mean.

The Ensign gestured to the console.

"It's set up for you," she told him. "It's one-twentieth normal speed and power, it won't be fast."

"That's fine," he replied and stepped up to it.

"*Avalon*, record for the record," he said loudly, his voice formal.

"Official recording confirmed," a tinny voice replied from the console.

"*Avalon*, please download the video file I am transmitting from my implant to the record," he told the computer. "Confirm once complete."

"File downloaded."

"*Avalon*, please note for the record that Captain Malcolm Blair, Commanding Officer of the Castle Federation deep space carrier *Avalon*, is deceased."

"I am activating Succession Protocol One," Kyle told the computer, his voice gentle for the benefit of his shipmates, not the machine. "I am assuming command."

"Succession Protocol One confirmed," the computer replied emotionlessly. "Command of DSC-001 *Avalon* is transferred to Acting Captain Senior Fleet Commander Kyle Roberts."

CHAPTER 32

Deep Space
00:45 September 16, 2735 Earth Standard Meridian Date/Time
DSC-001 Avalon – *Main Computer Core*

"All right," Kyle said into the silence that followed the computer's announcement. "Wong, what's our status?"

"We've got four antimatter plants up and running," the Chief Engineer replied. "That's enough that I should be able to start initializing zero point cells as soon as I have enough computer support."

"Can you spare any engineers to support Li?"

"I haven't been able to spare anyone to wake anybody who wasn't already awake," Wong said grimly. "Once the network is fully up, I can start pinging people's implants. Until then, anybody who's asleep is *staying* that way, and we're working with the hands we've got."

Kyle considered for a moment.

"The bridge is a write-off," he told Wong. "I'm going to check in with the infirmary, and then see what I can do about co-ordinating waking people up and searching the outer hull for survivors. Keep relaying through Secondary Control and keep me updated."

"Fine," Wong replied shortly and cut the channel.

"Are you okay to work up here on your own?" Kyle asked Li, glancing around the shadowy computer core.

"It'll be okay," the young ensign replied with a shrug. "You can't *help* me, in any case, and keeping me company seems a little much for the Acting Captain."

Kyle sighed and nodded.

"Relay through Secondary Control and Jackson if you need anything," he told her. "I don't know if we'll be able to send anyone up until we have full comms back, but we need these computers more than just about anything short of power."

"I'll get them back up, sir," she told him. "It won't be fast, and we won't get all of them, but I'll get them back up."

Deep Space
00:50 September 16, 2735 Earth Standard Meridian Date/Time
DSC-001 Avalon – *Main Infirmary*

The infirmary was as much of a chaotic mess as Kyle had been afraid it would be. With the only communications aboard ship via personal communicator, it seemed pretty clear no-one here had had a chance to even try and raise anyone.

Like Engineering, it looked like the night shift alone was trying to deal with the deluge. The scary part, to Kyle at least, was the certain knowledge that the only people who were making it to the infirmary were those awake enough to realize they were unwell, and capable of moving here under their own power.

That relatively small fraction of the crew was completely overwhelming the handful of medical Lieutenants and ratings trying to treat them and get them on their feet.

"Who's in charge here?" he asked of a passing attendant, trying to keep out of the man's way as he carried a tray of canisters full of anti-rad nanites.

"That's apparently me," a familiar, utterly exhausted, voice said from behind him. *Avalon's* Acting Captain turned to find Kelly Mason standing behind him, looking utterly shattered.

"Where's Doctor Pinochet?" he asked.

"She was off-duty," Mason replied. "I showed up here with Michael and nobody had a clue – the senior officer on duty is Carstairs."

Kyle winced. Xue Carstairs was *Avalon's* cybernetic specialist, and his own encounter with her after Hessian had left him... unimpressed with any of her skills beyond the purely technical.

"So you took charge," he concluded aloud.

"Yeah," she shrugged. "Got Michael into surgery, got the attendants dosing people with anti-rad, got beds lined up – but I know not everyone is making it here. We're getting crew from Decks Eight and Nine, which tells me that Two and Three are just as bad – and One and Ten are worse! The secondary infirmary on Deck Three has to be swamped too, and without the resources we have here."

"Deck Two is gone," Kyle said softly. "Everyone on the bridge and up is dead. I've assumed command," he concluded, "of such as there is *to* command for now."

"How's Michael?" he asked after a long moment. "You said he was in surgery?"

"Not rads," Kelly replied, clearly trying to process what she'd missed. "He got himself caught in an emergency airlock saving my life – lost both of his legs just above the knee. He'll *be* fine, but..."

"Not today, not in time to help," Kyle finished for her. He glanced around the infirmary.

"Do we have any walking wounded?" he asked finally. "Two thirds of the crew were *asleep* when this went down, and most won't have woken up. Some of them never will no matter what – and some of them won't if we don't wake them up soon."

"Plus," he continued grimly, "Doctor Pinochet's quarters were on Deck One. She's gone. So is everyone else on One, Ten, Two and probably Three."

Kelly inhaled as if he'd punched her in the gut. "That bad?"

"That bad," he confirmed. "We need to start waking people up – we don't have enough engineers to fix the ship or doctors to fix the crew – or to spare to wake up the rest!"

"The treated are this way," she said slowly, leading him through the infirmary. "We should be able to pull together a working party."

With the mass manipulators offline, getting a shuttle off of the flight deck was a slow, careful, exercise. Michelle wouldn't normally fully interface when flying a shuttle, as it didn't require the reaction speed and control of a starfighter.

Today, she was completely linked in, her physical body ignored in the front cockpit as she *was* the shuttle slowly maneuvering its way out of the deck with tiny bursts from the emergency thrusters.

Part of the problem was that while *almost* everything on the flight deck had been secured, there was still debris floating in the microgravity.

"Okay," she said over the shuttle's radio to Senior Chief Hammond. "I'm past the inner airlock door."

Mounted on superconducting magnetic bearings, the airlock doors for the main flight deck normally opened and closed so quickly and automatically that the starfighter crews were only vaguely aware of their existence.

With *Avalon*'s computers still focused on directing the search parties, that service was instead being provided by the senior Space Force NCO on the ship and a hand-picked team of Navy and Space Force techs.

"Hold one," the Chief replied. A second later, he continued. "Okay, Flight Lieutenant – *now* you're clear. I assumed you'd want to keep the last ten centimeters of your engine nozzles."

"Fair enough, Chief," Michelle replied. She wasn't sure how Hammond could be so cheerful – she knew, at least, that Angela was alive and fine, but so many of their crewmates weren't.

Hell, the *Captain* was dead. She'd have followed Kyle Roberts into the Starless Void as her CAG, but she had no idea what to think of him as the Captain.

The air transmitted the vibrating shock of the inner airlock door sliding home behind her. A moment later, the outer door opened and Shuttle Four was thrown out into space with the air and the garbage.

Finally free of the hull, she could at least bring up the *secondary* engines. Jets of fused plasma shot out, stabilizing the shuttle a hundred and ten meters away from *Avalon*. Michelle rotated the ship so her nose, with the shuttle's powerful sensor suite, was pointed back at the eight hundred meter bulk of the carrier.

Here, in the void between the stars, the ship looked... strange. Without running lights, without power, the ship was almost invisible in the darkness. Ignoring the shuttle's other sensors for a moment, Michelle looked on her home with just her eyes. All she could see was an impression of sharp edged darkness against the stars.

Sighing, she brought up the sensor suite.

"What exactly are we looking for?" she asked of her companion in the shuttle, one of Wong's senior engineers. "I'm not seeing much in terms of visible damage."

"We probably won't," the man admitted. "We need a full sensor sweep of the Stetson stabilizers though. Given what the XO said about the bridge, let's start with the top of the ship. If there's any visible damage, it'll be there."

Michelle nodded and gently nudged the shuttle up, slowly orbiting around the centerline of the carrier to bring them over the top of the ship.

"Watch that!"

Linked into the shuttle, it took Michelle less than a moment to identify the engineer's concern and adjust her course, pulling the ship significantly further away from the section of hull glowing a deep, dangerous, red in her sensors.

A piece of hull, a rough circle sixty or so meters in diameter, was radioactive, returning the energy dumped into it back into space in a slow and steady pulse of deadly energy.

"I didn't think our hull *got* radioactive?" Michelle asked, as her computer overlay the schematics of the ship over what she was seeing.

"It can," her companion replied grimly. "It takes a *lot* of the right kind of radiation – with a warp bubble failure? This much heat would take at least a full second more than it should have taken the failsafes to kick in."

When the wire frame schematic popped into her vision, Michelle wasn't surprised to see that the center of the circle was only fifteen meters from the bridge on Deck Two. The entire bridge was underneath a chunk of hull attempting to imitate nuclear waste.

CHAPTER 33

Deep Space
05:00 September 16, 2735 Earth Standard Meridian Date/Time
DSC-001 Avalon – *Deck Six Meeting Room Two*

The advantage to the extent of what Kyle could only call the bureaucracy of running a starship was that even with the main conference room a half-melted mess down the hall from the morgue that had been the bridge, there were still meeting rooms for the senior officers.

That there were only three of them standing meant that the meeting room intended for the ten-person logistics team still felt empty.

"The good news," Kyle said quietly, "is that both Pendez and Stanford will live. Neither is going to be back on active duty for a while though."

Stanford was going to have to have his legs regenerated, a process that would take at least two months. He was invalided out for that long.

Pendez was luckier. She'd been on Deck Three, in one of the sections that *had* been badly irradiated. Unlike anyone else in that section, though, she'd been awake. She'd woken up the Marine Lieutenant-Major whose quarters she'd been leaving, and between them they'd got seventeen of the thirty people in those berths to the secondary infirmary on Deck Four – before collapsing in a heap of radiation poisoning themselves.

She'd saved eighteen lives – and taken enough rads to compromise her skeleton and circulatory system. She'd be in the infirmary for weeks.

"No one has found Colonel Ardennes or Lieutenant-Major Khadem," he continued. "Both had quarters on Deck Two, which leaves me fearing the worst. I've confirmed Major Riesling as our acting Marine CO, and he's sorted his people into teams to sweep the outer hull for any survivors we've missed. They'll also," he finished quietly, "begin policing up the bodies."

"How bad is it, sir?" Kelly asked. The tactical officer – now acting executive officer – looked shaken and tired. So far as Kyle knew, she hadn't slept in almost twenty-four hours.

"We won't know the exact totals until the Marines and medics are done," Kyle told her. "But the com network is back up, and only two thousand and fifty-one people are linked in."

Avalon's crew, including the starfighter crews and their support staff and her embarked battalion of six hundred Marines, was just under thirty-one hundred. Over a thousand of their crewmates were almost certainly dead.

"Damn," Wong replied. The shaven-headed man looked even more exhausted than Kelly, for all that he *had* been asleep when it all went to hell.

"My good news, such as it is," the engineer continued, "is that most of our systems are back online. We have power, we have life support, we have computers and we have gravity. I *think* we have weapons and sublight engines, but I don't plan on firing off antimatter explosions I don't have to."

"What about FTL?" Kyle asked.

The Chief Engineer shook his head.

"I know what happened now," he admitted. "Flight Lieutenant Williams' survey let us know where to look, and we found it. One of the power couplings feeding the internal Stetson stabilizer field was *just* loose. Kept wiggling loose as we flew – every second we were under Alcubierre drive, it was weakening."

"When it finally blew, twelve Stetson emitters – directly above the bridge – went down. The failsafes recognized a problem *before* it blew, but it takes just over seven seconds to do an emergency Alcubierre emergence."

"The computers recognized the problem just under six seconds before it blew," he concluded grimly. "The entire ship took a quarter-second pulse of the radiation from the warp bubble – but everything under those twelve emitters took a *one and a quarter* second pulse."

"Damn," Kyle murmured. The artificial bubble of space-time created by an Alcubierre-Stetson drive caught up *every* particle that crossed their path, creating a pocket inside the bubble of radiation intense enough to melt even a starship's hull. The Stetson stabilizers contained that energy between an inner and outer bubble, and forced it out slowly as a ship decelerated. Not only did this prevent the bubble from destroying the ship, but it also avoided the massive radiation burst early theories had suggested an Alcubierre drive would emit on returning to sublight.

"What about the external failsafes?" he asked. They had stopped in mid-flight, still traveling at multiple light years a day. Stopping like that meant they *had* released that world-killing radiation blast.

"They worked perfectly," Wong answered. "The blast from our emergency stop was fired off on a vector with no system for at least three thousand light years."

Kyle glanced between his two senior officers and nodded slowly.

"Is the drive repairable?" he finally asked.

"Yes," Wong confirmed. "We'll need to replace about ten percent of the stabilizer emitters and re-calibrate the Class One manipulators. It's going to take at least twenty-four hours."

"That's all you have," Kyle warned him. "If we leave *in* twenty-four hours, we will arrive at Tranquility roughly when the Commonwealth battle group is scheduled to appear."

"You can't seriously intend to take this ship into action," Kelly snapped. "The only place we should be going is a shipyard!"

"If we go to a shipyard, Commander Mason, Tranquility falls," Kyle replied calmly. "From what Alistair has said, we are still capable of completing our mission. If we can, we *will*."

"You're nuts," she said flatly. "Alistair, please! You can't let him do this."

"He's the Captain," Wong said slowly. "And he's right – I'll test the weapons while we get the A-S drive back online, but the starfighters are fine either way. This ship can still fight, sir."

"Bullshit he's the Captain," Mason snapped, her glare turning on Kyle again. "You've been a Navy officer for a *week*, you have *no* idea how to command this ship. You're going to get us all killed and I *won't let you*."

"Commander Mason!" Kyle's hand slammed down on the table as he rose to his feet. She was a tall woman, but Kyle Roberts was a massive man – taller and broader than she was. Mason didn't even quiver facing him down, her eyes filled with fire as she glared at him.

"You are walking very close to the line of mutiny," he told her, his voice very slow and careful. "Of the people aboard this ship, I have spent more time in combat action than anyone left alive," he reminded her. "I have commanded an entire fighter wing for longer than you've run your department. I *am*, regardless of your opinion, qualified to command this vessel – and more importantly, by the Articles of our Navy, I *am in command*.

"Now, are you prepared to follow my orders, or do I need to relieve one of the few senior officers we have left?" His tone was flat as he met her gaze, but he knew his eyes were pleading. He *would* restrict her to quarters if he had to, but he *needed* her.

A long silence hung in the meeting room, with Wong looking hugely uncomfortable, and then Kelly exhaled sharply and nodded once.

"I apologize," she said stiffly. "I am... afraid. We have too many wounded aboard."

"I think we can all agree that nothing happened here that deserves comment," Kyle observed, his voice cheerful again as he returned her nod. "I'm concerned about the wounded myself," he continued. "I'm hoping to drop them on Tranquility before we have to fight, but it's going to depend on the situation."

Kelly nodded again, taking a sharp ragged breath.

"Now," he continued, "*I* need to go talk to our lords and masters. Both of *you* need to get some sleep – and that is an order. Understood?"

Both of his senior officers looked ready to argue with him for a moment, but they did nod their agreement. They knew he was right – being tired enough to yell at even the *Acting* Captain was a bad sign for their ability to do their jobs.

The XO's office was as close to Secondary Control as the Captain's was to the bridge, so Kyle was at least able to use his own desk to call Joint Command on Castle.

He'd fired off an initial text report before meeting with Mason and Wong, and the uniformed communications officer who answered his call was clearly expecting him.

"Senior Fleet Commander Roberts, correct?" he asked.

"Yes," Kyle replied, his voice tired. "Reporting in on the status of *Avalon*."

"Understood," the headquarters officer replied. "I'm to put you through to Admiral Blake immediately."

Kyle was suddenly both very aware that he hadn't showered, and glad that he *had* grabbed his uniform jacket, but he had barely moments before the image of the gray-haired Fleet Admiral appeared on his screen.

"If you try and salute after the night you've had, I will make personally sure your mother hears about today," Blake told him bluntly as he tried to rise. "At ease, Commander. What's your status?"

"Battered but unbroken, sir," Kyle replied, relaxing back into his chair. "Our starfighters are undamaged, we believe we have weapons and sublight engines, and we expect to have Alcubierre drive back within twenty-four hours."

"Damn, son," Blake replied. "How long a list of commendations should I be expecting?"

"Long," he admitted. "Not as long as the casualty list though. We've lost a third of the crew, and gods know Captain Blair is enough of a loss on his own."

"Indeed," Blake murmured. She looked down at her desk and keyed something. "I am confirming you in temporary command of *Avalon*, Commander Roberts. We don't have a lot of other options."

"I understand, ma'am," Kyle agreed. "Nonetheless, we remain able to carry out our mission. The timing will be tighter than any of us would like, but *Avalon* will reach Tranquility."

The Fleet Admiral's face tightened. He could almost *see* her desire to tell him to turn back. To save his people from the cauldron he was about to take them into.

"I can raise First Admiral Wu immediately," she said instead. "I think he deserves to be in this conversation."

"I understand, ma'am," Kyle said. "I can hold until you've raised the Admiral."

His senior uniformed commander nodded sharply, and then her image was replaced by the stylized castle and stars of the Federation.

Apparently, when the uniformed Commander-in-Chief of the preeminent power of the Alliance calls, even First Admirals pick up the phone. It was less than two minutes before the placeholder dissolved into a split screen of Fleet Admiral Blake on the left, and the pale, shaven-headed face of First Admiral Sagacity Wu.

"I understand that your ship is damaged, Commander Roberts," Wu said slowly. "What is your status?"

"We were forced to make an emergency Alcubierre exit, sir," Kyle summarized. "Captain Blair and a large portion of our crew were killed. Our ETA to Tranquility is now approximately three days."

The pale admiral blinked, considering Kyle carefully.

"How badly damaged is your vessel?" he finally asked.

"Not as badly as we feared," Kyle replied. "We will be fully functional before arrival in your system."

Wu glanced sideways, and Kyle knew he was meeting Admiral Blake's gaze.

"Commander, Admiral," he said slowly. "An emergency Alcubierre exit is a dangerous action, one which puts many hidden strains on a vessel. My government would understand if *Avalon* must detour. She is an old ship, and even a new one could not take...."

Glynn Stewart

"First Admiral," Kyle cut him off. "*Avalon* is a carrier, and her fighters are intact. She is also a warship of the Castle Federation, and the Federation Navy does *not* abandon our allies.

"As you yourself said to Captain Blair, it is right and it is proper that *Avalon* return to Tranquility to honor the promises made upon her decks."

Wu was silent, and then slowly bowed his head.

"I do not know if we can hold alone," he admitted. "My mind says to let you turn back, but my heart says to demand you come with all dispatch. Words do not – can not! – express our gratitude."

"This is our duty, First Admiral, nothing more," Kyle said quietly. "While *Avalon* flies, *Avalon* fights."

"Three days then," Wu accepted with a firm nod. "I will arrange for our defense telemetry to be forwarded to you via Q-com. Whatever happens, you will not arrive in Tranquility blind."

"Thank you, First Admiral."

Wu inclined his head and his image vanished, leaving Kyle facing only Blake again.

"I don't know if you're brave or crazy, Commander," she said bluntly. "Even with the Tranquility Space Fleet, you will be badly outnumbered by what we suspect is coming. Most would take the excuse to run."

"There may yet come a day, Admiral, when the Federation must break its word to its allies from necessity," Kyle said quietly. "But it is not today. And until that day, our honor – our *oath* – is part of the glue that binds this Alliance together.

"In all honesty, Admiral, I think we can afford to lose one obsolete carrier far better than we can afford to lose that honor."

CHAPTER 34

Deep Space
20:00 September 16, 2735 Earth Standard Meridian Date/Time
DSC-001 Avalon – *Main Infirmary*

Michael Stanford woke up.

That, given his last memories, was enough of a surprise.

He also woke up without pain, which was even more of a surprise until an interrogation of his implants informed him that he wasn't receiving nerve input from anything more than eleven centimeters below his pelvis.

Slowly, the fighter pilot opened his eyes. He was in one of the beds in *Avalon*'s infirmary, tucked off to one side with a curtain drawn around him. Knowing what he would see, he nonetheless looked down at his legs.

And sighed.

He'd hoped that his memories were somehow wrong, but the reason his nanites and implants weren't letting him feel his legs was that he didn't *have* any. From what he could see, he had all of twenty centimeters of thigh left, and the rest was gone.

The curtain whipped aside, allowing an unfamiliar blond Surgeon Lieutenant-Commander to slip into the room. The man looked Michael up and down calmly.

"You're awake, good," he said brusquely. "How do you feel?"

"I'm pretty sure my implants are *stopping* me from feeling anything," Michael told him dryly. "So how about you tell me? The legs are obvious."

"Yes," the doctor said slowly. "Your legs were completely severed, roughly where you see," he continued. "Your nanites automatically sealed the wounds and placed you into an induced coma. Commander Mason then carried you here."

"Along the way, you received what would have been a major dose of radiation poisoning in other circumstances, but is minor by today's standards," he finished. "I am Surgeon Lieutenant-Commander Cunningham, by the way," he introduced himself. "I normally run the night shift for the Deck Three secondary infirmary, but our resources are stretched thin."

Michael closed his eyes and breathed slowly.

"How bad is the ship, Lieutenant-Commander?" he asked.

"We've lost at least a thousand people," Cunningham told him. "A good quarter of those remaining have taken radiation doses equivalent to yours or worse. I think you're our worst physical injury, but some of the rad cases are just as bad in their own way."

He finished reviewing the scans next to Michael.

"You're going to live," he finished. "Legs will take seven to eight weeks to regen, though, so you're off-duty until then."

"The hell I am," Michael objected. "I don't need legs to fly a starfighter!"

A chuckle interrupted them, and *Avalon*'s CAG looked up to see Kyle Roberts ducking under the curtain.

"I'll deal with our stubborn ox of a CAG, doctor," the XO told Cunningham, dismissing the Lieutenant-Commander with a gesture. "You have other patients."

The doctor bowed out, and Stanford looked at Roberts, hard. The big man wasn't much of one to show strain, but there was something to his eyes.

"He said it was bad," Michael said quietly.

"He understated it," Roberts replied bluntly. "Blair is dead, along with one thousand and twenty-seven others. I'm in command, and, if Wong is as good as he thinks he is, we'll only be two days late to Tranquility."

"Damn," Stanford said slowly. "You're going to *need* me in that cockpit, Kyle," he concluded, "legs or no legs."

"For now, Commander Rokos is running things," Kyle told him. "I don't want you out there unless things have *really* hit the fan, Michael. But I'm also not having Cunningham lock you in here."

"I'll try not to do anything stupid," Stanford promised. "How are you holding up?"

"I'm in command," Kyle observed calmly.

"That doesn't answer the question."

"No," the Acting Captain agreed. "It was explaining why I won't. As for not doing anything stupid, are you going to fix things with Mason?"

Michael winced. They'd come to something of an agreement before everything had tried to explode.

"I don't know," he admitted. "It's a scary thought."

"I know all about scary thoughts," Kyle told him. "But I've got some food for yours: one, I checked: even with Kelly as Acting XO, she's *still* not in your chain and command, and it's not against regs. Two: the two of you have your heads *completely* off kilter. You were less compromised when you *were* together."

"So three," *Avalon*'s Acting Captain finished, his voice flat, "I need you *both* back on your game. If that requires you to fuck each other from one end of this carrier to another, all I ask for is your discretion. Do you follow me, Wing Commander Stanford?"

Michael couldn't help himself. The sudden crudity shocked a laugh from him. That turned into a smile, and a sudden moment of content relaxation.

"Thank you, sir" he said quietly. "I think... I needed to hear someone say that."

"Good," Kyle replied, his head cocking slightly as he received an implant comm. "Because she's here, and that means *I* need to be in Secondary Control."

The Acting Captain hung around in the cubicle for long enough to hold the curtain open for Kelly Mason, and then disappeared back to his duties.

For her part, Kelly had no words. She sat down on Michael's bed and took his hand in hers, looking at him in silence with tired eyes.

Michael smiled up at her. He still couldn't move much, but he could talk – and somehow, that wasn't as scary as it had been.

"I love you, you know," he began.

Deep Space
09:00 September 17, 2735 Earth Standard Meridian Date/Time
DSC-001 Avalon – *Secondary Control*

Per the book, Kelly, as acting XO, should have been in Secondary Control while Kyle held down the bridge.

Seeing as how all of Deck Two had been reduced to minus five Centigrade to hold the bodies until they could retrieve them and the bridge consoles were completely fried, she was instead holding down the tactical officer's console in Secondary Control.

This worked for Kyle, not least because her senior deputy's quarters had been on Deck Ten. With their casualties, *Avalon* really only had one full bridge shift to run the ship.

"Well, Alistair?" he asked finally, glancing at the clock. Twenty-seven hours had allowed them to bring what was left of the ship's crew mostly back onto their feet, have gravity back, and test the weapons and sublight engines.

Wong's image in the video link showed that the Engineer had been awake the entire time. His uniform was rumpled and his eyes were bloodshot, but he had a grin on his face.

"The good news is that we now have four Class One mass manipulators again," Wong replied. "All of the Stetson stabilizers are checking out green – we have *no* flutters this time."

"What's the bad news?" Kyle asked.

"Manipulator Three is garbage," the Chief Engineer said bluntly. "We gutted it for parts, and we may as well blast the shell off the hull as garbage. If we didn't have a spare, we'd be calling for help and floating in space."

"I can live with that," Kyle told him. They were lucky – like the atrium on Deck Six, having a full Class One mass manipulator as a spare was considered an unnecessary luxury by many of the Federation's allies. A Phoenix warship in the same position, for example, would have been waiting for a tow.

"Lieutenant Ivanov," he said, turning away from Wong's image to look over the senior surviving member of Pendez's department other than the hospitalized Navigator. "Do you have a course set in for Tranquility?"

"Yes, sir," the dark-haired young man replied crisply. "One light year per day squared for twenty-four hours, then decelerate at the same for twenty-four hours. We should arrive in Tranquility in just over forty-eight hours."

Kyle nodded and looked towards his acting XO and Chief Engineer.

"Do we have any reason to delay heading for Tranquility?" he asked quietly. "We're cutting it damned close, but we can't help anyone if we drop out of FTL again six light-months away."

"There's no guarantees at this point, Captain," Wong said simply. "Everything should hold together, but I won't be able to say for sure until we've been in FTL for a few hours. If you want to make Tranquility in time, we've got to go."

"Commander?" Kyle asked Kelly.

She shrugged. "We're as ready for battle as we'll be without finding replacement crew. If we're going to do this, then we need to do it."

"Agreed," he told them. Activating the ship's internal com, he gave the all-hands warning and then turned to Ivanov.

"Lieutenant Ivanov, please initiate Stetson stabilization fields," he ordered.

Kyle found himself holding his breath as the shimmer of the Stetson fields dropped over his screens smoothly and without issues.

"Interior Stetson field active," Ivanov reported. "Exterior field on standby, mass manipulators on standby."

"Thank you, Lieutenant," Kyle said softly. "You may warp space at your discretion."

It seemed to take longer than usual, though the timestamp on his implant told him he was imagining that. The space distortions of

Avalon's singularities filled up the screen, and then reality warped around them.

"Mr. Wong?"

"Running clean and clear, Captain. We'll keep an eye on it from here."

"Yes – *your staff* will keep an eye on it," Kyle told Wong pointedly. "*You* are going straight to sleep for at least ten hours unless something goes wrong. That's an order, Fleet Commander," he said sharply as Wong opened his mouth to protest. "Stims will only carry you so far."

The Engineer took a deep breath and nodded.

"Understood, sir."

That screen shut down, and Kyle looked back to the displays.

"Lieutenant Ivanov," he said quietly. "Put an ETA on the screen for me."

With a silent nod, the junior navigator obeyed. A timer started ticking down the seconds till their arrival, two days away.

"Commander Mason, what was the Commonwealth battle group's expected arrival time per their Operation Puppeteer plans?" Kyle asked. "Put it on the screen."

A second timer appeared immediately beneath the first, showing Alliance Intelligence's best estimate of when the attack on Tranquility would arrive.

If that estimate was correct, and if the Commonwealth kept their schedule, *Avalon* would beat them to Tranquility by less than an hour.

The Commonwealth battle group didn't know it, but it had just become a race.

One Tranquility couldn't afford *Avalon* to lose.

CHAPTER 35

Deep Space
19:00 September 18, 2735 Earth Standard Meridian Date/Time
DSC-001 Avalon – *Executive Officer's Office*

Kyle was sitting behind his desk, watching the two timers tick down on his screen and re-reading the Intelligence summary for Operation Puppeteer, when Ensign Li pinged him on his implant.

"Sir, something just came in over the Q-com network I think you want to see," the young computer specialist told him.

"What is it?" he asked.

"The same video just came in on every single channel that links from Commonwealth space," she replied. "It's being picked up by all the news media. I think... everyone is going to see this by tomorrow, and that's exactly what they want."

"Feed it to my wall-screen," Kyle ordered grimly. "Thank you, Ensign."

He recognized the scene on his monitor the moment it appeared. Even to someone born on a world far from Earth, the Star Chamber of the Interstellar Congress of the Terran Commonwealth was instantly recognizable.

The founders of the Commonwealth had spared no expense on the Star Chamber. The room had begun as a massive empty void, functionally a buoyancy tank for the immense floating platform anchoring the Skylink One space elevator. When the nine oldest colonies had combined with Earth to form the Commonwealth in the mid-twenty-fourth century, millions of dollars had been sunk into the chamber.

Now, massive floor to ceiling windows opened out onto the Atlantic Ocean along one wall, and the inner wall, an internal bulkhead that was moved every few decades to allow for new representatives, was lit up with floor mounted spotlights.

Around the walls were hung massive, twenty-meter long, banners with the images of each member world of the Commonwealth. With over a hundred star systems and seven hundred senators and Congressmen and -women, few worlds' representatives sat under their banner, but all of their worlds were represented on the walls.

At the front of the chamber, where the video they were receiving was focused, was a raised stage where whoever was speaking would sit. In the video, date-stamped two weeks prior, fifteen of the Congress' members occupied a long table on that stage, and a chill ran through Kyle.

"This special meeting of the Senate and Assembly of the Terran Commonwealth combined in Congress is called to order," a frail-looking woman with pale skin and hair announced calmly. A scrolling bar ran under her as she continued speaking, giving her name and position. The woman was Speaker Janet Lane, elected by the Congress itself to co-ordinate their meetings and generally considered the second most powerful person in the Commonwealth.

"I surrender the floor to the Committee on Unification," she concluded the remarks Kyle had mostly ignored, and his chill turned to ice.

The Committee on Unification was the sub-committee of Congress, selected from its membership by its membership via arcane rules no outsider would ever understand, charged with implementing the 'historical inevitability' of human unification. That Committee of democratically elected representatives had started more wars and shed more blood than any dictator in history.

The man sitting in the center of the fifteen-person Committee rose after Speaker Lane took her seat, and glanced around the Star Chamber. Another scrolling bar identified the heavy-set, white-haired, black man as Senator Michael Burns of Alpha Centauri.

"Esteemed officials of the Commonwealth Congress," Burns hailed his companions, "two days ago, in closed session, my fellow members of the Committee on Unification laid a proposal given to us before you. We recommended, and you, my fellow Congress members, agreed, that the proposal should be approved."

"We are here to begin the motions of that approval. The Committee calls on Fleet Admiral James Calvin Walkingstick to appear before us."

The Fleet Admiral had clearly been waiting just outside the doors to the Chamber. As Burns finished speaking, one of the formally clad but functionally armed Congressional Lictors opened the door and ushered the man in.

The camera zoomed in on Walkingstick as he approached the stage in front of the Congress. He wore the red and black uniform of a Commonwealth Fleet officer as if he'd been born in it, and the four stars on his collar had been polished so brightly they *gleamed* in the sunlight streaming in.

Walkingstick was a large man, with the heavy jowls and dark skin of a northwestern Amerindian. His auburn hair was tied in a braid that clung to his neck without restricting his movements. The Fleet Admiral walked forward as if he owned the Chamber – and for a few moments, some of the Congressmen took up a chant of "Walkingstick, Walkingstick!"

"Fleet Admiral Walkingstick," Burns greeted the Admiral. "You presented the Committee with a plan to forward the cause of human unification. We have reviewed this plan and presented to Congress. Do you have anything to add that was not in your proposal?"

Walkingstick nodded slowly, and Burns gestured for him to take the floor. The big man stepped into precisely the center of the space between the stage and the podium, and turned to face Congress while assuming a perfect parade rest.

"Leaders of the Commonwealth," he began, his voice carried the precise diction, odd to Kyle's ears, still taught in the British Isles, "given the resources laid out in the plan I presented, I believe I can deliver new members to this Congress."

"Some of these worlds will welcome us," he continued. "We offer all the benefits of Commonwealth membership, and many will see this as wise.

"Others, more foolish, will stand against the tide of history and the manifest destiny of the human race. They will resist with force, and there can be no guarantees in battle."

"I do not guarantee you victory, Senators, Congressmen," he finished. "But I promise you – the Cause will not fail!"

Now the chant of "Walkingstick, Walkingstick!" echoed through the chamber, and it took a good minute for Burns to gain the attention of his compatriots.

"Fleet Admiral James Calvin Walkingstick," the Senator finally said into a modicum of quiet, "this Congress offers you a Marshal's mace, to go into the stars and speak with our voice, act with our hands. We charge you to bring the worlds we place into your care to Unification.

"Do you accept this charge?"

Walkingstick bowed his head, an appearance at least of humility.

"I do," he answered, his voice echoing in the Star Chamber.

Burns picked the mace – a rod of platinum that concealed a DNA scanner and a chip that placed the bearer in command of vast Commonwealth resources – up from the table in front of him and offered it to the Admiral.

Walkingstick took it and the camera zoomed in on his smile.

"James Calvin Walkingstick, this Congress acclaims you Marshal of the Rimward Marches," Burns proclaimed.

The video ended, leaving Kyle staring at a blank wall for a long moment of silence.

"Fuck."

Then a priority ping began to sound on his console – Fleet Command was contacting *all* Federation capital ship commanders.

#

It took Kyle a moment to place the tanned man in the Federation Navy uniform and white turban facing the camera when the video link came up. For all that the man signed his deployment orders, Kyle had never *met* Vice Admiral Mohammed Kane.

From the list of names showing in a corner of his screen, Kyle wasn't the first starship commander to link in – but he was also far from the last.

"All right everyone," Kane said after waiting a moment, "anyone who isn't online yet can watch the recording – for some of you this is urgent."

"I assume you've all seen the transmission from the Commonwealth Congress," he continued. "For any of you who have forgotten your academy days, the 'Rimward Marches' in Commonwealth parlance is a region of space that basically coincides with the Alliance. There's some systems that aren't included, but we, the Coraline Imperium, the Renaissance Factor and Phoenix are all included."

"And the Commonwealth Congress just appointed a man to hold dictatorial authority over our worlds," Kane said grimly.

"Given our discovery of Operation Puppeteer, this isn't the shock to us they're likely hoping it is," the Admiral continued, "but we are still badly out of position. The Senate has decided that we have no choice but to take this video as a declaration of war."

"As of now, you are all operating under Rules of Engagement Alpha One. All Commonwealth warships are to be engaged on sight. All Commonwealth civilian shipping is to be seized and interned."

"Ladies, gentlemen – we don't want this war," Kane concluded. "We're not ready – but thanks to *Avalon*'s victory in Hessian, we're more ready they expect us to be."

"We don't want this war," he repeated, "but if the Commonwealth brings it to our shores, I fully expect you to kick it back through their teeth!"

"Good luck

Chapter 36

Kyle had set an alarm for well before emergence, so it took him a moment upon awakening to realize that the noise that had awakened him was *not* a wake-up alarm.

Finally, he managed to wake up enough to activate the communicator. "Roberts."

"It's Mason," Kelly said sharply. "We have a problem – looks like our battle group has a more efficient commander than Alliance Intelligence figured."

Kyle was upright and fully awake as that sank in.

"They've arrived."

"They've arrived," she confirmed. "Standard Commonwealth battle group, two battleships, two carriers. ETA to Tranquility orbit is three hours."

He checked the ETA clock for *Avalon* on his datapad, guessing what it would say.

They would arrive in Tranquility roughly fifteen minutes before the Commonwealth fleet settled into orbit of the main planet.

It would take them another three hours to reach the planet themselves, but it wouldn't matter. By the time they arrived, the Tranquility Space Fleet would be dead.

Michelle didn't quite sneak into the infirmary to meet Angela, but she was pretty sure 'skulking' was a valid descriptor. The main infirmary was quiet early in the morning, but she could tell that the nurses and doctors were all on duty.

The same feel was present throughout the ship – *Avalon* was going into battle, and her battered and depleted crew was going to be ready. Michelle herself was headed to the Flight Deck, and was already clad in the modified shipsuit she would wear in space.

"You shouldn't be here!" Angela hissed when she spotted Michelle. The nurse was smiling however, and quickly surrendered to a hug and kiss. She then held Michelle back at arm's length for a moment, studying her.

"What's wrong?" Angela asked. "You look like death."

"We're going to be too late," Michelle whispered. The news wasn't spread through the entire ship yet, but Flight Commander Rokos had warned the pilots. "The Commonwealth attack arrived early – unless the TSF does a lot more damage than we expect, we may have to run without a fight. If we do fight, it's going to be nasty."

The pilot shrugged helplessly. "I wanted to say goodbye, just in case."

Angela pulled her close again and held her for a long moment, and then a familiar voice cleared his throat behind them.

"I really do hate to interrupt," Michael Stanford told them softly. "But it seems that news isn't making it to the injured. *What* happened?"

Michelle turned to look at the CAG. The Wing Commander was in a wheelchair with a blanket covering the stumps of his legs. He wore a gown instead of a uniform, but his eyes were bright and alert as his gaze bore into her.

"The Commonwealth battle group arrived early," she repeated. She was relatively sure she *shouldn't* tell Stanford that, but he *was* her commanding officer, invalid or no. "They'll be engaging the Tranquility Space Fleet in about thirty minutes."

"Well, shit," a second, more feminine voice added as Lieutenant-Commander Pendez slipped out from behind the curtains of *her* cubicle. Like Stanford, she was in a wheelchair. The level of radiation poisoning the Navigator had taken left her unable to move without rapid exhaustion.

"Lieutenant Alverez, could you get me a uniform please?" Stanford asked calmly.

Michelle traded helpless looks with her lover. This was Angela's fight, not hers, and she stepped back out of way.

"You, Commander, aren't fit to be going *anywhere*," the nurse objected. "Except back to bed."

"You're not winning this fight, my dear," Pendez interjected from her own wheelchair. "All hell is going to break loose, and I don't know about the Wing Commander, but I have *no* interest in dying in bed because the ship blew up around me."

"*You*," Angela replied sharply, "are *definitely* not going anywhere. You can barely stand! And Stanford has *no legs*."

"I don't need legs to fly once I'm jacked in," Stanford pointed out with a small smile. "But you're right about Maria – she shouldn't do more than thinking, so you should accompany her to Secondary Control. Miss Williams is perfectly capable of escorting me to the Flight Deck."

Angela looked around, probably hoping for backup, but none of the doctors were paying attention to the long term care section. They were busy preparing for the influx of casualties when the battle started.

"We may not survive the next twenty-four hours, love," Michelle said quietly. "I think we'd all rather die on our feet, don't you?"

Deep Space
06:55 September 19, 2735 Earth Standard Meridian Date/Time
DSC-001 Avalon – *Main Flight Deck*

Stanford was aware that his 'functional' status was entirely based on the fact that his nanites were cutting off all of the nerve signals from the severed stumps of his legs. Unlike chemical painkillers, though, that process left him fully aware and cognizant of what was going on.

He changed into his uniform on his own and hustled Michelle to push his wheelchair down to the Flight Deck. Pendez, he knew, would take longer to be ready to move. In many ways, radiation poisoning at her level was a worse injury than his own gross physical trauma. Regenerating a lost limb was a late twenty-first century technology. Repairing pervasive cellular-level damage was a far younger science.

The Flight Deck was the chaotic storm he was expecting, and he gloried in it as Michelle pushed him towards the control officer.

"Hammond, Rokos," he bellowed when he spotted those two worthy souls. "Get over here!"

He gestured for Michelle to get to her ship, and the Flight Lieutenant promptly made herself scarce as the senior Space Force NCO and the acting CAG approached.

"What's our status?" Michael asked.

"All starfighters are fuelled and armed," Hammond replied crisply. "Crews aren't aboard yet, but we're still an hour from emergence."

"Shouldn't you be in the infirmary?" Rokos demanded bluntly. "You *are* missing both of your legs, in case you hadn't noticed."

"I don't need legs to fly," the CAG said calmly. "We're going to need every starfighter out there we can get. I assume command, Flight Commander Rokos."

The stocky Commander grinned and saluted. "I stand relieved, sir. The last plan *I* had was to co-ordinate with TSF Command. Do we have an updated one?"

"Not yet," Michael admitted. "But I have some thoughts. Hammond!"

"Sir?" the Senior Chief Petty Officer replied.

"Is everything clear for a full deck launch?"

"Somehow, I knew you were going to ask that," Hammond replied. "Yes, sir. We can have the birds prepped and the deck clear in sixty seconds once the pilots are aboard, but I'll be happier with ten minutes!"

"You'll get it," Michael promised. He glanced around, realizing that a growing knot of quiet people had been gathering around him. He smiled grimly.

Glynn Stewart

"I was going to ask someone to fetch you all," he said loudly, projecting across the crowd. By the time he was finished speaking, he was sure he had every pilot and most of the flight crews.

"By now, you know that the Commonwealth has beaten us to Tranquility," he told them. "And things don't look good for the Tranquility Space Fleet – we *cannot* get there in time to change the tide of that battle."

"But we know the Old Man!" The crews laughed and nodded in response to that, and Michael gave them a cold smile. "He was *ours* before he was *Avalon's* – so we know him."

"He's going to pull some crazy damned trick out of his hat, and while I don't know what it'll be, I do know one thing: the Commonwealth will *never* see him coming."

"So get in your ships, and prep for a full deck launch. When Commander Roberts asks us to pull off whatever crazy stunt he has in mind, I want us to be *ready. Do you follow*?"

"We follow, sir!"

"Then let's go save Tranquility, shall we?"

CHAPTER 37

Deep Space
07:20 September 19, 2735 Earth Standard Meridian Date/Time
DSC-001 Avalon *– Secondary Control*

Kyle was going to have a front row seat to the death of a star fleet.

They were receiving the full telemetry upload from every ship in the Tranquility Space Fleet, relayed through a Q-com link with a ground station at TSF Command. He could track where each of the TSF's guardships and starfighters were in real-time, and could even contact First Admiral Wu directly aboard the cruiser *Sapanā*.

He had no intention of jogging the elbows of a man about to defend his homeworld.

It looked like the TSF was going with a modified version of the original plan. The missile-heavy *Abhibhāvaka* and *Rakshaka* guardships had assembled in a sixteen-ship strong Force Beta, hidden in the ice rings of Tranquility itself.

Sapanā, escorted by two hundred *Hurricane* starfighters and the lance-armed *Śīlda* guardships, was advancing towards the Commonwealth battle group. There was no finesse to either the defenders' or attackers' approach. The Commonwealth had assembled a shield of starfighters in front of their battleships, and pulled the carriers back. They had the firepower to crush the Tranquility Space Fleet, and had assembled it into a giant hammer aimed at Tranquility itself.

The TSF really had no choice – they could defend the planet or surrender.

The starfighters went out first. All told, Tranquility had deployed just over two hundred of the fleet little ships.

The two Commonwealth heavy fleet carriers, between them, deployed two hundred and *eighty*.

As soon as the TSF ships launched forward from their larger brethren, the missile ships using Tranquility's rings for cover opened fire with the heavy capital ship missiles. Sixteen guardships launched sixty four missiles in a single salvo that made Kyle shiver.

When the missiles passed *Sapanā,* the cruiser launched her own missiles. Eighteen more missiles joined the salvo, which rapidly caught up to the starfighters – and passed through them, just as the two starfighter wings slammed into each other.

Kyle could see the echoes of the same trick he'd pulled on *Achilles*, but *this* time the Commonwealth starfighters had the numbers to split their attention. Eighty starfighters focused on the missiles, while the remainder went head to head with their Tranquility equivalents.

For someone watching through the scanners of other ships, from millions of kilometers away, the chaos that ensued was barely coherent. Fireball after fireball lit up the sky over Tranquility as positron lances and antimatter missiles reaped their deadly harvest.

Ninety-four seconds after the two fighter wings reached each other, a half-dozen Tranquility ships broke through – as much by luck as anything else. Behind them, still on course for *Sapanā*, one hundred and eighty-seven Commonwealth *Scimitars*, blasted forward.

Then the *second* wave of eighty-two missiles arrived – and detonated in a single massive swarm of explosions. They didn't take out all the Commonwealth fighters, but they opened a gaping hole in the heart of their formation.

The *Śīlda* class guardships followed those missiles in. Distracted by the sky-shattering force of the fighter clash, Kyle had almost forgotten about them. The handful of starfighters that had survived the missile salvo targeted in the center of their formation didn't stand a chance.

The eight vessels, tiny compared to a true starship, rode their pillars of antimatter flame just as well, just as agilely, as any starfighter –

GLYNN STEWART

and where a starfighter carried a single positron lance, the guardships carried *ten*.

They ripped through the remnants of the Commonwealth's center at top speed, ignoring the hundred-plus starfighters around them even as they annihilated the handful of ships in their path. A third wave of missiles rode their exhaust plumes, and followed them towards the Commonwealth battle group.

In response, the two mighty battleships opened fire. Their beams couldn't reach *Sapanā*, but they launched forty missiles between them, all targeted on the cruiser. Their positron lances slashed out into space, targeting the closing guardships and the missiles they were covering with their own hulls.

Kyle watched in horror, guessing without even having seen the revised plan what the guardships were doing. Those half-million ton ships couldn't take a single hit from even the lighter positron lances the battleships were firing – but they *could* take the lasers used to stop missiles. And their deflectors could shunt aside the positron lances.

For a while. A while the missiles wouldn't have survived on their own.

The fourth missile salvo, behind the guardships, ran into a slowing and prepared Commonwealth fighter shield. None of them made it through.

Avalon's Secondary Control was silent, and Kyle was certain he wasn't the only saying a silent prayer for the doughty little guardships as they charged forward, dancing a writhing path across space as they tried to guard their charges *and* survive.

Their fate was inevitable.

The first died moments after the Commonwealth found the range. The battleships' massive, one-and-a-half-megaton-per-second positron lances could burn through the guardships' deflectors long before the guardships' quarter-megaton weapons could return the favor.

Four more ships died without ever reaching the range of their enemies.

The three survivors opened fire. Beams of antimatter flickered across space, with even the mighty kilometer long battleships pirouetting in space to dodge their tormentors. A guardship died. Then another.

Then the last guardship violently blew apart. It hadn't been hit, its deflectors were still working – the ship simply exploded.

Kyle was shocked, looking stunned at the screen for a moment before it hit him. The *intentional* detonation of the guardship's zero point cells had saturated the space around them with an almost impenetrable level of radiation.

And the guardships' sacrifices had carried twenty missiles to striking distance of the Commonwealth battlegroup. No longer matching pace with the slower guardships, the last missiles of the salvo leapt forward.

Lasers and positron lances filled the air, trying to catch the radiation concealed missiles with blind fire. The programs behind that 'random' fire were smart, with nine hundred years of history behind human missiles to feed them. Blind or not, missiles began to die.

Then they emerged from the radiation cloud, and Kyle sucked in a sharp breath as he realized that the missiles were still there – and spreading out. Of the remaining missiles, three were targeting each battleship – and three were targeting each carrier.

There were only seconds between the missiles emerging visibly to *Sapanā's* sensors and their becoming lost in a haze of explosions and laser fire.

When the haze cleared, three ships were clearly damaged – near misses that had burnt off missiles, sensors and armor.

The forward battleship, closest to Tranquility, was shattered. A one-gigaton antimatter missile had struck her amidships and vaporized the middle half of the ship. The broke wreck of her stern and bow were rapidly separating, driven apart by the force of the explosion.

Cheers echoed in *Avalon's* bridge, but Kyle's gaze was drawn to *Sapanā*. The dying blow of that battleship closed in on the Tranquility cruiser, accompanied by the same starfighters that had destroyed every missile salvo the TSF had launched without an escort.

Sapanā was heavily refitted, but she was twenty years older than her enemies. Smaller. Less well armored, and less defended against missiles.

She took thirty-four starfighters with her, but moments after the missiles closed, *Avalon* lost their link to the old cruiser.

CHAPTER 38

Deep Space
07:50 September 19, 2735 Earth Standard Meridian Date/Time
DSC-001 Avalon *– Secondary Control*

Secondary Control was silent again, and Kyle looked around his crew. The screens now showed the Commonwealth fighter groups, still a hundred strong, closing in on Tranquility's rings. The ice rings would render positron lances useless at range, but the starfighters had enough missiles to close in and finish off the Tranquility Space Fleet.

Avalon would emerge *while* that butchery was occurring, but still three hours away. There was *nothing* they could do.

"We can't save them, can we?" Kelly whispered.

"Not the TSF, no," Kyle said grimly, his eyes on the ringed planet on their screen. "I don't know if I'm willing to give up on Tranquility, though."

"By the time we can get to engagement range, they'll have re-armed their fighters, and repaired any critical damage," Kelly pointed out. "If we could hit them *now* – hell, even in the next half hour! – we could clean their clocks."

Kyle blinked, looking at the screen again and then back at his console. A ship had to *enter* Alcubierre drive in a zone of effectively zero gravity, or risk ripping apart both themselves and any nearby fragile objects. Like planets.

But with all of the stabilizers and redirectors that Dr. Jessica Stetson had designed so longer ago, did they really *have* to emerge like that?

He hit a command.

"Wong, I have a question for you," Kyle said calmly.

"No, I can't make her go faster," the engineer said dryly. "Next, Captain?"

"If we push it – if we're willing to risk the ship – how close in can we emerge from Alcubierre?"

There was silence on the line, and Kyle brought up a video screen to be sure he hadn't lost the connection somewhere. The shaven-headed engineer was looking at him with unreadable dark eyes.

"You're serious," he finally concluded.

"As death," the Acting Captain told him. "How close?"

"It depends," Wong said slowly. "On how good a navigator we've got..."

"Someone's going to need to *put* me in my chair," a tired voice said from beside Kyle, "but I'm good enough for this."

Lieutenant-Commander Maria Pendez may have been in a wheelchair and may have had Lieutenant Angela Alverez managing to both push said wheelchair and hover, but her eyes were level and her face was determined.

"I should send you right back to the infirmary," Kyle told her.

"Yes, but there's no way my *assistant* can thread the needle for you," she replied, her voice sharp and fiery. "It *can* be done, Skipper. How close do you want?"

"Wong?" Kyle asked, turning back to the video.

The engineer shook his head, but when he looked up to meet Kyle's gaze he had a determined smile on his face.

"If she's mad enough to fly it, I'm mad enough to try and hold the manipulators together. How close boils down to one question, skipper," the Engineer said calmly. "Do you care if this ship can fly FTL again afterwards?"

"Commander Wong," Kyle said flatly, "if you can give me emergence within weapons range of those ships, I don't care if I have to *carry Avalon* home."

Wong glanced through the video screen at Pendez.

"If you can thread it that fine, Lieutenant-Commander, I *think* I can hold us together. You game?"

Pendez glanced past Kyle to the screen where the last warships of the Tranquility Space Fleet were making a hopeless last stand, praying for a rescue that even this trick wouldn't be able to bring there in time.

"Let's kill these sons of bitches."

Deep Space
08:00 September 19, 2735 Earth Standard Meridian Date/Time
SFG-001 Actual – Falcon-C *type command starfighter*

Stanford's flight crew had helped him get into the command chair in the cockpit of his starfighter, and then strapped him in tightly. He'd wanted to object to their mothering, but one level look from Rokos as he started to open his mouth and he'd meekly gone along with it.

Once he was linked into the ship, however, his body and its infirmities faded away. He *was* the little starfighter, and he quickly ran through the mental checklist to be sure everything was ready.

"All hands, all hands, this is the Captain," a voice cut in.

"We will *not* be emerging in Tranquility on schedule," Roberts announced, his voice calm. "Instead, we are going to attempt a late emergence. If everything goes as planned, we will arrive on top of the Commonwealth battlegroup."

"There will be no time for central control. We will launch all fighters as soon as we emerge and release all weapons to independent control. The Tranquility Space Fleet is gone," he continued grimly, "so if it crosses your sights and it isn't a *Falcon* or *Avalon* herself, kill it."

Roberts was silent for a moment.

"Good luck," he said finally. "From what I'm being told about this process, you'll want to strap yourself in if you can. It's going to get rough."

"Well, shit," Michael said aloud.

"Sir?"

"I doubt anyone else on this ship has ever threaded the needle before," he told his flight crew calmly. "*I*, on the other hand, have apparently had more than *one* lunatic captain. Strap in," he ordered. "'Rough' is an understatement."

Barely aware of his body as he was, he braced himself for what he knew was coming.

This was going to suck.

Deep Space
08:05 September 19, 2735 Earth Standard Meridian Date/Time
DSC-001 Avalon – Secondary Control

At eight hundred meters long and four hundred wide at the base, *Avalon* was shorter and squatter than more modern ships. With her heavy neutronium armor, however, only the latest and most massive battleships and super-carriers had eclipsed her immense mass.

Combined with dozens of mass manipulators of various sizes located throughout her hull serving so many different purposes, it took a mighty blow to make the old warship even shiver.

Acting Captain Kyle Roberts' orders were making her *scream*.

He held onto the arms of his command chair as the entire ship bucked like a drunken donkey, the air itself splitting and tearing to create the most godawful noise.

Pendez sat at her console, blank-eyed and completely linked into the ship's systems, riding the fine line between collapsing the warp bubble and ripping the ship apart from gravitic shear – 'threading the needle'.

In Engineering, Kyle knew that Wong and six of his engineers were linked in as well. They were manually managing the Stetson stabilizers and mass manipulators, desperately trying to keep the warp bubble a little bit more stable, to give Pendez that *little* bit more flexibility to keep them all alive.

And all the man who'd ordered all of their lives placed in the hands of that tiny handful of individuals could do was watch. Numbers and patterns flashed across his screen, an emergency

Glynn Stewart

klaxon began to ring, and *still* the air around him shrieked like a dying angel.

It seemed to last an eternity, even though he could do the math that told him they would cross the extra distance in less than ten minutes.

It ended with a sudden shock, and the viewscreen in front of them lit up with the sight of Tranquility.

And between them and Tranquility, directly ahead, was the surviving Commonwealth battleship.

Chapter 39

Tranquility System
08:15 September 19, 2735 Earth Standard Meridian Date/Time
SFG-001 Actual – Falcon-C *type command starfighter*

For a moment as his forty-two starfighters were blasted out of *Avalon*'s main flight deck, Stanford thought they were going to ram straight into the battleship in their path. Engines flicked on by mental control, twisting their courses away from the kilometer long warship, and Michael spared half of a second for a sigh of deep relief.

"Alpha, Bravo, Charlie Squadrons," he snapped over the net, his orders flying out at the speed of thought. "You're with Rokos, go right and kill me a carrier. Delta, Foxtrot, you're on me – we're going left and finding the other one!"

The squadrons split apart smoothly, hours upon hours of both simulated and real practice and combat experience showing.

"What about that battleship?" Rokos demanded on a private line.

Michael sighed and shook his head.

"Like it or not, Russell, she's *Avalon*'s problem," the CAG said softly.

There was no response from his senior squadron commander, and Michael focused on the here and now. Sixteen starfighters followed his as they vectored right, engines flaring antimatter into space as he tracked 'left' from *Avalon*'s launch bay.

"Oh *shit*," he cursed under his breath. The carrier must have been moving in to do search and rescue on the damaged battleship – she was *right there*, less than ten thousand kilometers away.

"Take her," Michael snapped, suiting actions to words as he triggered his *Falcon*'s positron lance.

The carrier's engines were barely starting to flare to life, the ship rotating to presumably present a less damaged broadside with more weapons.

She never completed the rotation. Seventeen fifty-kiloton-a-second positron lances ripped into her, and the rotation made the damage *worse*. Massive gaps opened in the carrier's hull as her own armor became an explosion of matter-antimatter annihilation.

Then one of the positron lances ripped open the antimatter capacitors in the ship's engineering bay, and the cigar-shaped, kilometer and a half long, warship vanished in a newborn sun.

Tranquility System
08:15 September 19, 2735 Earth Standard Meridian Date/Time
SFG-001 Alpha Six – Falcon-*type starfighter*

Michelle missed the battleship by less than a kilometer, close enough to *feel* the massive ship's electromagnetic deflectors try to shove her away. Focusing hard, she used that tiny bit of extra impetus to bounce her ship away from the Commonwealth warship and follow Rokos around towards the second carrier.

This one had been hanging back, potentially providing cover for the repairs of the other two, which bought the vessel time to react. By the time the Federation fighter squadrons crossed the fifty thousand kilometer mark, the carrier's weapons were active.

"Random-walk everybody," Rokos ordered. "Prep a Starfire salvo on my mark."

At a closing velocity of over five hundred kilometers a second, random-walking was *complicated*. Michelle threw her ship into a corkscrew, firing her positron lance as she did. The carrier was beginning its *own* evasive maneuvers – whoever was over there had reflexes like a cat.

A beam *just* missed her, the Commonwealth warship returning fire with its own positron lances, and a warning flashed up on her mental Heads Up Display as the carrier fired Javelin anti-fighter missiles.

"Missiles *now*," Rokos barked, and Michelle's gunner obeyed without her relaying the command. Twenty-four starfighters salvoed ninety-six missiles, flashing at the carrier at over a thousand gravities and interpenetrating the Commonwealth missiles coming the other way.

Michelle's computer calmly informed her that four of the missiles had been targeted on her, and she dismissed the Federation salvo from her thoughts as she focused on *surviving*.

Her positron lance cut through space in a spiraling pattern that caught the first missile, but the surviving three scattered – their networked intelligence smart enough to at least try to evade. It wasn't smart enough to come up with a pattern her starfighter's more capable computer couldn't crack, however, and she nabbed two more as they closed in.

At the last second, she fired one of the *Falcon*'s few precious decoys, cut her acceleration to a hundred gravities, and threw her ECM into overdrive.

The missile, confused by the high powered jamming, went for the target where its electronic brain said she should be – the decoy.

The bright light of the missile's explosion caused her mental screens to darken – and then they darkened *again*.

The officer on duty aboard the carrier had reacted immediately, and done everything right. The missile defenses had stopped dozens of the Starfires.

Dozens more had made it through, and Michelle's visual input darkened to pure black as over thirty one-gigaton explosions ripped the Commonwealth warship apart.

"Check in," Rokos ordered. "Who did we lose?"

The mental check-ins went by in a blink, and Michelle was stunned. Somehow, they hadn't lost *anybody*. Her scans showed all twenty-four starfighters still present.

Then she expanded the range of her scans and inhaled sharply.

Where was *Avalon*?

"Our God in heaven, hallowed by thy name, thy kingdom come, thy work be..."

"Shut up and *fire!*" Kelly snapped, shoving her senior assistant out of the way and grabbing the tactical console. "All weapons, target the battleship and *fire*," she snapped into the microphone.

Kyle watched in horror as the twenty million ton mass of the battleship grew in the screen. They couldn't *possibly* hit it – automated evasion sequences would activate on both ships, engaging random vectors to avoid collision.

His link to *Avalon's* systems told him they were evading, twisting 'up' to avoid the Commonwealth warship. Their prow cleared the other ship, and the starfighters blasted into space in the momentary clear space in front of the carrier.

Avalon rumbled as her weapons fired in anger, twelve battleship grade positron lances ripping into the armored hull ahead of them... an armored hull that was drifting *back* into their path.

He closed his eyes, but his link showed him the paths. By pure fluke, two computers had chosen the *same* vector to dodge along, and the battleship, with its more modern and powerful engines, was going to dodge right *back* into *Avalon's* path.

They had... seconds. He wasn't as fast as he had once been, but he was still linked into the battleship's computers, thinking and acting many times faster than an un-linked human.

With a thought, he pulled the missile batteries back into central control. Then he overrode the minimum distance safeties on the missiles' one-gigaton warheads and *fired*.

"Pendez," he bellowed. "Aim for the center! *Follow the missiles!*"

The Navigator didn't even hesitate. She saw the same disaster that Kyle did, and followed his missiles. *Avalon's* acceleration was a fifth of the missiles, barely two hundred gravities – not enough to avoid the collision now, but enough to control *where* they hit.

The battleship's defenses were active, running on automatic control. Four of Kyle's missiles were shot down, even as the positron lances tore the Commonwealth ship apart.

The last four slammed into the center of the battleship and detonated as one. The equivalent of four *billion* tons of TNT exploded in a moment, ripping a hole clean through the immense warship and spewing white fire in every direction.

That fire hadn't even *begun* to disperse before Pendez, with a precision Kyle couldn't have matched without his old implant bandwidth, took *Avalon*'s neutronium-armored bulk into the exact *center* of that fireball.

Kyle felt as much as saw the power readings go crazy as the old ship redirected every ounce of power into the mass manipulators serving as inertial dampeners. They collided at a combined velocity of eighty kilometers a second, and he *felt* even *Avalon*'s mighty armor buckle.

Finally, painfully, they ripped free of the wreckage, trailing fire behind them. For a moment, he breathed a sigh of relief as every system on his panel began to flash red.

And then the power died again.

#

Secondary Control was dark for fifteen seconds. Twenty.

Kyle was about to ask who was closest to the emergency supply closet when the lights came back on. The air circulation fans began to whir again, consoles slowly began to boot back up and his datapad lit up with the face of his Chief Engineer.

"Sorry about that," Wong said quickly. "The zero point cells tried to shut down from overload. We managed to keep enough up to reboot, but it took all of our power load for a few seconds."

"How bad are we?" Kyle asked without preamble.

"Twenty percent power and rising," the Chief Engineer replied. "I'll have exterior coms back for you in a few seconds, but we won't have sensors for at least five minutes."

"What about weapons?"

"He doesn't need to worry about powering those," Kelly interrupted grimly. "We *will* want to see if we can still vent those areas remotely."

Kyle turned back to his acting executive officer.

"What?"

"You flew us into an antimatter explosion, boss," she said calmly. "Best of a list of bad options – hell, it's not as if I had *any* ideas, let alone better ones! – but everything on our forward hull that wasn't covered in neutronium is *gone*."

"And we have fires in *all* of the weapon bays," she continued. "I'm getting reports," she tapped the side of her head, "and we've got most of our people out. Venting the air is the best option."

"You heard Mason, Chief?" Kyle asked.

"I got her," Wong replied. "I'll get my people on it." He paused, listening to someone who wasn't on this channel. "We've got coms back," he added.

"Get me Stanford," Kyle ordered Ensign Li, and slowly tried to relax back into his chair. The young Ensign nodded to him after a moment.

"Michael, please tell me you control the battlespace," *Avalon*'s Captain asked his CAG. "Because we are well and truly crispy over here."

"Hell, boss, I'm surprised to hear your voice," Stanford replied, his voice shakier than Kyle was expecting. "We *still* can't pick you out of the debris field from that battleship. We thought *Avalon* was gone and we were walking home!"

Kyle checked what status reports they had on the Flight Deck. The neutronium shutters had been closed and Hammond's note said they were 'welded the fuck shut', but also that he'd have them open soon.

"No, CAG, you aren't doing that," he replied with a soft chuckle. "You'll have to hang out outside for a bit until Chief Hammond gets your doors open, but the Flight Deck is otherwise fully operational."

"I hate to repeat myself," he continued, "but do you have control of the battlespace?"

Glynn Stewart

"Yeah," Michael replied slowly. "Yeah, we do. Scratch two carriers and a battleship, Kyle – though I would ask that you *not* take the next battleship out quite so dramatically!"

Kyle breathed a long sigh of relief.

"I'll take that under advisement, Michael," he told the other man with a cheer he was actually starting to feel. "Now, I'm going to deal with repairs. Could you and your people do me the *small* favor of making sure those Commonwealth starfighters don't interrupt?"

"They outnumber us two to one," Michael pointed out.

"And?"

"We have missiles and a carrier to go home to. They don't," the CAG finished. "I'll go see if the Terrans wanna play. You make sure we have a ride home."

"I'll do that," Senior Fleet Commander Kyle Roberts, Acting Captain of the Federation Space Carrier *Avalon*, said cheerfully.

Tranquility System
08:25 September 19, 2735 Earth Standard Meridian Date/Time
SFG-001 Actual – Falcon-C *type command starfighter*

Ten minutes. They'd been in the system barely ten minutes.

Michael could hardly believe it, but he doubted his computers were so broken as to give him the wrong time. In ten minutes, *Avalon* and her fighters had destroyed the equivalent of an entire star system's navy. Hell, a lot of systems were enough poorer than, say, Tranquility that they couldn't *afford* a fleet of three capital starships.

Of course, Tranquility didn't have a fleet of three starships anymore. One of their two remaining ships was in a dry dock space station tucked underneath the immense rings around the planet. Despite everything that had happened already, that station was still vulnerable.

There were still, after all, roughly a hundred Commonwealth *Scimitar*-type fighters in the system. The ships were primarily interceptors, armed with lighter missiles and positron lances than his own ships, but between them they would still be able to overwhelm the dry dock's defenses and see *Mauna* destroyed before it was deployed against the Commonwealth.

Which was why Michael was leading every fighter of SFG-001 in a deep dive towards the planet. If they were lucky, they could intercept the Commonwealth ships before they attacked the space station. If they were even luckier, the Commonwealth starfighters would come out to meet him and leave the station for later.

"Commonwealth starfighters," he transmitted. "You are a long way from home. You spent your munitions on Tranquility's defenders, and your carriers are dead."

"The Federation is here to defend Tranquility," he continued calmly. "My ships are fresh. We have full munition loads." Well, less the salvo that had killed one of the carriers, but no need to rub *that* in. "Your only sane option is to surrender before I am forced to kill you all."

There they were. Michael was still receiving relayed telemetry from the surface, and Tranquility's satellite network had detected the Commonwealth fighter group. They were cutting through the outer ring, staying just inside the debris field and taking the inevitable damage to try and sneak up on him.

"All ships, prep a Starfire salvo," he ordered. "Downloading targets from TSF Command."

There was enough of a delay, despite the Q-com and the short distance, that he couldn't hit them with lances, but the Starfires were smart enough to close in if he got them anywhere near them.

"Fire!" he ordered. Over a hundred and fifty missiles blasted into space, closing in on where he knew the Terran ships were hiding.

"Sir, incoming transmission!" his Flight Engineer reported. "Voice-only, he's ending it omni-directionally. Linking it through now."

"To the commander of the Federation starfighters," a clipped voice with a heavy accent began. "I am Wing Colonel Jakob Mbuntu, commanding the survivors of the Commonwealth strike groups."

"To prevent further loss of life on all sides, if you will guarantee the safety of my men and women under the honor of the Federation Navy, I offer the complete surrender of the forces under my command."

There was, Michael supposed, a chance it was a trick. Nonetheless...

"Suspend the missiles," he ordered. "Shut down their drives but hold them until it's too late for them to engage before detonating the failsafes. Then get me a link to this Colonel Mbuntu."

Moments passed, with the Federation missiles now sliding ballistically through space – but still on course for Mbuntu's fighters.

Finally, a channel opened, showing a heavyset black man strapped into his own chair and facing the camera.

"Wing Colonel Mbuntu?" Michael asked.

"I am," he said simply. "To whom am I speaking?"

"I am Wing Commander Michael Stanford, commanding SFG-001 off of *Avalon*," Michael told him. "My terms are simple, Colonel. You and your men will activate your emergency ejection pods and set a course for the surface. Tranquility SAR will retrieve you, but I will guarantee your safety under the honor of the Federation Navy."

Mbuntu seemed to hesitate. Ejecting would leave his starfighters – with all of their technology and computer cores – available for retrieval. It was a cost of his surrender he had to have expected, but it would still go against the grain.

"Colonel, every minute you and I are pointing missiles at each other is a minute Tranquility cannot launch SAR spacecraft to try and find all of *both* our people," Michael said softly. "Let's bring this to an end, shall we?"

The big man nodded sharply, once.

"It will be done," he answered.

CHAPTER 40

Tranquility System
21:00 September 19, 2735 Earth Standard Meridian Date/Time
Tranquility Space Fleet Orbital Dock

First Prelate Savitri Joshi of the Tranquility High Council looked far too young to be the head of state for an entire star system. Kyle admitted, at least to himself, that her faded brown skin, black eyes and long-braided hair could easily throw his guess off by a decade or more.

He bowed slightly as she entered the conference behind two *very* competent men in dark burgundy combat armor. They swept the rooms with eyes, implants, and hand-held scanners before letting her join him next to the table.

Before he could say anything, Joshi took his hands in hers and bowed deeply over them.

"Thank you, Captain," she said softly. "If you hadn't arrived when you did, I fear for what fate Tranquility would have faced."

He shifted uncomfortably, retrieving his hands with as much grace as he could manage. The First Prelate's closeness made him *very* aware of the frank way her tailored suit, the same dark burgundy as her guards', framed her figure, and the slightly spicy scent of her perfume.

Kyle cleared his throat carefully, and then caught a spark of a smile in her eyes. She knew *exactly* what she was doing, and he wondered for a moment how many of Savitri Joshi's political opponents had been thrown by her beauty – and ended up thrown to the wolves.

"I wish we had arrived earlier," he told her. "Had we arrived earlier, we could have saved more lives. I am sorry that we didn't arrive in time to save Admiral Wu. He seemed a good man."

"He was. But things happen as they happen, Captain Roberts," Joshi reminded him. "Had you not arrived at all, my world would now bow to Terra, and I have sworn to my people that this will not happen."

Kyle was saved from further awkwardness by the arrival of a gaunt, gray-haired man with another burgundy-clad guardsman – Tranquility's Director of Intelligence – followed immediately afterwards by Kelly Mason.

"Are we expecting anyone else, Madame Prelate?" he asked. He and Kelly were still up to their necks in trying to get *Avalon*'s many damages seen to, but when the local head of state asks you to attend a meeting, you attend.

"Mr. Richards and I are all," she replied, gesturing for the three of them to sit. "He's been keeping in the loop with Alliance Intelligence. I presume you haven't had a chance to catch up on the briefs?"

Kyle sighed and shook his head. It had taken eight hours to complete the initial SAR sweep of the battlespace for survivors of both the Tranquility and Commonwealth battle groups, even with *Avalon*'s starfighters playing spotter.

He'd kept *Avalon* out until that was complete, and then turned the task over to the Tranquility Orbit Guard when they'd finally brought in half a dozen sublight sloops to serve as bases for the search. They'd only been docked at the space station for an hour when Joshi's request for their attendance had arrived.

"If you would care to give us the highlights, Keith," Joshi told her intelligence head.

The sparse man gave the First Prelate a small bow as he stepped up to the head of the table. A holographic presentation of the new front line appeared over the table, called into place by the director's implant.

"Operation Puppeteer, from the Alliance's perspective, has been a barely mitigated disaster," he said bluntly. Eight systems flashed red on the hologram. "The Commonwealth hit us in each of these eight systems, including Tranquility, with between four and eight starships each."

"With the exception of Tranquility and Waterdeep, all of the systems have now fallen to the Commonwealth," he continued. "We were still *far* more out of position than we hoped, and losses on both sides have been heavy. The current estimate is that we lost twenty-six starships and the Commonwealth has lost twenty-eight."

That was ten percent of the *combined Alliance fleets*. The Commonwealth could afford its losses better – after all, they had over a hundred fully industrialized systems versus the Alliance's sixty-odd. Many of which were only industrialized by the loosest of definitions.

"What about Midori?" Kyle asked, noticing that the system with the big Alliance fleet base wasn't highlighted.

"From what Federation Intelligence has extracted from *Achilles'* data cores, the survivors of all the remaining strike groups will be moving on Midori within thirty-six hours," Richards said quietly. "Assuming they leave their more damaged vessels to garrison the seized systems, they will move on Midori with four battleships, three cruisers, and seven fleet carriers. Fourteen starships. A joint Federation-Imperial battle fleet is mustering in the system as we speak, and *should* match the Commonwealth's numbers when they arrive."

"*Tranquility* herself will remain in Midori until the battle there is resolved," Joshi informed Kyle. "At that point, I am assured that Alliance forces will be dispatched to Tranquility to relieve *Avalon*, allowing you to return home."

"We will do what we can until then," Kyle assured her. "We have some immediate repairs required, but as long as we can re-arm fighters, we can fight."

"I appreciate your courage, Captain," the First Prelate told him. "Of course, any resources we can provide are yours for the asking. My entire world is in your debt."

"Do you have any idea when *Mauna* will be ready to deploy?" Kyle asked the two Tranquility leaders.

"At least two weeks," Richards said calmly. "At this point, it will be as quick to complete her refit as it would be to re-activate her at all, so the engineers wish to finish the job."

Kyle nodded, and was about to comment on the wisdom of the choice when the door to the conference room burst open.

Despite the fact that there were at least two more of the burgundy-clad guards outside, all three of the bodyguards in the room had weapons out and trained on the intruder before Kyle had enough time to identify the out of breath woman as being in the Tranquility Space Force's navy blue uniform.

"I'm sorry, sirs, ma'ams," the officer managed to get out between breaths. "We just received an urgent priority message from the Assistant Director of Intelligence. We've cracked the encryption on the starfighter computer cores we retrieved."

Avalon's Captain watched the woman patiently, waiting for the other shoe that he knew had to be coming. The other shoe he had suspected since the moment the Commonwealth's fighters had surrendered without a fight.

"There's a second wave coming," he whispered, and the woman nodded as she regained her breath.

"Yes, sir," she concluded, offering a datapad that one of the guardsmen took from her. "All of the details are on the pad – she ordered me to deliver it immediately."

"Well done, Lieutenant-Commander Patil," Joshi said calmly, and Kyle found himself missing the ability to pull people's files at a glance *he'd* once had. "We will deal with this. Thank you."

#

Even as one of the guards was gently ushering Patil out of the conference room, the other was scanning the datapad for viruses and traps. Once assured that the device contained no dastardly schemes to assassinate the First Prelate, the guard flipped its main contents to the central hologram projector.

The projector quickly resolved into the image of a slim woman with pale skin, reminding Kyle vividly of Admiral Sagacity Wu.

"I am Assistant Director of Intelligence Jasmine Wu," she announced, in a calm and precise voice that drove home the resemblance to the First Admiral. "There is a complete set of the data extracted from the Commonwealth computer cores attached to this file, but I will summarize for the sake of time."

"The Commonwealth does not intend to keep any of their top-line warships tied up in garrisoning the systems they have seized. A second contingent, of older ships with less proven crews, will be arriving in each of the first wave systems twenty-four to thirty-six hours after the initial assault."

"We're still working on establishing an exact arrival time, but we have managed to identify the follow-up force intended for Tranquility: two *Paramount* class deep space carriers, with a total fighter strength of two hundred."

"We believe that their fighters will be *Scimitars* – the Commonwealth hasn't deployed a seventh generation starfighter yet, but all of their ships have been fully equipped with the *Scimitar*."

"I will forward more details as we manage to resolve them. The full dump has been transmitted to *Avalon*, in case they wish to review it themselves."

The hologram ended, leaving the occupants of the conference room staring at the empty space above the table in shock.

Finally, the First Prelate leaned back in her chair and met Kyle's gaze across the table.

"Captain, I appreciate your courage," she repeated quietly, "but I will *not* ask you and your people to die in a hopeless battle."

Kyle smiled grimly.

"Madame First Prelate, my mission is unchanged," he told her, his voice equally quiet. "*Avalon* was sent to Tranquility to hold this system. I do not intend to simply cut and run."

"You cannot fight two hundred starfighters with forty!" she snapped. "There is no point."

"We can't run, ma'am," Kelly interrupted quietly. "The stunt we pulled getting in as close as we did burned out our Alcubierre Drive."

"My engineer can't even give me an estimate on a timeline for repairs," Kyle told Savitri Joshi with a sigh. "As Commander Mason says, we cannot run, and I refuse to blithely surrender your world to the Commonwealth. *Avalon's* weapons may be gone, but we still have engines and a fighter wing. We can still fight."

"Your ship is already a legend, Captain," Richards said softly, the old Director's eyes sad. "Do you intend to make yourself a martyr to cap it?"

"No," Kyle replied. "I *will* request permission to offload my wounded and non-essential crew, just in case, but I have no intentions of dying to save Tranquility.

"But by all that is holy, I will *fight* for it."

CHAPTER 41

Tranquility System
23:55 September 19, 2735 Earth Standard Meridian Date/Time
DSC-001 Avalon – *Main Flight Deck*

At almost ship's midnight, less than sixteen hours after a major battle, *Avalon*'s Flight Deck was empty. Part of that tonight was the safety risk – in the end, they'd removed the carrier's main airlock doors with explosives.

The thin veil of glorified plastic wrap currently holding in the dock's atmosphere had transparency and replaceability as its main virtues. It could withstand the pressure of an atmosphere, but a starfighter hitting it would rip it to shreds. Launch-work would be done in vacuum when the time came.

For now, however, the plastic screen kept a breathable atmosphere on the deck while allowing Senior Fleet Commander Kyle Roberts to look out into space, at the glittering light show of Tranquility's rings.

It was a damn pretty planet and one, it turned out, that produced fantastic wine.

Avalon's Acting Captain wasn't drunk, but he had made a significant dent in the bottle Joshi had pressed on him before he'd returned to the ship. It might well be his last opportunity to enjoy a glass of wine, for that matter.

The Commonwealth second wave was due in-system at just after noon the next day. Part of him was hoping the wine contained some hidden drops of inspiration, because he still had no idea how he was going to fight two carriers, with a hundred starfighters apiece, with one functionally unarmed carrier with forty-two starfighters.

"Somehow, I figured I'd find you here," a voice said from behind him. Kyle looked up to see Michael Stanford slowly and carefully wheeling himself across the empty deck. "The wine is a surprise though. Willing to share?"

Kyle waved magnanimously. "I think the set the First Prelate gave me had a second glass."

Michael checked in the wooden box and rolled his chair up to where Kyle sat cross-legged on the desk, offering the glass out for his Captain to pour.

"Aren't you supposed to be planetside by now?" Kyle asked. "I seem to recall ordering all of the wounded off of the ship."

"Yes, you definitely did that," Michael replied, taking a sip. "Damn, I guess when a planetary head of state gives gifts, they give *niice* wine."

"Don't dodge the subject with me, Wing Commander," Kyle told him. "You shouldn't have flown out *today*. If you think you're going to fly out *tomorrow*, I will sic Kelly on you."

Michael sipped his wine, looking out at the ice ring floating in space in front of them.

"Threatening a man with his girlfriend is a low blow," he pointed out. "Who else would you trust to try and carry out whatever insane scheme you're plotting?"

"So you and Kelly are official now? Isn't that rather... high school for a warship?" Kyle pointed out.

"I can't say," Michael said slowly. "It's not *entirely* un-trod territory for me, but it's been a long damn time since I've been serious about anyone." He shrugged. "That said, I figure that if I'm willing to get my legs crushed saving her life, we should probably give things a shot."

"Don't look at *me* for relationship advice," Kyle warned, making a somewhat overdramatic gesture with his wine glass that risked spilling the liquid. "I figured out I wasn't cut out for the things shortly after I abandoned my pregnant girlfriend for the Navy."

"Wait," Michael said slowly. "Never since? Not even a single *date*?"

"Not one," the Captain admitted. "I can recognize when I'm not cut out for something, Michael," he continued quietly. "Two lives ruined is

Glynn Stewart

enough for one lifetime! Give me a battle to plan, a squadron to whip into shape? No worries. Families and relationships?! Ha!"

"Damn." The two men were silent for a long moment, drinking their excellent wine.

"Of the pair of us, I always figured *I* was the worse coward," Stanford finally said bluntly. "I may have run from relationships, but I didn't slam the door and salt the earth."

"I'm not afraid," Kyle protested, but his words fell hollow. "Okay, maybe I am – but it's not of relationships. I just feel... I don't know. That I owe *her* an apology before I could even look at someone else."

"Now, *that* I can see being terrifying," Michael told him. "Like something you'd need a damn good friend backing you up for."

"Not something I'd ask a friend to do," Kyle replied.

"Well, I think I just volunteered Kelly and me," the Wing Commander told him cheerfully. "Once whatever crazy plan you're cooking up sees off the Commonwealth, we're probably heading back to Castle, right? We'll drag you planetside and get your apology out of the way."

"You have *no* idea what you're threatening," Kyle told him dryly.

"We'll get you drunk first," Stanford told him, and Kyle laughed.

"You're insane. She'd never see it coming," he told his CAG.

"That's the point, isn't it? That's what you keep teaching us – hit them when they won't see it coming!"

Kyle stopped, his wine glass half-way to his lips.

"Boss?" Michael asked after a moment.

The Captain took a large swallow, finishing the rest of the wineglass, and slowly stood and turned to face Michael.

"I guess I'm keeping you aboard after all, Michael," he told the other man.

"Why?" Michael said slowly.

"Because you're right. I wouldn't trust anyone else to pull off the crazy stunt I'm planning."

Michelle was woken up by Flight Commander Rokos sticking his head into her room.

"Rise and shine, Lieutenant," he boomed. "We need to be in space ASAP – the Captain's got a plan!"

Michelle forgot that she wasn't alone in the narrow bunk, and outright tripped over Angela as she attempted to rise, falling flat on her face in front of her squadron commander, completely naked.

"Good morning, Lieutenant Alverez," Rokos calmly continued, his gaze suddenly fixed on an inexplicably interesting spot on the plain metal walls. "Don't worry, the wake-up call is only for Michelle – if this goes right, we'll leave you and the rest of the med-team *nice* and bored today."

With a wink and a grin, the big Commander vanished back out the door, re-engaging the privacy lock behind him.

Michelle, blushing bright red, looked back at her lover. Angela was, technically, not supposed to be in her quarters, especially with the ship at active readiness. That regulation was winked at as often as not.

Though not normally, she concluded, quite as literally as today.

"I've got to go," she said quietly. Before she'd even finished speaking, Angela was in her arms, holding her.

"I know," the nurse told her, following up with a desperate kiss. "I know. Good luck!"

Michelle smiled, a thrill of hope running down her spine.

"If Roberts has a plan, we may not even *need* luck!"

CHAPTER 42

Michael Stanford watched as his starfighters drifted out from *Avalon's* flight deck in pairs. They had the time to launch slowly today – but not by much.

"You know this plan leaves us with *no* margin," he said over his channel to Kyle. The total delta-V carried by a *Falcon*-type starfighter was difficult to calculate, but it was in the range of point six five of the speed of light.

"If the game were easy, everyone would play," Kyle told him dryly. "There's a reason a point three pass is the last resort of the mad and the desperate."

"Well, we are desperate," Michael agreed.

"It's a multiplier, Michael," his Captain said quietly. "We won't have surprise – they'll have seen the entire battle. But if we do this right, we *will* have shock, and fear – and those are weapons as deadly as any missile or positron lance."

A 'point three pass' meant hitting the enemy at point three cee – roughly ninety thousand kilometers a second, slightly *more* than a starfighter's maximum safe velocity. It would take Michael's starfighters five hours to build up that velocity, and as long to slow down from it again. *Avalon* had been flying away from the expected arrival point of the Commonwealth carriers for several hours to provide them enough distance to get up to speed.

If they got it right, they would pass through the range of the Commonwealth ships' weapons in a handful of seconds, firing on computer control as they went. They could destroy the carriers before they even launched their fighters and end the battle in a single pass.

If they failed… all of Michael's fighters would be heading out-system at a velocity that would take five hours to kill and leave them with almost no fuel. The only thing between any surviving Commonwealth warships and Tranquility would be one crippled carrier.

"They won't see us coming, boss," Michael promised. "I just hope Director Richards' people got their estimate of the emergence loci right – the margin for error is almost as narrow as my fuel reserves."

Tranquility Intelligence had narrowed the carriers' expected emergence to a roughly half light minute radius sphere and a ten minute window. Michael and Kyle had set the attack vector to allow them double both the space and time they could cover, but if they missed, it would be worse than if they'd never tried at all.

"We'll be behind you the whole way," Kyle told him. "We'll pick up anyone who falters."

Michael nodded silently, watching the last of Foxtrot Squadron's fighters drift out and form up.

"We'll see what happens," he said finally. "I never thought I'd say this, but let's hope the Commonwealth is punctual!"

"Good luck, CAG," *Avalon*'s Captain told him.

Tranquility System
012:00 September 20, 2735 Earth Standard Meridian Date/Time
SFG-001 Alpha Six – Falcon-*type starfighter*

There was something energizing about being able to point a starfighter at a target and open the engines all the way up. Cee-fractional encounters weren't *rare* in fighter combat, though they were unusual enough that having *two* of them in as many weeks was unexpected.

What was rare was for a fighter strike to have the *time* to build up a significant fraction of lightspeed under their own power. A starship would emerge from Alcubierre drive into a system at a relatively low velocity, but at a distance that only left a few hours to close with a world. Those few hours weren't enough to build up velocities of nearly a hundred thousand kilometers a second.

Inside the starfighter, there was no real sensation of speed or even acceleration, but Michelle still wore a broad grin as the indicator showing her velocity relative to Tranquility's star ticked over ninety thousand KPS.

"All ships, suspend acceleration."

With a mostly exaggerated sigh, Michelle cut the engines. The plume of annihilating matter and antimatter behind her flickered and faded to vacuum. Around her, the rest of SFG-001 did the same, leaving the forty-three starfighters hurtling through space at an almost unimaginable velocity.

She checked her sensors, focusing the fighter's passive scanners on the region of space they expected the Commonwealth carriers to appear in. Unless the enemy appeared in the exact middle of the target zone, the starfighters would need to maneuver to close, but they'd still have only seconds to react.

The clock ticked down to zero. The Commonwealth should arrive sometime in the next twenty minutes, and SFG-001 was in position to hit them anywhere in the expected zone once they did.

Michelle bared her teeth in what might charitably be called a smile.

Now, where were they?

Tranquility System
012:30 September 20, 2735 Earth Standard Meridian Date/Time
SFG-001 Actual – Falcon-C *type command starfighter*

The Commonwealth reinforcements were *late*.

Stanford cursed silently.

They should never have trusted what they knew to be second-tier crews to have left on time!

Now he watched as the maneuver cone of his starfighter group began to narrow. The edge of the target zone was already out of reach – even missiles wouldn't be able to change vectors enough to hit the carriers if they emerged there.

"All starfighters," he opened the channel. "Prep missiles for immediate launch and code for computer control. We're *in* the zone, we won't have time to fire ourselves."

Or to engage with positron lances, the most reliable ship-killer his people had. A handful of his people *might* get their antimatter beams on target, but for most, missiles would be all they'd be able to contribute.

More precious seconds ticked by, and Michael cursed himself for ever agreeing to this idea – and Roberts for ever even *suggesting* it.

"Emergence!" his gunner shouted, and the starfighter *lurched* as the missiles suddenly blasted away.

The two carriers erupted into space almost dead center in the target zone – which put them barely a hundred thousand kilometers ahead of Michael's ships, and about as far 'up' from them. *None* of his ships could bear on them with positron lances, and they were past them in barely a second.

In that second, forty-three fighters launched a hundred and seventy-two missiles, blazing in on their targets with blinding speed.

The two carriers had clearly heard about the fate of the first battle group. They emerged into the system with every sensor on full power, sweeping the space around them with radar, lidar, and every scanner man had yet invented.

Missile defenses began firing the instant the missiles launched: lasers, counter-missiles, even the lighter positron beams sweeping across space.

Dozens of missiles exploded, bursts of radiation that blinded Michael's sensors even as he strained to follow his strike in. Linked in to his computers, the second and a half flight time stretched out as he watched the trail of explosions reach across space and slam into the closer carrier.

That Commonwealth ship came apart in a blast of flame and radiation that blinded his sensors for a moment that seemed to last an eternity.

When the sensors finally cleared, several lengthy seconds later, for a moment all he saw was wreckage and he began to breathe a sigh of relief.

Then the vectors shifted, ever-so-slightly, and he saw Tranquility's doom emerging from the cloud of debris and radiation.

The second carrier had survived.

CHAPTER 43

Tranquility System
12:45 September 20, 2735 Earth Standard Meridian Date/Time
DSC-001 Avalon *– Secondary Control*

Secondary Control was silent as the data feeds streamed in from both SFG-001 and the Q-com equipped drones following behind them at a more sedate pace.

For a few minutes, the carrier had drifted and Kyle had hoped that they'd managed to carry the day after all, but then they'd began to launch starfighters.

Now, the Commonwealth ship's full complement of a hundred starfighters was in space, blazing after Stanford's fighter group. It would take them *hours* to catch up, but catch up they would. The ensuing battle would likely be a shock for the Commonwealth, as the seventh generation *Falcons* were more than a match for the *Scimitars* one for one.

Two to one odds, however, meant that SFG-001 was doomed. Whatever starfighters remained would return to their carrier, re-arm, and then finish off the damaged *Avalon* and seize Tranquility's orbitals.

"She's moving again, sir," Li reported. "Damned slow – I'm reading antimatter thrust but only twenty-five gravities."

Kyle nodded, staring at the screen in front of him as if some miracle would emerge from its stark graphical presentation of the star system.

The Commonwealth ship was ignoring *Avalon*. Slow as her acceleration was, she was using it to follow her starfighters to pick them up once they'd blown away *Avalon*'s starfighters. The other captain had drawn the right conclusions from the desperate strike Kyle had launched.

Twenty-five gravities was blood in the water. If the carrier was badly damaged enough that she could pull barely ten percent of her rated acceleration, it was a surprise she could launch at all. Old and damaged as she was, *Avalon* could still pull two hundred gravities.

If Kyle had had a single positron lance or missile left, his response would have been obvious – close and attempt to destroy the other carrier. Faced with any credible threat to their only way home, the starfighters would surrender with the carrier.

Even a single missile...

"Ensign Li," he said softly. "Throw their two-hour maneuver zone on the display."

The young officer paused in surprise and then obeyed. An orange cone expanded out from the damaged Commonwealth carrier, showing all possible paths they could follow at twenty five gravities. It was a wide zone, as their vector was currently towards Tranquility, but it was rapidly shrinking towards SFG-001 and their pursuers.

"Assume they're being gentle on their engines and can at least triple their acceleration if pushed," the Captain instructed, a plan – an *insane* plan – starting to take form in his mind.

The zone expanded into an elongated oval, shading out a large portion of the display.

"Lieutenant Ivanov," Kyle addressed Pendez's assistant, his Navigator having thankfully been convinced to go the surface with the rest of the wounded. "Show me *our* two-hour zone."

It took a moment, and a dark green ovoid extended out from *Avalon*'s current course. They couldn't go backwards, not with a velocity already over ten percent of the speed of light, but they could shape their forward vector almost any way they wanted.

The *entire* orange zone was inside the green zone. If Kyle had any weapons to engage with, they couldn't escape him.

"Second-tier crews," he said softly. "And a second-tier captain. He's no expert at starfighter tactics."

"Sir?" Ivanov asked.

"You *never* send all of your starfighters off in a single strike," Kyle told him. "Not unless you're desperate – or inexperienced. Our friend over there," he gestured at the icon of the Commonwealth carrier, "has assumed we wouldn't have launched the strike we did unless we were helpless, so he's ignoring us."

"But in his position, I'd have held back at least one squadron," he continued. "His starfighters are already far enough away they couldn't intercept us before we reached him."

"Before we reached him, sir?" Li asked. "He's right – we have no weapons!"

"But we have eight times his acceleration, slightly more mass in half the size, and a point one cee velocity advantage," Kyle pointed out. "Lieutenant Ivanov, please set a maximum velocity physical intercept course for that carrier."

"Sir?"

"A ramming course," Senior Fleet Commander Kyle Roberts clarified softly. "Set it to auto-update, then slave your console to mine and get to an escape pod."

Ivanov swallowed as Kyle activated the all hands channel.

"All hands, this is Acting Captain Roberts," he told his people. "I am setting a course that will take us directly at the surviving Commonwealth vessel. If we can eliminate her, we save Tranquility – regardless of the cost."

He let that sink in for a long moment.

"All personnel not directly essential to the operations of *Avalon*'s engines and defenses are to report to escape pods immediately," he ordered.

"God speed you," he finished quietly.

Secondary Control was silent again for a long minute.

"Course is set, sir," Ivanov said aloud. "Request permission to remain aboard, sir."

"Denied, Lieutenant," Kyle told him calmly. "I flew starfighters for ten years, I think I can guide the Old Lady the rest of the way."

He looked around his bridge crew. Kelly was staring at him in shock, her eyes dark with worry for her lover with the starfighters. Li was just plain in shock. Ivanov looked determined, despite having just set a suicide course for his ship.

"I can take this the rest of the way," he repeated. "All of you, get the hell off my ship."

#

"I've rigged the main positron capacitors," Wong told Kyle. "Uploading the command sequence to your datapad. Blow them, and *Avalon* turns into a giant shotgun blast in the sky."

The engineer paused.

"I'd wait as late as possible to use it, though," he pointed out. "Hell, *I'd* send a computer to do this, boss."

"There's a reason we don't run starfighters with just computers, Alistair," Kyle reminded him. "Too predictable. I doubt they've got much left in terms of on-board weapons, but if I'm doing this, I want to carry it all the way."

Wong sighed.

"Yeah. I figured whatever stunt you'd pull wouldn't involve us running away," he continued drily, "so I moved all of the remaining electromagnetic deflectors to the front of the ship. They'll have a hell of a time hitting you with lances, and you've got *some* anti-missile lasers. We've set them to automatic, but they should stop at least a few birds."

"Thank you, Commander," Kyle told him. "Now, I believe you have a shuttle?"

"Determined to die alone, huh?"

"'Duty is heavier than a mountain; death is lighter than a feather'," Kyle quoted. "We didn't come far this far to fail."

"You're nuts," Wong replied. "It's been an honor, Captain."

"Likewise," Kyle answered.

The channel went silent, and Kyle turned his gaze back to the main display. The icons of shuttles and escape pods littered the space behind *Avalon* as the tiny vessels carrying his crew set their course for Tranquility.

He was alone in Secondary Control now. Soon, he would be alone on *Avalon*. If he was *right*, it wouldn't matter. If he was wrong... Tranquility would still be saved.

He hated the old quote from the Japanese Imperial Rescript. He preferred the one about 'making the other bastard die for *his* country'.

So far as he could tell, the Commonwealth ship didn't have any Q-com equipped drones watching *Avalon*, meaning she would only see his people abandoning ship when the light reached them and their computers drew the conclusions.

Right about now.

Kyle *did* have Q-com equipped drones near the Commonwealth carrier, so he saw when they recognized his intent. The ship rotated ninety degrees 'up' relative to Tranquility's ecliptic plane and went to fifty-three gravities.

With a grim smile, Kyle adjusted his course. Without real-time information on him, and with a hundred and fifty gravity acceleration disadvantage, there was no chance for the carrier to escape.

Right now, they were three light minutes apart, and the distance was dropping rapidly as *Avalon* piled two kilometers a second onto her forty thousand KPS velocity.

Avalon's computer helpfully dropped a timer onto his screen. Twenty-two minutes to impact. If the carrier had missiles, she would be launching them shortly.

Kyle waited. It was funny, he realized, watching his own death grow in the screen. He wasn't afraid of dying. What bothered him was that if he died, he *wouldn't* be able to take Michael up on his offer of support when he went back to talk to Lisa.

But that wasn't quite it either, he realized.

It was simpler than that.

If he died, he would never be *able* to apologize to Lisa. And that, he realized, was even scarier to him than the thought of apologizing to her.

Of course, he was apparently less scared of *ramming another ship* than he was of talking to the mother of his child.

Kyle shook his head at his own foolishness, and checked the scanners.

The carrier hadn't launched any missiles. If he'd had any of his own, his current suicide course would be unnecessary.

Again, and again, and again, the carrier shifted course. Five decoys fired into space, each mimicking the electronic and infrared signatures of the carrier.

Unfortunately for the Commonwealth, his drones were close enough to pick them up as they launched and keep his course on the right track.

Ten minutes to impact. The Commonwealth starfighters had broken off their pursuit of SFG-001, but they couldn't possibly get back in time to prevent Kyle ramming *Avalon* into his enemy.

The question, he supposed, wasn't what *he* could do.

It was what his enemy would do when he realized he was doomed.

At forty light seconds, five minutes to impact, he received the first message.

"This is Captain Maria Jung of the Commonwealth warship *Majesty*," a crisply dressed woman with porcelain-white skin and jet-black hair in the Commonwealth Navy's red and black uniform informed him.

"As an alternative to this madness, I am prepared to accept the honorable surrender of your ship and starfighters," she continued. "I will personally guarantee your fair treatment and repatriation to your home nations."

It was a step in the right direction, but not what Kyle needed. He adjusted his course slightly, adding enough of a random spiral to throw off positron lances. Four minutes to impact. Three.

Captain Jung's skin was even paler when the second message arrived.

"Fine," she snapped. "I am prepared to negotiate the withdrawal of my forces from this system! Break off your course and I will pick up my fighters and leave!"

Kyle considered it. The problem here wasn't the offer – if the Commonwealth withdrew, he won.

The problem was that he couldn't *trust* her. Once she had the chance to retrieve her fighters, there was nothing stopping Captain Jung from sending them straight at *Avalon*. Right now he posed the only threat he could ever pose.

Two minutes to impact. Transmission time was down to sixteen seconds, and he *still* hadn't replied to any of Jung's transmissions. It was an open question in Kyle's mind whether or not the woman would crack – or if someone *around* her would crack.

Ninety seconds. Kyle could *probably* avoid impact with even seconds of notice, but he was starting to get nervous now. Eighty seconds. Seventy.

"This is Jung," the transmission finally said, her voice suddenly very small and afraid. The bridge behind her was a chaotic mess. Jung was bleeding from what looked like a bullet graze on her shoulder and was leaning on her command chair. Kyle's Q-com drones were now showing escape pods starting to fire off from her ship.

"To avoid further loss of life, I offer the unconditional surrender of all Commonwealth forces under my command. Please respond. *Please*."

Kyle smiled coldly. If he'd been a betting man, he'd have just owed himself twenty stellars.

"Captain Jung, this is Captain Roberts," he said calmly into the recorder. "You will stand down all zero point cells aboard your ship. Your starfighter crews will eject. If you do this, your surrender will be accepted." He checked the clock. "You have thirty seconds from receipt of this message to comply."

Captain Jung clearly still had a Q-com link to her starfighters. Less than *ten* seconds after she would have received his message, the one solitary drone with SFG-001 showed escape modules beginning to blast free of the Commonwealth fighters.

In the face of the potential destruction of their only way home, even starfighter pilots knew when the game was lost.

Kyle waited a few, painful, seconds to be sure the distinctive signature of the zero point cells had disappeared from *Majesty*, and then slammed an override into the computer.

With seventeen and a half seconds to spare, *Avalon* slewed aside from her suicide course.

CHAPTER 44

Castle System
14:00, October 10, 2735 Earth Standard Meridian Date/Time
Orbital Dry Dock Merlin Four

Doctor Lisa Kerensky, M.D. and a list of other letters that was *shortly* scheduled to include 'Ph. D. Neural Cybernetics', wasn't entirely sure the school tour was supposed to going quite this deep into the repair yard sections of *Merlin Four*.

She had her suspicions about just how the head of Jacob's expensive and prestigious private academy had wrangled getting the class of thirty eleven-year-olds the rarely granted privilege of a full tour of one of the Federation Navy's massive space stations. She couldn't really object, though. Jacob should, after all, get *some* benefit from having a famous war hero for a father.

More of a benefit than simply watching the man's face show up in every news cast for the last three days, anyway. Navy Public Relations had apparently wasted no time in getting newly-promoted Captain Kyle Roberts in front of a camera for an interview when the badly damaged *Avalon* had finally limped into Castle.

Since no matter what *she* did, Lisa was pretty sure *Jacob* was going to see it and ask questions, she'd watched it. They'd interlaced Kyle's matter of fact commentary with video of the battle – including *Avalon* flying *through* a Commonwealth warship in a blaze of fire.

Shaking her head to clear her vagaries, Lisa made sure that the collection of chaos makers she was helping chaperone were still mostly together. She concluded after a moment that they were doing better than expected, though the quartet of grim-faced Marines playing nursemaid as they walked through the semi-classified areas probably had something to do with it.

They came to a halt by a massive transparent window, and a voluptuous blond woman in a Navy uniform and three gold circles on her neck seemed to appear out of nowhere.

"That's *Avalon*, kids," she said cheerfully. "Most of us didn't think she was going to make it home, but Fleet Commander Wong did us proud."

A wheelchair-bound man in the same uniform and insignia, but with blue piping, rolled his chair up to join her.

"She was painted black," he pointed out to the kids, gesturing to the gray and black-charred hull. "The paint all burnt off though. The gray you see? That's neutronium. Still intact, despite everything the Captain did to her."

Lisa found herself off to the side as the two officers and Marines skilfully directed the children's attention to the unclassified parts of the ship and the repair yard around her. She couldn't help studying the ship.

At least one of the blackened holes in the surprisingly unmarked gray hull had to be fifty meters deep. The old ship looked like she'd been through hell.

"I'd say you should see the other guy," a familiar voice said from behind her, "but the truth is that none of them were intact enough to drag home."

Lisa turned around. The voice was familiar. The face was older, carrying lines she was sure hadn't been in the last images her landlady – Jacob's grandmother – had shown her a few months ago. The uniform was different too – gold-piped instead of blue, and with a single gold planet on the collar instead of two gold circles.

"So they didn't just conjure with the name of a hero to get us aboard then?" she asked.

"Honestly? I had nothing to do with Jacob's class getting the trip," Kyle told her. "I *did*, however, get them this deep into the repair yard."

He shrugged. "Nothing classified about *Avalon* anymore. She's due to be decommissioned in two days."

She'd forgotten how fast Kyle moved for being so large a man. Suddenly he was next to her, just out of reach and looking down at her.

"I wanted to see you," he said quietly. "And Jacob too, if you're okay with that."

"If I'm okay with that?" she asked. "This is your territory, Kyle."

"And you are his mother," her old lover replied, his voice still soft. "I... wronged you. Deeply. You owe me *nothing*, Lisa – and if you want me to walk away from Jacob and never bother either of you again, I will do so. Child support will keep coming. Nothing will change."

He paused and swallowed.

"I am sorry," he said continued. "I'm not here to ask for forgiveness. I am simply here to tell you that it was always me. I was afraid, and I wronged you, and I was too afraid for too long to make it right."

Somehow, Lisa's occasional dreams – and, honestly, fantasies – about this moment had never included her stomach being full of butterflies or her hands being sweaty. She was so angry with him – almost twelve *years* of anger – but she'd never really considered the possibility he would truly show up and apologize.

"I won't pretend I didn't know where the money that pays for Jacob's school came from," she said quietly. "Or that you were paying more child support than you had to. I wouldn't be where I am without the support you gave, even if you did leave us in the lurch. It helped, no matter how angry I was, to remind that somewhere inside, you *cared*."

"It's not right. Not yet," Lisa told him. "But..."

"Mommy!" came a twelve year old yell, and both of them turned around to see Jacob round the corner at maximum speed. He came careening up to Lisa – he was already up to her shoulder, looking to rival his father's height eventually – and stopped dead about four feet away.

He looked Kyle up and down, his face suddenly very mature.

"Mom," he said slowly, "is that...?"

"I know you've watched that interview, Jacob," Lisa told him with a smile and a laugh. Suddenly, her heart was at ease for the first time in years.

"Yes, Jacob, this is your father."

Kyle was suddenly on his knees, and Lisa noted, absently, that her son was as tall as his father like that. It seemed... right.

"Hi Jacob," he said quietly. "I'm sorry it took so long."

The boy glanced from his father, to his mother, then to the battered spaceship outside the window.

"You were on that," he whispered.

"I was," Kyle said gravely.

"Did you... almost not come back?" Jacob asked, and Lisa's heart dropped out of her chest. Angry as she'd been at Kyle, when she'd heard about the Battle of Tranquility and *Avalon*'s losses, *she'd* been terrified for days.

She'd never even *thought* that Jacob might be just as scared for the father he'd never met.

"I did," the boy's father replied, his voice heavy. "I did come back – I *had* to. I owed you and Lisa that much."

Lisa found herself blinking back tears as Jacob suddenly *threw* himself into Kyle's embrace. The big officer held his son gently, carefully.

Behind him, the wheelchair bound officer corralling the rest of her school tour smiled brightly, and threw Lisa a perfect salute.

###

If you enjoyed the novel, please leave a review!

To be notified of future releases, join my mailing list by visiting my website at http://www.faolanspen.com

Other books by Glynn Stewart

Castle Federation
Space Carrier Avalon
Stellar Fox
Battle Group Avalon
Q-Ship Chameleon (upcoming, see www.faolanspen.com for latest estimated launch date)

Starship's Mage
Starship's Mage: Omnibus
Hand of Mars
Voice of Mars
Alien Arcana (upcoming, see www.faolanspen.com for latest estimated launch date)

Stand Alone Novels
Children of Prophecy
City in the Sky

21891377R00207

Printed in Great Britain
by Amazon